Sunday Times

'Superior Scandinavian crime . . . nail-biting' *Woman & Home*

'For fans of Jo Nesbø, this dark tale by Nesser is set to be one of the autumn's biggest thrillers . . . an intense read' *Stylist*

'Will have you howling with pleasure' *Evening Standard*

'Håkan Nesser is in the front rank of Swedish crime writers . . . A novel with superior plot and characters' *The Times*

'The atmosphere of the small town, the mysterious fringes of the forest full of aspens and blueberries, are evocatively drawn . . . The clarity of Nesser's vision, the inner problems of good and evil with which Van Veeteran struggles, recall the films of Bergman' *Independent*

'Håkan Nesser's Chief Inspector Van Veeteren has earned his place among the great Swedish detectives with a series of intriguing investigations . . . This is Van Veeteren at his quirkiest and most engaging' *Sunday Telegraph*

'Veeteren is a terrific character, and the courtroom scenes that begin this novel are cracking' *Daily Telegraph*

'The novel's prime asset is the mordant clarity of Nesser's voice. Its understatement is a pleasure in itself'

Times Literary Supplement

'A richly atmospheric addition to the series . . . Nesser contrives an impressive balance between a twisty thriller plotline and satisfying characters with believable quirks . . . his subtle touch when it comes to psychological insight and his confident storytelling make for an enthralling read' *Metro*

'Nesser produces crime writing that is so rivetingly written that it makes most contemporary crime fare – Scandinavian or otherwise – seem rather thin gruel. Nesser's tenacious copper, Chief Inspector Van Veeteren, is one of the most distinctive protagonists in the field, and the baffling, labyrinthine cases he tackles have a rigour and logic all too rarely encountered'

Guardian

THE STRANGLER'S HONEYMOON

Håkan Nesser is one of Sweden's most popular crime writers, receiving numerous awards for his novels featuring Inspector Van Veeteren, including the European Crime Fiction Star Award (Ripper Award) 2010/11, the Swedish Crime Writers' Academy Prize (three times) and Scandinavia's Glass Key Award. The Van Veeteren series is published in over 25 countries and has sold over 10 million copies worldwide. Håkan Nesser lives in Gotland with his wife, and spends part of each year in the UK.

Also by Håkan Nesser

THE MIND'S EYE
BORKMANN'S POINT
THE RETURN
WOMAN WITH A BIRTHMARK
THE INSPECTOR AND SILENCE
THE UNLUCKY LOTTERY
HOUR OF THE WOLF
THE WEEPING GIRL

HÅKAN NESSER

THE STRANGLER'S HONEYMOON

A VAN VEETEREN MYSTERY

Translated from the Swedish by
Laurie Thompson

PAN BOOKS

First published in the UK 2013 by Mantle

This paperback edition published 2014 by Pan Books
an imprint of Pan Macmillan, a division of Macmillan Publishers Limited
Pan Macmillan, 20 New Wharf Road, London N1 9RR
Basingstoke and Oxford
Associated companies throughout the world
www.panmacmillan.com

ISBN 978-1-4472-1733-6

Originally published in 2001 as *Svalan, Katten, Rosen, Döden* by
Albert Bonniers förlag, Stockholm.

1 3 5 7 9 8 6 4 2

A CIP catalogue record for this book is available from the British Library.

Typeset by Ellipsis Digital Limited, Glasgow
Printed and bound by CPI Group (UK) Ltd, Croydon, CR0 4YY

Visit www.panmacmillan.com to read more about all our books
and to buy them. You will also find features, author interviews and
news of any author events, and you can sign up for e-newsletters
so that you're always first to hear about our new releases.

Killing a human being takes a minute at most.
Living a normal life can take seventy-five years.

Henry Moll, author

1

'In the next life I want to be an olive tree.'

She gestured vaguely towards the hills where dusk was falling fast.

'It can live for several hundred years, according to what I've read. That sounds pretty reassuring, don't you think?'

Afterwards, he would occasionally recall that these were her last words. That comment about olive trees and reassurance. It was remarkable. As if she was taking something big and sublime with her to the other side. An inspiration, a trace of some kind of insight that she didn't really possess.

At the same time, of course, it seemed to him a little odd that she should make such a general – and actually rather meaningless – comment, immediately after those terrible words that had sealed her fate so definitively. Which ended her life and gave their relationship its final destiny.

I love somebody else.

Needless to say, it never occurred to her that things would develop the way they did. That what happened next was the only way out – not until the very last seconds, presumably – but in a way it was typical, both of her naivety and of their relationship in general. It had frequently happened that she

1

didn't grasp the full significance of things until it was too late. At a stage when it was pointless trying to put things right, and when all that could be said – absolutely everything – had already been said. When the only possibility available was decisive action. He had thought about that before.

'I've made up my mind. I know I'm hurting you, but we must go our separate ways from now on. I love somebody else.'

Then silence.

Then that comment about the olive tree.

He didn't answer. Had she expected him to answer?

It wasn't actually a question she had asked. Merely a statement. A fait accompli. What the hell could he have answered?

The balcony was not large. Six to eight square metres. A little white table with two chairs that looked exactly like all other plastic chairs and all other plastic tables in every part of the world. The same applied to the hotel. Only two floors, no dining room – hardly even a reception. They had booked the holiday at the last minute and hadn't bothered to pick and choose.

Olympos. Just a few minutes' walk up from the beach, the landlady had a moustache and it had about a dozen rooms, probably fewer.

Their colourful patterned beach towels were folded over the balcony rail to dry. They each had a glass of ouzo and were sitting within half a metre of each other; she had just had a shower, was suntanned and radiant after a whole afternoon on the beach.

A whiff of thyme from the hills formed an unholy alliance

with the stench of low-octane petrol wafting up from the main road. And that was more or less it.

That and those words. A note suddenly began to resound in his head.

Faint and difficult to pin down, but somehow persistent. It can be heard like the trickling of a little rivulet babbling through the sound of the cicadas churring drowsily after a hot day. They sound like several hundreds, but there are probably no more than two or three of them. He stands up. Knocks back the rest of the ouzo in one swig, takes a few deep breaths.

Stands behind her; moves her hair to one side, places his hands on her naked shoulders.

She stiffens. She becomes more tense, almost impercept-ibly, just a few muscles – but he notices it immediately. The tips of his fingers on her warm skin are as sensitive as tiny seismographs. He feels his way along the sharp edges of her collarbones. Feels her heart beating. She says nothing. Her left hand lets go of the wine glass on the table. Then she sits there, still. As if she were waiting.

He moves his hands in towards her neck. Notices that he has an erection.

A motorcycle with a very badly damaged silencer clatters past in the street down below. His blood starts racing through his veins, both in his hands and down below in his genitals.

Now, he thinks. Now.

*

At first her struggles are like a sort of orgasm, he registers this similarity even while it is taking place. An orgasm? he thinks. Her body is arched from the soles of her bare feet on the balcony floor to his hands around her throat. The plastic chair overturns, her left hand hits the ouzo glass, which falls over backwards and lands on one of his flip-flops, rolls over a few times but doesn't break. She grabs hold of his wrists, her thin fingers squeeze so hard that her knuckles turn white, but he is stronger. Very much stronger. The motorcycle clatters up the narrow asphalt path between the olive groves – it has evidently turned off the main road. He squeezes even harder, the note inside his head is still resounding, he still has an erection.

It takes no longer than forty to fifty seconds, but those seconds seem never-ending. He doesn't think of anything in particular and when her body suddenly goes limp, he shifts his grip but maintains the pressure, goes down onto his knees and bends over her from in front. Her eyes are wide open, the edges of her contact lenses are clearly visible, her tongue is protruding slightly between her even, white teeth. He wonders fleetingly what to do with the present he has bought for her birthday. The African wooden statuette he found in the market in Argostoli that morning. An antelope leaping. Perhaps he can keep it for himself.

Or maybe he'll throw it away.

He also wonders how he will spend the remaining days of the holiday as he slowly relaxes his grip and straightens his back. Her short dress has ridden up and revealed her extremely skimpy white panties. He contemplates her dark triangle that can be seen through the thin cotton, strokes it a few times and is aware of his steel-hard penis.

He stands up. Goes to the bathroom and masturbates. In so far as he feels anything at all afterwards, it feels odd.

Odd, and somewhat empty.

While waiting for the right moment, he lies down on his bed in the darkness of the hotel room, and smokes.

Smokes and thinks about his mother. About her undeniable gentleness, and the strange, empty feeling of freedom she left behind. *His* freedom. After her death last winter he no longer feels her eyes staring at his back all the time. There is no longer anybody who sees him exactly as he is, in every respect; nobody who rings once a week to hear how he is.

Nobody to send holiday postcards to, nobody to keep reporting to.

As long as she was alive, what he had just done would have been inconceivable, he was certain of that. Not in the way it had happened, at least. But now that the blood-relationship had been severed, quite a lot of things had become easier. For better or worse. It simply happened.

Better but also rather pointless. His personality no longer seemed to have any real substance, no backbone. That was a conclusion he kept coming back to over and over again during the past six months. Often. Life had suddenly lost its *raison d'être*. And now here he was, lying on a hotel bed on a Greek island just like any other, smoking and seeing her gentle but also stern face in his mind's eye, while his wife lies dead on the balcony, going cold. He has moved her closer to the wall and placed a blanket over her, and he can't really make up his mind whether or not his mother in some mysterious way – in some totally incomprehensible sense – knows what has really happened this evening. Despite everything.

He is a little annoyed at not being able to answer this question satisfactorily – nor how she would have reacted to what he has just done this hot Mediterranean evening: and after his tenth or possibly his eleventh cigarette he gets up. It is only half past midnight: night life in the bars and discotheques is still as vibrant as ever – there is no question of getting rid of the body just yet. Not by a long way. He goes out onto the balcony and stands for a while, his hands on the rail, wondering what he should do. It is not easy to lug a dead body out of a hotel without being seen – even if the place is off the beaten track, even if it is dark outside: but he is used to taking on difficult tasks. He often finds the difficulty stimulating, it makes his heart beat that bit faster and supplies some of that *raison d'être*. It is no doubt thanks to that aspect of his character that he has progressed as far in his career as he has. He has often thought about that before, it is a recurrent reflection of his. The challenge. The gamble. The *raison d'être*.

He inhales the fragrance from the olive groves, tries to experience it as if it were coming from the world's first olive tree – or the world's oldest – but he can't manage it. Her last words get in the way, and the cigarettes have deadened his sense of smell considerably.

He goes back indoors, fetches the packet from the bedside table and lights another one. Then sits down on the white plastic chair on the balcony again, and thinks about the fact that they had been married for nearly eight years. That is a fifth of his life, and much longer than his mother predicted when he told her that he had found a woman with whom he was going to enter a serious relationship. Much more.

Even if she had never passed her opinion as explicitly as that.

When he has finished smoking this cigarette as well, he picks up his dead wife and carries her into the room. Lays her down at an angle over the double bed, takes off her T-shirt and panties, gets another erection but ignores it.

Lucky that she's so light, he thinks. She weighs nothing at all.

He picks her up again and drapes her over his shoulders – as he will have to carry her eventually: he has only a vague idea of how rigor mortis works, and when he drops her back down onto the bed he leaves her lying in the U-shape she had assumed while hanging round the back of his head and over his powerful shoulders.

In case she starts stiffening up now.

Then he takes the tent out of the wardrobe – the light-weight nylon tent he had insisted they should take with them – and starts wrapping it round the corpse. He trusses it up, using all the loose nylon cords, and decides that it looks quite neat.

It could easily be a carpet or something of the sort.

Or a giant dolmade.

But in fact it is his wife. Naked, dead, and neatly packed

into a two-man tent, brand Exploor. There we have it, all neat and tidy.

He wakes up at half past two after dozing off briefly. The hotel seems to be fast asleep, but there are still rowdy noises from the nightclubs along the street and the promenade. He decides to wait for another hour.

Exactly sixty minutes. He drinks coffee to keep himself awake. The night seems to be an accomplice.

His rented car is a Ford Fiesta, not one of the tiniest models, and there is plenty of room for her in the boot, thanks to the fact that she is doubled up. He opens the boot lid with his left hand and eases her down from his left shoulder by leaning forward and slightly to one side. Closes the boot, looks around then settles behind the wheel. No problem, he thinks. No sign of life anywhere. Not inside the hotel, nor out in the street. On the way out of the town he sees three living creatures: a thin little cat slinking along in the shadow of a house wall, and a street cleaner with his donkey. None of them pay him any attention. Easy, he thinks. Killing is easy.

He has known that in theory all his life, but now he has transferred theory into practice. He has a vague idea to the effect that this is the point of life. Man's actions are God's thoughts.

*

The ravine has also been hovering in the back of his mind, but it is a somewhat shaky memory and he is forced to wait for the first pink light of dawn in order to find his way there. They passed by it a couple of days ago, travelling over the mountains on their way from Sami and the east side of the island: he remembers that she had wanted to stop there and take some photographs, that he did as she wished, but that she had difficulty in establishing the right camera angles.

Now they are here again. It's really a crevice rather than a ravine. A deep cleft inside a hairpin bend, a thirty- or forty-metre almost perpendicular drop, the bottom hidden by a tangle of thorny bushes and rubbish thrown out of car windows by less than scrupulous car passengers.

He switches off the engine and clambers out. Looks around. Listens. It's ten minutes past five: an early bird of prey hovers motionless over the barren mountainside to the south-west. Down at the bottom of the V between two other rocky precipices he can just catch a glimpse of the sea.

All is silence. And the distinct smell of a herb he recognizes but can't identify. Oregano or thyme, most probably. Or basil. He opens the boot. Wonders for a moment if he should remove the tent inside which she is wrapped, but decides not to. Nobody will ever find the body down there, and nobody will ever ask him to explain what happened to his tent. He has use of the car for two more days and will be able to drive over to the other side of the island again. Get rid of the pegs, the ropes and the bag in some other crevice. Or in the sea.

Nothing could be simpler. Nothing at all.

He looks round one more time. He picks up the big bundle

and heaves it over the low rail. It bounces off the steep cliff walls once or twice, then crashes through the dry bushes and disappears. The bird of prey seems to react to the noise and the movement, and moves further westward.

He stands up straight. It's hard to imagine that it really is her, he thinks. Hard to believe that he really is here, doing this.

He lights another cigarette. He has smoked so much during the night that his chest is aching, but that is of minor importance. He gets back into the car and continues over the crest of the mountains.

Twelve hours later – in the middle of the hottest hour of the siesta – he opens the glass door of the travel agent's air-conditioned office in the big town square in Argostoli – the angora, as it's called. Sits down patiently on the sticky plastic chair and waits while two overweight and over-tanned women complain about the shortcomings of their hotel to the blonde girl in a blue suit behind the counter.

When he is alone with the blonde girl he adopts the most agitated tone of voice he can conjure up and explains that he has a problem with his wife.

He's lost her.

She seems to have disappeared. Just like that.

Late last night. She was going out for a late-night swim. Needless to say there might be a perfectly natural explanation, but he is worried even so. She doesn't usually vanish like this.

So perhaps he ought to do something?

Maybe he should contact the authorities?

Or the hospital?

What did she think he ought to do?

The girl offers him a glass of water and shakes her Nordic hair in a gesture of sympathetic concern. She comes from a different country, but they understand each other well even so. They don't even need to speak English. When she turns to one side and reaches for the telephone, he catches a glimpse of one of her breasts right down to the nipple, and he feels a sudden surge of sexual excitement.

And while she tries in vain to make telephone contact during the hottest hour of the day, he begins to wonder who that other person could be, the one his wife had talked about.

The one she claimed to be in love with.

MAARDAM

AUGUST–SEPTEMBER 2000

2

Typical, thought Monica Kammerle as she replaced the receiver. So bloody typical. I hate her.

Her conscience pricked her immediately. As usual. As soon as she had a negative thought about her mother it emerged from the shadows and made her feel ashamed. Conscience. That internal, reproachful voice, telling her that you shouldn't have negative thoughts about your mother. That you must be a good daughter, and acclaim rather than defame.

Be grateful, not hateful, as she had read in some girl's magazine or other several years ago. At the time she thought the advice sounded so wise that she cut it out and pinned it up over her bed when they were living in Palitzerlaan.

Now they lived in Moerckstraat. The four-roomed flat in the Deijkstraat district – with high ceilings and views over the Rinderpark and the canal and the green patinated roof of the Czekar Church – had become too expensive now that there were only the two of them. They had managed to live there for three more years after her father died, but in the end the money he had left them ran out. Of course. She had known all along that they would have to move out, there was no point in pretending otherwise. Sooner or later. Her mother had explained that to her in great detail and unusually clearly on more than one occasion, and last spring they had moved here.

Moerckstraat.

She didn't like it.

Not the name of the street. Not the drab, brown-coloured building with its three low-ceilinged storeys. Not her room, not the flat, nor the dull, characterless district with its straight, narrow streets and dirty cars and shops, and not even a single tree.

I'm sixteen years old now, she had begun to think. Three more years at grammar school, then I can move away from here. Then I can look after myself.

Her conscience pricked her once more as she remained standing by the telephone, looking out of the window over the top of the net curtains at the equally dirty-brown façades on the other side of the street. The narrow, dark windows that were in the shade for eleven hours out of twelve even on quite sunny days like today.

She remembered a line in a play by Strindberg: 'You have to feel sorry for human beings.' Not just sorry for myself or for Mum, but for everybody. Every man jack. But being aware of that doesn't make it any better.

She liked having little conversations about life with herself. She didn't write them down, but kept them in the back of her mind and thought about them occasionally. Perhaps because it helped to place her in a context with other people. A sort of gloomy solidarity.

Reminded her that she wasn't so different, despite everything. That life was like this.

That her mother was just the same as the mothers of other
sixteen-year-old girls, and that loneliness was just as devastat-
ing for everybody else as well.

And maybe her mum would get well again one of these
days – even if that fat psychologist woman hardly made it
sound as if she believed it would happen. Better to keep an
eye on it and try to keep it under control with the aid of
medication. Better not to hope for too much. Better to keep
your sights low.

Manic depression. That was what it was called. And it was
disciplined medication, the psychologist had said.

Monica sighed. Shrugged, and took the recipe out of the
file.

Chicken in orange with rice and broccoli sauce.

The chicken pieces had already been purchased and were
in the refrigerator – she would need to buy the rest at Rijk-
man's. The rice, spices, oranges, salad. And ice cream sorbet
for afters. She had noted it all down, and her mother had
made her read out the whole list over the telephone.

Manic, she thought. A sure sign that her mother was
moving into a manic phase. That was presumably why she
had missed her train. She had been to tend the grave in
Herzenhoeg and stayed there too long – not for the first time.

But her late arrival and the evening meal business were not
a problem. Not as far as her mother was concerned: there
were virtually no problems when she was in this state. She
was experiencing what would be a brief high – it seldom

lasted longer than a week. While it lasted there was no reason why everything shouldn't go like clockwork.

And the medicine was doubtless here at home in the bathroom cupboard. As usual. Monica didn't even need to check in order to know that.

Wouldn't it be better to postpone the dinner? she had suggested. He was due to arrive at eight o'clock; surely he wouldn't want to hang around until half past eleven waiting for her mother to get home?

Her mother had explained that of course he would want to hang around: that was something an innocent sixteen-year-old couldn't possibly understand. She had already checked with him when he rang her mobile. So could she please be a good daughter and do what her mother had asked her to do?

Monica tore the page out of her notebook and took the necessary money out of the housekeeping kitty. She saw that it was already half past five, so she had better get moving if she was going to avoid disappointing her mother's lover.

Lover? she thought as she pushed her trolley around the shelves, trying to find what she was looking for. She didn't like the word, but that's what her mother called him.

My lover.

Monica preferred the actual person to what her mother called him, in fact. Thought he was much better. For once.

Just think if this could be it, she thought. Just think if they could make up their minds to try and live together.

But it seemed pretty unlikely. As far as she knew they had

only met a few times – and most of them did a runner after three or four.

Nevertheless she allowed herself the childish hope that he would move in with them, and she tried to conjure up his image in her mind's eye. Quite tall and well built. Probably around forty. Hair greying at the temples, and warm eyes that reminded her a little of her dad's.

And he had such a nice voice, that was perhaps the most important thing of all. Yes, now that she came to think of it, that was nearly always how she judged people.

By their voice, and the way in which they shook hands. Those were two things that couldn't be falsified. That was no doubt something she had read in another girls' magazine ages ago, but it didn't matter. It was true, that was the main thing. You could lie with so many other things: your lips, your eyes, your gestures.

But never with your voice and the way you shook hands.

As far as she was concerned, he scored especially highly on those two aspects of character: a calm, deep voice which gave words exactly their right value and never rushed things, and a hand which was big and warm and neither pressed too hard nor felt as if the owner would rather pull it away. It was almost a pleasure in itself to shake hands with him.

She smiled slightly at her thoughts, and turned her attention to her shopping list. What a brilliant assessor of human character I am, she thought. I've only met him for about ten minutes in all. I ought to become a psychologist or something.

★

As she prepared the food, she began thinking – as usual – about Loneliness. With a capital L: that was how she often saw it written. Presumably in order to give it some sort of extra dignity.

Wondering whether she would be able to overcome it now that she was starting in a new class at school, or if everything would turn out to be the same old story. Loneliness, her only reliable companion.

Would she still not dare to invite new classmates to her home? Because of a mum who put both herself and her daughter to shame the moment anybody new stepped over the threshold.

Or posed a threat of doing so, at least. Who could lie under a blanket on the sofa in the living room in broad daylight – with a carving knife and a bottle of sleeping pills on the coffee table beside her, begging in a loud voice for her daughter to help her to commit suicide.

Or float around in the bathtub barely alive, surrounded by her own vomit and with two empty wine bottles standing on the floor.

Or at the other extreme: as high as a kite, instructing young twelve-year-olds about the most efficient ways of masturbating – since sex lessons at school nowadays were such a lot of rubbish.

No, she thought. No, three more years will be more than enough – I don't want to end up like that.

And the men. The boyfriends who came and went, always during the manic weeks in the spring and the autumn, each of them even worse than the previous one, none of whom she ever saw more than three or four times.

Apart from Henry Schitt, who claimed to be a writer and smoked hash all day long for four weeks, either in the bathroom or out on the balcony, until Monica plucked up enough courage to phone Auntie Barbara up in Chadow.

Auntie Barbara hadn't intervened personally, of course: she never did. But she had arranged for two social workers to call round and throw out Henry. And for her sister to be placed in medical care for a few hours.

And to be given some more medicine.

That was in the spring, a year-and-a-half ago; and things had in fact become rather better after that. As long as the medication wasn't left unused in the bathroom cupboard because her mother had been feeling so well that she didn't think she needed to take it any more.

And now this Benjamin Kerran.

When she thought about him, it occurred to her that this was the first time during all those years that she hadn't heard the shout for her father echoing inside her chest. Her own shout inside her own body.

Benjamin? The only thing she had against him was in fact his name. He was much too big to be called Benjamin. And vigorous and warm and lively. A Benjamin ought to be small and skinny with misted-up glasses and a face covered in pimples and blackheads. And bad breath – just like Benjamin Kuhnpomp, who had spent a term in her class in year five, and who was, as far as she was concerned, the model for all Benjamins the world over.

But now here she was, cooking a meal for a quite different Benjamin.

A Benjamin who was her mother's lover, and was welcome to stay with them for as long as he wished.

As far as Monica was concerned, she was keen to do her best not to frighten him off – that much was clear, and she was determined to carry it off. She checked the temperature and put the casserole with the chicken into the oven. It was only half past seven: if she skipped washing her hair, she would have time for a shower before he arrived.

'You don't need to sit here entertaining an old fart just because your mum was delayed. You mustn't let me interfere with your plans.'

She laughed and scraped up the final, runny lump of sorbet from her plate.

'You are not an old fart, and I don't have any plans for this evening. Have you had enough?'

He smiled and patted his stomach.

'I couldn't even force down another raisin. Is it your mum who's taught you how to cook? That was really delicious. An old bachelor like me isn't used to feasts of this quality, believe you me.'

'Oh, come off it!' she managed to come out with, and could feel that she was blushing.

'Let's put some foil over the remains, so that we can warm

them up when your mum gets back. I'll see to the washing up.'

'No, I . . .'

'Enough of that. Sit down and watch the telly, and I'll sort all this out. Or read a book. Incidentally, speaking of books . . .'

He stood up and went out into the hall. Fished around in a plastic carrier bag he had left on the hat shelf, then came back in.

'Here you are. A little present as a thank you for the meal.'

He placed a flat, gift-wrapped little parcel on the table in front of her.

'For me? But why?'

'Why not?'

He started clearing the table.

'You might not like it, but you sometimes have to take a chance.'

She ran her finger over the fancy ribbons.

'Aren't you going to open it? I've got something for your mum as well, so she won't need to feel jealous.'

She slid the ribbon over the corner of the packet and tore open the wine-red paper. She took out the book, and couldn't conceal her delight.

'Blake!' she exclaimed. 'How did you know?'

He came over to her and stood behind her with his hands on the back of her chair.

'*Songs of Innocence and of Experience*. I happened to notice that you had *Tyger, Tyger, burning bright* pinned up on your noticeboard – it was your mum who insisted that I should take a look at your room – forgive me for intruding. Anyway,

I thought he must be a favourite of yours . . . And it's a beautiful book, with all the paintings and so on.'

She started thumbing through, and when she saw the mystical illustrations and the ornate script, she could feel that tears were not far distant. In order to keep them at bay she stood up and gave him a hug.

He laughed, and hugged her as well.

'So there, little lady – that wasn't much, let's be honest! Time to leave me in peace now here in the kitchen.'

'You're so nice. I hope . . .'

'Well, what do you hope?'

'I hope everything goes well with you and my mum. You would be so good for her . . . For us.'

She hadn't meant to say that, but it was done now. He held her shoulders, at arm's length, and eyed her with a somewhat confused expression on his face.

'We'll see what happens,' he said.

Then he steered her out of the kitchen.

When he came and sat beside her on the sofa, it was twenty past ten. There was over an hour to go before her mother would arrive. She had started watching a French film on the telly, but switched off after a quarter of an hour. She switched on the reading lamp and went over to Blake instead.

'Read something for me,' he said.

She suddenly felt her mouth go dry.

'My English isn't all that good.'

'Nor is mine. But I think all young people speak like native

24

Brits nowadays. Do you have a favourite poem? You don't need to feel embarrassed if you slip up.'

She thought for a moment, then leafed back through a few pages.

'Maybe this one.'

'Let's hear it.'

She cleared her throat, closed her eyes for two seconds, then started reading.

'*O Rose thou art sick*
The invisible worm
That flies in the night
In the howling storm

Has found out thy bed
Of crimson joy
And his dark secret love
Does thy life destroy'

She closed the book and waited for his reaction.

'Lovely,' he said. 'And sad. It's called "The Sick Rose", isn't it?'

She nodded.

'But it's really about people. I realize that you've had a bit of a rough time. If you want to tell me about it I'd be glad to listen.'

She knew immediately that that was exactly what she wanted to do. But was it appropriate? she wondered. And if she did tell him, how far should she go? And where should she begin?

'If you don't want to, then of course you shouldn't. We can sit here in silence, Or talk about football. Or ropey TV programmes, or the perilous state of hedgehogs in the contemporary world . . .'

'You are just like my dad,' she said with a laugh. 'You really are. We used to sit here on this sofa, reading aloud to each other. When I was little, that is – he did most of the reading, of course. I used to sit on his lap.'

Three seconds passed before she burst out crying.

Then she sat on his lap.

Afterwards she had trouble in remembering what they had talked about.

If they had said all that much in fact, or just sat there in silence for most of the time.

Probably the latter.

But she remembered that he smelled nice. She remembered the rough texture of his shirt, and his regular, deep breaths against her back. The warmth he radiated, and his strong hands that occasionally caressed her arms and her hair.

And she remembered that it was shortly after the old wall clock over the television struck eleven that she felt that sudden movement inside her that ought not to have stirred at all.

And that at almost exactly the same moment a part of him also moved and made its presence felt, in a way that was absolutely forbidden.

3

He rang to apologize the very next day.

In the late afternoon: her mother was at some preliminary meeting for people who had been out of work for quite a long time, but were now being launched back into the labour market. Perhaps she had told him about that, so that he knew when it would be a suitable time to phone her.

'Please forgive me, Monica,' he said. 'No, you shouldn't do that, in fact. It was unforgivable.'

She didn't know what to say.

'There were two of us involved,' she said.

'No,' he insisted. 'It was entirely my fault. I don't understand how I could have let it happen. I was a bit tired, of course, and I'm only human – but for God's sake, that's no excuse. It's probably best if you don't ever see me again.'

He fell silent, and she thought she could hear his bad conscience in the receiver.

'We didn't go all that far,' she said. 'And I must accept some of the blame. You're not a child any longer when you're sixteen years old.'

'Rubbish,' he said. 'I'm in a relationship with your mother. This is the kind of thing you read about in dodgy magazines.'

'Do you read dodgy magazines?' she asked. 'I didn't realize that.'

He burst out laughing, but checked himself.

'No,' he said. 'But maybe I should, in order to discover what I shouldn't do. But it won't happen any more, I promise you that. It's probably best that I put an end to my relationship with your mother as well . . .'

'No,' she said. 'Don't do that.'

He paused before responding.

'Why not?'

'Because . . . Because you are good for her. She likes you and you like her. I like you as well – not like last night, that was an accident.'

He seemed to hesitate again.

'I rang to apologize, and . . . and to say that I thought it was best to accept the consequences and leave both of you in peace from now on.'

'But you didn't tell Mum that?'

He sighed.

'No, I didn't tell your mum that. That would have been the correct thing to do, of course, but I didn't know how she would take it. And if you're a coward, that's what you are. So you see what a shit I am.'

'You're not a shit. Pack it in now, there were two of us on that sofa and I'm not utterly unaccountable for my actions.'

'I'm sorry.'

Silence once again. She could feel thoughts buzzing round inside her head like a swarm of bees.

'I must say I think you are treating this less seriously than you should,' he said in the end. 'Maybe we should meet and talk it over properly.'

She thought for a moment.

'Why not?' she said. 'It wouldn't do any harm. When and where?'

'When do you have time?'

'Whenever suits you. I don't go back to school until next week.'

He proposed a walk in Wollerims Park the following evening, and she thought that sounded like a good idea.

The following evening was a Wednesday, and one of the hottest days of the whole summer. After quite a short walk they sat down on a bench under one of the weeping willow trees next to the canal, and talked for over an hour. Afterwards they went for a walk through the town. Along Langgraacht, through Landsloorn and out to Megsje Bojs. She did most of the talking. Spoke about her childhood, her father's death, her mother. About her difficulties at school, and her girlfriends who kept letting her down. He listened and asked a few questions. When they turned off onto one of the pedestrian paths through the woods, she linked arms with him; when they had come deeper into the woods where there were no more lights, he put an arm around her shoulder, and by shortly after midnight they had become lovers for real.

*

And they carried on meeting.

After the evening and the night in Megsje Bojs, she heard nothing from him for almost four days. Then he rang late on the Sunday evening when she was alone at home again. He apologized once again, insisted that what he had done was unforgivable, and that what they had been doing must stop before it ended up disastrously.

They talked for about ten minutes, then arranged to meet for one last time and sort everything out. He collected her from school on the Tuesday, they drove out to the coast in his car, and after a long walk along the beach they made love in a dip among the dunes.

When they went their separate ways neither of them said a word about putting a stop to what was now happening, and during the first couple of weeks she was back at school he came to visit them in Moerckstraat twice. On both occasions he spent the night with her mother, and in the badly sound-proofed flat she could hear them making love until well into the early hours.

But she knew that one of these days he would come back to her. It's madness, she thought. It's sheer lunacy.

But she did nothing – nothing at all – to put a stop to it.

Not yet.

School was the same old story. Her hopes that things would change now that she was starting in the sixth form were soon shattered.

At the venerable old Bungeläroverket Sixth Form College –

which her father had attended in his day – she found herself in a class consisting mainly of new and unknown faces. But there were quite a few well-known faces as well, and it wasn't long before she realized that these old so-called friends from the Deijkstraaskola had made up their minds to keep her in the role they had carved out and assigned to her alone, once and for all.

It was not difficult to see that her new classmates had been informed about various things. That they knew quite a bit about her already, despite the fact that they were only a few days into the new term. Her home circumstances, and the state of her mother, for instance. The story about the vomit in the bathtub that she had confided to a very reliable girlfriend a few years ago was by no means a thing of the past just because she had moved to a new school. And the same applied to her mother's masturbation lesson. Indeed, it would be more accurate to say that such stories had acquired new legs.

In other words, her reputation was already established. Monica Kammerle was a bit odd. No wonder. With a mother like she had. Not surprising that she tended to keep herself to herself, the poor thing.

And when she thought about Benjamin and what went on in her home, she had to admit that they were right.

She really was odd. She was different from the others.

She and her mother as well.

Possibly even Benjamin. When she made love with him for the third time – at home in Moerckstraat one morning when her mother was attending her work experience course and she was playing truant from a sports day – it struck her how little she knew about him.

His name. Benjamin Kerran.

His age. Thirty-nine. Exactly the same age her father would have been, and one year younger than her mother. The occasional strands of grey hair around Benjamin's temples might have led most people to assume that he was a little older than that. Forty-odd, perhaps.

Job? She didn't really know. He worked in local government – she didn't recall his ever having been more precise than that.

Home address? No idea. Surely it was preposterous that she didn't know where he lived? They had never met in his home – only outdoors, or at her flat in Moerckstraat when her mother was out of the way. Surely it was a bit odd that they had never made use of his home – always assuming that he lived alone. She decided that she would find out his address the next time they met. He wasn't in the telephone directory, she had established that as soon as she had started to wonder about the question.

Of course, she could ask her mother about such details. Obviously, Monica had legitimate reasons to know some details about her mother's lover no matter what the circumstances.

Even in circumstances that were rather more normal than these.

And what about his life in general? What did she know about his life?

THE STRANGLER'S HONEYMOON

Hardly anything. He had been married, he had mentioned that: but it was evidently a long time ago. He had never said anything about any children.

So presumably there aren't any, Monica thought.

It's strange, she thought. Strange that I know so little about the only lover I've had in my life. Still have.

But at the same time she realized that it wasn't really all that odd. The main topic of conversation between them had always been her. Every time they had met.

Monica Kammerle. Monica Kammerle's childhood and youth. Her mum and dad. Her teachers, her old unreliable friends, her favourite hobbies and favourite books. Her thoughts about everything under the sun, and how she felt when he touched her in various ways. And when he was inside her.

But what about him? Nothing. It was hardly his fault. She liked to talk, and she liked him listening to her. To be perfectly honest, you could say that she wasn't much more than a self-centred sixteen-year-old who liked to contemplate her own navel and never looked beyond the end of her own nose.

On the other hand, she had never had anybody to listen to her since her father died. That's life, she supposed. You have certain needs, and if you had an opportunity to satisfy them, that was what you did of course.

Apart from the phenomenon of Monica Kammerle there was really only one topic of conversation to which they devoted any time.

Their relationship.

The forbidden fact that she had the same lover as her mother. The fact that she, Monica Kammerle, sixteen years of age, and he, Benjamin Kerran, thirty-nine, spent their time *screwing* each other. From in front and from behind. With mouths and tongues and hands and everything possible. Screwing away like the very devil. She soon realized that she felt a sort of delight mixed with horror, a rather stimulating dismay, as soon as they began talking about it.

As if they had invented it. As if no other person was aware that you could act like that.

Or as if putting all the disgusting actions into words somehow made it all acceptable. By talking about it. She was quite sure that he felt the same way about it as she did.

We are well aware that we are doing wrong, and so we can allow ourselves to do it, she said on one occasion.

And so we can allow ourselves to do it?

At first she believed that.

At first she was really no more than a willing victim in his arms – she was bright enough to be aware of that.

Because she enjoyed what he did to her. Everything – almost everything.

And she enjoyed what he allowed her to do with him. And the fact that he enjoyed it as well.

He told her on one occasion that there are other cultures in which they introduce young girls to sex by letting them go with experienced, grown-up men. Perhaps that's not a bad idea.

Monica agreed. Not a bad idea at all.

After a night that Benjamin had spent in her mother's bed before leaving shortly before dawn, she confided in her daughter that he was the best lover she had ever had.

Monica was inclined to agree, but she said nothing. There was no doubt that Benjamin had a strong and positive influence on her mother, it was impossible not to notice that. The manic high she had enjoyed during the latter part of August had come to an end. She was taking her medicine regularly – as far as Monica could judge by checking the medicine cupboard – and she seemed to be healthier and more relaxed than Monica could recall her being at any time since her father's death.

She was attending her work therapy classes four times a week, cooking meals, shopping and doing the laundry. Almost like a real mother. She had never been so patient and focused. Not as far as Monica could remember, in any case.

So touch wood, she thought. What we are doing might be lunacy – but we are living in a different culture, as it were.

She smiled at the thought. If only her classmates knew . . .

The need to confide in somebody, to tell at least one other person what was going on, cropped up a few days later: to be more precise, the early morning when he left her mother in her bedroom and came to hers instead.

It was early one Wednesday morning at the beginning of September. Shortly after five o'clock. As far as she could make out Benjamin and her mother had been on a trip to Behrensee, and got back home quite late. She was already asleep in bed when they returned, and had only a vague recollection of hearing them in the hall.

She was woken up by him caressing her nipple. He held a warning finger to his lips and nodded in the direction of her mother's bedroom. Took her hand, placed it on his rock-hard penis and looked suggestively at her.

There was something hungry in his eyes, she noted, but at the same time something entreating, almost like a dog.

And although she was only sixteen years old – and had been a virgin as recently as eighteen days ago – she read in that look of his something about the balancing act that is a hidden component of bodily love. Had crystal-clear insight – although she was only half awake – into all the bottomless pits that lurked behind the most gentle touches and modest glances.

How quickly something could go wrong. And how easily something could go wrong.

She hesitated for a moment. Made sure that he at least closed the door properly. Then nodded and allowed him to penetrate her doggy-fashion.

It hurt, wasn't at all like it usually was. She hadn't been properly prepared, it hurt and he was much rougher than usual. He seemed to be interested only in satisfying his own needs, and after a minute or so he ejaculated all over her back without her having been anywhere near to an orgasm.

Without her having experienced an ounce of pleasure.

He mumbled an apology and went back to her mother's bedroom. No, this was nothing like it usually was, and for the first time she was filled with a surge of extreme disgust.

No doubt he would tell her mother that he'd just nipped out to the loo. If she happened to wake up. Hell's bells.

She got out of bed. Staggered to the bathroom and threw up until she felt completely drained. Showered and showered and showered.

His dark secret love does thy life destroy, she thought. No, I can't go on like this. I need to talk to somebody.

4

'Can you tell me what this is?'

The young shop assistant smiled nervously and fingered his moustache. Van Veeteren wiped the counter with his shirt sleeve and placed the object in the middle of the bright, shiny surface. The young man leaned forward to examine it, but when he realized what it was he straightened his back and watered down his smile.

'Of course. It's an olive stone.'

Van Veeteren raised an eyebrow.

'Really? Are you absolutely sure of that?'

'Of course.'

He picked it up carefully between his thumb and index finger and eyed it closely.

'No doubt about it. An olive stone.'

'Good,' said Van Veeteren. 'We're in agreement so far.'

He gingerly took a rolled-up handkerchief from his pocket and unfolded it meticulously.

'What about this, then?'

It seemed as if the young man was about to give this object the once-over as well, but for some reason changed his mind. He remained halfway bent over the counter with an odd expression on his freckly face.

'It looks like a tooth filling.'

'Precisely!' exclaimed Van Veeteren, sliding the olive stone towards the little dark-coloured lump of metal until they were more or less side by side, with only a centimetre or so between them. 'And might I ask if you have any idea who you have the great pleasure of conversing with on a beautiful September day like this one?'

The shop assistant tried to smile again, but it wouldn't come. He glanced several times at the display window and the door, as if hoping that a rather more normal customer might turn up and relieve the somewhat tense atmosphere inside the shop. But no such saviour appeared, and so he put his hands into the pockets of his white smock and tried to appear rather more self-assured.

'Of course. You are Chief Inspector Van Veeteren. What are you getting at?'

'What am I getting at?' enquired Van Veeteren. 'Let me inform you. I want to go to Rome, and I'll be damned if I don't make sure I get there. Tomorrow morning, to be more precise, when I have a flight booked from Sechshafen. However, I must say that I had hoped to make that journey in the best possible condition – namely with all my teeth present and correct.'

'Your teeth?'

'My teeth, yes. Incidentally, it is true that my name is Van Veeteren: but when it comes to my occupation, allow me to inform you that I ceased to be a member of the police force three years ago.'

'Yes, of course,' said the youth apologetically. 'But they say you get dragged back in from time to time.'

Get dragged back in? Van Veeteren thought, losing his concentration for a moment. Do they say I get dragged back in? What the hell . . . ?

He thought quickly about the four years that had passed since he handed in his resignation to Hiller – but the chief of police changed the request on his own initiative to a sort of permanent leave, an arrangement for which there was no precedent in the rulebook. Was the situation really as the callow youth had described it? That he got dragged back in now and then? That he had difficulty in staying away?

Three or four times, he decided. Maybe five or six, it depended on how you counted.

But no more often than that. Once or twice a year. Not much to speak about, in fact, and he had never been the one to take the initiative. Apart from just once, perhaps. It had usually been Münster or Reinhart who had proposed something over a beer at Adenaar's or Kraus's place. Asked a tricky little question or requested some advice, as they and their colleagues were getting nowhere in a particular case.

Asked for help, in fact: yes, that's the way it was. Sometimes he had declined to be of assistance, sometimes he had been interested. But *dragged back in*? No, that was going too far. Definitely an exaggeration: he hadn't been involved in any police work in the real meaning of the term since he had become an antiquarian book dealer. In that respect his conscience was as clear and pure white as both innocence and arsenic.

He glared at the shop assistant, who was shuffling his feet

and seemed to be having difficulty in remaining silent. Van Veeteren himself had never found it difficult to remain silent. On the contrary, he and silence were old mates, and sometimes he found it advantageous to use silence as a weapon.

'Rubbish,' he said in the end. 'I work with old books at Krantze's antiquarian bookshop. Full stop. But the point has nothing to do with my personal circumstances, but with this olive stone.'

'I see,' said the shop assistant.

'And this filling.'

'And so?'

'You acknowledge that you know me?'

'Er, yes . . . Of course.'

'Do you also acknowledge that you sold me a sandwich this morning?'

The shop assistant took a deep breath, as if to build up some strength.

'As I have done every morning for the past year or so, yes.'

'Not every morning,' said Van Veeteren. 'Not by any means. Let's say three or four times a week. And nowhere near a year either, as I used to shop at Semmelmann's until January when they closed down. I very much doubt if I would ever have had a problem like this in that shop, incidentally.'

The young man nodded submissively and hesitated.

'But what the hell . . . What is the point you are making?' he managed to force himself to ask as the blush began to make its way up from under his shirt collar.

'The content of the sandwich, of course,' said Van Veeteren.

'The content?'

'Precisely. According to what you said and in accordance with what I expected, you sold me this morning a lunchtime sandwich with a filling of mozzarella cheese – made from buffalo milk, of course – cucumber, sun-dried tomatoes, fresh basil, onion, radicchio and stoneless Greek olives.'

The blush on the assistant's face blossomed forth like a sunrise.

'I repeat: *stoneless* olives!'

With a restrained gesture Van Veeteren pointed out to the youth the small objects on the counter. The young man cleared his throat and clasped his hands.

'I understand. We apologize, of course, and if what you are saying is . . .'

'That is what I am saying,' said Van Veeteren. 'To be more precise, the fact is that I have been forced to make an appointment with Schenck, the dentist in Meijkstraat. One of the most expensive dentists in town, unfortunately, but as I am due to leave tomorrow morning I had no choice. I just wanted to make you aware of the circumstances, so that you are not surprised when the invoice arrives.'

'Of course. My father . . .'

'I have no doubt that you will be able to explain it all in a convincing manner to your father, but now you must excuse me – I simply don't have the time to stand here arguing the toss any longer. You may keep the stone and the filling. As a souvenir and a sort of reminder, I don't need either of them any longer. Thank you and goodbye.'

'Thank you, thank you,' stammered the young man. 'We shall be seeing you again, I hope?'

'I shall think about the possibility,' said Van Veeteren, stepping out into the sunshine.

He spent the rest of the afternoon in the inner room of the antiquarian bookshop, working. Answered eleven requests from bookshops and libraries – eight of them negative, three positive. Listed and annotated a collection of maps that Krantze had found in a cellar in the Prague old town (how on earth had he managed to make such a journey and also go down into a cellar, afflicted as he was by rheumatism, sciatica, vascular spasms and chronic bronchitis?). Began sorting out four bags of odds and ends brought in that same morning by the heirs of a recently deceased man, and bought for a song.

He allowed the few customers who came into the shop to wander around freely, and the only transaction was the sale of half a dozen old crime novels for rather a good price to a German tourist. At a quarter past five Ulrike rang to ask what time he would be coming home. He told her about the olive stone and the tooth filling, and thought that she found it more amusing than she ought to have done. They agreed to meet at Adenaar's at about seven – or as soon after that as possible, depending on when he had been allowed to leave the dentist's chair. Neither of them had any great desire to cook a meal the evening before a journey; and in any case it was by no means certain that he would be able to chew anything so soon after being fitted with new false teeth, Ulrike thought.

'It's not a matter of new false teeth,' Van Veeteren pointed out. 'It's just a filling.'

'They usually have pretty good soup at Adenaar's,' Ulrike reminded him.

'Their beer is usually drinkable,' said Van Veeteren. 'I know nothing about their soup.'

When they had hung up he remained sitting there with his hands clasped behind his head for a while. He suddenly noticed that something warm was stirring inside him, and wondered what on earth that could be. An unobtrusive, barely noticeable emotion, perhaps, but even so . . .

Happiness?

The word burst as a result of its own presumptuousness, and soon various other thoughts had occurred to him. No, not happiness, he thought. Good God, no! But it could have been worse. And there were other lives that had been even more of a failure than his.

Then he started thinking about relativism. About whether other people's unhappiness actually made his own unhappiness greater or less – whether the world really was constituted in such a penny-pinching and cheese-paring way that this relativism was the only basis on which good and evil could be judged: but then something seemed to be intent on distracting him . . .

A few fake coughs and a cautious 'hello' penetrated his consciousness from the other room. He wondered briefly if

he should respond or not. But then he stood up and acknowledged his presence.

Six months later he was still not sure if that had been the
right thing to do.

The man was in his thirties. Tall and thin, and with a face
that did its best to remain unseen behind a long fringe, a
dark beard and dark glasses. He seemed to be enveloped by
an aura of nervous unease, rather like BO, and Van Veeteren
couldn't help thinking about similarities with a suspect trying
to pull himself together before a crucial interrogation.

'Hello there,' he said. 'Can I help you with anything?'

'I hope so,' said the man, holding out his hand. 'Assuming
you are Van Veeteren, that is. My name is Gassel. Tomas
Gassel.'

Van Veeteren shook his hand, and confirmed that he was
who he was.

'Please forgive me for contacting you like this. What I have
to say is a bit on the delicate side. Do you have a moment?'

Van Veeteren checked his watch.

'Not really,' he said. 'I have an appointment at the dentist's
half an hour from now. I was just about to shut up shop for
the day, in fact.'

'I understand. Perhaps tomorrow would suit you better?'

Van Veeteren shook his head.

'I'm afraid not. I'm going away on holiday tomorrow.
What is it you want?'

Gassel hesitated.

'I need to talk to you. But a couple of minutes won't be enough. The fact is that I find myself in a situation that I can't cope with. Not professionally, nor as a private person.'

'What do you mean by "professionally"?'

Gassel looked at him in surprise for a moment. Then he stretched his neck and brushed his beard to one side. Van Veeteren saw the man's dog collar.

'Oh, I see.'

'Please excuse me. I forget that my status isn't obvious. I'm a curate in the parish of Leimaar here in Maardam.'

'I see,' said Van Veeteren, waiting for what came next.

Gassel adjusted his beard and cleared his throat.

'The fact is that I need somebody to talk to. To consult, if you prefer. I find myself in a situation in which . . . in which my vow of silence is in conflict with what my moral conscience tells me I ought to do. To put it in simple terms. Time has passed, and I'm afraid that something very unpleasant might happen if I don't do something about it. Something very nasty and . . . criminal.'

Van Veeteren searched around for a toothpick in his breast pocket, but then remembered that he'd given them up eighteen months ago.

'But why are you turning to me? Surely you must have a vicar in Leimaar who must be better placed to help you than somebody like me?'

Gassel shook his head.

'You might think so. But we're not exactly on the same wavelength on matters like this, Pastor Brunner and I. Unfortunately. Obviously, I've thought about it a lot, and . . . No, it's not possible to handle it in that way. You've got to believe me.'

'But why should I be able to handle it any better? As far as I recall we've never met before.'

'Forgive me,' said Gassel, somewhat awkwardly. 'I'd better explain how it is that I know about you. I know that you've resigned from the police force – that's the key fact. I've given her a sacrosanct promise not to go to the police with the information I have at my disposal. If I hadn't promised her that, I'd never have found out anything about what was going on – even, of course, if I'd been able to work out that something very nasty was afoot. Very nasty indeed. I got your name from Sister Marianne in Groenstadt – I don't know if you remember her. She's only met you once, but she remembers you very well and recommended that I should try to talk to you . . . Marianne is an aunt of mine. My mother's elder sister.'

Van Veeteren frowned. Transported himself rapidly back six years in time, and suddenly saw in his mind's eye the spartan whitewashed room where he had sat for an hour, talking to the old woman. Sister Marianne . . . The Roman Catholic Sister of Mercy and the newly operated-on Detective Chief Inspector who between them, very slowly – and filled with deep, mutual respect – resolved the final unanswered questions in the Leopold Verhaven case. The double murderer who wasn't in fact a double murderer. An innocent man who had been in prison for twenty-four years – oh yes, he certainly remembered Sister Marianne.

And he also recalled the final act in the Verhaven case. No matter how much he would have preferred to forget it.

I knew it would come back to haunt me, he thought. I knew it would turn up again one of these days.

But in this way? Was he really going to have to pay his debts via this worried young priest?

That's absurd, he thought. Preposterous. I'm pulling on too many strings. There's such a thing as coincidence as well, it's not only a matter of these confounded patterns all the time.

'Do you remember her?' Gassel wondered.

Van Veeteren sighed and looked at the clock.

'Oh yes, of course I do. I remember your aunt very well. An impressive lady, no doubt about that. But I'm afraid that time is running out. And I'm far from convinced that I can be of any help to you. For many years my capacity has been somewhat overestimated.'

'I don't believe that,' said Gassel.

'Huh,' muttered Van Veeteren. 'Be that as it may. But in any case, I simply don't have the time today, and tomorrow I'm off to Rome for three weeks. But if you are prepared to wait that long, of course I can listen to what you have to say when I get back to Maardam. But don't be under the illusion that I shall be able to help you.'

Gassel contemplated the bookshelves while he seemed to be thinking that over. Then he shrugged and looked unhappy.

'All right,' he said. 'I can't see any alternative. When exactly will you be back?'

'On the seventh of October,' said Van Veeteren. 'That's a Saturday.'

Gassel took a little notebook out of his inside pocket and wrote that down.

'Thank you for listening to what I had to say, in any case,' he said. 'I just hope nothing awful happens between now and then.'

Then he shook hands once more and left the shop. Van Veeteren watched the tall, stooping man walk past the window and out into the alley.

A young priest in a quandary, he thought. Seeking help from an agnostic ex-detective chief inspector. God moves in a mysterious way.

Then he went out, locked the shop door and hurried off to the dentist's in Meijkstraat.

5

Monica Kammerle sat waiting outside the school welfare officer's office.

While she was waiting, she wondered why she was in fact sitting there. To be honest there were two reasons, but they weren't really connected. Not directly, at least.

In the first place she had promised that priest to go to the school welfare officer and talk to her about her situation. He had both nagged at her and appealed to her, and in the end she had agreed to go along with it. Not that she was going to tell the welfare officer everything – that was what Pastor Gassel had intended, of course, but she was not going to go quite that far. If she had really wanted to do that, there would have been no need to call in at the church – he ought to have realized that. And there was professional secrecy and there was professional secrecy, that was something she had gathered long ago.

The whole business had disturbed him deeply, that was obvious. She had tried to explain that quite a lot might look worse from the outside than it did from the inside, but he had dismissed any such thought.

'Look here, my girl! You simply cannot go on like this, you

must surely see that!' he had said when she met him for the second time. 'What you have confided in me goes against all ethical and moral values, and will end in disaster. You are too young to escape unscathed from anything like that. You won't be able to cope with it!'

And you are too inexperienced to understand, she had thought.

Anyway, in the end she had promised to talk to the welfare officer: but before making an appointment she made sure she had thought up a rather more seemly reason. It hadn't been all that difficult: her relationship with her schoolmates was sufficiently poor for it to merit a meeting, anybody could see that. As long as she was able to describe it convincingly.

When she had come that far, she had decided to take matters a step further.

A change of school. It was a good idea to have a specific proposal to make. She intended to explain to this washed-out fifty-year-old woman – who called herself a welfare officer, but hadn't made a very convincing impression when she was introduced to the pupils at a special assembly in the hall soon after her appointment – to explain certain carefully selected parts of her situation as comprehensively as possible, and make her understand that a school transfer was the only plausible solution for a pupil with Monica Kammerle's problem profile.

As it was called. She had been there before.

The Joannis Grammar School out at Löhr, for instance.

As far as she had been able to discover there were eleven

grammar schools in the Maardam area, and if there was one which might be able to give her the opportunity of a new start, it must surely be Joannis. If there was a school where she stood a chance of being completely unknown to her new unprejudiced schoolmates, this was the one. No pupil from Deijkstraa had ever attended a school in Löhr – one lunchtime she had checked through all local school record books for the last four years in the library, where they were kept in large black files. Yes, she felt confident that she would be able to convince the welfare officer that taking this step would be reasonable and necessary. The business of bus passes and choice of subjects and other practical and technical details – well, if she really was a welfare officer she should be able to sort out such matters.

Monica laughed when she thought about this and her own sudden ability to act positively. Perhaps it was the young priest who had inspired her to such decisiveness, despite everything; but something had also happened after that latest embrace with Benjamin. Just happened, apparently of its own accord.

Embrace? She didn't really know what to call it, but after having come to terms with the feelings of disgust and the almost shocking re-evaluation of their relationship, some sort of inner strength seemed to have germinated inside her. She had noticed it even before she went to confession for the first time: obviously it was far from certain that it would last – she had been through periods of depression before, and there were those who maintained that manic depression was a hereditary illness. But why not take this opportunity of doing something positive if she was on a high for once?

Why not, indeed? She looked at the clock and established that the welfare officer was running ten minutes late. Or that her current client was going on at length. The little lamp over her door shone red and insistently. In a way Monica felt comforted to discover that there seemed to be other pupils with problems. That she wasn't the only one. That there was evidently some other confused and lonely teenager in there, who didn't know what he should do next. Or she.

Or was the old witch just sitting there, gossiping on the phone and drinking coffee?

Monica sighed, sat up straight and began thinking about Benjamin Kerran instead.

Nine days had passed, and he hadn't been in touch.

She couldn't make up her mind if this surprised her or not. She didn't know if her mother had been seeing him: in any case, they hadn't been seen together at home in Moerckstraat, she was quite sure of that.

But she had been talking about him, she certainly had. In a way and in such words that Monica suspected her mother was becoming rather dependent on him. On having a relationship with him. And that she probably hoped it would develop into something more serious.

There wasn't much doubt about it – her mother was not the type to hide her feelings and her thoughts. Not from her daughter. And she never bothered even to try to do so, even if that might have been best at times.

No, it seemed her mother wanted to carry on seeing Benjamin Kerran. Monica had begun to notice the first signs that her stability was starting to waver, but the more she was able to hold that Sunday morning experience at arm's length, the more convinced she became that it might be possible to sort things out somehow or other.

That her mother and Benjamin might be able to have a perfectly normal relationship, and that this shameful triangular affair in the early days might gradually fade away and be forgotten.

Why not? she thought again, and wondered if perhaps this was how it felt when you weren't seeing problems from a slightly manic point of view.

Mind you, how she would react when she met Benjamin the next time was something she was not at all sure about.

And she had no desire to think about it, either. *Que sera sera*, as they say. And how would he react?

She noticed that sitting there on the chair was becoming uncomfortable, and that she was becoming impatient.

Turn green now, you little bastard! she thought in irritation as she gazed at the lamp over the welfare officer's door – and as if as a result of a telepathic miracle, it suddenly did just that.

'Wow!' Monica whispered to herself. She stood up and opened the door.

*

It went more easily than she had imagined.

Much more. The welfare officer listened to her account of the situation at school, and to her proposed solution. Nodded encouragingly and promised to make contact with Joannis that very afternoon and see if there might be a place for her there. If Monica called in at the same time tomorrow, she would find out what decision had been made.

It was almost as if she wanted to get rid of me, Monica thought as she walked back to her classroom; but she dismissed the thought.

And when she found herself sitting once more on the comfortable green sofa in the welfare officer's room the next morning, she was informed that everything was done and dusted. There was no reason why Monica couldn't start at the Joannis Grammar School this coming Friday: there was a biology class with only twenty-three pupils, and if she found that she would be happy in it, she could transfer straight away.

She was given the name of another welfare officer at the new school who would help her on Friday, then she could spend the weekend thinking things over, and make up her mind.

So easy, Monica thought. But perhaps these matters weren't so difficult after all, provided you applied yourself to getting to grips with things.

And she hadn't said a word about Benjamin Karren.

That same evening, Thursday 21 September, she noticed definite signs that her mother was on the way down again.

When she came home from school her mother was in bed, half asleep. Monica woke her up and explained that she was thinking about changing schools and would be travelling out to Löhr the next day: but her mother only nodded and muttered something about that no doubt being a good idea.

She had a sore throat, she claimed, and had skipped today's course – but it was a crappy course anyway, so it didn't really matter.

She hadn't done any shopping, so if Monica wanted a meal that evening she would either have to go to the shops or see what was available in the freezer. She wasn't hungry.

There was virtually no money in the housekeeping kitty, so Monica made an omelette and a sandwich. She had just finished eating and washing up when the phone rang. She expected her mother to answer, but gathered she had probably pulled the plug out in the bedroom. Monica hurried into the living room and took the call.

It was Benjamin.

He was in his car, outside their front door, talking on his mobile, he explained. He asked if she had anything against meeting him for a little chat. It might be a good idea to discuss a few matters, he suggested.

She hesitated for a few moments, made a quick calculation and concluded that it was now eleven days since he had slunk out of her bedroom.

Then she said yes.

Provided it didn't take too long, she added. She had quite a few things to see to.

Benjamin accepted this, and five minutes later she was sitting in the passenger seat of his car. He was wearing the same shirt as he'd had on that first evening on the sofa, she noted.

6

'I've been a bit busy,' he said. 'That's why you haven't heard from me. Please forgive me.'

She wondered how many times he had apologized or begged for forgiveness during the short time she had known him. It somehow seemed to be his built-in opening line every time he met anybody: apologize, draw a line under everything that had happened and start afresh. Raring to go and without prejudice.

But perhaps it wasn't such a good strategy in the long run.

'Me too,' she said. 'School is causing a lot of problems. I'm going to change, I think.'

'Change what?'

'Schools.'

'I see.'

He didn't sound especially interested. Perhaps he had a voice that always gave him away. She had been so taken by it to start with, but perhaps that had been mainly because that was what he wanted her to feel. Maybe he used his voice as a sort of tool.

He stroked her arm gently with the back of his hand before starting the car. She tried to assess her reaction to that gesture – to determine what she really felt about it – but she couldn't. It was too superficial and insignificant.

'Where would you like to go?'

She shrugged. Pointed out that he was the one who wanted to talk, not she. As far as she was concerned, it didn't matter where they did it.

'Have you eaten?'

She admitted that she had only had an omelette and a sandwich, as her mother was ill.

'Ill?' he said as he drove off in the direction of Zwille. 'She hasn't said anything about that to me.'

'It started today. When did you last speak to her?'

'Yesterday. We spoke on the phone yesterday.'

'But you haven't actually met her for quite a while?'

'Not for a week. I've been a bit busy, as I said.'

There was only a slight hint of irritation in his voice, but she noticed it. A vague reminder that . . . well, what? she wondered. That not just one person was to blame if two people were not in touch with each other? Not even when one was thirty-nine and the other sixteen.

'But you have time to meet me?'

He turned onto the Fourth of September Bridge, turned his head and looked at her for so long that she was about to tell him to keep his eyes on the road instead. Then he cleared his throat, wound down the side window and lit a cigarette. She had never seen him smoking before, and had never noticed that he smelled or tasted of tobacco.

'Do you smoke?'

He laughed.

'I've given it up. Although I buy the odd packet now and again when work gets a bit too stressful. Would you like one?'

He held out the packet. She shook her head.

'The important thing is that I'm in control of it. I can stop whenever I want.'

'Do it then,' she said. 'Stop now, smoke inside a car makes me feel sick.'

'I'm sorry,' he said again, throwing the cigarette out of the window. 'I didn't know that. Are you angry with me?'

'Why do you ask that?'

'Because I think you sound negative. Quite clearly annoyed. Can I invite you to dinner even so?'

She thought it was odd that he wanted to invite her to dinner if he thought she sounded negative and annoyed, and didn't know what to say. She suddenly began to think she was being nasty to him: if she didn't want to talk to him at all, she could have said so on the telephone instead. Declined to join him in the car, that would have been more honest. What she had done in fact was a half measure, as her mother usually called it. A typical, rotten half measure.

And in any case, surely he hadn't done anything to deserve being treated in this childish way? Six of one and half a dozen of the other, after all.

Thus far, at least.

'Okay,' she said. 'Let's have a bite to eat somewhere.'

He nodded.

'I don't want to appear negative, it's just that I think we have to put a stop to these goings-on that we've embarked upon,' she began. 'I felt that it was wrong even before the last time, and it would be catastrophic if my mum got to hear about it.'

'We can talk it over,' he said. 'How about Czerpinski's Mill?'

She'd heard about that restaurant by the Maar out at Bossingen, but she had never been there. As far as she knew – and as the name suggested – it was a restored and revamped mill. Rather an elegant venue, in fact. White tablecloths and all that. She glanced at the clothes she was wearing – a pair of dark corduroy trousers and a wine-red tunic – and decided they would pass muster. Let's face it, teenagers were teenagers after all.

'That's fine by me,' she said. 'As long as we don't stay there too long – I ought to be home before ten.'

'No problem,' he assured her.

For a brief moment, while they were waiting for the food to be served, a mad thought flashed through her mind.

She would stand up and leave their little table hidden away in a corner. Step out into the middle of the restaurant and hold forth for the other guests sitting at tables next to the walls in the low, oblong room with its big oak tables and exposed roof beams.

'Perhaps you think that the pair of us sitting at this table are a father and his daughter,' she would say. 'You no doubt assume that a generous dad is inviting his daughter to have a top-class meal in order to celebrate a birthday, or something of that sort. But that's not the way it is at all. This man is my lover, and he's my mum's lover as well – just so that you know. Thank you for listening, please carry on with your meal.'

Just to see how they reacted. Him and the other guests at this sophisticated restaurant – which didn't in fact have any white tablecloths, but whose class was clear from other subtle details, such as the weight of the cutlery, the thick hammered paper on which the menu was printed, the stiff-starched linen table napkins and the even stiffer-starched waiters.

'I often give him a blow job,' she might add. 'Suck him off. Just so that you know.'

'What are you sitting there thinking about?' he wondered.

She could feel that she was blushing, and tried to cool things down with a drop or two of Coca-Cola.

'Here comes the food,' she said.

'Does it torment you?' he asked. 'This affair between you and me.'

She thought for a moment.

'I wouldn't say it torments me,' she said. 'But it will have to stop now. I thought you'd grasped that.'

She noticed that he stiffened. Sat motionless for a few seconds before calmly but firmly putting his knife and fork down.

'I had the impression that there were two of us involved,' he said. 'I seem to recall that those were the words you used.'

She didn't answer, nor did she look at him.

'If I accept you as a real woman – and isn't that what you

wanted? – you must also act like a real woman. And accept that I am a man. Do you know what I mean?'

A real woman? she thought. No, I don't know what you mean.

But she said nothing.

'I know full well that it wasn't very good for you last time,' he went on. 'But that happens. You shouldn't give up just because it's not the same intense experience every time. You have to learn to forget it and move on.'

'I don't think I really understand what you're talking about,' she said. 'So you think we should carry on as before?'

He nodded.

'Of course. Why not?'

'Because I don't want to, for instance.'

He smiled and put his hand on hers.

'How can you know whether or not you want to continue if we don't give it a try?'

She thought for a moment. Tried to find words that would somehow make holes in his stubborn self-assurance.

'It wasn't just that last time,' she said. 'It's the whole situation, as it were. I can't cope with it. I like you, but not as my lover. I simply can't handle that . . . It was okay for a short time, but it can't go on any longer. You are more than twice as old as me, and you're in a relationship with my mother.'

He didn't remove his hand. Sat there in silence for a few seconds and looked thoughtful. Contemplated different parts of her face. Mouth, hairline, eyes.

'Are you quite sure about that?'

'As sure as I can be.'

'All right,' he said, leaning back. 'Maybe it's best to do as you say. Shall we pay the bill and leave?'

She nodded, excused herself and went to the toilet.

It started raining as they were driving back towards the centre of Maardam. Instead of turning right at the Richter Stadium, he continued straight on past the Pixner Brewery and Keymer church.

'How's your mum?' he asked.

'She's ill today, I told you that. Why are we going this way? Aren't you going to drive me home?'

'I don't mean how your mother is feeling today: I mean in general.'

She shrugged.

'So-so. You know what her problem is. Why are we going this way?'

'I just thought I'd show you where I live. You don't have anything against that, I hope?'

She glanced at her watch and hesitated. It was a quarter past nine. She sat in silence for a while, staring out into the rain.

'I want to be home before ten.'

He patted her forearm.

'Don't worry. Couldn't we talk a bit how you feel, at least? It's not good to break off relationships willy nilly. Believe you me, you have to make sure the scars heal over as well.'

'I think I've talked enough about that.'

She was feeling quite angry now. He put his hand back on the steering wheel.

'Talked enough about it? What do you mean by that?'

'What I say. I've discussed it long enough.'

'I don't understand. With whom have you discussed it?'

She could hear that tone in his voice again. The tone she had noticed when she first got into the car. Like a dash of spice that didn't suit the taste. Something acrid, a little bitter. The word 'dangerous' came into her mind for the first time.

'With a priest.'

'A priest?'

'Yes.'

'Why have you spoken to a priest?'

'Because I needed somebody to talk to about it, of course.'

'I didn't know you had a priest among your friends.'

'I don't. He was visiting the school and telling us what programmes the church was organizing for young people. I went to see him after that.'

'Which church?'

She tried in haste to decide whether or not she wanted to reveal the name of the church, and made up her mind that she did. I might as well, she thought, so that he doesn't get the impression that I'm making it all up. It struck her also that it was a sort of insurance – an independent person who knew all about it. Even if it was only a priest bound by vows of silence.

She didn't have time to ask herself why on earth she should need that kind of insurance.

'Which church?' he asked again.

'The one out at Leimaar. Pastor Gassel. I've met him twice – it's part of their job description to listen to what people tell them, but not say anything about it to anybody else. A sort of confession, although they are not Catholics.'

He nodded vaguely, and scratched his neck.

'But you haven't told your mother at least?'

'Of course not.'

He turned left behind the university into Geldenerstraat, and parked in one of the lanes leading up to the Keymer churchyard. It was raining quite heavily now, and there was not a soul to be seen in the dark alley. He switched off the engine and took out the key, but made no move to get out of the car. He just sat there, tapping his fingers on the steering wheel.

'And what do you think would happen if she found out about it? If somebody were to tell her what we'd been up to?'

'What do you mean? She's not going to know anything about it.'

'Of course not. But how do you think she would take it if she did find out? Hypothetically, that is.'

'I don't understand why you're asking about that. It's pretty obvious that she would have a nasty shock – we've talked about that before.'

He carried on drumming on the wheel.

'So you don't think it would be a good idea for me to tell her?'

Monica stared at him.

'Why would you . . .'

'Because I also feel that I need to be honest about things. More of a need than either you or she has, it seems.'

In a split second the penny dropped for her. And just as

quickly she knew what the implications might be. It wasn't he or she, the guilty parties, who would be worst affected if their affair became known: it would be her mother. No doubt about it. Twofold treachery of this nature – on the part of her lover and her only daughter – given her fragile state and her emotionally unstable situation . . . No, anything but that was Monica's reluctant reaction. And in the circumstances she seemed to be ending up in, to make things even worse . . .

An image of her mother's washed-out face as she lay in bed earlier that afternoon found its way into Monica's mind's eye, and she felt the tears welling up behind her eyes. She swallowed, and tried to pull herself together.

'You mustn't do that,' she said. 'Do you hear? You really must not do that!'

He took a deep breath and let go of the steering wheel.

'No,' he said. 'I know. But can't we go up for a while and talk it over, at least?'

She looked out through the rain-soaked side window at the building they were parked outside.

'Is this where you live?'

'It certainly is. Shall we go in?'

She glanced at her watch again, but realized that it no longer mattered much what time it was. Whether she got home at ten or eleven or even later. She opened the door and stepped out onto the pavement.

He hurried round the car, put his arm round her shoulders and steered her rapidly through the rain and in through the entrance door, which was some ten metres further up the alley in the direction of the churchyard. She had time to note that the building was four or five storeys high, quite old and with stone walls. The entrance door led into an inner courtyard with bicycle stands, a shed for rubbish, and some benches under a large tree she thought was an elm. It was all a bit reminiscent of Palitzerlaan, and she felt a slight pang of nostalgia.

'What a lovely building,' she said.

'Art Nouveau,' he said. 'Built exactly a hundred years ago. Yes, it's pretty impressive.'

His flat was also impressive. To say the least. Four rooms plus a kitchen, as far as she could tell; large parquet floor tiles made of light-coloured, grained wood and an open fire in the large living room. Heavy, dark furniture widely spaced – and well-filled bookshelves covering almost all of every wall. Two large, low sofas and soft carpets. She compared it with Moerckstraat, and felt a somewhat different pang.

He must be rich, she thought. Why is he bothering with the likes of us?

'What was that name on your door?' she asked. 'It wasn't yours.'

'What did you say?' he shouted from the kitchen.

'It didn't say Kerran on your door.'

He came back into the living room.

'Oh, that . . . I had a lodger last spring. A student. He insisted on having his name on the door, so that visitors could find his pad. I forgot to take it away. Would you like something to drink?'

She shook her head.

'Can we do the talking now, and get it over with?'

She sat down on one of the sofas, and he flopped down beside her after a moment's hesitation.

'I hadn't thought of restricting ourselves to talking.'

Before she had time to respond he stood up again and disappeared into the kitchen. Came back carrying a single candle in a holder. He turned off the ceiling light using the switch in the doorway, lit the candle with a cigarette lighter and put it on the table. Sat down next to her again. She began to catch on to what was going to happen next.

I don't want to, she thought. Not again.

'So it wouldn't be very good if your mother found out about us?' he said.

'No . . .'

'If you can be nice to me just one more time, I promise I won't breathe a word.'

She wouldn't have thought it was possible to combine an emotional entreaty and an ice-cold threat in such an ingenious way, but it evidently was. She tried to swallow, but her mouth was so dry that it was no more than a facial twitch. He put his arm round her shoulders and hugged her closer to him.

'I don't want to,' she said.

For a few seconds the only sound to be heard was his calm, regular breathing and the pattering of rain on the windows. When he started speaking again, she thought for a confused moment that it was somebody else. That it wasn't him.

'I couldn't give a damn if you want to or not, you diabolical little whore,' he said. 'You will kindly allow me to fuck you, otherwise I shall make sure that your bloody mother ends up in a loony bin for the rest of her life.'

He said it in an almost normal conversational tone of voice, and at first she thought she had misheard him. Then she realized that he meant exactly what he had said. He held her tightly with one arm round her back and shoulders, and started pawing at her lap with his other hand. For the first time it dawned on her how strong he was, and how incapable she would be of resisting if he were to force himself on her.

'Is that clear, you silly little bitch? Take your clothes off!'

Everything went black before her eyes; she had always thought that this kind of thing only happened in tenth-rate books or in old girls' magazines – but it was happening to her, here and now. It became black in reality. The candle's little flickering flame suddenly vanished as if someone had blown it out, and it was several seconds before it was lit again.

Help, she thought. God. Mum . . .

He pulled her closer and started kissing her. Forced her jaws apart and thrust his tongue so far into her mouth that she could scarcely breathe.

Then he let go of her.

'Or perhaps you would prefer it a bit more gently?'

She was gasping and tried to think a sensible thought. Just one would do.

'Yes,' she said. 'Yes please.'

The thought came. Slowly, like a thief in the night. I must kill him, it said.

Somehow or other. Kill him.

'Take off your tunic,' he said.

She did as she was told.

'And your bra.'

She leaned forward on the sofa and unhooked the straps with her hands behind her back. But he didn't bother about her breasts. He stood up instead and placed himself behind her. Moved her hair out of the way and put his hands on her bare shoulders. She felt herself going stiff.

'You are tense,' he said, stroking his fingers along the sharp edges of her collarbones, moving them inwards towards her neck. 'My fingertips are like small seismographs. I can almost feel your thoughts . . . My sick rose. My sick, sick rose . . .'

'I need a pee,' she said. 'Where's the bathroom?'

'Pee?'

'Yes.'

'I'll come with you,' he said.

She stood up. He walked behind her into the hall, keeping his fingers on her shoulders, as if it were some silly kind of follow-my-leader game.

I must kill him, sang a voice inside her. Must find a way . . .

'Like seismographs,' he said again.

LONDON

AUGUST 1998

7

At first there were two of them.

Both in their thirties. Both of them jolly and a bit merry after visits to the cinema followed by a restaurant meal together. They lived in Camden Town: this pub was more or less halfway between home and Oxford Street, and this wasn't the first time they had dropped in after a night out.

He had been to see a play at the old Garrick Theatre – one of those incredibly thin and pointless West End hits that ran before packed houses for tourist season after tourist season. Thank the Lord there had been an interval, and he was able to sneak out and call in at three pubs on the way back to his hotel near Regent's Park. This was his fourth.

The Green Stallion. It was turned eleven, but this was evidently one of the establishments that no longer observed the old opening hours. He had just collected another Lauder's and another pint when they came in and asked if the empty chairs at his table were taken. The pub was full and noisy both around the long bar and at the tables. There didn't seem to be any other empty chairs anywhere, as far as he could see. So why not? He beckoned with his hand, and smiled.

The women smiled back, and sat down. Each of them lit a

cigarette, and introduced herself. Beth and Svetlana. Obviously keen to talk.

Svetlana was Russian, but born in Luton. By hook or by crook her parents had managed to wriggle out of the Soviet Union during the thaw in the early sixties, and of course it was anybody's guess why they had given their first-born child, born in the West, the same name as Stalin's daughter. 'A fucking mystery!' said Beth, laughing and displaying her forty-eight perfect teeth.

'Beth is just another London bitch who knows nothing about anything,' explained Svetlana. 'Who are you, please?'

He didn't tell them who he was. For some mysterious intuitive reason he gave them a different name and a different nationality.

But he did tell them his profession. He could see that both of them were quite impressed, and he knew immediately that he wanted them.

Or one of them. It didn't matter which, certainly not: but for the first time for ages and ages he felt that he really must have sex with a woman.

It wasn't clear why this was. Perhaps it was his being in a foreign but even so very familiar city. A sort of reunion – he had been there a dozen times before, but when he worked it out he realized that it must be six years since the last time. Six years . . .

Perhaps it was the warm summer's evening, perhaps it was the booze. He was agreeably drunk, and when he drank a toast with the two women, he made sure he looked them both in the eye. He couldn't detect any trace of reluctance. On the contrary. In vino veritas, he thought, and drank deeply.

Or perhaps it was just the passage of time. He had needed three years, and now they were over. It didn't need to be any more remarkable than that. You must learn how to wait, his mother used to say. If you are able to be patient, you will be able to achieve anything you want, my boy. No woman will ever refuse you anything, never ever – remember that.

Not even your mother.

He realized that he was sitting there and thinking about those very words while Beth and Svetlana had briefly taken their leave to powder their noses.

No woman will ever . . .

It was Beth.

Presumably they reached an agreement during the afore-mentioned visit to the toilets, because shortly after they returned to the table Svetlana announced that she really ought to be thinking about making her way home. A few minutes after midnight she took her leave and hoped they would continue to have a pleasant evening. With unambiguous looks and routine cheek kisses.

They continued talking for another half-hour, then they took a taxi to Beth's little flat in Camden Town Road. His hotel would have been nearer, but a home is always a home – and she had a bottle of white wine in the fridge and a chicken that only needed heating up.

★

Shortly after two, she suddenly didn't want to go through with it.

By that time he was completely naked, and she was wearing only her knickers when out of the blue she decided that enough was enough. They were half-lying on her cramped sofa, the wine bottle was almost empty, the remains of the chicken were on the table, and she had been stroking his stiff penis.

'I can do it for you,' she said.

But she didn't want to go to bed with him tonight. Another time, perhaps, if he would be staying on in London?

But it just wasn't on right now. Could he understand that?

He said that he could. Moved her hand away and sat there for a while as they drank what was left of the wine. Then he heaved himself up and stood behind her with his hands on her shoulders. Brushed her red hair to one side and began stroking his fingers over her soft, naked skin and the sharp edges of her collarbones.

Asked if he could give her a bit of a massage.

She nodded hesitantly, and straightened her back.

He massaged her gently for a few minutes, until her shoulders relaxed and began to sink. She said she liked it. He said that he did as well. He could feel that she was a sensuous and warm-blooded woman.

Then he felt his own blood reaching boiling point, and strangled her.

It was probably all over within about ninety seconds. He removed her red knickers and laid her down on the floor, on her back. Opened her legs wide and placed her in a position with her pussy exposed and naively inviting. Her dead pussy.

He masturbated, and wiped himself dry with her knickers.

He was back in his hotel room an hour later. Went to bed and slept until noon the following day.

His flight left Heathrow on time that same evening, and as he watched the multi-million city shrinking away into insignificance through his cabin window, he was convinced that they would never find Beth Lindley's murderer.

Never ever.

He also thought that he had better be careful when it came to women in future. Maybe he should give them a wide berth, that would be the safest bet, of course – but if he found himself in similar circumstances at some point in the future even so, he would be well advised to think ahead.

Very well advised. He ordered a whisky from the stewardess, and noted that he was sitting there smiling.

MAARDAM

SEPTEMBER–OCTOBER 2000

8

She didn't go out for three days.

Three nights and three days. She spent exactly seventy-two-and-a-half hours in her room with ridiculously short breaks in order to go to the lavatory. Or to the kitchen to have a drink of water and something to eat. A sandwich. A cup of yoghurt. Or just a lump of bread, there wasn't much food in the flat – and it was a mystery how all that time, all those endless hours and those absurdly long-drawn-out minutes passed through her consciousness without driving her mad.

Or perhaps she was mad. Afterwards – the moment she emerged into the rain-drenched street at a quarter to twelve on Sunday evening – it felt as if those locked-in days had already passed.

As if they had been and gone without touching her.

She was in her room, her mother in hers. Three small rooms and a kitchen. Moerckstraat. Rain, more rain, and no food in the fridge. A manic-depressive woman and her mad daughter, who had just murdered their shared lover.

No wonder they were not exactly memorable days.

'I'm ill,' her mother had said when they bumped into

HÅKAN NESSER

each other on Friday afternoon. Coughed a little, perhaps to prove it.

As if Monica hadn't known. As if she was an easily fooled idiot on top of everything else.

'Me too,' she had answered.

And frightened, she could have added if her mother had looked as if she were interested in listening. Or if she had been a different sort of mother.

And mad. And desperate. And scared to death.

No, perhaps she wouldn't have been able to say that. Might not even have been able to say it if she had been a member of the best of families.

'I'm going for a lie-down,' her mother had said. 'You should do the same. It'll pass.'

So, in bed, on her back. Staring at the ceiling or with her eyes closed, it didn't make any difference. The images came. The same images, the same film. Over and over again in a never-ending stream, until she had the urge to dig her fingers deep down into her eye sockets and dig out those disgusting projectors by the roots and put an end to everything once and for all, and fall down into darkness and silence and eternal merciful rest and forgetfulness . . . These images.

Benjamin Kerran.

Standing there in the bathroom, watching her.

Just standing there, while she squatted on the lavatory seat, emptying her bladder, then trying to press out a few more drops while frenetically trying to work out a plan in her head. Frustratedly and desperately she rejected all possibilities even before they came to the surface of her flickering consciousness. He dug his hand down inside his trousers, contemplating her with glazed-over eyes and an increasingly warped smile, then suddenly he whipped his penis out of his flies, in a sort of perverted triumph, and ordered her to give him head while she was still sitting on the lavatory. That gave him extra stimulus, he said. No, he didn't order her: Benjamin Kerran didn't order her to do it, the circumstances didn't need that. This was different. Instead he used the same remarkable blend of entreaty and threat as before, that was sufficient. 'You wouldn't want your mother to find out about us, would you?' he said. 'Just one more time. It'll be easy . . . Don't you think we should grant ourselves an enjoyable finish, especially as it started so well?'

And she did what he wanted. Was almost sick as he thrust his penis a long way into her throat, but she was even closer to being sick when she thought of the possibility of biting off his glans penis. Just bite him as hard as she could – would that save her? she wondered. Is that enough to kill a man, biting off his cock? Would one strong bite be enough?

She didn't know, and didn't do it anyway. It wasn't necessary, as at that very moment she caught sight of a pair of scissors lying on a shelf diagonally behind his back: no more planning was necessary, none at all. All that was needed was to remain cool and calculating and wait for the right moment. That was all.

And in the insistent cinema of her memory she watches herself flush the lavatory and stand up. Sees herself both from the outside and the inside – these pictures that are three days old, but nevertheless seem to her to be older than life itself . . . She forces him out of her mouth but grasps his penis in her hand instead and tosses him off, just as he has taught her to do during the short and bewitched time they have known each other, and slowly manoeuvres herself into a position behind his back. She holds his stiff cock in her left hand, stretches round from behind his back, meets his green eyes in the bathroom mirror, and out of his line of vision reaches out with her right hand for the scissors, takes hold of them silently and then stabs them into his stomach with one violent thrust. Without a thought in her head.

Sees his face reflected in the mirror, sees it dilating and expressing first genuine surprise for a fraction of a second. The pain. Then nothing.

She feels his virility deflating in her hand, just as quickly as the air gushing out of a balloon.

Sees – and feels – him collapse without a sound, no more than a slight hiss like the flow of air from the one of those balloons, albeit a bigger one. He falls like a felled ox, like a shot beast, onto the blue-green clinker floor with its small goose pimples and false fossils and genuine heating coils, and sticking out just over his right hip are the shiny handle loops of the scissors, like a magic, mythological symbol. The blades have penetrated him as far as they could go, ten centimetres at least, and even as she stands there staring at the body and at her own face in the mirror, she wonders if he is dead. Already dead? Is it so easy? Doesn't it take any longer than that? Is that all that's involved?

And she sees – in the unremitting cinema of her memory – how she leaves the bathroom, rushes out of the flat. How she slams the door behind her with a loud bang that echoes in the staircase and hangs in the air until she is outside in the court-yard with its bicycle stands and rubbish shed and elm tree and bench, because it is a sound-film running in the cinema of her memory. And there is another sound lingering in the air: she doesn't know if it is real or merely an illusion – a hallucination or an audible mirage: just as she slammed the door, perhaps half a second beforehand, did she hear him shout her name?

Monica!

Is that possible? Did she really hear that?

And just look how she is running through the rain. Racing here and there along the dark streets that seem to be rocking and swaying and branching off in hitherto unknown direc-tions, so that she loses all sense of where she is and of the way home. She continues in this manner for at least an hour – perhaps she doesn't really want to reach home . . . She pauses three or four times, leans against walls and tries to throw up: she succeeds on one occasion, but not on the others, and when she staggers into the kitchen in Moerck-straat the clock, the old, everlasting brass mantelpiece clock that she and her father bought at an auction when she was only five, is showing a quarter past eleven and her mother is sitting in the living room gaping at a blue-coloured crime series on the telly, and doesn't even say hello.

She doesn't even say hello, nor does she ask where her daughter has been.

And her daughter doesn't tell her that she has just killed their shared lover. She simply stands there for a while in the doorway of the big room, which is certainly one of the smallest big rooms in the whole of the town, staring at the uncombed back of her mother's head and the fast-moving, jerky pictures on the television screen. Then she goes into her own room and stays there for three days.

Three nights and three days.

Seventy-two-and-a-half hours.

Then she goes out.

The cafe was called Duisart's, and was evidently open until three.

It was in one of the alleys between Armastenplejn and Langgraacht: she had never seen it before, but then, this was not her home district. The light was dirty yellow and the premises seemed a bit on the shabby side, but she found a corner where she was hidden away and didn't have to look at any other of the sparsely distributed customers crouching over small plastic tables with their coffees, drinks and cigarettes. Men, almost exclusively men. Aged between thirty-five and a hundred. On their own or in pairs. An elderly, intoxicated lady with a spotted dog sat in a corner.

She ordered coffee and a glass of cognac: the waiter, with a ponytail, a nose ring and a flower tattooed on one cheek seemed to be wondering how old she might be, then shrugged and came back after less than a minute with the cup and the glass on a tray.

She sipped at the coffee and at the strong drink in the glass. She was not used to drinking alcohol, far from it: but a voice inside her told her that she needed it now. Something strong. Something uncompromising.

She needed to think straight, quite simply. And needed help in order to be able to think straight.

Needed to switch off that worn-out film show that filled her memory, and get to grips with things. Here and now. She emptied her glass in one gulp, and beckoned the waiter to bring her another one.

I have killed somebody, she began.

A man who was my mother's lover. And my lover.

Who deserved to die. Didn't deserve to live.

Not any more.

Why? Why did he deserve to die?

Because he had been exploiting them. Herself and her mother and their extraordinary fragility.

My guilt is light, she thought. As light as a feather. I shall be able to bear it, and nobody need know about it. Nobody knows what I have done, nobody knows about Benjamin Kerran and me, it is all and has all been exclusively between me and him, and now it is hidden away in my head, nowhere else. It hurts and chafes and drives me mad, but that is the only place where it exists. And it will pass . . . my mother suspects nothing and will not be given any reason to suspect anything; if anybody else finds out about our connection with Benjamin Kerran, there is no reason to link that connection with his death . . . My mother, I mean, my mother will not be connected with his death, there is no reason to do so, he has no doubt kept her just as secret as he has kept me, and when they find him nobody will suspect anything . . . They've probably only met about five or six times in all . . . no, there are no clues linking him to my mother or to me. They will look for a murderer, of course, male or female; but it will never occur to anybody to start looking around in a cramped little flat in Moerckstraat with ceilings so low that even a domestic pet would have to crouch down in order to move around, there's no reason for anybody to search for anything in a place like that. No reason to be afraid, no reason to be scared any more, no reason to . . .

The waiter arrived with her new glass and she broke off her train of thought. Just like cutting off a piece of thread that was too long. Paid, and waited until he had gone away. Then emptied the glass into her half-drunk cup of coffee, as she had seen her mother do, and as she remembered her father doing, and tasted the brew. Added a spoonful of sugar, stirred it and tried again. Much better, it almost tasted good, and warmed her up inside. She had never smoked – apart from a few giggly puffs at less than elegant dances when she was in class five or six – but now she suddenly fancied a cigarette to suck at as she sat in this gloomy cafe as the rain poured down outside.

But instead that voice came back to her. The thought of that voice. It burst into her head like a sour-tasting belch – Benjamin Kerran's cry from the bathroom just before she slammed the door and raced down the stairs.

Monica!

Was it possible? Wasn't it just her imagination? A hallucinatory cry from beyond the grave?

Or could it be that she really had heard him? That he really had shouted from that warm clinker floor in the bathroom with a pair of scissors stuck ten centimetres into his gut, his cock hanging helplessly like a piece of rag and his trousers crumpled around his ankles?

That he hadn't died?

That he was still alive, despite everything?

Then, at least: that he was still alive then, at the moment when she left him and rushed out into the night like a terrified madwoman, her brains crushed like a crust of ice by the heavy boot of reality?

Where do all these words come from? she wondered. *The heavy boot of reality?* Something she had read, presumably. Lonely girls read more books than anybody else in the world, a woman teacher had told a gathering of parents when she was in class four. She wondered what pedagogical value such a disclosure could have; but of course there was little point in wondering about that just now, in sitting there and trying to trace the dodgy origins of her dodgy thoughts . . . It was more important to sharpen them, to focus them and introduce a modicum of clarity. Decide what to do next. Was she drunk? Intoxicated already after no more than one-and-a-half glasses? It wasn't impossible. She hadn't had much to eat these last three days, next to nothing in fact, and alcohol had a greater effect on people if they had an empty stomach, even she knew that. Even Monica Kammerle knew that – but there was something else she didn't know, and that was in fact the most important thing in the world for her to know just now.

Was he dead?

Had Benjamin Kerran really died up there in the bathroom? Had she finished him off by stabbing him with a pair of scissors, or had she only wounded him?

Oh hell, she thought, emptying her cup. Bloody hell, I simply don't know. I'm such a damned useless idiot that I don't even know if I've killed him or not! Idiot, Monica Kammerle, you are just a poor little idiot, and you'll soon be as mad as your mother and the pair of you will end up in the loony bin. It's only a matter of time before the pair of you are lying there under yellow blankets, keeping each other company amid the faint smell of fading carnations and badly washed bodies . . .

Almost as a confirmation of this last thought, two men at another table burst out laughing.

A crude, wheezing belly laugh as if from an old horror film, accompanied by curses, a thumping of fists on the table and stamping on the floor. She leaned forward and looked at them through an apology of a trellis which should have been covered by some climbing plant or other, but wasn't and never would be. Saw how one of the men dug into his right ear with the handle of a teaspoon while the other was convulsed by a coughing attack, which brought the fun and games to a full stop.

She checked her watch and stood up. Five minutes past

one. Time to go home, no doubt about that. This wasn't a place for young girls to while away the night at, Duisart's, definitely not.

Time to find out how things were in the real world.

To snuggle down into bed in Moerckstraat and make plans, in fact.

I'm a pain, she thought when she was out in the alley again. My thoughts keep nagging away at me. I'm drunk. Some people go downhill rapidly. I'm a drunken murderess, even though I'm only sixteen.

And I feel sick – holy shit!

The night air and walking through the cold rain sobered her up, and by the time she returned to Moerckstraat, fear had once again begun to swirl around inside her.

Her mother was sitting in front of the television, where a different blue-coloured crime series was now trundling along with the sound on low. It was half past one. There was a smell of something unpleasant oozing out from the kitchen, but no doubt it was just the slop bucket.

'What are you watching?' she asked.

'I don't know,' said her mother.

'Shouldn't you go to bed now?'

'I've only just woken up,' said her mother.

'I see. Well, I'm going to bed now.'

'Mmm.'

'Good night.'

'Mmm.'

She went to the bathroom. Brushed her teeth. She smelled of sweat, but who the hell cared? Looked for a moment or two at the bottles of tablets, but desisted from checking.

What was the point?

When I'm dead I'll see Dad again, she thought.

9

After darkness cometh light, after strength cometh weakness.

She had read this somewhere or other, so perhaps it wasn't surprising that a few days passed after her risky outing to the cafe on Sunday before she plucked up courage to go out again.

Once, just once, her mother went to the corner shop and bought in a few necessities, but Monica stayed put. She in her room, her mother in hers, full stop. Time passed, and yet again seemed not to affect them. When her mother summoned up all the pathetic sense of duty she was capable of and asked why her daughter wasn't at school, Monica said she had the flu, and that was accepted as a sufficient explanation.

She read, then hid what she had been reading. Wrote, and threw away what she had written. It was not until Wednesday evening that she could summon up sufficient strength and energy to dare to venture as far as the library in Ruidsenallé.

She had a plan. It was simple, and she had been considering it ever since it came to her during one of her sleepless nights.

If Benjamin Kerran had been found dead in his bathroom nearly a week ago – she had concluded – there must be something about it in the newspapers. It would be implausible for there not to be.

And so all she needed to do was to check. She asked for copies of *Neuwe Blatt* and *Telegraaf* for the last six days, sat down at an empty table and started leafing through them. Calmly and methodically, leaving nothing to chance. Page by page, newspaper by newspaper. No hurry. It took twenty minutes.

Not a word.

Not a single word about a man stabbed with a pair of scissors in a flat near the university. No death notice. Nothing.

Ergo? she asked herself as she gazed out of the aquarium-like windows at the square, and listened to the blood pounding in her temples. What does this mean? What has actually happened?

The answer was obvious. Or rather, the alternatives were obvious.

Either he had survived. The scissors had not damaged any vital organ. He had simply fainted as a result of the pain, come round again and pulled out the scissors. Driven to the hospital and had his wound dressed. Or managed it himself.

Or – the other alternative – he was simply lying dead on his bathroom floor, just as she had left him, waiting to be discovered.

It would soon be a whole week. Was that plausible? Was it possible? How soon does a body start to smell? When would the neighbours begin to suspect foul play? His colleagues at work?

She slid the pile of newspapers to one side and allowed her thoughts to wander between the two possibilities. Trying to weigh them up and working out which one was the more likely.

If he had survived, if he was still alive, she thought – trying to ignore the cold and remarkably slow shudder working its way up along her spine – shouldn't he have been in touch? Shouldn't she have known by now?

She took a few deep breaths and tried to think clearly. Surely it was extremely odd that he hadn't made some sort of counter-move? He couldn't possibly have failed to see that she had tried to kill him. Even if he hadn't registered what happened during the critical moments, the scissors must surely have indicated what had happened. They couldn't have landed there of their own accord. She – that crafty sixteen-year-old Monica Kammerle – had tried to finish him off, there was no mistaking that.

Attempted murder. She wondered how long a sentence such a charge would involve.

A few years? That was for sure. But of course, not as many as it would have been if she had succeeded in her attempt.

Self-defence, of course. And perhaps it was classified as manslaughter. Attempted manslaughter? That didn't sound so bad. And surely one had a right to defend oneself against unwanted sexual advances? Surely she would be able to plead attempted rape and self-defence?

She gave a start when she realized that she was beginning to lose sight of the basic facts. She had had sex with him several times of her own free will, and there was not really much point in sitting there speculating about the possible consequences of that.

Besides, he's dead! she suddenly decided, gritting her teeth. He can't possibly be still alive without getting in touch somehow or other! Impossible. He's lying up there in his bathroom, rotting away: old buildings made of stone are solidly constructed, and it can take months before the stench starts to become noticeable. Weeks in any case. Art Nouveau, wasn't that what he'd said?

But then, it wasn't the stench from the corpse that was the crucial point, she realized. His employers and workmates must start wondering what was going on – in local government, she seemed to recall he had said – and sooner or later they would begin to suspect foul play. In fact, they had probably already started to do so: colleagues and close friends . . . relatives as well, assuming he had any he was in regular touch with, she didn't know . . . They must surely catch on to the fact that something odd must have happened – not everybody was as isolated as a certain mother and a certain daughter in a poky little flat in Moerckstraat.

She stood up and carried the newspapers back to the issuing counter. Dead, she told herself once again. I have murdered Benjamin Kerran. It's only a matter of time before his body is found, and the whole of Maardam will be able to read about it.

But just as she was about to thank the well-upholstered librarian for her help, once again that shout echoed inside her head.

Monica!

She felt herself shaking, and hurried out through the entrance hall. I'm a sick rose, she thought. A sick, sick rose.

Thy dark secret love does my life destroy.

It was not until an afternoon four days later that she left her flat the next time. Four days. As heavy as lead and as empty as a vacuum.

She had only come as far as the corner of Falckstraat and Zwille when she bumped into her English teacher, fröken Kluivert; and a few minutes later she saw a group of class-mates crossing over Grote Torg. Girls with their arms around each other's shoulders, laughing away somewhat artificially. It was Saturday, a free day.

She survived both incidents, just about, but made up her mind to postpone what she planned to do next until that evening, when it would be dark. She had realized that daylight, and the pale September sunshine, were not a com-bination likely to assist her in achieving her aims.

Not that anybody would have been especially interested, put two and two together and wondered why she had been off school for over a week. Certainly not.

But she had no desire to meet anybody. The bottom line was that it was her interests at stake, nobody else's. She didn't want to talk to anybody, or to look anybody else in the eye. These people had nothing to do with her, had never had any importance, and even less now. Everything was as it always had been, she thought, but her life had acquired a sort of sig-nificance that it hadn't had before. A sort of transparency.

When she got back home she found her mother on the telephone. For a moment she thought it might have been Benjamin, and her heart felt as if it had just been kicked by a horse. Then she heard that it was in fact her aunt Barbara, and it was just the routine check, the call that came every third or fourth week, like clockwork, and which contained about as much empathy and sisterly love as there was blood in an ice crystal – to use an expression her father used occasionally. An expression based on deeply felt emotions.

Her mother kept a stiff upper lip to the best of her ability, and the call was terminated after less than a minute.

'Have you met that Benjamin again lately?' – the words slipped out of Monica's mouth before she could stop them. She hadn't planned to say that, but it seemed that her words had suddenly acquired an uncontrollable will of their own. She knew after all that her mother hadn't set foot outside the door for a week.

'Benjamin?' said her mother, as if she had already forgotten who that was. 'No, I don't think there would be much point.'

'Has he been in touch at all lately?'

That was also a pretty pointless question. She had barely been more than ten metres away from her mother recently.

'No.'

'Okay, I was just asking.'

'I see.'

Monica went back to her room. Lay down on her bed and prepared to wait for the arrival of dusk. Stared up at the ceiling. Thought for a moment about Pastor Gassel, but pushed any such thoughts to one side as she had already done several times before. She had never really managed to believe wholly in him, and to do so now was a step too far. Much too far. She took out her Blake instead, and picked out a poem at random.

> *Cruelty has a Human Heart*
> *And Jealousy a Human Face*
> *Terror, the Human Form Divine*
> *And Secrecy, the Human Dress*

She read those lines over and over again until she was sure that she knew them off by heart. Then lay down with her eyes closed and repeated them over and over again, until she fell asleep under her blanket.

There was no Benjamin Kerran in the Maardam section of the telephone directory. Nobody by the name of Kerran at all, in fact.

An ex-directory number, then; but if things had been different, she could have asked her mother, of course.

There was nothing in her mother's room either, in fact: she took the opportunity of making a search while her mother was in the bath with a glass of wine. Nothing in the address book. No number scribbled down on a scrap of paper or in the margin of a newspaper, places her mother liked to use for noting down important things.

So she would have to drop the idea of phoning him. There was nothing she could do about it, she thought. Never mind – perhaps she wouldn't have dared to anyway, when the chips were down.

And directory enquiries had no current number for anybody called Kerran, no subscriber by that name . . . And no, of course it was not possible to supply information about so-called ex-directory numbers: why did she think people took the trouble of keeping their private lives private?

Monica sighed. Back to plan A, then. Another little visit to see if it was possible to find out anything.

If there was a light in one of his windows, perhaps.

Or in the chink under the door.

Or if the mailbox down in the entrance hall seemed to be chock-full. There ought to be several indications to look for and interpret, without her needing to go so far as to press her nose against the keyhole and sniff for the smell of rotting flesh. Even if she couldn't be certain, surely there would be a pointer or two.

A clear pointer, and with a bit of luck, certainty. Plan A it would have to be.

She left Moerckstraat at about nine. She noticed to her surprise that the evening was quite warm. Fifteen degrees or thereabouts. As far as she could recall it hadn't rained all day, and the wind that had died away to become no more than a mild whisper was distinctly friendly as it wafted in from the south, despite the fact that it was almost October. She took the route past the canals and Keymer Plejn: it was a bit of a detour, but she felt that the walk would do her good. She also decided to skirt round the cemetery rather than cut through it, and when she turned into the right alley and could see the dreary old university building in the background, it was already turned half past nine.

She stopped on the pavement opposite, just in front of the steps down to some sort of zoological shop. She gazed up at the dark façade on the other side of the street. Five storeys, just as she had remembered it – the bottom floor some way above ground level so that nosy parkers peeping in through the windows were not a problem.

But Benjamin Kerran didn't live on the bottom floor, and she suddenly realized that she wasn't sure if it was on the third or fourth.

But surely it must be the fourth, she thought. The top floor, that must be it. In any case, he had windows both looking out over the street and into the courtyard, she was sure of that.

But which ones were they? Which windows? The building extended along the whole length of the alley, from the university at one end and the cemetery wall at the other, and she counted up to eighteen windows on the top floor, under the overhanging roof. Unless she was completely mistaken, the ones she was looking for should be slightly to the left of the centrally placed entrance door, from where she was standing.

But how many to the left?

At least four, she thought; and with the aid of some kind of obscure, intuitive sense of direction she picked out the four most likely ones. It was dark in two of them, light in the other two – a warm, yellow, slightly subdued light. No cold blue light from the television through lace curtains in this block. There were also lights in the windows to the right of the ones she had picked out, while on the other side everything was dark all the way to the cemetery. The shortcomings and uncertainties in these observations and calculations struck her at about the same time as she realized that the whole business of light and dark windows was nothing much to go by in any case.

If Benjamin Kerran was alive and at home, then of course he was likely to have lights on at this time in the evening.

But if he was at home and lying dead in the bathroom, it was at least as likely that he wouldn't have had the strength to heave himself to his feet in order to switch off the lights that she must have left burning nine days ago. There had only been a candle burning in the living room, she remembered that: but all the lights had been on in the bathroom and the hall.

She congratulated herself on reaching those brilliant conclusions, then plucked up courage, crossed over the street and tried the entrance door.

It was not locked. She hesitated for a moment, then opened it and went into the courtyard. Paused and looked around.

A dark-haired young woman appeared, carrying a basket of newly washed clothes. There was a smell of cooking coming from an open window on the ground floor on the right. The old wrought-iron lantern in the corner by the bicycle stands was switched on, as were the small yellow lamps over the various staircases. The woman went in through one of them, but that wasn't Benjamin Kerran's door. Monica took a deep breath and established that there was no stench of rotting flesh lurking in the air in the courtyard, only that cooking smell. Something with mushrooms and garlic, no doubt, and she suddenly felt hungry. She hadn't had a cooked meal for over a week now, so that was hardly surprising. Not surprising at all.

She scanned the façade of the building from this side as well, from the inside as it were, but didn't bother to try to work out which windows were relevant. It looked as if people were at home in most flats, in about two-thirds of them in fact, she estimated. Some of the windows were even open – it was such a warm evening, so why not? She could hear noises from televisions and radios here and there, and the occasional conversation, muted somewhat by the thick walls and the dense atmosphere of . . . well, of middle-class civilization. She noted that the overall impression was of unambiguous homeliness – a feeling of homeliness impervious to pressures from the outside – and she could feel a lump forming in her throat.

I mustn't start crying now, she thought – and at that same moment she realized that she couldn't remember the name on the door of the flat.

It had been something different: not Kerran . . . But the name of a lodger who had since moved out, and she hadn't a clue as to what that name was. How come she had over-looked this state of affairs? Until now?

In other words, was she sure that she would be able to find the right door? And come to think of it, how about the entrance doors out here in the courtyard, leading up to the various staircases? Surely they wouldn't be unlocked as late as this in the evening, allowing any old riff-raff to gain entry?

Hell's bells, she thought. I must have forgotten that I'm just an idiot. What am I doing here? What the hell was that for a daft impulse, sending me back to the scene of the crime? Standing here in the courtyard like a halfwit, totally unable to take any steps likely to throw light on the fate of the dead body!

She shook her head, walked forward and tried the door in question – the one she thought she remembered, at least.

Locked. Just as anybody with a brain more functional than a walnut could have worked out. I might just as well give up, she thought. Just as well go home and continue to stare up at the ceiling, waiting for my collapse, the arrival of the social services and the Day of Judgement . . . Bloody fucking hell!

She was just about to turn on her heel and turn this decision into reality when a light was switched on, visible through the small, frosted glass panes in the upper part of the door.

She had no time to consider. To make a decision. A balding, middle-aged man in tracksuit and trainers came out. Nodded to her, ran out into the courtyard and vanished into the street within three seconds.

She managed to catch the door before it closed and automatically locked itself, and before she knew where she was, she found herself inside. Paused for a moment and felt a sort of whirlpool welling up inside her. Gritted her teeth and clasped her hands. Looked around.

Now, she thought. Please, God, give me a chance.

On the wall to the left, before the stairs up to the lift, was a noticeboard inside a glass case, with the names of the tenants, floor by floor: and when she read it, she suddenly remembered – she recognized the name of the student. On the fourth floor, just as she had thought. At the top of the building.

If the circumstances had been different and her head clearer, she might have wondered why his name wasn't here either, just that of the student lodger who had moved out some time ago – wondered for a moment about whether there was something odd about the correct name not being displayed in such obvious places.

But she didn't. She didn't question anything at all. The whirlpool inside her was too strong. Having come this far, Monica didn't give herself time to reflect about anything. Even forgot to check the state of the mailboxes, which were lined up on the wall opposite the list of names.

Simply stepped into the lift – it was a well-lit and inviting old-fashioned wooden lift with folding seats covered in red velvet. She remembered it. Closed the noisy barred door and pressed the button.

The lift cage, which presumably dated back to . . . did he say 1905? . . . started moving and slowly, rattling and squeaking, raised her up inside the building – and as she stood there, swaying from side to side and watching floor after floor pass by, she remembered to start sniffing, wondering if she would be able to recognize the smell.

The sweetish smell of her lover's rotting body.

But she didn't smell it at all. Not even when she stepped out of the lift and stood in front of his door was there any trace of a suspicious stench.

Nor was there any sign of a chink of light under the door to his flat. But then, that would have been impossible in any circumstances, she realized, because there wasn't so much as a millimetre's gap under the bottom of the door. On the contrary, the door was just as dark and well-fitting and solid as everything else in the building, and the keyhole was certainly not of the type that you could peer through. Definitely not.

Monica swallowed, and stood there with her arms dangling by her sides. She felt that the whirlpool was fading away, and that she was once more close to crying – but at that very moment she heard footsteps on the staircase below.

She hadn't heard a door opening and closing again, but perhaps somebody had come in through the door while she was still in the noisy lift.

Somebody was on the way up the stairs. She looked around, and wondered what to do. There was one more door on the landing where she was standing, a bit further down a short corridor. And four steps up was a solid-looking door made of iron or steel. Presumably leading into the attic space. It looked as securely locked as a safe in Switzerland.

She listened. The footsteps continued to approach.

Getting closer.

You are standing at the door of the flat in which you murdered your lover, an inner voice informed her. Somebody is on his way up the stairs, and he'll discover you within the next ten seconds . . .

Unless that Somebody isn't on his way up to the top floor.

She pressed herself close to the wall next to the door and held her breath.

The footsteps paused on the landing below, and she heard the sound of a man coughing – then the jingling sound of keys being taken out of a jacket pocket.

Then the footsteps continued upwards.

She didn't make a decision now either – there was no time. She simply acted.

Took hold of the door handle. Pressed it down.

It was unlocked. She stepped inside and closed the door behind her.

10

On Sunday, 8 October, a stray swallow flew in through Van Veeteren's bedroom window.

It had just turned half past five in the morning, and the unfortunate bird was probably one of the very few phenomena in the whole world that could have woken him up. The flight from Rome had been over four hours late, and they hadn't got to bed until about three o'clock.

Two-and-a-half hours' sleep, then, and how Ulrike managed to stay asleep despite all the persistent fluttering of wings was beyond him . . . A mystery that on reflection he assigned to the inherent feeling of security in her warm, feminine being.

Or something biological along those lines.

But someone definitely not affected by symptoms of weariness in connection with the unexpected visitor was Stravinsky.

Stravinsky was a cat, and in a way Ulrike Femdli's most noticeable contribution to their shared home. This state of affairs had been in existence for no more than five months: it ought to have happened much sooner, but Van Veeteren's idiotic dithering had delayed the project and, indeed, almost wrecked it altogether – but thank goodness her persistence had eventually won him over. Thank God, he frequently thought.

They had known each other for five years. Van Veeteren knew that for the rest of his life he would not want any other woman. The weeks in Rome had brought him much satisfaction, including an awareness of this fact.

For his part, Stravinsky was eight years old, almost nine. He had been given his name because of a partiality unusual in cats for *The Rite of Spring*: he couldn't care less about any other music, classical or modern, but whenever he heard this work he would always lie there as if petrified, on tenterhooks from the first note to the last, brooding over some esoteric mystery that presumably existed only in his own (and perhaps the composer's?) imagination.

In outward appearance Stravinsky was black and white, in a pattern rather similar to that on a Gruyderfelder cow. He had been neutered at the age of two, and was normally quite gentle and quiet. On the whole. But as he lay on the window ledge as usual this early morning in autumn – and to his surprise saw a meal fluttering into the room – it mattered little that he was both sterile and fairly full already.

With all due deference to Whiskas and Kitteners, a living booty was not to be sniffed at. It took him no more than three or four leaps, no more than five or six seconds, before he was able to get his teeth into it.

By the time Van Veeteren heaved himself up onto his feet, his heart pounding like a piston in his chest, it was too late. Stravinsky had already dropped the swallow, which was slithering around on the floor, flapping away with its two broken wings. The cat sat there, watching intently as the bird tried in vain to escape, while Van Veeteren wondered for one confused second (a) what the hell had happened, and (b) what the hell he could do about it.

When that second was over, he hissed at the cat – with the immediate result that he hyperventilated and almost collapsed in a heap. Stravinsky grabbed his prey in his mouth once again, rushed off into the living room with it and took cover under the sofa.

Van Veeteren closed his eyes, recovered and rushed after it. Swore loudly and pointlessly, and hammered several times on the cushions, but the only response was a muted growl and a few heartbreaking peeps. He staggered into the kitchen, took a carpet-beater out of the broom cupboard and tried in vain to poke it under the sofa. Stravinsky stayed put for a while, then sprinted out with the bird in his mouth and sprang up onto the top of a bookcase.

Van Veeteren stood up, and paused to think. Contemplated the cat up there just under the ceiling. It had dropped its prey once again, and was examining it with what seemed to be almost scientific interest. Studied it in all seriousness, with the same neutral expression on its triangular cat-face as usual. Van Veeteren couldn't help but wonder what on earth was going on inside the animal's head. In Stravinsky's head, that is: nothing at all was going on any more in the swallow's head, it seemed.

He stood there, carpet-beater in hand, wondering what to do, and allowed his train of thought to continue.

Just what was it in the cat's programmed instincts that made it drop its booty and study it in this way?

It was impossible not to reflect and be surprised by it. To keep letting its victim go free like this – a highly illusory freedom, of course – simply so that he could sit in peace and quiet at a convenient distance and observe its death throes. What was the point when the fate of the bird was already sealed? What forces lay behind this wicked game? Why did he do it? The beast of prey and its victim.

Were they biological or culinary? Perhaps it didn't matter, although he recalled that human beings prefer to eat meat that has been killed in conditions as unstressful as possible. He had read somewhere that pork and ham tasted best if the slaughterer was able to lull the pig into a false sense of security before its death. A shot through the back of the head while it was asleep, perhaps?

Did cats – cat-like creatures in general – prefer meat that was filled with the bitter fluids caused by the fear of death? Could that be the explanation?

Yes, probably. So infernally banal. And from the point of view of the victim, what pointless cruelty! A long-drawn-out death struggle simply to please the executioner's taste-buds?

My God, he thought. You must be a wicked devil.

He shook his head at all these questionable speculations, raised the carpet-beater and hammered away at the bookcase. Stravinsky picked the swallow up again in his mouth and jumped down. Dashed out into the hall with Van Veeteren on his heels, then paused for a moment in front of the shoe shelf. He seemed to be wondering where next to retreat to, in order to escape being hounded by this madman with the carpet-beater – he had been living with him for quite a while now, and he'd seemed to be a reasonable and balanced person. Well, not all that barmy: but you could never tell with humans.

Van Veeteren made use of the brief pause for thought to open the door out onto the landing, and Stravinsky took advantage of this opportunity to escape. He raced down the stairs like a flash, with the swallow – now no doubt as dead as a doornail – looking like a bushy but well-trimmed moustache.

Van Veeteren had no doubt that the confounded little beast must go out into the courtyard, and chased after him – stark naked, hoping that none of the neighbours were up and about at this unholy hour (especially old fru Grambowska: a naked confrontation on the stairs would have ruined their good relationship once and for all, that was obvious, and she had looked after both Stravinsky and the potted plants while he and Ulrike were away in Rome). With a little difficulty he eventually managed to shoo the cat out through the back door, and left it ajar with the aid of the sweeping brush that was usually kept there. When he went back to the flat he felt as wide awake as if he had just taken a plunge into eight-degree seawater and survived.

He checked the clock in the kitchen: seventeen minutes to six in the morning. He pinched his arm. It hurt, so he hadn't been dreaming.

*

Expecting some kind of tiredness to kick in after his surreal morning exertions, he went first to check if Ulrike had really managed to sleep through all the hullabaloo.

She certainly had. She lay there on her side, sniffling peacefully, the obligatory pillow between her knees and a faint, slightly mysterious smile on her lips. He stood by the bed for a few moments, watching her. It had been an exceptional morning, but even now he simply couldn't understand what benevolent higher power had brought her into contact with him. Or him with her. If there was anything for which he had to thank the God in whom he didn't believe, it was Ulrike Fremdli. No doubt at all about that.

Which had not just brought them into contact with each other, but had guided her here. To share his home and his bed and his life. Nothing – he was quite certain of it – nothing he had achieved during his erratic journey on this earth had made him worthy of her; but he had slowly begun to accept it as a fact, and just as slowly to adopt a sort of humility, which no doubt did not always reveal itself in his day-to-day activities but was present nevertheless, rooted ever more deeply inside him, like . . . like a slowly growing benign tumour of gratitude and peace of mind.

Or how the hell could he describe it on a morning like this one? In his darkest moments – when he succumbed to his old weakness of regarding life as an equation and not much more – he sometimes saw Ulrike as a sort of substitute for Erich, his son, who had passed away two years ago, and naturally left a wound inside him which would continue to bleed for the rest of his life.

But such equivalences did not exist. A dead son could never be compensated for, he knew that now – had always known it of course – just as little as good deeds, no matter what they were, could balance out evil ones. It was no coincidence that Schopenhauer had been his household god for a while in his youth, and over thirty years in the police force had hardly served to contradict those basic pessimistic maxims about the facts of life. On the contrary.

And in recent years he had begun to think that Good also has a right to exist on its own account in this world. A much greater right than what he used to regard as a mere pawn in the struggle with Evil. The powers of darkness. How else could one allocate the true value of a child's laughter or the eyes of a woman who loves you?

If these things have to be weighed up and compared. Balanced.

He closed the bedroom door and returned to the kitchen. Put the kettle on and flopped down at the table with the heap of newspapers in front of him. Copies of the *Allgemejne* for the last twenty days.

I might as well start working my way through them, he thought. They ought to be able to keep him occupied until his tiredness hit him once again, if nothing else. He adjusted the pile and started chronologically from the back. It was now eleven minutes to six. There was a scratching at the door, but he was damned if he was going to make it up with that confounded cat already.

★

116

An hour and three cups of tea later the lack of sleep had caught up with him. He had also given way and allowed Stravinsky back in: the cat had miaowed reproachfully and gone back to the same window ledge, presumably hoping against hope for the arrival of the next delicacy on this day of miracles when grilled swallows were flying around all over the place.

Or perhaps he's forgotten all about it already, Van Veeteren thought. Cats' memories are short. Enviably short. What he had done with the bird – or the remains of it – seemed to be written in the stars.

The newspapers were nothing special. He read at most two or three articles to the end, but leafed dutifully through every copy and glanced at every single page. He cut out the chess columns and put them in a pile, and by the time he had dealt with the fifteenth copy of the *Allgemejne* he could tell by the gravelly feeling behind his eyes that he wouldn't be able to keep going for much longer. And there wasn't much point anyway. He folded the newspaper up, placed it on top of the bundle of those he had read already and glanced at the first page of the one on top of the pile of unread copies.

Then his heart missed a beat.

The priest was glaring at him.

Glaring. There was no other word for it. His eyes were prominent under the long quiff of hair carefully combed to one side. His expression had something reproachful and at the same time aggressive in it. His dark beard was slightly better trimmed than Van Veeteren recalled it from the visit to

117

the antiquarian bookshop. Presumably a little shorter as well, because his dog collar could be seen quite clearly.

He shook his head and stared at the headline.

PRIEST FELL UNDER A TRAIN

The text was only about ten lines long, and there was no continuation on an inside page.

> The 29-year-old priest Tomas Gassel was killed late yesterday evening when for some unknown reason he fell down onto the lines just as a local train was pulling into Maardam Central Station. There were no witnesses, the platform where the accident happened was empty at the time and it has not yet been possible to interrogate the driver as he was in severe shock and was taken immediately to the New Rumford hospital. The police say there is no reason to suspect foul play. Tomas Gassel was a curate in Leimaar parish, and a special mass in his memory will take place next Sunday.

Van Veeteren stared at the photograph once more. His tiredness had disintegrated.

Bloody hell, he thought. This is a black Sunday if ever there was one.

It was not easy to wake Ulrike up, but he managed to do so.

'What time is it?' she muttered, without opening her eyes.

'Er,' said Van Veeteren. 'Just turned seven . . . Getting on for half past, in fact. Quite a lot has been happening.'

'Been happening? We haven't slept for more than four hours.'

'I know. You have an amazing ability to avoid waking up, no matter what's happening in the world. Stravinsky killed a swallow.'

'Oh dear. But these things happen.'

She rolled over and placed a pillow over her head.

'In here,' said Van Veeteren.

Time passed without her saying anything, and he began to wonder if she had fallen asleep again.

'There aren't any swallows in here,' she maintained in the end.

'It came in.'

'Came in?'

'Through the window. Stravinsky grabbed it. I must say it's odd that they have to torture their prey so horribly. There's a degree of cruelty in that old lazy-bones that is beyond comprehension. It makes you think . . .'

'What did you do about it?' asked Ulrike, without removing the pillow.

'I managed to get him outside in the end. There was a right shemozzle – he lay first under the sofa and then up on the bookcase.'

'Ugh,' said Ulrike. 'But the poor bird is out of the flat now, I hope?'

'Yes,' said Van Veeteren. 'Then there was that business with the priest.'

There was silence for three seconds.

'The priest?'

'Yes, I think I told you about him. He called in at the bookshop the day before we went on holiday, and wanted me to help him with something. And now he's dead.'

'Dead?'

'As dead as the swallow, although it went a bit more quickly in his case. He fell under a train. I reckon we could do with quieter mornings when we get home in the middle of the night. Cats and priests and the devil and his grandmother. I wonder what he wanted.'

Ulrike removed the pillow and looked at him.

'Who?'

'The priest, of course. Don't you think it's a bit odd that he should fall under a train only a week after he came to see me?'

Ulrike continued looking at him, with a furrow between her prettily arched eyebrows. Stretched, and pulled the covers up under her chin. Five more silent seconds passed.

'Why are you looking at me like that?' he asked.

'To be honest,' she said.

'To be honest what?'

She diverted her gaze to Stravinsky, who was curled up fast asleep on the window ledge.

'Just a thought. Can it be that you've been dreaming all this? It sounds a bit on the bizarre side, if you'll forgive me for saying so.'

'What the hell?' exclaimed Van Veeteren. 'It's in the newspaper – do you want me to go and fetch it?'

She hesitated a moment.

'Not just now. I think we ought to get a bit more sleep, no

matter what . . . Then we can talk it over when we wake up again. Come back to bed and give me a hug.'

Van Veeteren had several valid objections on the tip of his tongue, but after a brief internal struggle he gave up and did as he was bidden.

11

In the early hours of Monday morning he dreamt about a train hurtling at high speed through the world and running over hordes of black cats with white patches; and early the following morning he woke up in a cold sweat after being chased through a deserted and unlit town by a mad, bearded priest with a gigantic dead swallow in his mouth and a carpet-beater in his hand.

The message could hardly be clearer, and when Ulrike had left for work at about half past eight, he telephoned the Maardam CID.

After the obligatory wrong connections, he finally got through to Münster.

'That priest,' he said.

'What priest?' wondered Münster.

'The one that died. Who fell in front of a train.'

'Oh, him,' said Münster. 'I know nothing about it. It was Moreno who took charge of that.'

'Moreno?'

'Yes. Why do you ask, Chief Inspector?'

Hell and damnation, Van Veeteren thought. Four years

have passed, and he still calls me that. No doubt it will say *Chief Inspector* on my gravestone.

'Sorry about that,' said Münster, who had drawn conclusions from the silence in his receiver. 'I obviously have trouble in getting used to it.'

'Never mind,' said Van Veeteren. 'Can you put me through to Moreno?'

'I can always try,' said Münster. 'But I don't think there was anything for us to worry about. No suspicious circumstances at all. I suppose you don't want to tell me why you're ringing?'

'Quite right,' said Van Veeteren. 'Put me through to Moreno now.'

Detective Inspector Ewa Moreno was not in her office, but he eventually caught up with her via her mobile in a car between Linzhuisen and Weill. It was true that she had been dealing with the case of the priest who fell under a train – and what Münster said was also true, i.e. that there was no reason to suspect anything out of the ordinary.

Apart from the possibility that Gassel might have done it of his own free will, that is. The train driver had been interrogated, but had noticed nothing unusual apart from a person appearing out of nowhere and suddenly falling down in front of the engine. Obviously, it had been a traumatic experience for him – every train driver's nightmare – but Moreno had not managed to squeeze anything else out of him, despite talking to him for two hours, she said. Or trying to talk to him.

Van Veeteren pondered for a moment. Then he asked if

she might possibly have time to indulge in a glass of beer with him that evening at Adenaar's: and she had.

What's he after? she wondered.

He didn't want to go into that over the phone, but promised to do so while they were enjoying their beers.

She turned up a quarter of an hour late, and what struck him immediately was how beautiful she was. The most attractive inspector in the whole world, he thought. She seemed to get prettier and prettier as the years went by: he wondered what kept her in the force, and how old she actually was. No more than thirty-five in any case. A year had passed since he saw her last, in fact – in connection with the deplorable case involving Intendent deBries – and the situation then had been so awful that even an attractive woman had been unable to distract attention from the horror of it all.

'I'm afraid I'm a bit late, Chief Inspector. I hope you haven't been waiting for too long.'

'Go to hell,' he said. 'Drop that *Chief Inspector* crap or I'll have an epileptic fit.'

She laughed.

'Sorry,' she said. 'It takes time to get used to it.'

'Four years,' Van Veeteren pointed out. 'Is it all that difficult to get used to it over four years?'

'We police are a bit slow to catch on,' said Moreno. 'As is well known.'

'Hmm,' said Van Veeteren, beckoning to the waiter. 'You can say that again.'

'So, Gassel,' said Moreno after they had ordered. 'What's it all about? I have to admit I was a bit curious.'

Van Veeteren scratched his head impassively and took out his cigarette machine.

'I don't really know,' he admitted. 'I started to smell a rat, but no doubt it has to do with my age and impending Alzheimer's.'

'Shall we take a bet on it?' Moreno asked.

Van Veeteren fed tobacco into the machine and said nothing for a while.

'He came to see me,' he said eventually. 'That's the rat.'

'Came to see you?' said Moreno. 'Gassel came to see you?'

'Yes.'

'Why?'

'I don't know. I never got round to talking to him, unfortunately. I had an appointment at the dentist's, and the following day I was flying to Rome with Ulrike. You've never met her, but she's my better half . . . Much better, in fact. Anyway, that was three weeks ago – just over, to be precise: we agreed to meet when I got back, but now he's dead. It could be pure coincidence, of course, but you sometimes wonder.'

Moreno said nothing, but a furrow appeared in her brow.

'I did get a hint of what he wanted, though,' said Van Veeteren. 'He wanted to get something off his chest.'

'Get something off his chest?'

'Yes. Somehow or other. He'd evidently got to hear of something that came within his duty of confidentiality and so he couldn't tell me what – a confessor who wanted to confess, as you might say.'

'Confession?' said Moreno. 'But he wasn't a Catholic priest.'

Van Veeteren lit his cigarette.

'No,' he said. 'But as far as I can make out most other denominations use a sort of modified variation of confession. I suppose they've begun to understand that our conscience can sometimes become too heavy to bear.'

Moreno smiled.

'Didn't he say anything else?'

Van Veeteren shook his head gloomily.

'Not as far as I remember. But he did make a decidedly nervous impression, and that's what worries me. If it hadn't been for that damned olive stone, I'd have sat down and listened to what he had to say, of course.'

'Olive stone?' said Moreno. 'Now then, Chief . . . Now you're talking in riddles.'

'I broke a filling on an olive stone,' explained Van Veeteren, pulling a face. 'The same day as we were due to fly to Rome . . . or the day before, to be precise. That was why I had to go to the dentist's. My fangs are in pretty good shape apart from that.'

'I don't doubt that for a second,' said Moreno, deepening the furrow in her brow somewhat.

The waiter came with the beers. They drank a toast, then sat in silence for a while.

'Do you think there's something illegal lurking in the background? Is that what you're saying?'

Van Veeteren inhaled deeply, then peered through the smoke as he breathed out.

'I don't know,' he said. 'It's impossible to say, but he'd picked me out in order to take me into his confidence because of what I was – a former chief inspector. *Former*, kindly take note of that. It was no coincidence – if I remember rightly, he let slip that he'd promised not to go to the police, that was the point. So what the hell could it be all about, if there wasn't something illegal going on?'

Moreno shrugged.

'Who knows?' she said. 'What do you think? Your intuition is not exactly an unknown concept, after all.'

'Bah,' muttered Van Veeteren, taking a swig of beer. 'I don't think as much as a chicken's fart. Perhaps it's the latest fad in the criminal underworld to go to confession, how should I know? But what about you, Inspector? Have you no suggestion to make? I assume there must have been some sort of investigation?'

Moreno sighed and looked slightly worried.

'Not much of one,' she said. 'We haven't written it off yet – it's only a week after it happened, of course; but we haven't found anything to suggest that . . . well, to suggest that there are evil spirits behind it, as it were.'

'Who have you spoken to?'

'His father,' said Moreno. 'He's a retired former self-employed businessman up in Saaren. He took it very hard. It was his only son, his wife died a year ago. A colleague out at Leimaar as well, and quite a few people in the station, of course. Gassel lived alone. Not many friends. It's possible he was depressed, but based on what we know there's no reason to make a song and dance about it. We simply don't have any evidence to suggest anything improper.'

'And nothing odd?'

Moreno paused to think that over.

'I see what you're getting at,' she said. 'I'm not as sensitive as a certain former chief inspector used to be, but I haven't noticed anything odd. Nothing at all. It would no doubt have been different if there had been any witnesses, somebody who'd seen or noticed something, but nobody has come forward. It was wet and windy that evening, and pretty dark on the platform where it happened. And there was nobody waiting to get onto the train – it was the terminus.'

'I understand,' said Van Veeteren. 'And the engine driver didn't notice anything?'

'No. He happened to be looking down at the controls at the moment when it happened. That's what he says, at least. All he noticed was a jolt.'

'A jolt?'

'Yes, that's how he put it.'

'And it hasn't been established what Gassel was doing there? Whether he was waiting to meet somebody in, or something like that?'

'No.'

'Do you know what he'd been doing earlier in the evening? Before he fell onto the tracks, that is?'

Moreno shook her head.

'No. It seems he was running a confirmation class until six o'clock. Out at Leimaar. Then he presumably went home. He lived in Maagerweg in the town centre. He should have been home by about half past six, but that's only a guess. He fell under the train at 22.46, but what he'd been doing before that we have no idea.'

'Had he bought a ticket?'

'No. Not at the station, in any case. And he didn't have one on him.'

'So you don't know why he was at the station at all? Unless of course he'd gone there to jump under a train . . .'

'No. As I said.'

Van Veeteren looked out of the window and sighed.

'And you haven't made much of an effort to find out, either?'

'No,' said Moreno. 'Presumably he was at home all evening, but who knows? We have other things to do to keep us busy, you know.'

'You don't say,' said Van Veeteren. 'Anyway, I suspect this is about as far as we're going to get. Thank you for coming to listen to my high-flown rhetoric. Do you mind if I ask you a personal question before we pack up?'

'Please do,' said Moreno.

'You are probably the most beautiful copper I've ever seen. I'm old enough to dare to say that. Haven't you got married yet?'

He watched her blush, and noted that she waited until it had passed.

'Thank you,' she said. 'No, not yet. I keep myself young by not doing so.'

'How old are you, in fact?'

'Old enough to have the sense to say thank you for a compliment,' said Inspector Moreno.

The vicar of Leimaar parish was Franz Brunner, and he received Van Veeteren at his vicarage. It was the oldest building in the area, he claimed – a low, handsome, wooden building from the early nineteenth century with wings covered in ivy, Virginia creeper and rambler roses gleaming in the sudden autumn sunshine.

Van Veeteren enquired tactfully if the church itself wasn't a little older, but Brunner explained that it had burnt to the ground at the end of the nineteenth century, and the new one wasn't consecrated until 1908.

Leimaar was also one of the most recently built parts of Maardam, Van Veeteren was aware of that. Not until after the Second World War, in three or four stages: in the fifties, sixties and eighties. Nearly all the buildings were blocks of flats, rather ordinary in appearance: but being on a ridge with views for miles over the plain leading to the sea, it was considered to be one of the more attractive parts of the town. He recalled once having interrogated an elderly woman in a conservatory right at the top of one of the blocks of flats, and making a mental note that Leimaar was one of the places he might consider as a suitable environment in which to spend the autumn of his life.

But not the vicarage. And he wasn't yet in the autumn of his life, even if he was well past sixty and it was the beginning of October.

'As I said,' he began, 'it's about Pastor Gassel.'

The vicar assumed an expression of pious professional sorrow and served coffee.

'Ah yes, Gassel,' he said. 'That was a sad story.'

Van Veeteren waited in order to give him an opportunity of enlarging upon that platitude, but the vicar showed no sign of doing so. Instead he selected a biscuit and began chewing thoughtfully.

As far as Van Veeteren could tell he was in his fifties, perhaps fifty-five, but there was hardly a wrinkle on his pale face, and his ash-blond hair was parted in a way that made him look like a confirmation candidate. His hands, which only just peeped out of the sleeves of his black priestly jacket, were as smooth as a communion wafer, and Van Veeteren decided provisionally that he was one of those unfortunate people who manage to grow old without looking old. Who have lived so carefully and with such respect for the rules of morality and virtue that time has not succeeded in leaving any traces on their bodies.

He also wondered if he had ever come across this phenomenon outside the ranks of religious practitioners. Presumably not, he decided: it had to do with Sodom and Gomorrah, of course.

'How long had he been working in your parish?' he asked after his host had swallowed the biscuit and started looking round for another one.

'Not all that long,' said Brunner, withdrawing his hand. 'Just over a year. This was his first post after qualifying – he had studied various other subjects before coming round to theology.'

He made it sound like a mild but fully justified rebuke.

'I see,' said Van Veeteren. 'Were you on good terms with him?'

'Of course. There are only three priests in this parish, and we must share out the chores fairly.'

'Chores?' Van Veeteren took the opportunity of remarking, and a faint glow spread over the vicar's white-bread cheeks.

'I was joking,' he said. 'Yes, we work together every day – or worked – me, Pastor Hartlew and Pastor Gassel. We devote ourselves to quite a lot of social work, which not everybody realizes. Hartlew has been with me since 1992, and Gassel joined us last year when the diocese finally agreed to estab-lish a new living in the parish. I should point out that we take care of forty thousand souls, more than any other parish in Maardam.'

. A hard job, Van Veeteren thought, but refrained from expressing his admiration.

'What was he like?' he asked instead.

'What do you mean?' asked the vicar.

'When I ask what he was like, it means that I would like to know what he was like,' Van Veeteren explained, tasting the coffee. As expected, and as usual, it was like dishwater. They base all their activities on the drinking of coffee, he thought, but even so they never learn how to make it properly.

'I'm not really sure exactly what you want to know,' said Brunner. 'I gather he had been to see you, is that right?'

'Yes,' said Van Veeteren. 'He had a few problems connected with his work.'

'Problems? I don't think I understand what you—'

'That's the impression I had. That something had happened in connection with his work.'

The vicar flung his hands out wide.

'What could that have been?'

'That's what I'm asking you. Could you do that again?'

'What? What should I do again?'

'Fling your hands out once again. Forgive me for saying so, but you look like an actor who is being forced to play the same scene for the twentieth time. No offence intended.'

Brunner opened his mouth for two seconds, then closed it again. Van Veeteren took a biscuit, and congratulated himself on rather a successful opening move.

'What is it you're actually after?' asked Brunner when he had recovered. 'You don't really have any authorization any more, am I right? You've left the police force, haven't you?'

'True,' said Van Veeteren. 'Why do you ask? Have you something to hide?'

'Of course not. It's just that I think you are acting a bit aggressively. Why should I have anything to hide?'

'God moves in a mysterious way,' said Van Veeteren. 'But it is quite obvious to me that you are uncomfortable about this conversation. If you asked me to say what I think, I would say that you were not on very good terms with Pastor Gassel. Am I right?'

Brunner had problems with the colour of his face again.

'We respected each other,' he said. 'You must . . . you must understand that to a large extent the work of a parish priest is just like any other job. As vicar, I am of course in charge of everything when it comes to responsibilities and duties . . .'

'So you had different views when it came to beliefs?'

The vicar thought for a moment.

'In one respect, yes.'

'On something important?'

Brunner stood up and started walking backwards and forwards around the room.

'Why are you insisting on this?' he asked after half a minute's silence. 'Is it so important for you?'

'I don't know yet,' said Van Veeteren. 'Maybe, maybe not. But the fact is that Pastor Gassel came to me to confess, fundamentally speaking. One might have thought it would have been more natural for him to go to his own vicar. Or at any rate to somebody inside the church's organization. Personally, I'm a defector, an agnostic detective chief inspector.'

Brunner stopped.

'What did he want?' he asked.

It seemed to occur to him almost immediately that he didn't really have any right to ask such a question, and he sat down in the armchair again and sighed.

'I never discovered what he wanted,' explained Van Veeteren. 'But I had hoped that you might be able to point me in the right direction.'

'I see. Let me think for a moment.'

Brunner clasped his hands in his lap and closed his eyes. Van Veeteren assumed that in this simple way he was obtain-

ing permission to proceed from a higher authority, and wondered in passing if this might be one of the motives for all
religious activities: the need to pass responsibility on to somebody else.

The unwillingness to bear the burden.

'All right,' said Brunner in a matter-of-fact tone of voice,
opening his eyes. 'Yes, we had several differences of opinion,
Pastor Gassel and I. You are right in that respect.'

Van Veeteren looked up at the ceiling and gave silent
thanks for the praise accorded to him.

'What differences?' he asked.

'Pastor Gassel was homosexual.'

'Really?' said Van Veeteren.

There followed a moment's silence.

'One can have different views on homosexuality,' said
Brunner.

'Can one?' said Van Veeteren.

'Personally I have a liberal attitude based on biological and
Christian points of view.'

'Meaning what?' wondered Van Veeteren.

'Nobody should be condemned because he – or she – has a
deviant sexuality.'

'I agree.'

'But the person concerned must make the best of the situation. Acknowledging one's homosexuality is of course a
vital and necessary step – Pastor Gassel and I were in complete agreement on that score. But we had different opinions
when it came to the next step.'

'Which is?' wondered Van Veeteren.

'Fighting against it, of course,' said the vicar, sitting up straight. 'There are natural circumstances, and unnatural circumstances, and in the church we must pray for and help those who find themselves in unnatural circumstances. For me, this has always been obvious and a guiding principle. One can perhaps understand individuals who are unable – who don't have the strength – to fight against their illness: but when a priest doesn't even understand the importance of fighting against it at all, well, he is on the wrong path. His own illness, and what is more . . . well, perhaps you can understand our different points of view now?'

Van Veeteren nodded.

'I think so. Did you notice anything unusual in Pastor Gassel's behaviour shortly before his death?'

The vicar shook his head slowly.

'No, I don't think so. Not that I can recall, at least.'

'Was he depressed?'

'Not as far as I know.'

'Do you know if anything special happened during the autumn or the late summer that might have been traumatic for him?'

'Traumatic? No, I've no idea of anything like that. But then we didn't have the sort of relationship that would lead to him confiding in me, because . . . well, because of what we've just been talking about.'

'I understand,' said Van Veeteren. 'I assume you can't comment on the likelihood of him committing suicide or that sort of thing?'

'When it comes to matters of faith we are not as rigid

as the Roman Catholics,' said Brunner, clearing his throat. 'Of course it is never right to take your own life: but it is not for us to judge a desperate person who turns to desperate measures . . .'

'If we leave matters of faith to one side,' said Van Veeteren, 'would you say it was possible rather than out of the question that Gassel might have committed suicide?'

The vicar pursed his lips and seemed to be thinking hard.

'I really can't say,' he said eventually. 'I don't think he would have done, of course, and know of nothing that would suggest he might have done. But on the other hand, I can't exclude the possibility altogether.'

'Do you know if he was in a relationship? Did he live with a partner, for instance?'

The vicar blushed again.

'A partner? No, certainly not . . . But I have no idea about . . . about that sort of thing.'

'I see. Was it public knowledge in the parish – his deviant sexuality, as you called it?'

'The fact that he was homosexual?'

'Yes.'

'I hope not. It would have come to my notice if it had been, and we had at least come to an agreement that he wouldn't make a song and dance about it. It's a very sensitive matter in connection with the teaching of confirmands, and of course it is the vicar who must accept ultimate responsibility. I hope you realize that all this hasn't been exactly easy for me.'

No, Van Veeteren thought. You poor thing – you manage to persuade the diocese to award you an extra post, and you end up with a clockwork orange. It must be a bit annoying, to be sure.

But hardly so annoying that the vicar would feel it necessary to dispatch Gassel into the Twilight Zone by shoving him under a train? His face seemed to be too mild and innocent for anything like that.

'So it was because of these little differences of opinion that he was unwilling to go and confess to you? Do you agree to that as a reasonable conclusion to draw?'

Brunner thought for a moment.

'Yes,' he said. 'That's the way things were, unfortunately. And I don't think he would have turned to Pastor Hartlew either. As you know, confession is not a sacrament in our church, but of course there is always the possibility of getting things off one's chest. In the knowledge that whatever one says will go no further. But I don't understand why he turned to you, of all people.'

'Neither do I,' said Van Veeteren, who saw no point in mentioning Gassel's Catholic aunt. 'Does Pastor Hartlew share your views on homosexuality?'

'I'm sure he does.'

'How was it you put it?'

'Put what?'

'Your views. "A liberal attitude based on biological and Christian points of view," I think you said.'

Brunner thought for five seconds.

'I don't remember,' he said in due course, with a tired shrug of the shoulders.

'Even if he didn't want to talk to the vicar, surely it was quite a long step from that to going to talk to you?' commented Ulrike Fremdli later that same day. 'If you have any homosexual traits, you've been pretty successful in hiding them from me. But perhaps that wasn't why he came to see you?'

'Presumably not,' said Van Veeteren. 'No, I prefer women, full stop. But joking apart, it's a hell of an odd coincidence, there's no getting away from that. Gassel comes to me and asks for help, and a week or so later he's run over by a train. If he really wanted to take his own life, surely he could have waited a couple of days and got off his chest whatever it was he wanted to say? Or left me out of it in the first place? And for Christ's sake, you don't just happen to fall off a railway platform by mistake.'

'Was he drunk?'

'Not even half a pint of beer in his blood, according to Moreno.'

'And you had no indication of what it was all about? When he came to see you, I mean.'

'Not as far as I remember,' said Van Veeteren. 'That's what's so damned annoying, the fact that I don't remember. I think he said something about a woman . . . a woman who had confided in him, I assume. And he'd promised to say nothing about it, and above all not to go to the police. I had the impression that he was afraid something would happen:

but that could be something that came to me with hindsight . . . There again, I'm pretty sure he did say something to that effect. Something would happen, if precautions were not taken . . . Bloody hell!'

Ulrike lifted Stravinsky up from the sofa and started tickling him under his chin.

'But he wasn't the one who was in danger?'

'Not as I understood it. I suppose we could find out if he'd noted down who had come to confess to him – but for Christ's sake, I'm not in the police force any more, isn't that true?'

'Yes,' said Ulrike. 'As far as I'm aware.'

'Huh,' said Van Veeteren. 'Damn and blast, I don't think I can just ignore this business.'

Ulrike put Stravinsky down on the floor and leaned against him on the sofa. Sat quietly for a few seconds, stroking the veins on the back of his hand.

'What alternatives do you have?'

Van Veeteren sighed.

'A few names, for instance,' he said. 'People who knew him. And also a nasty feeling that if I don't continue to poke away at this business, nothing much will happen. It's not good, wandering around with a dead priest on your conscience . . . Anyway, I suppose we can wait and see if anything occurs to me.'

'I expect it will,' said Ulrike. 'If I know you right.'

'What on earth do you mean by that?' said Van Veeteren.

MAARDAM

NOVEMBER 2000

12

Sunday 5 November 2000, was the day when a sneeze threatened to ruin Egon Traut's marriage.

At least, that gloomy prospect hovered over him for several long hours in the evening, and there is after all a certain difference between a grim outlook and ruins.

Egon Traut was a self-employed businessman. He had a firm making and selling display stands for opticians and shops selling spectacles. The factory was located in Chadow, where he also lived in a spacious, hacienda-inspired villa with his wife and five children, of whom two had flown the nest (for most of the time, at least), two were twins in their teens (and quite a handful), and the fifth (an afterthought called Arnold) suffered from Hörndli's syndrome and was autistic.

The firm was called GROTTENAU, an anagram of his own name, and at the end of the eighties and throughout the nineties it had slowly but surely increased its market share, at first in Chadow, then in the surrounding area, and eventually the whole country – to such an extent that by the beginning of the new millennium it claimed sixty per cent of the whole cake. In opticians' circles F/B GROTTENAU was, if not a

143

concept, then at least a name associated with expertise, quality and reliable delivery.

Since 1996 Egon Traut had employed a staff of four. Three of them worked on the production of the display stands in Chadow's new industrial estate, and the fourth dealt with the paperwork. The last was Betty Klingerweijk, who was exactly ten years younger than he was, and owned a pair of breasts that sometimes kept him awake at night, unable to expunge their image from his head.

When he was lying in the matrimonial bed, that is. It sometimes happened that, instead, he was in the same bed as the aforementioned breasts, and on those (unfortunately all too sporadic) occasions, of course, he did not need to worry about expunging them from his head. On the contrary. Getting them into his head (via his mouth) was something he was only too happy to spend time and effort on. Betty Klingerweijk had been his lover for rather more than three years by this time, and she was the one who sneezed so unfortunately on this rainy November Sunday.

It happened on the motorway between Linzhuisen and Maardam: they were on the way home from a three-day sales trip in the southern provinces, and Traut had just rung his wife on his mobile to ask her for some information.

'What was that?' asked his wife.
'What was what?' said Traut.
'That noise. It sounded like somebody sneezing.'
'Eh? . . . I didn't hear anything.'

'You don't have somebody in the car with you, do you?'

'No. Why should I have?'

'That's a good question. It sounded like a woman sneezing in any case.'

'How odd. Perhaps there was somebody on the line.'

'Somebody on the line? That's the daftest thing I've ever heard. I'm absolutely certain that I heard a sneeze. You have another woman with you in the car, don't you?'

'I swear I don't,' said Traut.

'Huh, tell that to the marines,' said his wife. 'But it's what you don't tell the marines that I'm interested in. What's her name? Is it somebody I know, or have you just picked her up?'

Traut tried to hit on a counter-move, but his mind was pretty sluggish today and nothing plausible occurred to him.

'It's not that vulgar little hussy fröken Klingerweijk, is it?' yelled his wife as loudly as she could, to make sure she could be heard clearly in the car. Traut glanced at his passenger, and could see she had heard what was said.

Bugger it, he thought. Death to the inventor of the mobile phone.

'I can assure you,' he assured her. 'I'm as much alone in the car as . . . as a herring in a church.'

'A herring in a church? What are you raving on about? There aren't any herrings in a church. Are you not even sober?'

'Of course I'm sober. You know I'm always very careful about what I drink when I'm travelling on business. And if there were a herring in a church, it would be feeling pretty lonely, wouldn't it? Can I get to the point now, or are you going to go on and on, accusing me of God knows what?'

That was quite a clever ploy, and the receiver was silent for a few seconds. But it was not a good silence, he could hear quite clearly that she didn't believe him. And in the corner of his eye he could see that Betty Klingerweijk was glaring at him, and seemed to be preparing to sneeze again. Out of sheer cussedness.

'What point?' asked his wife.

'Your barmy sister, of course. What's her new address – you said they'd just moved. I'll be in Maardam in five minutes.'

That was enough to shift the focus of the conversation – for the time being, at least. His sister-in-law was in fact the reason he had made the call, and doing so was bound to portray him in a more favourable light. His wife had gone on and on about how he really must call in and check on how she was, seeing as he was passing though Maardam in any case. Her sister hadn't answered the phone for over a month, and something must have happened to her. That was as clear as day, and blood is thicker than daylight.

They had discussed the matter at considerable length on the Thursday morning before he had set off, but he hadn't actually promised to call on her sister. Not as far as he could recall, at least. So the fact that he was ringing her now and offering to do so must surely be seen as a reasonable and humane thing to do. He was prepared to put himself out and call on her lunatic sister in her flat in order to make sure she was okay – wasn't that proof of how highly he valued his wife and their married life together?

He didn't say any of this outright, but he felt he could interpret his wife's soft humming – presumably while she was looking through the address book – along those lines. At least she was no longer harping on about that damned sneeze.

'Moerckstraat,' she said in the end. 'Moerckstraat 16. God only knows where that is, but no doubt you can ask somebody. And make sure you take whatever steps are necessary if she doesn't answer the door.'

Necessary steps? thought Traut. What the hell might they be?

It took over half an hour to find Moerckstraat, which was in an unusually grim 1970s district on the northern side of the Maar, and Betty Klingerweijk was already moaning about the delay.

'You promised we'd be home before ten,' she said. 'We'll never make that now.'

'Promised and promised,' said Egon Traut. 'But it's great if we can be together a bit longer.'

'Huh,' said Klingerweijk, and he was not at all sure how he should interpret that.

He switched off the engine and stepped out into the rain. Turned up the collar of his jacket and ran ten metres up a little asphalt ramp. That was about as far as Traut was able to run – especially if it was uphill – and he stopped to get his breath back under a roof overhang that ran all the way along the row of houses. He found the name Kammerle on a glass-covered nameplate, barely legible under all the graffiti, and worked out that the flat must be on the first floor.

He couldn't find a lift, so he walked up the stairs.

The Kammerle hovel – it really was a hovel – overlooked the courtyard. Traut found it difficult to imagine how people could live like this. It was somehow inhuman. He could see right into the flat through a narrow window, presumably a kitchen ditto – or rather, would have been able to if there had been a light on. But there wasn't. All he could see in fact was his own reflection, which more or less filled the whole window, at least in width.

He rang the bell. There was no humming nor ringing sound, so he assumed the bell was broken. He belted hard on the door several times with his fist, and waited. No response. He tried knocking on the window several times as well, but there was no sign of life inside.

Bugger, he thought. There's nobody in, that's obvious. What shall I do now?

Necessary steps, Barbara had gone on about.

He looked around and thought. Most of the tenants seemed to be at home on this miserable November evening. There was a light in almost every window. Perhaps he could ask a neighbour? Or try to contact some kind of caretaker – there must surely be a caretaker in a place like this?

And Betty was sitting in the car, growing more annoyed for every minute that passed.

And Barbara had heard her sneezing in his mobile. Damn

and blast, he thought. I'd rather be sitting with a beer some-where in the sun, a long way away from here.

He looked up at the blue-grey sky and decided that just now, this very moment, these very hours of his life were something he could happily have done without.

And he was a little surprised to realize that this was by no means a new thought.

When he lowered his gaze again, he saw that a door a few metres further along the corridor formed by the roof over-hang had opened, and a woman's head was poking out, looking at him. A short, dark-skinned immigrant woman. Kurdish or Iranian, perhaps: but he was not all that well up on foreign cultures and so she might well have been from some other country.

'You looking for Kammerle?' the woman asked, with barely a trace of a foreign accent. She must have been living here for several years, Traut thought.

'Yes. They don't seem to be in.'

'There is something that is not good with them in there.'

'Not good? What do you mean?'

She opened the door, wrapped the patterned shawl more tightly around her head and shoulders, and came out to him. She was small and dumpy, and moved awkwardly; but her eyes were large and expressive. It was not difficult to see that she was genuinely worried.

'I worry for them,' she said. 'Something is not right, I haven't seen the mum, not the girl, none of them for a whole month.'

'Perhaps they are away on holiday? Or have moved?'

'Not moved, that can't be so. You notice when somebody moves, and I'm at home for all of every day. They had washing in the machines as well.'

'Washing?' wondered Traut, who had little idea about communal laundry facilities in blocks of flats.

'Yes, a month ago. Fru Kammerle left two machines full with washed clothes without taking care of them. I have hung and dried, we have them in carrier bags in our flat, but something must have happened. Why would anybody leave fine clothes in that way?'

Traut had no answer to that, and began rummaging in his pockets for a cigarette.

'Who are you, by the way?'

'Ah, I'm sorry,' he said. 'I forgot to introduce myself. Egon Traut.' He held out his hand, and the woman shook it with a firm, warm grip. 'I'm married to a sister of Martina Kammerle. We have also begun to wonder, as she hasn't answered the telephone for . . . yes, as you say, for a whole month.'

She let go of his hand and shook her head anxiously.

'My name's Violeta Paraskevi,' she said. 'I don't know your relative at all, we just say hello, as you do in the country. But we never meet, nor do my girl and her girl. It's sad and I'm so worried that something must happen to them.'

Traut thought for a moment.

'Do you know if somebody has a key to their flat?' he asked. 'A caretaker, or somebody like that?'

Violeta Paraskevi nodded energetically.

'Herr Klimkowski,' she said. 'He's the landlord, I have his telephone number. I have told him an earlier time, but he just says we shouldn't interfere and wait some more time. I say to him that he's wrong, but he doesn't want to listen to a fat little woman from another country with a hijab and lots of oddities. He is one of those who . . . you know, who don't like us. Who thinks we should go home and be followed and killed instead of living here and having it good . . .'

'I see,' said Traut. 'Anyway, if you give me the number, I'll give him a ring.'

'Good. Come in and ring from me.'

Traut tapped his jacket pocket, but realized that he'd left his mobile in the car with Betty. He followed the woman into her flat.

It was another half an hour before herr Klimkowski appeared in Moerckstraat. He was a small, sturdy man of about sixty with a limp in his right leg, and he made no secret of what he thought about being dragged out on a pointless exercise on a rainy Sunday evening in November.

Betty Klingersweijk wasn't in a much better mood, despite the fact that Traut had been to the pizzeria on the corner and bought her a beer and pizza with chips.

Women, he thought, after sitting in the car for over a quarter of an hour, trying to entertain her with a little small talk. I simply don't understand you. I'll be damned if I do.

'Well, here I bloody well am,' said Klimkowski. 'People think I'm a fucking priest, on call 24/7.'

'I do apologize,' said Traut. 'I don't think that at all, believe me. It's just that we happen to be passing through Maardam and we're a bit worried about my sister-in-law. Obviously I shall pay you for your trouble.'

'Huh,' said Klimkowski, rattling his bunch of keys. 'Keep your money. Now, let's see . . . 16D, Kammerle, is that right?'

Traut nodded and they climbed the stairs once again. Violeta Paraskevi met them on the landing and pointed to the door in question with an exaggerated gesture typical of somebody from the south.

'I know, I know,' muttered Klimkowski. 'Get out of the way.'

He fitted the key in the lock and opened the door.

'You'll have to sign a form as well,' he said, turning to Traut. 'It has to be a relative or the police for me to be authorized to open the door. I don't want to find myself in the shit if I can avoid it.'

'Of course,' said Traut. 'So, let's go in and see what there is to see.'

It took them less than half a minute to find the body, and it was above all the smell that guided them. Martina Kammerle's rotting corpse was packed into two black rubbish bags under her own bed. One bag was pulled down from the top, the other pulled up from the bottom. When Klimkowski pulled out the corpse and exposed the upper part, Egon Traut realized that the last thing one ought to do before discovering a dead body is to drink beer and eat a pizza.

When he had finished throwing up, he also realized – with a vague trace of gratitude amidst all the gloom – that the sneeze picked up by his mobile phone was not going to have as much significance for the future of his marriage as he had been fearing it would for the last few hours.

Every cloud has a silver lining, he thought, with a slight trace of guilt.

13

It was Detective Inspectors Jung and Rooth who were delegated to supervise the first few hours at Moerckstraat 16, and neither of them would write anything about the experience in their diaries.

Or at least, wouldn't have done even if they had kept a diary. It was just too depressing. Too grim, too macabre. They wandered about in the cramped little flat, kept their eyes skinned for anything of importance worth noting down, tried to keep out of the way of the scene-of-crime team – and to breathe with their mouths wide open in order to avoid the smell.

'What a lot of bloody crap,' said Rooth. 'I find it hard to cope with this sort of thing.'

'You get paid to cope with this sort of thing,' said Jung.

It was a few minutes after half past nine before Chief Inspector Reinhart turned up, just in time to hear a preliminary assessment from the medical team and an even more preliminary assessment from the technical specialists.

Martina Kammerle – assuming it really was her in the rubbish bags under the bed (there was no obvious reason to suspect that it might be somebody else, but because of the advanced state of decomposition of the body and his own indisposition at the time, Egon Traut had been unable to make a definitive identification) – had apparently died quite a long time ago. At least three weeks, it seemed, but in order to make a more precise judgement it was necessary to analyse more data, such as textile tests, blood status, average daily temperatures in the flat, and so on.

It was not possible to establish the cause of death at this early stage, but because it seemed likely that the woman hadn't died of natural causes in two plastic sacks under her bed, Jung at least concluded that, as it was stated officially, she had been killed by a person or several persons unknown.

And there was nothing to suggest that anybody had been in the flat for at least three or four weeks. Whether or not Martina Kammerle had managed to collect fragments of her murderer's skin under her fingernails, or possibly even drawn his blood – and hence, with a large dose of luck, enabled a DNA analysis – remained to be seen, after the National Laboratories for Forensic Chemistry and Forensic Medicine had played their part. In any case, no obvious clues had been discovered; but needless to say the flat would be cordoned off for as long as it was considered necessary, so that high-ranking detective officers would have the right to wander around and search for clues – always assuming that it was concluded that there was anything worth searching for.

That was more or less the attitude behind the statement issued by Inspector le Houde, who was in charge of the scene-of-crime group – and who had been summoned from a cup match in the Richter Stadium ten minutes before half time, and two minutes before the home side equalized – a goal that, according to all sensible spectators, had been dream-like, and executed by a recently bought Dane: the ovation had been echoing inside le Houde's head ever since he was about to enter the patrol car.

'Ah well, we'll have to wait and see,' said Reinhart. 'I'm sorry you missed the match. Personally I couldn't care less about football, but we won five–two, I gather. Not a bad performance,'

'Shut up,' said le Houde.

Reinhart spent five minutes inspecting the room and the flat. Then he decided to return to the police station together with Egon Traut, but he instructed Jung and Rooth to stay at the scene and begin interviewing the neighbours.

'It's a quarter to ten,' Rooth pointed out.

'Keep going until twelve,' said Reinhart. 'Nobody's going to bed after this palaver. I'll send you some back-up as soon as I find anybody,'

'All right,' said Rooth. 'We'll start by a trip to the pizzeria – it's just round the corner. No point in working on an empty stomach, you just don't function properly.'

Reinhart glared at him, then left with Traut. Jung declared that in the circumstances, he wasn't all that hungry, and instead went to the neighbouring flat to talk to the woman from Yugoslavia who he had already exchanged a few words with.

And who seemed to have some idea of who the victim really was.

But only a bit of an idea. If this Kammerle woman had

been lying here dead for a month or more, the idea of good neighbours couldn't very well have been all that effective.

Thought Inspector Jung, as he dug out a pen and some paper.

'What's been going on?' asked Münster, sitting down opposite Reinhart.

Reinhart pulled a face and placed his feet conveniently on a bookshelf.

'I'm glad you've come,' he said. 'Murder. A woman who seems to be called Martina Kammerle. Lived in Moerckstraat. She was strangled, and has been lying dead under her bed for about a month.'

'Under?' said Münster.

'Yes, under,' said Reinhart. 'The murderer had tucked her into a couple of rubbish sacks so that she didn't have to feel too cold. Very thoughtful of him. It's a right bugger. As usual.'

'As usual,' said Münster. 'Was she raped as well?'

'Possibly,' said Reinhart. 'But she was wearing a few clothes, so she might have escaped that. Knickers and a night-dress . . . Or the remains of those garments, to be more precise. If a body has been lying at room temperature for a month or so, certain chemical processes take place – I presume I don't need to go on about that.'

'I'd rather you didn't,' said Intendent Münster with a sigh. 'You don't need to. Who is she?'

Reinhart sat up straight and started scraping out his pipe.

'I don't know,' he said, 'but we have a bloke here who might know. His name is Traut – he was the one who found her. He's a relative, it seems. Runs a business of his own. To be honest he's not exactly my type – but being honest doesn't really help us . . .'

'Have you interrogated him?'

'Not yet. I thought there ought to be two of us – that's why I rang you.'

Münster nodded.

'Anything else before we get going?'

'Not as far as I know at this stage,' said Reinhart. 'Shall we have a go at him? I think he's been waiting for long enough now.'

'It's eleven o'clock now,' said Münster. 'High time we got started if we're going to get any beauty sleep tonight.'

'You're right,' said Reinhart, standing up. 'There's a time for everything. Just hang on a minute – I must have some tobacco handy: I reckon I can allow myself a bit of pleasure.'

'What a depressing area this is,' said Rooth after a while. 'Thank God we don't have to live here.'

Jung, who had grown up less than three hundred metres away from Moerckstraat, had no comment to make. He suggested instead that they should call it a day and sum up their impressions in the car. Rooth had no objections: they said goodnight to le Houde and his team of officers, and hoped they would have a fruitful night.

Le Houde was so tired that he didn't even have the

strength to swear at them, and when Rooth offered him half a bar of chocolate he simply turned his back on them.

'Good to know that we have such well-brought-up colleagues,' said Rooth, putting the chocolate into his own mouth. 'Well, how did you get on? Have you found a strangler?'

'I don't think so,' said Jung. 'But then, I've only managed two flats so far.'

'I did three,' said Rooth. 'They don't seem to know much about anybody else around here. But I expect fru Paraskevi must have had plenty to say for herself?'

Jung shrugged.

'Not really,' he said. 'She was there when they went into the flat, and she said she'd been feeling that something was wrong for quite some time. She's on a disability pension, and is at home all day – presumably she notices things, as you might say. Her husband's a Serb, incidentally: she's a Croat. She thinks he's living somewhere in the Balkans, but she hasn't heard from him for five years.'

'Great,' said Rooth.

'Yes, terrific. They have a daughter as well. She last saw her father when she was eight: she's sixteen now. Martina Kammerle also had a daughter, according to Paraskevi. About as old as her own. Where the hell is she? you have to ask. It seems that nobody has seen her for a month either.'

'Could she be the one who's done it?' wondered Rooth. 'Strangled her mother then done a runner?'

Jung pulled a face.

'That sounds a bit steep, but you never know. Surely there

must be quite a lot of people who knew the Kammerles – relatives and friends, and suchlike. Not to mention enemies. Fru Paraskevi says fru Kammerle had a gentleman friend for a while in August–September. She never saw him, but she heard them talking.'

'A gentleman friend?' said Rooth. 'Does that mean there wasn't what you might call a steady relationship, then?'

'I've no idea,' said Jung. 'Nothing that we've heard about so far, at least. Did your interviews produce anything of interest?'

'Nothing more than a bit of heartburn,' said Rooth with a sigh. 'I must stop drinking coffee this late at night. No, nobody seems to know anything at all. None of the people I've spoken to were even quite sure of her name. That of the dead woman, I mean. Despite the fact that they've been living here for . . . er, for how long? Two years, was it?'

'One-and-a-half, I think,' said Jung.

'But no doubt this Traut bloke will be able to clarify a few things. There doesn't seem to be much point in our running around and disturbing people when we haven't got a clue about the background. For Christ's sake, all we know so far is her name. Not much more than that, in any case.'

'Very true,' said Jung. 'So what do you reckon we should do?'

'Go home and get some sleep,' said Rooth, after a split second's thought. 'I expect we'll be spending all tomorrow knocking on doors around here, so no doubt we'll get to know the place pretty well.'

Inspector Jung realized that for once, he was in full agreement with his colleague, and after having emptied his bladder of all that coffee and tea and more coffee – plus a tiny little glass of plum brandy fru Paraskevi had insisted on – in a well-hidden corner of the courtyard, they went back to the car.

'Sorry to keep you waiting,' said Reinhart. 'But as I'm sure you realize, this business has created an awful lot of work for us.'

'No problem,' said Egon Traut accommodatingly. 'I've rung the missus and told her I'll be coming home tomorrow instead.'

He tapped the breast pocket of his jacket, where the top part of a mobile telephone was sticking up. Münster and Reinhart sat down at the table opposite him, and Reinhart lit his pipe.

'She's pretty shaken, my wife is,' said Traut. 'But that's understandable. They weren't all that close, but a sister is a sister, let's face it.'

'Are there any other siblings?' wondered Münster.

'Were,' said Traut. 'A brother. He died . . . Committed suicide, to be honest.'

'There is every reason to be honest in this situation,' stressed Reinhart. 'Your sister-in-law has been brutally murdered, there's no doubt about that, and we must catch whoever did it.'

'Of course, obviously,' Traut hastened to say. 'I'll do anything I can to help you get on the right track . . .'

He broke off and raised the palms of his hands towards the

ceiling, a gesture presumably meant to demonstrate the genuineness of his intentions. Münster regarded him with a feeling of mild distaste. Traut was about the same age as he was, around forty-five, but he looked heavy and bloated. The passage of time had taken its toll on him, but it was hardly as a result of work and hard effort, Münster suspected. More like living the good life. Sitting around doing nothing. Creamy sauces and strong booze. And a minimum of exercise. His red-coloured hair was sparse and lifeless, and combed in an odd sort of way from below his ears and upwards, apparently in a vain and rather pathetic attempt to conceal a well-developed bald patch.

Ah well, Münster thought, it's not outward appearance that matters.

'So you live up in Chadow,' said Reinhart. 'What brought you down here to Maardam?'

Traut cleared his throat and began to explain.

'I was just passing through,' he said. 'On business. I usually make a little trip to Groenstadt and Bissenhof and other places around there at this time of year. Usually two or three days – it's important to be in personal contact with your customers, that's something I've never doubted. There are those who think that—'

'What exactly is your business?' interrupted Münster.

'Optical display stands,' said Traut with a professional half-smile. 'I sell them to opticians and spectacle shop chains all over the country. My firm is called GROTTENAU, and it's doing pretty well, though I say so myself . . . Anyway, I went by car as usual, and I'd promised my old lady that on the way home I'd call in on her sister. She was a bit worried because she hasn't heard anything from her for over a month. I did so, of course – blood is thicker than water after all – and when I realized that there didn't seem to be anybody at home in the flat in Moerckstraat today either, I began to suspect that there was something wrong . . .'

'Why?' wondered Reinhart. 'They might have been at the cinema, or somewhere else.'

'True enough,' said Traut, digging out a cigarette. 'Of course. But as she hadn't answered the phone for such a long time and wasn't at home this evening, I thought I ought to look into the situation. Try to get to the bottom of it while I was on the spot anyway. And the rest you know.'

He lit the cigarette and leaned back.

'Tell us about Martina Kammerle,' said Reinhart.

Traut inhaled deeply, coughed and looked worried.

'Huh, what can one say?' he said. 'We didn't have a lot of contact, as I said. None at all, really. I don't think I've met her more than four or five times, ever, even though I've been married to her sister for twenty-three years . . . Time passes, that's one thing there's no doubt about. She was a bit odd, Martina. Ill, in fact – you ought to be clear about that.'

'Ill in what way?' asked Münster.

'Her psyche,' said Traut, making a vague gesture in the direction of his own head as if to indicate where in the body the psyche was to be found. 'Manic depressive, as it's called. She's suffered from it all her life. Spent time in care homes a few times, although that was quite a long time ago . . .'

'But she had a daughter, we gather,' said Münster. 'Who lived with her, is that right?'

'That's right,' said Traut. 'Mar . . . Monica.'

'Monica Kammerle?'

'Yes.'

'How old?'

Traut flung out his arms.

'I don't really know. In her teens. About fifteen or sixteen, I'd guess.'

'And presumably you had no contact with her either?'

'None at all.'

'And who was Monica's dad?'

Traut frowned and tried to think.

'I can't remember his name. Apart from Kammerle, of course. Yes, they were married, Martina and him, but he died. Four or five years ago, I'd say, but time passes so quickly. Car accident. He fell asleep at the wheel – that's what they say, at least. I only met him once, briefly . . . Ah yes, his name was Klaus of course, I remember now. I think things have gone downhill for Martina since she's been on her own. Hasn't been able to hold down a proper job and so on, that's what my old lady says in any case. No, she didn't exactly lead a happy life – but that it should end like this is . . . well, a bit much, don't you think?'

He looked at Reinhart and Münster in turn a few times, as if he was expecting them to enlighten him on how things really stood.

'Do you know if she had a job at the moment?' asked Münster.

'*Keine Ahnung*, as they say in France,' said Traut. 'I think it would be better if you talked to my old lady about this. She's taken it pretty hard, but of course she'd be pleased to give you any help she could. What kind of a loony could do something like this? I mean, you read about it in the papers and see it on the telly, but you don't believe—'

'We'll talk to your wife in the next few days,' interrupted Reinhart. 'Possibly even tomorrow. Do you know if there's anybody else who might be able to give us information? Anybody who knew Martina Kammerle or knows a bit more about her?'

Traut shook his head.

'Or her daughter?'

'No, no, I'm sorry. It's as I said, we haven't been in touch very much at all. There were six years between the sisters as well, and Martina was never easy to handle, you must be clear about that.'

'How do you know that if you've hardly ever been in contact with her?' wondered Münster.

Traut seemed to be thinking that one over.

'The old lady told me,' he said. 'She keeps ringing her, although all she gets back is nearly always a lot of shit . . . Or used to get a lot of shit, I should say. We've lent her money a few times, by the way, but we've never received anything back. Not even any shit. A pretty crappy investment, I must say . . .'

'When was that?' Reinhart asked. 'When you lent her money.'

'Ages ago,' said Traut. 'Before she got married. Twenty

years ago, something like that . . . She'd just come out of a home, and we lent her some money so that she could get a flat. Not the kind of sum to make a fuss about, of course, and we didn't do so.'

'Hmm,' said Reinhart, looking at the clock. 'It's getting a bit late. I gather you have a hotel room for tonight, and intend driving up to Chadow tomorrow morning, is that right?'

'Exactly,' said Traut. 'The Palace in Rejmer Plejn. If you need me for anything else I'll be there until about eleven tomorrow morning.'

'Excellent,' said Reinhart. 'I think we can leave it at that for now. I suppose there's no point in asking you what you think might have happened – who might have murdered your sister-in-law, that is?'

'No,' said Traut, displaying the palms of his hands again. 'How the devil would I know?'

'Two questions,' said Reinhart when Traut had left them alone. 'If you can answer them, maybe we can get some-where.'

'Only two?' said Münster. 'I have a hundred. And we haven't even started yet.'

'No,' said Reinhart. 'We haven't. But I can't help wonder-ing about the daughter. Where the hell is she? A fifteen- or sixteen-year-old girl can't simply disappear into thin air. Did you notice that Traut didn't even seem to be able to remem-ber her name?'

Münster stood up and wriggled his way into his jacket.

'Yes,' he said, 'I noted that. But even if people have forgotten about you, it's a bit hard simply to go up in smoke. Do you think she's lying in another rubbish bag somewhere? Or do you think she strangled her mother after a row over pocket money?'

Reinhart snorted, but didn't answer.

'What was your other question?' asked Münster. 'You said you had two.'

'Traut,' said Reinhart. 'I have the feeling he's keeping something from us, but I can't work out what.'

Münster nodded.

'I had the same impression, in fact. Anyway, I don't suppose we've seen him for the last time. Shall we say goodnight now? It's past midnight.'

'Goodnight,' said Detective Chief Inspector Reinhart. 'I expect to see you here at nine o'clock tomorrow morning. As clear in the head as a chess computer.'

'I've always thought that Monday mornings have a special shimmer about them,' said Münster. 'Especially at this time of year. Was it half past nine you said?'

14

Ewa Moreno took an early flight and was in Chadow by eight o'clock.

The town was shrouded in smoke from the factory chimneys, sea mist and the grey light of dawn which seemed to be reflecting her own inner landscape. November, Monday morning and blocked sinuses. She had a quick breakfast in the lugubrious cafeteria in the airport terminal, as no food had been served on the flight, and took a taxi to Pelikaanallé, where Barbara Traut lived.

Three children had just been sent off to various schools, and fru Traut asked Moreno if she could have a shower before they started their conversation – she had hardly slept a wink during the night, she explained, and after all, they had the whole morning at their disposal.

Moreno abandoned all hope of catching the eleven o'clock flight back home, and assured fru Traut that there was no hurry. She sat down at the half-cleared breakfast table with yet another cup of tea and the local morning paper, which was called the *Kurijr*. She glanced absent-mindedly through its pages, and wondered – as she had done on the plane – about points of contact between Barbara Traut and herself.

Or point of contact, rather: on the basis of what little she had seen of fru Traut, she hoped there was only one.

Having lost a sister.

On her own part Inspector Moreno had not actually lost a sister – not in the horrendous way that her hostess had, at least. But it was over three years since she had heard from Maud, and there were certainly reasons to assume that she was unlikely to appear again in Moreno's life. Good reasons.

No, not good ones. Awful reasons. Rootlessness. Drugs. A constant shortage of money and consequential prostitution – plus some sort of warped and inadequate relationship with her family that presumably was at the bottom of it all, and that Moreno preferred not to think about: all those desperate factors that seemed somehow to be legion among her generation, and dragged Maud relentlessly down into the cold, man-eating swamp that seemed to claim so many victims in the late twentieth century. That was simply the way it was. Perhaps she was clinging to a sort of life in one of those big cities where there was still a need for broken people with no safety net who could be ruthlessly exploited. In the social machinery that nobody was servicing any more, or bothered to oil.

As she had seen it described somewhere.

Or perhaps she's dead, Moreno thought. Vanished in the anonymous and unidentified way that people, young people, are simply wiped off the ethnographical map of the new Europe. Victims, victims of the post-modern age.

Without leaving any trace behind.

Lives as substantial as footprints in water.

Yes, Maud has no doubt vanished for ever, she decided with

the same cold bitterness as always. Dead, or enduring a living death. There was nothing Moreno could do about it: a continuation of the amusing and happy thirteen-year-old that had been her little sister when she flew the nest was simply non-existent. Moreno had realized that several years ago: the fact that she thought about it now was simply due to the parallel she had now come across. What happened to be on today's agenda. Barbara Traut and Martina Kammerle.

And echoed by the dull greyness of the November day. She recalled something Van Veeteren had said a few years ago. We must unfortunately be aware, he had maintained, that for many people, life ends before they die.

All she could do was to bow down once again before the *Chief Inspector*'s superior wisdom. And it seemed there was plenty to suggest that Barbara Traut's sister belonged to this category. To those who hadn't had much of a life before she lost it and passed over into the next one.

Assuming of course that the scant amount of information that had so far emerged turned out to be true.

But why anybody should help her along the way in such a hideous fashion was another question. Murder her. Why would anybody have wanted to get rid of Martina Kammerle?

And what had happened to her daughter?

Good questions, thought Inspector Moreno as she sipped her cup of tea. Hopelessly good.

And of course the reason why she was hanging around in the Trauts' over-decorated kitchen, waiting for the shower to come to an end, was to receive an answer to those questions.

*

'Martina and I never really got on,' said Barbara Traut, blowing her nose. 'I ought to make that clear from the start, even if it sounds awful at a time like this.'

She was a morose woman who seemed to exude a sort of self-justified dissatisfaction, both in her facial expression and in her voice. As if the world had failed to fulfil her expectations of it. Her shower had taken a long time, and Moreno gathered that making herself up had no doubt been a laborious process. She seemed to be about forty-five. Pale and somewhat colourless, but with hair of many colours that seemed to need non-stop care. She put on water for more tea and coffee, produced some biscuits and muffins and a third of a rillen cake from the pantry, breathing hard and chain-smoking all the while.

'We've gathered that things were not all they might have been,' said Moreno. 'But it's important that we get a good idea of her life and general circumstances to begin with, and you are the obvious person to turn to. We haven't yet found anybody in Maardam who knew her well.'

'No,' said fru Traut, blinking away the tears that threatened to well up into her eyes. 'She led a pretty solitary life.'

'But she used to be married, I gather?'

'To Klaus, yes. He was a big support for her, no doubt about that; but he died. Since then – that was 1996 – things haven't been easy for her. I assume and hope you've found Monica?'

Moreno shook her head.

'I'm afraid not. Have you any idea where she might be?'

'Me? No, I haven't a clue. We didn't socialize, I haven't seen the girl since Klaus's funeral. She was twelve then. A really nice girl, poor thing.'

'Klaus Kammerle died in a car accident, is that right?'

'Yes. Drove off the road and into a tree. Somewhere between Oostwerdingen and Ulming – there wasn't much left of him . . . They say he fell asleep at the wheel.'

'They say?' said Moreno. 'Do you mean you are not convinced?'

'No, no, of course not,' said fru Traut. 'Certainly not. It was at night, and he was on his way home from some course or other. No doubt he just dozed off.'

Moreno took another sip of tea, and changed tack.

'Let's concentrate on your sister,' she said. 'How was she? Was she in difficulty?'

Fru Traut inhaled deeply and coughed.

'Difficulty? You can say that again. She swung this way and that like a weathercock – that was her problem, and it started while she was still at school . . . She was always in a mess. Manic depressive – do you understand what that means?'

Moreno nodded and made a note.

'Before she met Klaus she was taken into care several times. There are medicines to treat the condition, but she never took them as she should. Refused to take any tablets when she was feeling good, and of course, she suffered as a result. When she was on a high she would start up one daft project after another, and behaved in such a way that nobody could put up with her. Then she would fall to pieces, get into a state of anxiety, and she tried to commit suicide. It was like that all the time. She cut her wrists several times as well, but that was mainly cries for help and they managed to save her.'

'But things got better when she met Klaus, is that right?'

'Yes. At least there was always somebody close to her who could ride her punches and make sure that she kept going. I don't know, but I suspect that she got pregnant the very first time they met. In any case, she told me about both things at the same time – that she was pregnant and they were going to get married. That was 1984. I think she'd had a few abortions before then, incidentally. Or one at least . . .'

'But you didn't start socializing with them then? When they were going to start a family?'

Fru Traut paused and stirred another lump of sugar into her coffee.

'They came here once,' she said. 'Stayed for an hour and a half and had lunch. Monica was three or four. But that's all, I'm afraid. She wasn't easy to be together with, my sister. Klaus didn't always have an easy time either.'

'What was he like?'

'Calm. As safe as a parking place, as far as I could tell. Maybe things would have turned out all right, if only he'd been able to keep going . . .'

Her voice started to tremble, and she blew her nose again.

'What a bloody mess,' she said. 'I can't get it into my head that somebody would have wanted to murder her. What kind of a lunatic could have done such a thing? Do you have any idea?'

'Not yet,' said Moreno. 'The body's been lying there in

the flat for quite a long time – that makes things more complicated.'

'Didn't anybody go and ask about her?" asked fru Traut with a sob – she had been crying silently now for a while. 'Wasn't there anybody who wondered where she'd been all that time?'

'We don't know,' said Moreno.

'But what about Monica? Where is she? Are you suggesting that she's also dead and that nobody's bothering about her either?'

Moreno suddenly felt how the bitterness of this large woman was beginning to infect her as well.

Was that really possible? she thought. That a mother and her daughter could vanish, without anybody asking about their disappearance for a whole month? Surrounded by lots of people in the centre of a town?

And this was supposed to be civilization?

She looked down at her notebook and tried to concentrate.

'Do you know anything at all about her circle of friends?' she asked. 'Any names of people she used to mix with?'

'No. I know nothing at all about things like that.'

'But you used to phone her occasionally. Isn't that right?'

'Yes, of course. I used to ring her at least once every month. To find out how she was and so on. But I hardly ever found out anything at all. And she never phoned me. Never – can you believe that? Since Klaus died I haven't received a single telephone call from my little sister.'

'I understand,' said Moreno. 'But have you any idea whether

she had any friends at all? I mean, you did speak to her now and again.'

Fru Traut frowned even more intensely, and thought for a moment.

'I don't think she had any friends,' she said. 'No, she was a pretty lonely person. In the old days she often used to bring new people into her life when she was in a manic phase, but I think she stopped that . . . I gather that's a normal development.'

'Did you use to speak to her daughter as well?'

'Never. If she was the one who answered the phone, she always used to hand over to her mother the moment she realized it was me. If Martina wasn't at home, she would say so and put down the receiver without more ado. It would be a lie to pretend that I felt appreciated, let's face it.'

'And if your sister had met a new man, that's not something she would have told you about?'

'It would never have occurred to her to do so.'

'This autumn, for instance?'

'No. Not a word. I haven't heard her mention a man since Klaus died. But no doubt she had a few. One of them even answered.'

'You mean he answered the phone when you rang?'

'Yes.'

'When was that?'

Fru Traut shrugged.

'I don't remember. Last summer, I suppose.'

'Just that one occasion?'

'Yes.'

'And he didn't mention his name?'

'No.'

Moreno turned over a page in her notebook. Fru Traut lit another cigarette.

'So your sister didn't have a steady job, is that right?'

'I think she was on sick leave. Long-term or half-time or something along those lines. No, she hasn't really been able to cope with a job since Klaus left the scene.'

'But she used to work before that, did she?'

'On and off. Mostly off. She was a hotel receptionist for a while. Then a cleaner at a hospital . . . I think she worked in an office for a while as well. She didn't have any educational qualifications – she didn't even finish her GCEs. She just couldn't cope with anything formal.'

'Do you know if she had a doctor . . . A therapist or a psychologist who used to see her regularly?'

'I've no idea,' said fru Traut, scratching her lower arm where she had some kind of rash. 'I wouldn't have thought so. Martina had trouble in coping with anything that required regular attendance. She always used to think that people were letting her down although in fact it was the other way round.'

'I think I understand,' said Moreno. 'I'm sorry to keep harping on, but can you really not recall any name at all when it comes to your sister's circle of friends? There must surely be somebody. If you think really hard?'

Fru Traut took the challenge *ad notam* and sat there quietly for half a minute.

'No,' she said eventually. 'I'll be damned if I can think of a single person at all.'

Just over an hour after Inspector Moreno left the Traut mansion in Chadow, she was very nearly run over.

A pale sun had begun to force its way through the thick cloud, the mists had lifted, and she decided to walk to the little airport. It was several kilometres away from the town, but she had a good two hours to fill.

The last of those kilometres was along a very busy road with only a narrow shoulder for cyclists and pedestrians, and it was there it happened. A motorcyclist suddenly cut in directly in front of a large long-distance lorry, and Moreno had to jump into the ditch and escaped being hit by a whisker.

The only tangible outcome of the incident was that she got her feet wet, but she also received a sharp reminder of the inherent fragility of life, and when she turned into the road leading to the little airport, thankfully much safer for pedestrians, she suddenly found herself longing for Mikael Bau.

A strong and powerful longing for him to wrap his arms around her and give her a big hug, and she promised herself to contact him the moment she got home that evening.

The feeling of being weak and vulnerable had of course to do with both her sinuses and the conversation with Barbara Traut, she was aware of that.

And with the murdered Martina Kammerle, whose life and death somehow seemed remarkably petty. She couldn't shake off that impression – it was as if the poor woman's brutal end had merely been a grotesquely exaggerated exclamation mark after a totally pointless and insignificant existence.

When Moreno was at secondary school – and hence was roughly the same age as the murdered woman's missing daughter – she used to have two maxims printed on a piece of paper pinned over her bed:

It's up to you to give significance to your life.

It's better to regret what you have done,
than what you never did.

She knew that the second saying was a quotation from Nietzsche; she wasn't sure where the first one came from, but that didn't matter. Just now, as she walked through the almost white sunshine on her way to Chadow's little airport, she felt that the words were of immense topical significance.

So topical, in fact, that she didn't dare to wait until evening before telephoning Mikael Bau. She did so as soon as she entered the terminal building instead.

Needless to say he wasn't at home, but she left a message on his answering machine: that she was longing to be with him, and that he should prepare something tasty as she intended to call round at his place for dinner that evening.

At about nine o'clock or thereabouts.

When she had switched off her mobile, she felt a little bit alive at last.

15

It was not until half past six on Monday evening that they were able to acknowledge anything resembling a breakthrough in the Martina Kammerle case.

But, as Reinhart said, the murderer had had plenty of time in which to cover his tracks, so perhaps matters were not as urgent as the media hacks – always keen to apply pressure – seemed to think. The investigation team had issued a press release at the routine media briefing at three o'clock, but had explained that there would be no press conference as such until Tuesday afternoon at the earliest.

In response to this, a young and obviously unbalanced reporter from the *Telegraaf* had called Reinhart a secrecy-obsessed turnip, and Reinhart had asked him if he had been accepted for training at the College of Journalism as part of a quota reserved for sticks of asparagus without heads.

Relations between the head of Maardam CID and the fourth estate were nothing to write home about.

In addition to Reinhart, Moreno and Münster, also present at the run-through were Jung, Rooth and Krause – the last-named had just been promoted to the rank of inspector – so it was obvious that plenty of resources had been mobilized at this early stage of the investigation.

Apart from that, as Reinhart stressed, things were not looking exactly rosy.

'Unless a murderer full of regrets, or a five-star witness, turns up within the next few days, we shall no doubt have to resign ourselves to a long, hard slog. People who lie under a bed dead for a month without being discovered have not normally been living in the spotlight either. Does anybody disagree about that?'

Nobody did. Reinhart took out his pipe and tobacco, and handed over to Münster for a summary of what had been discovered during the day with regard to what are usually but somewhat inappropriately called 'technical matters'.

'A month seems about right,' Münster began. 'That's what Meusse reckons at least, and we all know the status of an estimation by Meusse, right? The cause of death is obvious: strangulation. Persistent and hard pressure applied to the larynx. Only the hands were used, presumably from behind, probably by somebody who is pretty strong. No rape, no sign of any sort of struggle. Nothing odd at all, one could say.'

He paused, and looked around.

'Go on,' said Reinhart.

'The scene of the crime and the place where the body was discovered seem to be identical. Somebody had been to visit Martina Kammerle four or five weeks ago. He killed her and put the body in rubbish bags – there are several in the broom cupboard by the way, so he might well have taken them from there – and then he shoved her under the bed and left the scene. The door can be locked without a key. There is no indication of anything having been removed from the flat, nor that it was searched, although of course we can't be certain of that. There was no alcohol in the victim's body, no sign of any unwashed plates or glasses. If we eventually find that he removed jewellery worth a million or two from the flat, we shall obviously have to consider the possibility of robbery with murder: but there is nothing to suggest that at the moment.'

'Is there anything to suggest anything at all?' wondered Rooth, but he received no reply.

'Fingerprints?' asked Krause.

'Nix,' said Münster. 'It looks as if the murderer was careful to wipe everything clean before leaving. There are hardly any prints in the flat at all. Mulder says it seems that somebody spent several hours cleaning and dusting all surfaces. There were a few prints on crockery and books and suchlike, but most of them are those of the victim herself. It's fairly obvious that the others are probably those of the daughter.'

'A very cautious type, then,' said Rooth. 'So nothing to hope for there?'

'Presumably not,' said Münster.

'I don't suppose we have any of the usual suspects on the run, do we?' asked Rooth. 'Characters who enjoy strangling women now and then?'

Münster shook his head.

'I've started looking into that,' he said. 'But I don't think so. Not in the vicinity of Maardam, at least.'

Reinhart had lit his pipe by now, and blew a cloud of smoke over all those present.

'So we're looking for a loony making his debut, in other words,' he said. 'Anything else?'

'Nothing of significance,' said Münster. 'All the reports are available for people to read.'

'Very true,' said Reinhart. 'That will be the homework for tomorrow. I don't know how long we'll be allowed to continue on the case with as many officers as we have now, but for the time being it would be as well if everybody could make sure they were familiar with all aspects of it. There's not all that much, and of course, three eyes see better than one.'

'No doubt,' said Rooth. 'And coffee without any cake is better than no coffee at all. Are we going to get any refreshments?'

Reinhart ignored that question as well.

'What about the neighbours?' he asked instead. 'Jung, Rooth, over to you.'

Jung explained that together with Constables Klempje, Dillinger and Joensuu, they had spent six hours knocking on doors in Moerckstraat, and the result had been depressingly thin. Nobody – not a single soul of the ninety-two persons listed as having been contacted – had known anything at all about Martina Kammerle.

And precisely the same number had been able to comment on her daughter, Monica.

'It makes you think,' said Jung. 'And leaves you depressed. Violeta Paraskevi, who lives next door to the Kammerles, is the only one who noticed that there might be something wrong. *Might be*, note that. And it was thanks to her that this Traut character decided to call in the caretaker.'

'And what about him?' wondered Münster. 'What did the caretaker have to say?'

'Not a dicky bird,' said Rooth. 'As long as you pay your rent on time and don't trash anything, you are as familiar as a paving stone in his eyes. And valued just about as much. Nice chap – it's a pity we don't have a standard punishment for being a bastard. But where's the daughter? We should be talking about that instead. We can forget about the neighbours, despite the fact that Dillinger and Joensuu still have a few more doors to knock on tomorrow.'

'Ah yes, the daughter,' said Reinhart. 'That's another disaster, to say the least.'

'Really?' said Münster. 'What do you mean by that?'

Reinhart had no desire to enlarge upon his comment, but delegated this question as well.

'Inspector Krause,' he said. 'Over to you!'

'Hmm, yes, thank you,' said Krause leaning forward on his elbows. 'It looks as if Monica Kammerle hasn't attended school since the twenty-first of September – assuming the information we have received is correct, and no doubt it is in this case. She's in the first year at the Bunge Grammar School, but nobody has reacted to the fact that she's been absent. I've spoken to the headmaster, to one of the teachers and a few of her classmates, and there seem to be quite a few points that are unclear.'

'Points that are unclear?' wondered Moreno. 'What, for instance?'

'It seems to have been assumed that she had transferred to another school, but she hasn't been registered at any of the other grammar schools in Maardam and district. There's a social worker who ought to know a bit more about it, but she's been at a funeral down in Groenstadt today. We shall be talking to her tomorrow.'

'So you're saying that the daughter has been missing for as long as her mother has been lying dead, are you?' said Moreno.

'It seems so,' said Krause. 'On the face of it.'

'But that's deplorable,' said Rooth.

'That's exactly what I said,' agreed Reinhart. 'If nobody notices that a child has been missing for a month and a half, you have to ask what the hell is going on there.'

'Precisely,' said Krause. 'The headmaster seemed flabbergasted, to be fair.'

'No wonder,' said Münster. 'Perhaps we ought to say a few words about this at the press conference?'

'When I played truant at secondary school, they nabbed me after no more than an hour,' said Rooth. 'Every bloody time.'

There followed a few moments of silence. Reinhart leafed through his papers and blew out another cloud of smoke.

'That's the way things are nowadays,' he muttered eventually. 'And however they are, it's bonkers. But I suppose this isn't really anything unprecedented . . . The world is a madhouse, and has been that way for as long as I can remember. Münster, did you make contact with any of the medics?'

Münster nodded.

'After considerable difficulty,' he said. 'Martina Kammerle was a manic depressive, and she was taken into care a few times. The first time she was only eighteen, and had tried to take her own life. She's been on medication ever since then, but Dr Klimke – the one I spoke to – suggested that she some-times used to skip it. It seems that is not uncommon, when patients are on a high. The usual medicines are Lithium and Calvonal. Martina Kammerle has been on both of them: they are used to try to level out the ups and downs of the manic-depressive psyche, as they say. Klimke works at Gemejnte Hospital and came into contact with Kammerle four years ago, in connection with the death of her husband – I expect you know about that car accident business?'

He looked round the table.

'Yep,' said Rooth. 'Was she on the sick list now?'

'Klimke thought so – we'll check that tomorrow. He didn't really know all that much about her. He'd signed prescrip-tions for her and phoned the pharmacy once or twice, when she had been in touch; but he says he hasn't actually met her for about three years.'

'Top class psychiatric care,' said Rooth.

'Brilliant,' said Reinhart. 'But that's not exactly anything new either. Medicine is cheaper than therapy. Anyway, all this boils down to the fact that Martina Kammerle hasn't had a steady job – or any job at all, come to that – for the last five years. She had no social contacts, not that we know about, at least; and apart from her daughter her only living close rela-tive is her sister up in Chadow. Perhaps Inspector Moreno could be so kind as to inject a little light into the compact darkness and tell us something substantial about her visit to Chadow?'

Moreno did as she was asked, without feeling that anything had become any clearer. She was tempted to mention the incident with the motorcycle, in order to increase the degree of substantiality asked of her, but desisted.

'A testament to sisterly love, in other words,' said Reinhart when she had finished. 'Is there a single person who has anything to say about Martina Kammerle? Didn't she ever undergo a course of treatment, by the way?'

Krause cleared his throat and took the floor once more.

'It depends what you mean by "undergo",' he said. 'She started on a sort of work aptitude course in August, and was paid a subsidy to attend. She seems to have turned up three or four times, but the man responsible for it doesn't recall ever speaking to her about it. It apparently involved mainly watching videos and then filling in aptitude forms . . . But he promised to send us a list of all those taking part so that we can maybe check on whether she made any contacts there.'

'Good,' said Reinhart. 'Not much chance of that, I suspect, but this is the kind of thing we have to hope comes up with a lead. Somebody who might be able to tell us a little bit about her. Every little helps, as they say.'

'Let's face it,' said Rooth, 'Everything that is more than nothing is something.'

'You don't say?' said Reinhart. 'Anyway, we'll make sure her picture appears in tomorrow's papers, come what may. And urge people to come forward – especially if anybody has seen her in the company of a man.'

'A man?' said Rooth. 'Why?'

'Surely that's obvious,' said Reinhart, beginning to look annoyed. 'It's got to have been a man who killed her, and next-door-neighbour Paraskevi said something – pretty vague, for God's sake, but still. Something about having seen a man around. At the end of August or thereabouts.'

'But she never actually saw him, did she?' asked Krause.

'Apparently not,' sighed Reinhart, sitting up straight. 'Unfortunately. Anyway, to sum up: this is a case about which we know next to nothing – I take it we can all agree on that? We know so damned little that we ought to be ashamed – if it helps for police officers to be ashamed, and maybe it doesn't. Has anybody anything to add before we start deciding who is going to do what?'

Rooth stood up.

'I think I must go and fetch something to eat before we go any further,' he said. 'Bearing in mind my blood sugar levels and all that. But there's one other thing I wonder about.'

'What's that?' asked Jung.

'Well, if this Martina Kammerle woman was so cut off from contact with anybody else, how come that anybody should bother to murder her? Eh? If she was so insignificant?'

Reinhart nodded vaguely, but said nothing.

'There's something in that,' said Münster. 'Anybody who had a reason for murdering her must have been acquainted with her – a little bit, at least. Bearing in mind how she was killed. You don't strangle somebody on the spur of the moment. I wouldn't, at least.'

'Nor would I,' said Reinhart. 'Anyway, let's take a five-minute pause, so that Inspector Rooth doesn't starve to death.'

⋆

Once Tuesday's work programme had been drawn up, Münster invited Moreno into his office for a brief chat.

'You didn't say very much during the meeting,' he said when they had sat down.

'I know,' said Moreno. 'I'm sorry, but I find this Martina Kammerle business very depressing.'

'So do I,' said Münster.

'If you live in such a way that nobody notices your presence, why should anybody want to kill you? I agree with Rooth. Getting murdered seems to suggest an interest in you that you haven't deserved.'

'Indeed,' said Münster. 'That thought struck me as well. But I suppose it's possible that she possessed some sort of inner light that we're unaware of. Qualities of life that we don't see. We're only rooting around in the afterbirth, as it were.'

'Do you think so? That there was some kind of inner light?'

Münster shrugged.

'I don't think anything. But what we've gathered about the daughter is very perplexing.'

'You can say that again,' said Moreno. 'I wonder if in fact she's the one behind it all. The murderer seems to have been a very strong man, but you never know – she might have hired a contract killer.'

Münster sighed and looked grim.

'Some sort of showdown between a psychologically disturbed woman and her daughter, you mean?'

'Something like that. What do you think?'

'Why not? The girl must be involved in some way, seeing as she's disappeared . . . Huh, it's not exactly a bundle of laughs, this case.'

'A bundle of laughs?' said Moreno, twisting her mouth into a clownish grin. 'When did we last have a case that was a bundle of laughs? I must have missed it.'

Münster said nothing, but eyed her up and down for a while.

'How are you?' he asked eventually. 'If one dare ask.'

Moreno laughed.

'I'm okay,' she said. 'It's just that being a human being is so hard. And so pointless. I'm afraid I've started thinking seriously along those lines . . . Look at deBries, for instance. It's only about a year since he died, but it seems as if we've forgotten about him already. I know he was a swine in a way, but still.'

'Yes,' said Münster. 'I'm afraid you're right.'

'And Heinemann is struggling with his prostate cancer. Has anybody been in touch with him since he left? Proper contact, I mean. He was a cop for forty years, after all.'

Münster made no reply.

'So no doubt that's what you and I have to look forward to, unfortunately,' said Moreno. 'That's what I mean. We're so insignificant. Oblivion lies in store for us all. Unless we happen to be murdered, like Martina Kammerle, of course. Or shot while on duty. Then we might receive a bit of attention. Briefly.'

'A damned perverted sort of attention,' said Münster, looking over her shoulder and out of the window. 'I think I'd prefer to fall asleep in peace and quiet. Why don't you get married and have some children? That would give your existence a bit more substance.'

As he said that, he couldn't avoid the fact that the love he had once felt for her surged up again inside him – and he found it necessary to keep gazing out of the window when she looked at him.

'Thanks for the tip,' she said. 'I might well be on the way to doing that, in fact. It might be a makeshift solution, but rather one of those than none at all.'

'Good,' said Münster. 'I'm also about to give my existence a bit more substance. We're going to have another one.'

'A baby, you mean?'

'A baby, yes. What did you think I meant? A hamster?'

Moreno laughed. Genuinely, at last.

'I'm delighted to hear it,' she said, looking at her watch. 'No, I'd better go – there's a dinner waiting for me. We can carry on philosophizing tomorrow.'

'By all means,' said Münster. 'Mind you, tomorrow is deeper than a camel's soul.'

'Eh?' said Moreno. 'What does that mean?'

'I've no idea,' said Münster. 'I must have read it somewhere.'

16

'Monica Kammerle,' said Detective Inspector Krause. 'What can you tell me about her?'

Welfare Officer Stroop tried hard to produce a smile hinting at mutual understanding before answering, but it looked somewhat ambiguous. She raised her narrow eyebrows and looked at him as one would look at an old but not entirely reliable ally. Krause clicked his biro a couple of times and looked out of the window. It was raining.

'Well, what can one say?' said the welfare officer hesitantly. 'We're so understaffed that we simply can't keep up. There are over nine hundred pupils in this school.'

'Minus one,' said Krause. 'You were in contact with Monica Kammerle at the beginning of this term – perhaps you remember that, at least? What did she want?'

'I'm not allowed to discuss such matters with third parties . . .' said Stroop slowly, rotating a ring with a large green stone round and round her little finger.

'Rubbish,' said Krause.

'Rubbish?'

'Her mother has been murdered and the girl has been missing for at least six weeks. If you don't tell me what you

191

know, I shall report you to the authorities this afternoon. No matter how busy you are, you have a duty to keep tabs on all the pupils in this school.'

Stroop blushed well into her bleached hair. She fiddled nervously with the various piles of papers on her desk, and drank something out of a china mug with blue flowers on.

'I'm sorry,' she said. 'These are . . . well, these are extraordinary circumstances. Yes, she came to see me. She wanted to transfer to another school, it was as simple as that.'

'As simple as that?'

'Yes. She told me about her situation, and said she wanted to transfer to another grammar school.'

'Why did she want to transfer?'

'Because of the situation in her class. She thought she was being bullied.'

'Was she?'

The welfare officer shrugged.

'I only saw her once. That's what she said, in any case – but I don't always have time to dig more deeply into every individual case. Girls at that age are very sensitive, and you have to be very careful about how you handle them. And besides, the term had only just started.'

'So what did you do?' asked Krause.

Stroop looked down and clasped her hands.

'Well, I decided that her situation could justify a school transfer. Especially as she had thought it through herself, and come up with a specific proposal. I contacted the Joannis Grammar School in Löhr, and arranged for her to go there for an interview. Monica was supposed to visit the school and see if she liked it.'

'And?'

'Well, she went there: and as she didn't come back here we took it for granted that she had made up her mind. It was already decided which class she would join, and so on . . .'

'You assumed that she had transferred to the Joannis Grammar School?'

'Yes.'

'And no doubt you checked up in accordance with the official procedures?'

'Well . . . various other things cropped up that needed dealing with. You must understand the working conditions we are landed with here, and—'

'No,' interrupted Krause. 'I don't understand that at all. Did you even check that she had been there?'

'Er . . . well, I can't really remember what we did.'

'Remember?' said Krause. 'Surely you must know if you rang them and checked that she had been there?'

Stroop took another sip from her mug, and fiddled with the green stone.

'It's possible that it was overlooked. I had a trainee to supervise, and . . . well, I assumed of course that everything had gone according to plan.'

'What do you mean? What plan?'

'The procedures we had drawn up. We'd all agreed that she could start out at Löhr immediately, if that's what she wanted . . . And when she didn't turn up here any more, well . . . we assumed that everything was done and dusted.'

Krause paused and made notes.

'Do you know for sure that she actually did visit the school in Löhr?'

'Yes, she was supposed to do that. It was a Friday . . .'

'Supposed to?' said Krause. 'Have you spoken to your colleague at Löhr since you sent Monica there?'

'Yes . . .'

'When?'

'I . . . I phoned her this morning, and . . . well, it's not absolutely clear whether or not she turned up on that Friday. They are looking into it . . .'

'Not clear?' said Krause. 'I think it's crystal clear. Monica Kammerle never set foot in Joannis Grammar School. She's been missing since Thursday the twenty-first of September, and to say the very least I think it's remarkable that nobody at the school where she is registered has reacted at all. Six weeks have passed.'

Stroop made as if to say something, but changed her mind. Krause closed his notebook and put his pen in his breast pocket.

'I'll be back,' he said. 'Have you anything to add that might throw light on the girl's disappearance? Anything at all – but let's have no more prevarication.'

The welfare officer shook her head and looked decidedly shifty.

'I'm sorry,' she whispered. 'My personal circumstances have been difficult. I attended my brother's funeral yesterday . . . That's not an excuse, but . . .'

Her voice broke, and Krause suddenly felt embarrassed. He stood up.

'I'm only doing my job,' he said, and when he had closed the door behind him he wondered why on earth he had made such an idiotic comment.

But then, you have to say something in your own defence.

As agreed, Moreno met the two girls in the Bunge Grammar School cafeteria: but after a brief discussion they decided it would be better to adjourn to a more neutral location.

They ended up at the Café Lamprecht, which was only a stone's throw away, and at this time of day had plenty of little corners where they could talk without being overheard.

Both girls were dressed in black, both smoked like chimneys and both ordered coffee drinks called Black & Brown. More or less the only thing that distinguished between the two young ladies was their names: Betty Schaafens and Edwina Boekman. Moreno tried to recall what she looked like when she was sixteen, getting on for seventeen, but no really clear images came to mind. Even so, she found it hard to believe that she had ever gone through a similar phase.

But you can never be sure . . .

'As I said, it's about your classmate Monica Kammerle,' she began by saying. 'We'd like some information about her.'

'Why?' asked Betty.

'What kind of information?' wondered Edwina.

'I'm afraid I can't go into that at the moment,' said Moreno in a friendly tone. 'Maybe I can tell you more on another occasion.'

The girls inhaled deeply and exchanged glances.

'Okay,' said Betty.

'All right,' said Edwina. 'But she's not in our class any more.'

'So I gather,' said Moreno. 'But you were in the same class even before you started at the grammar school, weren't you?'

'Yes, for three years,' said Edwina. 'Deijkstraaskolan.'

'Four years in my case,' said Betty. What do you want to know?'

'Just a few general things. What she's like and how she gets on with the rest of the class. With her friends, and that sort of thing.'

'We don't socialize with her,' said Edwina. 'Never have done. She doesn't like us, and has never made a secret of the fact.'

'Really?' said Moreno. 'How come?'

Edwina shrugged. Betty blew out a cloud of smoke and pulled a face.

'She's odd,' she said. 'Sort of superior. Always wants to do things that nobody else does. Nobody misses her, in fact.'

'Does she have any friends in your class? Anybody who knows her a bit better than you seem to do?'

The girls shook their black heads.

'No, Monica doesn't have any friends. She sort of doesn't want to have any. It was like that in those other classes, and it's the same now. Or was, if she really has transferred . . .'

'I see,' said Moreno. 'Have you seen her at all since she changed schools?'

'No,' said Edwina. 'I haven't seen a trace of her.'

'No,' said Betty, 'me neither.'

'But surely she must have had some friends in your old class?' said Moreno. 'Surely everybody has a friend or two? I need to talk to somebody who knows a bit about her.'

The girls sat there in silence, thinking. Exchanging doubtful glances and stubbing out their cigarettes.

'I can't think of anybody,' said Betty. 'Can you?'

Edwina shook her head.

'No, she was very much a loner. Some people are like that, and Monica was one of them. She did mix a bit with Federica Mannen, but Federica moved away when we were in class nine.'

Moreno made a note of the name and asked where the girl had moved to, but neither Edwina nor Betty could remember.

'Why did Monica change schools?' she asked instead.

'Huh,' said Betty. 'I suppose she didn't like it here. Why don't you ask her?'

Moreno didn't respond.

'Have you met her mother at all?'

Judging by their feeble reaction, the news of Martina Kammerle's death hadn't yet reached them. They shook their heads again, and Edwina said they had never seen any sign of either of Monica Kammerle's parents. But they had heard that her mother was a bit of a weirdo. A lot of a weirdo, in fact. She hadn't even turned up to some parents' meetings before a school trip when they were in class nine – but Betty thought that maybe wasn't so odd as Monica didn't take part in the trip anyway.

'Where did you go to?' wondered Moreno.

The girls explained that they had gone to London, and that it was fab. All the class had been there apart from Monica and a fat slob called Dimitri.

'A really, really fat slob,' agreed Betty, lighting another cigarette.

Moreno had a sudden urge to snatch the cigarette out of her excessively made-up mouth, squash it in the ashtray – the cigarette, that is, not her mouth – and tell her and her friend to go to hell. Or at least to go out jogging.

Or to eat an apple. No, she thought, if I really passed through a phase like this I must have suppressed all memory of it.

And rightly so. Some things need burying.

'What's going on?' asked Edwina. 'Has something happened to her?'

'I can't go into that,' said Moreno again. 'But if you come across anybody who's seen Monica recently, please give me a ring. Ask among your classmates if you have time.'

She took out a couple of business cards and gave them one each. The girls took them, and suddenly their heavily made-up faces took on a more serious, unforced expression.

As if a child were peeping out from behind all the make-up, Moreno thought. She guessed that it was the italicized words on the cards that had brought about the change: *Detective Inspector Moreno*.

'Yes, of course,' said Betty. 'We'll . . . we'll ask around. Is it . . . I mean, is it serious? What's—'

'I'm sorry, but I can't tell you any details,' said Moreno for the third time. 'Thank you very much for speaking to me. I might be in touch again before long.'

'Great,' said Edwina Boekman.

Inspector Moreno stood up and left the Café Lamprecht. Neither of the girls showed any sign of going back to school, and when she came out into the street Moreno caught a glimpse of their black heads through the dirty window, deep in conversation. Enveloped in fresh clouds of smoke from newly lit cigarettes.

They'll have cellulite and drooping breasts before they are twenty, she thought, sighing deeply. Serves them right.

'I know what's the worst aspect of this bloody job of ours,' said Rooth.

'Really?' said Jung. 'Let's hear it, then.'

'The constant confrontation with life and death,' said Rooth. 'It's so hard to handle that you're just not able to cope. You either have to be so damned serious and profound and gloomy all the time – and my petty brain's not really up to that . . .'

'I know,' said Jung. 'Or?'

'Don't interrupt,' said Rooth. 'Or you have to back off and keep it all at arm's length. Be cynical, or however you'd like to put it . . . And my big bleeding heart can't manage that in the long run. Do you understand what I mean?'

Jung thought for a moment.

'Yes, of course,' he said. 'You're absolutely right, for once. You're constantly veering from one extreme to the other.

Facing up to Death, or waving two fingers at him. That's what it's all about.'

Rooth scratched his head.

'Very well put, dammit!' he said. 'Facing up or two fingers! That's what I shall call my schizophrenic memoirs. No wonder we grow prematurely old. If only we could look after rabbits instead, or something of that sort.'

'That will come in the next life,' Jung assured him. 'Anyway, shall we go in and get going?'

'Let's do that,' said Rooth. He put the key into the lock and turned it. 'The murderer's name is what we're after!'

They entered Martina Kammerle's flat. There was a sort of grey light inside, but nevertheless Jung began by walking from room to room and switching on every light he could find.

Rooth put a packet of sandwiches and two bottles of mineral water on the kitchen table, and looked around.

'An interesting job, this,' he said. 'Believe it or not.'

It was Rooth himself who had proposed it, so Jung refrained from comment. Besides, he was inclined to agree: if the person who had put his hands round Martina Kammerle's neck just over a month ago and squeezed tightly – if that person was known to his victim, no matter how slightly, was Rooth's point – then the probability was that she had written down his name somewhere.

If not in blood on the wall under the bed where her body was discovered, then in some other place. In an address book, perhaps. A note pad. On a scrap of paper . . . Anywhere at all. There were indications that the killer had cleaned up the flat and removed any traces of his presence: but he had been most concerned about fingerprints, and surely he couldn't have checked absolutely everything?

There was nothing to suggest that Martina Kammerle or her missing daughter had had a wide circle of friends – on the contrary. If for instance they were to find fifty names – Rooth had maintained – there was a good chance that one of them would be the person they were looking for. The murderer.

To be honest, this was a routine measure that was carried out in eleven out of ten investigations: but with a bit of luck the chances of finding a vital clue were greater in this case than usual. The investigation team had been in agreement on that point.

So, it was time for Inspectors Rooth and Jung to get going. It was ten o'clock in the morning, and they had promised Reinhart to report by five in the afternoon.

Or to be pedantic, that was when Reinhart had said he expected them to report.

'I'll take the mother's room, and you take the daughter's,' said Rooth. 'To start with, at least. We'll meet in the kitchen two hours from now over a sandwich.'

'Two hours?' wondered Jung. 'Can you really last as long as that without food?'

'Character,' said Rooth. 'It's all a question of character and strength of mind. I'll explain it to you in more detail some other time.'

'I'll look forward to that,' said Jung, opening the door to Monica Kammerle's teenage room.

17

A picture of the murdered Martina Kammerle appeared in the three most important Maardam newspapers on Tuesday – the *Telegraaf*, the *Allgemejne* and the *Neuwe Blatt* – and by four o'clock, in response to the police's appeal for tips and assistance, three people had telephoned the switchboard and been passed on to Chief Inspector Reinhart in person.

The first was a social worker by the name of Elena Piirinen. She reported that on and off – mostly off – she had been in contact with Martina Kammerle until about a year ago, when she changed jobs and was given more administrative work. The assistance she had given Martina Kammerle had mainly been in connection with financial matters: Piirinen had helped her to apply for various grants, and also – once or twice – arranged for her to receive regular social care. But she was adamant that she had not had much of an insight into her client's private life. However, it was horrendous that she had been murdered.

Reinhart agreed, and wondered if she had any more concrete tips to give him.

No, she hadn't, she assured him. She had decided to get in touch because she thought it her duty as a responsible citizen to do so, nothing else. Reinhart thanked her for her laudable public spirit, and said he might be in touch again if developments in the investigation suggested that it might be helpful to do so.

Number two was a certain fru Dorffkluster, who had lived next door to the Kammerles in Palitzerlaan in Deijkstraa for five years, but unfortunately had even less information to impart than Elena Piirinen. Fru Dorffkluster was eighty-seven years old, and recalled clearly that there were two small, badly brought-up boys in the neighbouring family, and that Martina Kammerle herself had been a very successful television presenter who liked to play golf and ride thoroughbred Arabian horses in her spare time. She presented one of those question-and-answer programmes that everybody watched, and that changed its name more often than a cat scratched itself . . . Or a pig. Some sort of quiz . . .

Reinhart also thanked this public-spirited citizen, and thought briefly about his own mother who had passed away at this lady's age, eighty-seven. That was six years ago, and he recalled that whenever he visited her in hospital during her final months she always thought he was her father rather than her son. Which certainly made their conversations somewhat bizarre – but not without interest even so.

Perhaps that is what ought to happen in one's twilight years, he thought. A right to populate one's environment with the people one wanted to be surrounded by, and talk to. So that everything can be cleared up before it is time to pass over to the other side. After all, it was often one's environment that caused the most distress when one's memory started dancing around, Reinhart thought as he lit his pipe. Yes indeed. Of course Mum was as mad as a hatter, but she was in no pain.

The third person who phoned in that day with information about Martina Kammerle was also a woman. Her name was Irene Vargas, she was in her forties, if he was able to judge her voice correctly, and he realized immediately that she had information to impart that justified a face-to-face interview rather than a one-dimensional telephone conversation. As he had seventeen irons in the fire at the time, he contacted Münster and arranged a meeting between him and fröken Vargas in the intendent's office an hour later. Irene Vargas lived in Gerckstraat, a ten-minute walk from the police station, but needed to sort out a few errands first.

Nothing could be simpler.

'Please sit down,' said Münster, gesturing towards the visitor's chair.

Irene Vargas thanked him, and sat down. Looked around the room a little anxiously, as if wanting to make sure she wasn't locked in. Münster had the overall impression that she radiated an aura of anxiety. She was a thin woman of about his own age, with pale skin, pale hair and pale clothes. He guessed that she was afflicted by some chronic illness – fibromyalgia or a mild form of rheumatism, perhaps – but it could just be because he had read an article about hidden suffering in one of Synn's magazines the other evening.

In any case, she had not come to talk to him as a patient.

'You phoned us,' he began. 'Chief Inspector Reinhart, who you spoke to, is unfortunately busy and out of his office, but no doubt we can get by without him. My name's Münster.'

Vargas met his gaze, and nodded somewhat hesitantly.

'Would you like something to drink? I can arrange for tea or coffee, or—'

'No thank you, that's not necessary.'

Münster cleared his throat.

'Well, if I understand it rightly, you have some information about Martina Kammerle, who was found dead in her home the other day.'

'Yes,' said Vargas. 'I knew her slightly.'

'We'd be grateful for anything you can tell us,' said Münster. 'We've found it hard to find anybody who knew her.'

'Martina was quite a solitary person.'

'We have gathered that.'

'She didn't know many people. She didn't really know me either, come to that. We met at the hospital three or four years ago. We attended the same little therapy group, but we haven't seen much of each other since then . . . We're not exactly friends, as they say.'

'But you did meet occasionally?'

'Never by arrangement. But we sometimes bumped into each other in town. I've never been to her flat, but she did come to my place for tea, three years ago.'

'Did you talk on the phone?'

'Very rarely nowadays. More frequently when we first got to know each other – we used to chat a few times a month then.'

'When did you last speak to her?'

'In August. That's why I phoned you. The rest might not be very important – nor this either, perhaps, but . . .'

'In what circumstances did you meet Martina Kammerle in August?'

Vargas swallowed, and stroked a few strands of her sparse hair behind her ears.

'It was in town. We just bumped into each other, and I mean that literally. It was one evening in the middle of August, the fifteenth or sixteenth I'd guess. I was on the way to the Rialto cinema with a woman friend of mine, and we were a bit late. We hurried round a corner in Rejmer Plejn, and I literally bumped into Martina, who was coming from the other direction.'

Münster nodded encouragingly.

'Go on,' he said.

Vargas shrugged.

'Well, there's not much more to say, but the policeman I spoke to on the phone evidently thought it was important . . .'

'It certainly is,' said Münster. 'Then what happened? Did you stop and talk for a while?'

'Not really,' said Vargas with a somewhat guilty smile, as if she now felt she ought to have done. 'There were only a few minutes to go before the film started, and . . . Well, to be honest, I didn't really want to talk to her. Martina seemed to be a bit high, I could see that, and she could go on a bit . . .'

'High?' said Münster.

'I mean manic, of course. Nothing to do with drugs or anything like that . . . I assume you know she was a manic depressive?'

'Yes,' said Münster. 'We are aware of that. So you were with a friend. What about Martina? Was she alone, or was she also with a friend?'

'She was with a man,' said Vargas.

The way she pronounced the word 'man' made Münster suspect that this was a fact she had struggled for some time to come to terms with. Probably without success.

'A man?' he said. 'Did you recognize him?'

'No.'

'But you spoke briefly to them?'

'Not to him. We just spoke about bumping into each other, Martina and I. Laughed a bit and agreed that it was funny. And after ten or fifteen seconds, we continued on our way to the cinema, my friend and I. I'm sorry if you had the impression I had something more important to tell you. I tried to explain that to the chief inspector, but he—'

'Don't worry about that,' said Münster encouragingly. 'You can never tell what is significant and what isn't as early as this in an investigation. But let's concentrate on this man . . . Did you have the impression that . . . that they were a couple, as it were? Monica Kammerle and him?'

'I think so,' said Vargas after a second's hesitation. 'But that's only the impression I got. He might just have been somebody she knew.'

'And she didn't introduce him?'

'No.'

'You don't happen to know if she was having an affair at this time?'

Vargas shrugged again.

'I have no idea. I hadn't spoken to her for nearly six months.'

'Do you know anything about other men in her life? After that tragic accident involving her husband, that is.'

'No. Although she did mention once that she'd been with somebody, but we never discussed it. I don't think she had any steady relationships.'

'But occasional ones?'

'Now and then, yes, that's possible. I do know she picked up a bloke for a one-night stand once. We were at a restaurant together, and she pulled him. It was rather painful, in fact.'

'When was that?'

'Maybe three years ago . . . Yes, it was while we were still attending that group.'

'I see,' said Münster. 'Let's go back to that collision in August – you weren't introduced to the man?'

'No,' said Vargas. 'As I said, my friend and I rushed off to the cinema.'

'And you'd never seen him before?'

'No.'

'What did he look like?'

She thought for a moment.

'I don't really remember,' she said. 'Quite tall, quite power-fully built, I seem to recall. But pretty ordinary at the same time. There was nothing especially remarkable about him, in any case. No, I can't really describe him.'

'Try,' Münster urged her.

'Darkish – well, fairly dark. Between forty and fifty, maybe . . .'

'Beard? Glasses?'

'No. Er, yes, maybe a little beard . . .'

'Would you recognize him if you saw him again?'

Vargas sucked in her lips, and said nothing for a while.

'I suppose I might do,' she said. 'But I doubt it . . . He looked pretty much like everybody else.'

'And you'd never met him before?'

'I don't think so, no.'

'Were they holding on to each other? Arm-in-arm or anything like that?'

'I don't remember . . . No, I don't think so.'

'And Martina Kammerle said nothing at all about him?'

'No, I'm sure she didn't.'

'Have you spoken to any of your friends about this?'

'No. My best friend's in Australia at the moment. She won't be back until March. She's an artist.'

'I understand,' said Münster again, wondering at the same time what there was to understand.

He leaned back on his desk chair and switched off the tape recorder he'd switched on when Vargas entered the room.

'Okay,' he said. 'I think we'll leave it at that for the time being. Many thanks for coming to help us along the way, fröken Vargas. If you remember anything else, don't hesitate to contact us again. It's possible we might be in touch with you again.'

'Thank you,' said Irene Vargas. 'Sorry I had so little to offer.'

Yes, thought Münster after she had gone. It really wasn't much at all.

Martina Kammerle had been out walking with a man in Maardam in the middle of August.

That was all. And to make matters worse, that was more or less the sum total of what they had discovered about the case in general so far.

Intendent Münster sighed. He got up and walked over to the window. Stood there, as he usually did when an investigation seemed to be stuck in the mud. Perhaps he was trying to create a sort of illusion of having an overview by gazing out over the town: that was a thought that had occurred to him before. In any case, it looked pretty grey out there. It was only half past three, but darkness was already on the way in. Rain was in the air, he noticed – but was doubtless waiting for the right moment to bucket down, when people were going home from work. That was what usually happened.

Reinhart nodded grimly.

'So they admit that they've been behaving like donkeys, do they?' he said. 'That's something to be grateful for, I suppose.'

'They don't put it quite like that,' said Krause. 'But basically, that's what they are saying. It'll be the welfare officer who's made the scapegoat – she was the one who arranged the school transfer. But you have to wonder . . .'

He hesitated and leafed through his notebook.

'What?' said Rooth. 'What do you have to wonder?'

Krause tried to glare at him, but seemed to realize that he was too young to glare.

'Whether it was pure chance that she disappeared when she did,' he said instead. 'Or if they are connected, as it were . . . That Monica Kammerle vanished because she was changing schools. Of course it must have to do with what happened to her mother, but why did Monica leave Bunge Grammar School at exactly the same time?'

Nobody had any immediate comment to make about that. The question was presumably something nobody had thought about before – or at least, it was for Moreno. As she thought it over, she allowed her eyes to wander around the room and noted that all her colleagues who had been on the case were still there: Reinhart, Münster, Jung, Rooth, Krause and herself. The meeting was taking place in Reinhart's office, and they had just been hearing the reports on their sallies into the world of education. Her own and Krause's.

'Coincidence,' decided Reinhart, clasping his hands behind the back of his head. 'Even if I'm sceptical about the concept, I think we are dealing with two things which just happened to take place at the same time – but for Christ's sake correct me if I'm wrong. It's pretty bad luck for that welfare officer as well, let's not forget that. In normal circumstances they would surely have discovered that the girl was missing rather earlier?'

'Yes,' said Krause. 'No doubt they would. I agree with the chief inspector, by the way. And I don't think she made the most of the opportunity to vanish purely because it presented itself. She doesn't seem to be that type. But of course, I'm only guessing.'

'The worst thing is that we still don't have a clue what's happened to her,' said Münster. 'Where the hell is the girl?'

'You mean you believe she's still alive?' said Moreno in surprise.

'Not believe,' he said. 'Hope.'

Reinhart dug a document out of the pile of papers on his desk.

'Let me just inform you about this,' he said, 'before we hear what Rooth and Jung have to say. We're busy sifting through old cases that are a bit like the one we're wrestling with just now. I've had some help from Intendent Klemmerer from Missing Persons – both solved and unsolved cases. Out-and-out stranglers aren't all that common, after all. We've only had fifteen of them in the whole country during the last ten years – I thought that was a sufficient time span. Twelve are solved, three as yet unsolved, and I've just received a hundred-and-twenty pages of data about all those cases from Klemmerer. I'll try to glance through them before tomorrow. A fundamental thought is that we can't be sure that Martina Kammerle is the murderer's first victim – she could be number two or number five or number any-bloody-thing. Please make any comments you might have now, by all means: but we shall be coming back to this topic tomorrow when I've done a bit of weeding out.'

'Did you say twelve–three?' asked Rooth.

'Yes,' said Reinhart. 'It's possible that several of those cases are nothing like ours, so those numbers are likely to shrink a bit. This is a shot in the dark, of course, but when we have so few damned facts to go on, it seems well worth a try. Don't you think?'

'No doubt about that,' said Rooth. 'The solved cases must be quite easy to check on, in any case. It's just a matter of hauling in the stranglers and squeezing an alibi out of them.'

'It might not be all that easy,' said Jung. 'We don't know exactly when she died.'

'That's true,' said Reinhart. 'But if they've been found guilty of murder we can cross our fingers and hope they are still under lock and key. But in any case, Rooth's probably right: the unsolved cases are the most interesting ones. But as I said, we shall go into that tomorrow. Tell us what you've been doing all day in Moerckstraat instead!'

'With pleasure,' said Rooth, opening his briefcase. 'Let's see. Comrade Jung and yours truly have been sweating away and going through the flat where the murder took place with a fine-tooth comb, searching for names. As you can imagine that involved both patience and cunning – but to cut a long story short, here are the results!'

He produced a bundle of photocopies, and handed them round.

'Forty-six names, all of them originally handwritten by either mother or daughter Kammerle. We've listed them in alphabetical order. The letters in brackets after individual names indicate where they were found. K equals kitchen. M

213

means mother's bedroom – or the murder room, if you prefer that. D is the daughter's room, and L the living room. We've edited out several names from inside schoolbooks or of public figures such as Winston Churchill, Socrates and Whitney Houston. Maybe I should mention that more than half the names come from a little address book in the victim's bedside table. So, any questions?'

'This verges on the impressive,' said Moreno, looking at the sheet of paper she had just been handed. 'If we're lucky, the murderer's name will be one of these. But of course, we have no idea which.'

'Exactly,' said Rooth. 'One out of forty-six. We've had worse odds than that, I suspect.'

'We certainly have,' said Reinhart. 'Anyway, take the lists home and work your way through them. Obviously we shall have to investigate every single name in due course, but we're not going to start this evening. Is there anything else we need to discuss before we draw the curtains?'

'Just one thing, perhaps,' said Jung. 'Shouldn't we put the girl's picture in the newspapers as well? And on the telly? Surely there's no need to keep quiet about her disappearance any more.'

'That's already been taken care of,' said Reinhart. 'She'll be in tomorrow's papers – and maybe even on the late news this evening.'

'I have the feeling we'll have this bastard cornered any time now,' said Rooth. 'Today we've been as efficient as an earthquake.'

'Does anybody else have an intelligent thought?' asked

Reinhart, looking round the room. 'If not, you're welcome to clear off. We'll meet under a cold star tomorrow morning – and never fear, we'll solve this case sooner or later.'

Later, Münster thought. I'll put money on that.

18

After the brief run-through in Reinhart's office on Tuesday afternoon, Inspector Rooth paid a visit to the gym in the basement of the police station.

He pumped iron and pedalled away for almost twenty minutes, then showered and loitered in the sauna for forty. Sweated himself dry, rested and got dressed – almost another hour's effort.

When he emerged into Wejmarstraat it was still only half past seven, and he had plenty of time. His table at Kraus was reserved for half past eight, and since for some incomprehensible reason it wasn't raining, he went for a long and invigorating walk along Wejmargraacht and back – as far as the allotments next to the Richter Stadium.

Why not, now that the fitness gremlin had sneaked its way into his being?

As he was walking, he tried to imagine how the evening would turn out. He had no difficulty in conjuring up the face of Jasmina Teuwers in his mind's eye. No difficulty at all. Her high cheekbones. Her long neck and blonde hair. Her blue-green eyes that were so bright, he had been tongue-tied the first time he gazed into them. Her smile, that was like sunrise over the sea.

Che bella donna! Rooth thought – they had first met when they both attended a course in Italian. That was no coincidence, of course: last summer he had phoned his good friend Maarten Hoeght, whose job involved organizing evening courses, and asked which beginners' courses attracted the most eligible young ladies. French and Italian, Hoeght had declared without a moment's hesitation: and since Rooth had studied French at grammar school and achieved less than satisfactory grades, he had chosen Italian.

Italiano! The language of Dante and Boccaccio. And Corleone. One evening a week. Thursdays, between eight and ten o'clock. At the very first class it had struck him that choosing this course was a stroke of genius. Twenty-two women, three men: one of the other men was a Greek Orthodox priest in his sixties; the other was a cripple, but had nevertheless done a runner after only two sessions.

Easy meat, polyglot Rooth had thought: and he still thought so two months later.

Like the experienced if somewhat wounded courtesan he was, he had proceeded with caution. He had restricted himself to non-alcoholic drinks, and chatted urbanely with three different women on three different Thursday evenings: but in the end nature and fate had asserted themselves, and he had selected Jasmina Teuwers.

It was after the latest class the previous week that he had eventually plucked up enough courage to ask – without any beating about the bush – if she might be prepared to have dinner with him: nothing special. When, after an exceedingly brief hesitation (which wasn't really a hesitation at all, Rooth decided, but merely a perfectly understandable palpitation), she said yes, he had felt once again like the awkwardly blushing fifteen-year-old he had been at school dances.

Incredible, Rooth thought. The wings of love will transport you through fire and water. He wondered what such thoughts might be in Italian. Perhaps that was a question they could discuss while eating their dessert?

Amore . . . acqua . . . fue . . . ?

He arrived at Kraus a quarter of an hour early, but the table was free and so he sat down and waited.

As he sat there he recalled the little distinction he and Jung had discussed that morning. Facing up to facts of life and death, or waving two fingers at them.

What was his own approach, in fact? Did he want to face up to the facts of his own life? Did he dare to?

He ordered a beer, and thought about it.

Forty-two is old. Unmarried, not engaged. Detective inspector with prospects of promotion to intendent in three or four years' time.

What difference did it make, for God's sake? Inspector or intendent?

A few hundred a month more. What would he do with the extra money? Buy a bigger aquarium?

Not much more is going to happen in my life, he thought in a moment of grim insight. Unless I'm shot in the course of duty, that is. That's always a possibility.

And nothing much has really happened thus far either, he

added. Nothing to speak of, that is. Why don't I have a wife and children and a context, like Münster and Reinhart?

Even Jung seemed to have solid ground under his feet, since he moved in with Maureen. Why was it only Inspector Rooth who chased after women without success, year after year?

But then again, he thought philosophically and took a swig of beer, then again it's not a hundred per cent clear that such aspirations are worth bothering about. Just look at my poor sisters!

Rooth had four sisters. They were younger than he was, and had all been in such a rush to find a man and a house and children that you could be forgiven for thinking it was some sort of competition. At the last Christmas dinner at his seventy-odd-year-old parents' place out at Penderdixte, if he remembered and had counted correctly, the number of nephews and nieces amounted to nine. And at least two of the sisters had been pregnant. His father had commented that the situation was very Icelandic – with a meaningful look at Rooth's mother, who had come over from Rejkjavik shortly after the war. Or maybe he had gone there to fetch her: there were several uncertainties in the family history.

Anyway, thought Rooth laconically, whatever the circumstances I'll never be able to survive without relations. But I prefer women of my own to networks of relatives.

At that point the image of Jasmina Teuwers floated up into his consciousness again, and he forgot all about that business of facing up to facts or waving two fingers.

But it was already five minutes after half past. Why hadn't she arrived?

A quarter of an hour later she still hadn't turned up, and he had sent the waitress away twice without having ordered.

What the hell had happened? Rooth began to think that it was embarrassing to sit there alone at the table. All around him were diners chatting away merrily, devouring their main courses and draining bottles of wine: it was only at his corner table, set for two, that there was a lonely, middle-aged detective inspector with shattered hopes and a receding hairline.

Bugger this for a lark, he thought. I'll wait for another five minutes, then I'll phone her.

In fact he held out for ten minutes; and then when he furtively took his mobile out of his briefcase, he realized that he didn't have her number.

'*Sacramento diabolo basta,*' Rooth muttered silently to himself. '*Madre mia*, what the hell should I do? Something must have happened to her. No doubt she's been run over by a tram on the way here. Or been mugged. Or been arrested by the police.'

After a little more thought that last possibility seemed to be somewhat unlikely – and it suddenly occurred to him that he had given her his telephone number. Yes indeed: he hadn't received hers, but she'd got his. For some reason or other.

Has something cropped up? he wondered, and rang his own home number in order to listen to his answering machine.

There was only one message, and it was from her. Recorded at 18.21. Round about the time he was in the sauna.

She was terribly sorry, she said, but there was a problem. A colleague had suddenly been taken ill, and she'd been forced to work over. She probably wouldn't get home until about eleven, but she left her number so that he could ring her.

Rooth switched off his mobile and stared at it for a while.

Sorry, she had said. Terribly sorry.

And she had left her number and asked him to ring her.

Hmm, he thought. Maybe that's not a bad sign after all. He'd just have to be patient.

He beckoned to the waitress, ordered another beer plus a salad and a large steak.

It wasn't that he particularly felt like working, but sitting there drinking coffee and cognac with nothing to look at apart from the china and his own hands did not seem especially satisfactory.

That was why he took the list of names out of his briefcase.

That was why he started studying those forty-six names rather more closely.

That was why he suddenly reacted to one of them.

Just because he'd been reading casually through the list in a typically two-fingered sort of way. His brain switched off, but nevertheless receptive in that remarkable way he remembered from talking to Van Veeteren on some occasion or other.

There was a D in brackets after the name. D as in daughter.

It was Jung who'd found it. He remembered it now. Monica Kammerle's little notebook, to be precise: it hadn't meant a thing when he first wrote it down together with all the other names, but now it rang a bell. Surely that was the man's name? Surely it was? . . .

He checked his watch. Five past ten. The night was yet young. He took out his address book and dialled Ewa Moreno's number.

'Good evening,' said Rooth. 'It's your favourite colleague.'

'So I hear,' said Moreno.

'I hope you hadn't gone to bed?'

'At ten o'clock? Who do you think I am?'

'We'd better not go into that,' said Rooth. 'Anyway, have you looked at the list?'

'What list?'

'What list! For Christ's sake! We work our guts out and produce a very instructive list of names, and then discover that our sisters and brothers in the force haven't even—'

'Oh,' said Moreno, 'that list. No, I haven't had time yet. Why do you ask?'

'Huh,' said Rooth. 'There's a name on it that it's suddenly occurred to me that I recognize.'

'Suddenly?'

'Yes. I didn't think about it when we were slaving away and writing down all the names, Jung and I; but now I'm sitting here at Kraus with the list in my hand, and it jumps off the page at me . . .'

'Eh?' said Moreno.

He broke off, and the line was silent for a few seconds.

'Are you telling me that you're sitting at Kraus and working?'

'Not really, but a girl I was supposed to have dinner with didn't turn up, and so – but bollocks to that. Are you going to get your list out or aren't you?'

'Okay,' said Moreno. 'Just a minute.'

Rooth waited and drank the rest of his cognac.

'Number eleven,' he said when Moreno returned. 'Tomas Gassel. Does that ring a bell?'

Moreno said nothing, and for a moment he wondered if there was a fault on the line.

'Hello. Are you still there?'

'Yes, of course,' said Moreno. 'Of course I'm still here. It's just that I was a bit surprised. You're absolutely right. Tomas Gassel must be that priest . . . the one who fell under the train. There surely can't be anybody else with that name. What the hell does he have to do with all this?'

'That's exactly what I'm wondering,' said Rooth. 'What happened to that investigation? It was you who was in charge of it, I seem to remember.'

'Shelved,' said Moreno. 'It will be closed down altogether shortly, I assume. There's nothing to suggest a crime.'

'Until now,' said Rooth.

'What do you mean by that?'

'Until now,' said Rooth again.

'Okay,' said Moreno.

She thought for a moment.

'Hmm, maybe there was a bit more than we thought earlier as well,' she said. 'With regard to Gassel. To be honest . . . Yes, to be honest I think this changes the whole situation. It might be pure coincidence, of course, but I have the feeling that it isn't. It would be much too . . . too improbable.'

'Really?' said Rooth. 'Would you kindly stop talking in riddles, woman. What the hell are you saying?'

But Moreno evidently had no desire to fill him in on that point.

'Gassel?' she mumbled instead. 'What the hell's going on? Anyway, we must look into this in more detail tomorrow – and obviously, I must get in touch with the *Chief Inspector* again.'

'The *Chief Inspector*?' wondered Rooth. 'Do you mean . . . ?'

'Yes,' said Moreno. 'I mean him. I'll explain everything tomorrow. Thank you for ringing – I shan't sleep a wink now all night.'

Rooth thought for a moment.

'Would you like me to pop over?' he said: but Ewa Moreno only laughed and hung up.

He put his mobile away, and looked around the almost full, buzzing restaurant.

Checked his watch.

Saw that it was still only a quarter past ten, and decided to round off with a dark beer.

Then he would go home and phone Jasmina Teuwers.

The *Chief Inspector*? he thought, when his drink had been served. What the hell has he got to do with this?

WALLBURG

JUNE 1999

19

Kristine Kortsmaa was annoyed.

It ought to have been a lovely evening . . . well, it *was* of course a lovely evening – apart from that damned bloke. 'A pain in the ass,' as Birthe used to say. The moment she stepped onto the dance floor, he was there, forcing his attentions on her. No matter how much she ignored him and tried to move away from him, he still chased her up. Which wasn't all that difficult of course: it wasn't ballroom dancing, people were swaying from side to side and jumping around, and doing whatever they wanted to do. The band was called Zimmermans, and was playing almost exclusively old Dylan songs. Everybody was in high spirits, sweaty, and to say the least contented. Kristine Kortsmaa had always been a fan of Dylan, despite the fact that her dad was younger than her guru.

And she liked dancing. Prancing around artistically and uninhibitedly in time with the music – well, in time with anything you liked, to be honest. Yes indeed, it would have been a perfect evening if it hadn't been for that berk.

Berk . . . That was a good name for him, she thought. He had a crew cut, more or less; big ears and a crooked nose. Much older than she was as well – he must have been getting on for forty. Couldn't he see that she wasn't interested? Purple shirt. Purple! He had asked her to dance with him twice: on both occasions she had shaken her head, and looked away. But when she had a rest and sat down at her table, listening to the music – or chatting to Claude and Birthe and Sissel – she could see that he was watching her all the time.

She had come here with Claude and Birthe. Sissel and Maarten and a couple of their friends had joined them, and they had been lucky enough to find a table quite near the front. They had eaten various Mexican fancy dishes and drunk a few bottles of wine before Zimmermans got going. There had been a party mood right from the start, and it was still going swimmingly. Kristine had every reason to get a bit drunk and enjoy an evening of dancing and good music – every reason: after no end of trials and tribulations she had at last completed her training to become a physiotherapist. At last. She had been awarded her licence and diploma the previous day, and today had spent over five hours filling in forms and applying for jobs. Eight jobs. She was confident of having a job from the middle of August onwards: there was a shortage of good qualified physiotherapists . . . But for now, and for another seven weeks, it was summer. Nothing but summer and summer and summer. And she was free – she had enough money to last her for a few months, and no Ditmar: he seemed to have gathered at last that it was all over between them. At long last.

So there was nothing unresolved, lurking in the background, she thought. No skeletons in the cupboard, casting a shadow over her future. Nothing at all.

Apart from that bloke. The berk. She wondered if he was high on drugs: there was something about his eyes. He seemed to be in another world, but at the same time very intense – just like junkies always did. As if they were operating on a different frequency from everybody else.

Which they were, not to put too fine a point on it. She danced away from him, and joined Birthe, Claude and the others. Sissel and Maarten seemed to have found each other, and had eyes for nothing else: but there was still a little group out there, dancing away without inhibitions. Claude looked at her approvingly, and she wondered if he fancied her. Or maybe he was a bit drunk: he tended to start flirting when he'd had too much to drink – or so Birthe maintained.

But what the hell? she thought, continuing to look at him and wiggling her hips, sufficiently innocently but attractively to confirm what his eyes had already concluded. That was her intention, at least.

'I'll Be Your Baby Tonight' came to an end. Applause, shouts and whistles made clear the audience's approval. The band acknowledged the applause and bowed, and the singer announced that there would now be something a bit softer. Three of the musicians left the stage: only the solo guitarist and one of the girl back-up team remained.

'Tomorrow Night' from the album *Good as I Been to You*, the singer announced. Oh, shit! Kristine thought. That means dancing with a partner. Sissel and Maarten were already facing each other and swaying from side to side. Birthe had her arms round Claude, and something similar was being enacted all over the dance floor. The guitarist strummed the first chord, and the Berk suddenly appeared in front of her with a new gleam in his eye. She glanced quickly around, and saw a possible escape route.

He was leaning against one of the pillars with a beer in his hand. Looked nice. Normal, at least. Black jeans and a short-sleeved white shirt. Slightly tanned. A bit on the old side, perhaps, but what the hell . . . A second later she was standing in front of him.

'Please dance with me.'

'Eh?' said the man, looking surprised.

'May I have the pleasure of this dance? There's a bloke who's pestering me.'

She gestured back over her shoulder, and the man nodded. Caught on to the situation immediately. Put his beer glass down on a table and laughed.

'All right. I'll be your bodyguard tonight.'

Kristine Kortsmaa suddenly felt that she wasn't annoyed in the slightest any more.

She realized how drunk she must be when he had to help her to fit her key into the lock.

'Oh my God,' she said. 'But I had good reason to celebrate tonight.'

'Really?' he said, holding the door open for her. 'What reason was that?'

'Passing my exams. I finished my physiotherapist training today. Or yesterday, to be precise. No more swotting, thank God. Would you like to come in? I don't normally invite men into my flat, but maybe we could chat for a while. If you wanted to, that is . . .'

He looked at his watch.

'I don't know. The conference programme is pretty intense. I have to be up and about by nine tomorrow morning.'

'Just a few minutes.'

'All right,' he said. 'A quarter of an hour.'

Half an hour later they were dancing again. Or perhaps you couldn't really call it dancing. They were standing there, swaying from side to side – she in her bare feet, he in his stockinged feet. Dylan again, but now on her latest CD. It was dark in the room, but only a pleasant sort of summer darkness – the balcony door was open, letting in a pungent scent of blossoming jasmine and honeysuckle. She could feel his erection against her stomach, and closed her eyes.

She shouldn't have done that. Closed her eyes.

The room started swimming, and she felt sick.

'I'm sorry,' she said. 'I don't feel well.'

She pushed him away and hurried into the bathroom.

It took some time, and when she returned to the living room she couldn't see him. Has he left? she thought, walking out onto the balcony. I hope so.

She felt clearer in the head after being sick, washing herself and brushing her teeth. She realized to her horror that she had brought back into her home a man she didn't know at all. Pleasant enough, and courteous: but there are limits, as

231

Birthe used to say. Kristine hadn't had sex with anybody after Ditmar – that was three months ago by now, and doing something about it was naturally enough high on the list of her priorities for the summer. But she hadn't intended it to be a one-night stand like this. Somebody attending a conference that she'd picked up at Dorrit's. Certainly not, for Christ's sake!

She leaned over the balcony rail and breathed in the warm smells of the summer evening. Great! she thought. Free all summer, then a steady job in August! You've done pretty well for yourself, Kristine Kortsmaa! Very well indeed!

Then she heard him moving inside the flat. She took another deep breath, and went back inside.

'I'm sorry,' she said.

'Why?'

He was lying on the sofa in the darkest corner of the room, that was why she hadn't noticed him. He suddenly moved, only a little, but she caught sight of bare skin and realized that he was naked.

'I think it's time to say goodnight now,' she said. 'It was silly of me to invite you in. I'm sorry if I aroused your expectations, but I'd be grateful if you got dressed.'

He said nothing, and didn't move.

'I'm sorry,' she said. 'I got a bit drunk, that's why I lost the plot. I didn't intend things to turn out like this.'

She found his clothes on one of the chairs.

'Here you are. Put them on now. Would you like a cup of coffee before you go?'

He sat up.

'Coffee isn't what I want.'

He didn't sound offended or angry. The slight trace of menace she sensed immediately was not in his voice, but in his words.

'What do you mean?'

'I mean that I don't want any coffee just now,' he said, standing up and ignoring his clothes. He took two paces towards her and placed his hands on her shoulders. Stood there for a while as if uncertain what to do next, and she wondered if she ought to make her rejection even more clear. She felt both stupid and guilty with regard to her behaviour: she was the one who had taken the initiative at Dorrit's, she was the one who had invited him to dance with her – not only to protect herself from the Berk, she had assured him over and over again – and she was the one who had invited him in after he had escorted her home.

So it wasn't very surprising if he felt a little disappointed.

'I'm sorry,' she said again.

'It's a pity,' he said. 'May I massage your shoulders for a while? I think you need it.'

She hesitated, but before she could say yes or no he was standing behind her. Moved her hair out of the way and began exploring with his fingers over her bare shoulders. But not massaging. He followed the sharp outline of her collar-bone towards her neck, and she could feel that he was trembling.

And she was holding her breath.

'My finger tips . . .' he said. 'My finger tips are like little seismographs. They register everything you feel in your body,

233

and your thoughts as well – that's pretty remarkable, don't you think?'

She decided that things had gone far enough now, but it was too late.

Much too late for Kristine Kortsmaa.

MAARDAM

NOVEMBER 2000

20

Van Veeteren lifted the carrier bags onto the counter, and began taking out the books.

Forty in all, Professor Baertenow had said. He couldn't carry any more than that nowadays, unfortunately. A mixed bag, you could say: but mainly novels in foreign languages.

He thought it was a pity he needed to offload them: but at least he knew that giving them to Krantze's antiquarian book-shop meant they were in good hands. Or rather, that they had been delivered into good hands. Which would have been necessary sooner or later, no matter what. No, he didn't want paying for them this time either. Money was of no use to him any more.

Van Veeteren studied the titles, one after an other, and was surprised yet again by the range of languages – Russian, Czech, Hungarian, Finnish. A collection of poetry in Basque. Norwegian, Danish and Swedish.

An impressive character, this Baertenow, to say the least. An old philologist, retired several years ago, and now in the habit of turning up several times a year, bringing with him a couple of carrier bags of books. They say he spoke fifty-five living languages. Plus an unknown number of dead ones.

He used to say that he was busy tidying up his bookshelves – you have to sort things out when death is breathing down your neck.

Van Veeteren used to pay him with a glass of port wine, sometimes two, and a chat: but today the professor didn't have time. He was planning to move into a somewhat smaller and rather more convenient flat, it seemed: there simply wasn't room for all his books . . . That was life – there was a time for collecting and a time for getting rid. Or, as the Estonians say, *Kui oikk in vahe hauakivil kahe aastaarvu vahel.*

'Very true,' Van Veeteren had said.

But what immediately attracted his attention was not any of the Estonian books: there was another title that sent his mind spinning

The Determinant.

That really was the title. His eyes were not deceiving him. Two books, in fact. He stood there with one of them in each hand, staring at them. One was white with a woman's face on the front cover, and with the subtitle *Eva.* The other was pale red with lots of strange configurations in some sort of system of coordinates.

The author's name: Leon Rappaport. Language: Swedish.

Rappaport didn't sound all that Swedish. Jewish, rather. Van Veeteren investigated and found the years when the books had been copyrighted: 1962 and 1978. The first book was evidently written in Polish, with the original title *Determinanta.* The second one, with the woman's face, seemed to have been written in Swedish.

He shook his head. Very odd, he thought. Would he now

THE STRANGLER'S HONEYMOON

have to teach himself Polish and Swedish? In order to get to the bottom of it all. He had spent half his life believing in a concept that he thought he had invented: but now he was standing here with two books that had been written about it. Or at least had been called that.

The Determinant.

Very odd, to say the least. He thought for a while. Then put both the books into his briefcase, and took out his cigarette machine. Time for the day's first cigarette, no doubt about that. What was needed now was time to think things over; to keep things at arm's length . . .

Before he'd had time to light his cigarette, Moreno rang.

And he sat there with it unlighted throughout the whole of the conversation.

'Come in,' Van Veeteren said an hour and a half later. 'Let's withdraw to the kitchenette, we can be undisturbed there.'

He pulled down the blind over the glass pane in the door, and locked up. Moreno took off her jacket and hung it round the back of a chair.

'Fire away,' he said. 'I had a feeling that damned priest wouldn't leave me alone for long. A premonition, it seems.'

'Yes, indeed,' said Moreno, flopping down into one of the Greek armchairs in the cramped kitchenette. 'You can say that again. As I said, we discovered his name when we searched through that flat yesterday . . . Martina Kammerle's flat in Moerckstraat. She was found murdered last Sunday evening, but the body had been lying there for over a month – I don't know if you've read about it, Chief Inspector—'

'Belay there!' warned Van Veeteren.

'Oops!' said Moreno. 'A slip of the tongue. Anyway, I don't know if you've read about it?'

Van Veeteren nodded.

'Yes,' he said. 'I still plough my way through a few newspapers. *Allgemejne* had quite a detailed article about it today, in fact. A strangled woman . . . and a missing girl as well, is that right?'

'Correct,' said Moreno. 'Although we didn't discover the link with that priest until yesterday, so there hasn't been anything about that in the newspapers. We don't really know any more than I said on the phone. It might be a blind alley, of course, but to be honest that seems a bit unlikely. Or what do you think?'

Van Veeteren opened a cupboard and dug out a couple of cups.

'Blind alley?' he said. 'Like hell. I take it you fancy some coffee?'

Moreno nodded; he put the kettle on and started rummaging in another cupboard.

'Shall we take things in chronological order?' he suggested, putting a tray of cinnamon biscuits on the table. 'That might make sense. As far as I'm aware causes still usually come before effects in most circumstances. So, where do we begin? . . .'

'Well,' said Moreno, 'if we look at the cards we have in our hands at present, it all starts when Pastor Gassel comes to see you . . .'

She looked around and made a hesitant gesture.

'. . . in this very room, if I've understood it rightly.'

Van Veeteren nodded and scattered some coffee powder in the two mugs.

'Some time around the middle of September?'

'The fifteenth, I seem to recall.'

'The fifteenth? In that case it was just over two weeks before he was found dead under a train in Maardam's Central Station. At about the same time, or possibly slightly later, a certain Martina Kammerle was murdered in her flat in Moerckstraat. Her sixteen-year-old daughter Monica disappeared at the same time, and is still missing. Martina's body was lying there for over a month before it was discovered, and in a notebook in her daughter's room we found the name Tomas Gassel . . . Well, that's about it in a nutshell, you could say.'

'Nothing else?' asked Van Veeteren after a few moments' thought. 'Was there nothing else apart from the name in that notebook? Telephone number or address, for instance?'

'No. She'd written it at the very bottom of an empty page. There was nothing else at all.'

Van Veeteren nodded and poured hot water into the mugs.

'It's not exactly a common name.'

'No.'

'But not all that uncommon either.'

'No.'

'Can there be any doubt that he's the one?'

'No doubt at all. Krause has checked. There's one other person in the area with the same name, but he's only four years old. Lives in Linzhuisen and has no links with the Kammerles whatsoever.'

'Hmm,' muttered Van Veeteren. 'So it hangs together, does it?'

'It certainly does,' said Moreno. 'Thus far, at least. It's obviously possible that Monica Kammerle has some kind of normal link with Pastor Gassel, something that has nothing to do with his death or her disappearance, but, well . . . we'll find that out in due course. At the moment we must assume that there is a more significant connection, of course . . .'

'Of course,' said Van Veeteren.

'We can naturally speculate about how that contact came about.'

'One can always speculate,' said Van Veeteren, adding milk to the coffee. 'How long is it since you caught onto this?'

Moreno took a sip and smiled innocently.

'Can you tell by looking at me?' she asked. 'Can you really? Can you see that I haven't slept a wink, lying in bed, thinking about nothing but this? Rooth caught on last night, and was kind enough to phone me right away.'

'I can't see a single trace,' said Van Veeteren. 'I can assure you that you are the most delicate and fragrant violet in the whole bookshop. Anyway, where exactly are your thoughts leading you?'

Moreno coughed away a smile.

'It's pretty self-evident,' she said. 'Somebody has killed Martina Kammerle for some reason or other. The same person has removed Pastor Gassel from the stage . . . possibly because he knew the reason for the murder. Monica Kammerle might well have suffered the same fate. It's just that we haven't found her yet . . . To reduce matters to basics, that is.'

'Why complicate matters?' said Van Veeteren. 'It will get more complicated of its own accord, and second-degree equations have never been one of my strengths . . . But if a certain antiquarian bookseller hadn't sent a certain priest packing because he had an urgent dental appointment, the Maardam CID wouldn't be sitting in this hole. That's what you're getting at, of course.'

'I'm not getting at anything,' Moreno assured him, 'but let's face it: there is something in that. The fact is that I have a little request as well.'

'A request?' said Van Veeteren, raising an eyebrow.

'Maybe I should call it a formal invitation. From Reinhart. He wants you to turn up and answer some questions.'

Van Veeteren spilled some coffee on the table.

'Answer . . . ?'

'Yes, it follows naturally if you think about it,' said Moreno. 'We clearly need to find out as much as possible about that meeting between you and the priest . . .'

'So you're going to interrogate me, are you?'

'Have a chat,' said Moreno. 'Not interrogate. Shall we do it now, or leave it until later?'

'Well, I'll be damned. But now you mention it, I suppose . . .'

He glanced at his watch.

'Now,' he said.

'Just one condition,' said Van Veeteren as they clambered out of the car in the police station's basement garage. 'If we bump into Hiller I shall do an about-turn and disappear. You'll have to fetch me by patrol car at Klagenburg instead.'

'Of course,' said Moreno, pressing the lift button.

No chief of police put in an appearance in fact, and two minutes later the *Chief Inspector* was sitting in Reinhart's smoke-filled office with its owner and Intendent Münster.

'Nice to see you here,' said Reinhart with a wry smile. 'I'll be damned if you don't look younger every time I see you.'

'Natural beauty can't be repressed in the long run,' said Van Veeteren. 'How are things?'

'We get what we deserve, I suppose,' said Reinhart. 'Or what do you think, Münster?'

'We get what Reinhart deserves, unfortunately,' said Münster. 'Hence all the misery. How are things in the book trade?'

'There are still one or two citizens around who can read,' said Van Veeteren. 'But there are fewer of them by the day, alas. Anyway, enough of this nonsense. This business with the priest is pretty damned awful . . . and the rest of it. Is the connection any more definite than Moreno indicated?'

Reinhart scratched the back of his neck and pulled a face.

'I don't really know,' he said. 'Krause and Jung are looking into it. Gassel's furniture and belongings have already been put in storage, unfortunately, and his flat has been let. But as I see it, it's only a matter of time before we're a hundred per cent certain . . . Everything fits in, and I'm sure that's how it will turn out. But what I'm most interested in just now is whether we can squeeze out of you any more details of that meeting you had with the priest.'

'Yes, I can understand that,' said Van Veeteren, taking out his cigarette machine. 'But I think I've already remembered everything it's possible to remember. I spoke to Moreno about it a month ago, after all. On my initiative, note that.'

'Yes, I know about that,' said Reinhart. 'We don't intend to arrest you just yet. Have you anything against my trying to reel off what you said, and you can squeal whenever I put a foot wrong?'

'Fire away,' said Van Veeteren. 'As long as I can smoke in peace and quiet.'

Reinhart leaned back, took a deep breath, and started off.

'Pastor Gassel comes in to see you at Krantze's and wants to talk to you. Date: fifteenth of September. Is that right?'

'Yes.'

'You turn him down, but nevertheless you have the impression there's something he wants to get off his chest ... Something he's been told, that is covered by his vow of silence. He mentions the word "she".'

Van Veeteren nodded and began rolling a cigarette.

'A reasonable assumption to make, in the light of what happened later, is that he was referring to Monica Kammerle. Or possibly her mother, although that is significantly less likely as it was in the girl's room that we found his name, and it was in her handwriting. In any case, "she" must have told this priest about some problem or other. Central to this problem is an unknown person, probably a man, who eventually makes sure all those involved are removed out of the way. Gassel. Martina Kammerle. Monica Kammerle. We haven't yet found the last-named, but unfortunately that's probably only a matter of time. Anyway, that's more or less the scenario as we see it. One of the possibilities, at least.'

Van Veeteren lit his cigarette.

'Yes,' he said. 'It fits together, just as you say. There's only one question mark, as far as I can see.'

'Really?' said Reinhart.

'I know what the chief . . . I know what you mean,' said Münster. 'You are referring to the minor detail of who did it. The perpetrator. Is that right?'

'Yes,' said Van Veeteren. 'There must be some bastard behind all this.'

Reinhart started working on his pipe and tobacco.

'That thought had occurred to me as well,' he muttered. 'Believe it or not. It's amazing how a former chief inspector can still hit the nail on the head in certain circumstances. Anyway, what indications did you get of a perpetrator of this nature during your conversation with the priest?'

Van Veeteren thought that over for about five seconds.

'None at all,' he said. 'It was hardly a conversation, incidentally. He was with me for about two minutes at most.'

'Are you sure? There's nothing you've forgotten?'

Van Veeteren snorted.

'Of course I'm damned well sure. What are you getting at? If there's one place in this world where I feel at home, it's inside my own head.'

'Congratulations,' said Reinhart. 'Forgive my insistent style – it would be great fun to submit you to a proper interrogation one of these days, but I don't suppose that's likely to happen . . .'

'I tread the straight and narrow,' said Van Veeteren grumpily. 'I don't suppose you've ever heard of that.'

Reinhart lit his pipe and transformed his mouth into something that might – just possibly – be interpreted as a smile.

'Anyway,' he said, 'back to business. I spent four hours this morning studying old cases involving strangulation. I can tell you that it made inspiring reading. But I suppose I ought to devote myself now to cases involving victims being pushed under trains . . .'

'Sounds interesting,' said Münster. 'And it would be even more interesting to hear if you found anything.'

'Keep plodding away and eventually you'll come across something,' said Reinhart. 'Yes, I think so. If we accept the ten-year time limit, as I suggested yesterday, there are only two unsolved cases in the whole country similar to this one – strangulation cases, that is. If I were pressed to be more rigorous, I'd say in fact just one.'

'So you're saying he's been at it before?' asked Van Veeteren.

'Yes,' said Reinhart, pulling a face again. 'I think that's what I'm saying. It's all hypothetical, of course, but the more it rains, the more flourishing theories tend to look. There was a case up at Wallburg last summer which could well have involved a murderer like ours. A twenty-six-year-old woman strangled in her flat. From behind. I'm told it's more difficult to do from behind. Bare hands. No clues and no suspects. I'm waiting for a call from Wallburg, but I intend to ask Meusse to take a look into it at any event, and come up with an informed guess.'

'Meusse doesn't know the meaning of the term uninformed guess,' said Münster.

'Exactly,' said Reinhart.

Van Veeteren stood up and walked over to the window.

'Stranglers are not among my favourite people,' he said, gazing out over Wejmargraacht and the misty-grey Wollerimsparken. 'There's something extra unpleasant about a murderer who doesn't even need a weapon.'

'Perhaps he's an Eco-murderer?' suggested Münster. 'No environmentally damaging aids needed. All natural and healthy.'

'For Christ's sake,' said Reinhart. 'If I had thoughts like that I'd seek help.'

'I'm not saying I'm guilty of anything,' said Van Veeteren, swirling the wine around in his glass. 'I'm just saying that if . . . *if* I'd made time to listen to him, maybe two people, and possibly even three, would still be alive, instead of . . . Ah well, that's all I'm saying. Nothing more.'

'So I gather,' said Ulrike Fremdli. 'You've explained that three times now.'

'Have I?' said Van Veeteren, staring at his glass in genuine surprise. 'I suppose that must mean I'm going gaga . . . This is a very good wine, where did you get it from?'

'The supermarket in Löhr,' said Ulrike. 'It's Californian.'

'Californian?'

'Yes.'

'The times are out of joint,' muttered Van Veeteren. 'I'd have sworn it was Saint-Émilion at the very least.'

'I don't think it's got anything at all to do with going gaga,' said Ulrike after a while, contemplating him over the top of her reading glasses. 'You have a policeman's soul deep down inside you, and that's what drives you when something like this crops up. And as you often say, if something keeps us awake at night, we have to come to grips with it. No matter what it is. And anything we dream of more than twice.'

'Is that what I say?' asked Van Veeteren. 'I must be pretty brainy.'

Ulrike laughed and stroked his cheek.

'I like you so very, very much – do you know that? My mature and serious lover.'

'Huh. Reinhart maintained that I was looking much younger. But in any case, you're right. And I'm right as well. There's somebody at large in this town who in all probability has killed three people, and maybe more. With his bare hands. I don't like it. I wish I could stop thinking about it, but I can't . . . What did you say it was, a copper's soul?'

'A policeman's soul,' said Ulrike. 'You could also call it your conscience if you wanted to be pedantic about it. Or your duty. Are you intending to devote all your efforts to this business?'

Van Veeteren emptied his glass and sighed.

'I don't think so,' he said. 'I might do if they ask me to, but I don't suppose they dare . . . We'll see. Anyway, while we're on the subject . . . I've told you all about this business, but there's one aspect I'm starting to wonder more and more about.'

'What's that?'

'What's behind it all. What exactly it was that the priest wanted to tell me, and what made the killer murder three people – assuming the girl is also dead.'

Ulrike took off her glasses and stared up at the ceiling.

'I can see your problem,' she said. 'Something must have been badly wrong even when he came to see you, of course. No, I have no idea. Have you?'

Van Veeteren shook his head and sat in silence for a while.

'Speaking of coincidences,' he said eventually, 'do you know what turned up at the bookshop today?'

He stood up and went to fetch some books from his brief-case in the study. He handed them over to Ulrike.

'*Deter . . . The Determinant*?' she said in surprise. That's what you keep going on about and I can never understand. What's it all about?'

Van Veeteren thought for a moment.

'What you've just said might be the best way of describing it,' he said. 'The tiny driving force that governs everything that happens, although we don't realize that it's doing so. Something we don't have a name for yet. I'm looking for the question whose answer is "life", as it were.'

'Rappaport?' said Ulrike, scrutinizing the covers, one mainly red and the other mainly white. 'Have you read them?'

'No,' said Van Veeteren. 'I can't read Swedish, unfortunately.'

21

'Inspector Baasteuwel from Wallburg. Am I speaking to Chief Inspector Reinhart?'

'You certainly are. What did you say your name was? Baas- . . . ?'

'. . . -teuwel. I'm ringing in connection with that strangulation case last summer you were wondering about. I was in charge of it. We got nowhere, unfortunately – but that happens in the best of families.'

'So they say,' said Reinhart.

'Incidentally, I know a pretty young cop in Maardam by the name of Moreno: I met her out at Lejnice last summer. Give her a kiss from me, assuming you haven't cocked things up and let her slip through your fingers.'

Reinhart thought for a moment,

'Baasteuwel?' he said. 'I do believe we've met. Are you small and ugly and smoke like a chimney?'

'That's me,' said Baasteuwel. 'An IQ of two hundred and ten, and the favourite of all the ladies as well. Where do you reckon we met?'

'Wernerhaven, if I'm not much mistaken,' said Reinhart. 'Five or six years ago. A conference about the reorganization

251

of the police force or some similar crap, I don't remember exactly.'

'Aha,' said Baasteuwel. 'Yes, I forget the details as well. But I do remember this damned Kristine Kortsmaa case. A sad business. I spent an awful lot of time on it, in fact . . . last June, it was, but we didn't get anywhere. Which annoyed me no end, to tell you the truth.'

'I've read about it,' said Reinhart. 'You don't even have a suspect, is that right?'

'Not a trace of one. The lady was found dead in her flat. Naked, strangled. As clear as day. She'd been out eating and dancing, picked up a bloke and took him home. There wasn't even anything to suggest they'd had sex . . . The bloody irritating thing is that there were loads of witnesses who saw them dancing at that restaurant. We even had a mock-up image of him to work with, but it didn't help. Most irritating.'

'What did he look like?' asked Reinhart.

'Quite tall, quite strong, according to what everybody said. About forty or just over, most of them thought. The colour of his hair varied between medium blond and coal black, and some people thought he had the beginnings of a beard . . . Obviously it wasn't easy to build up a good phantom image, but I can fax you the one we used, if you like. If you think there's any point.'

'Yes, please do send it,' said Reinhart. 'But I'll keep it to myself for the time being, for safety's sake. It would be silly to give the team preconceived ideas. I assume you checked back as well – cases similar to that one?'

'Oh yes,' sighed Baasteuwel, 'you can bet your bloody life I did. I rooted around among a few dozen attractive women's bodies . . . Great fun, but no luck, of course. We drew another blank. This girl Kortsmaa had passed her exams the same week as it happened, by the way. Qualified as a physiotherapist after three years of studies – that's why she was out celebrating. He gave her an excellent present, there's no denying that.'

'A lovely present,' said Reinhart.

'It would bring great satisfaction into my black copper's soul if we can catch the bugger this time round, make no mistake about that. Assuming it's the same swine, that is.'

'It's certainly a possibility, to say the least,' said Reinhart. 'We'll do the best we can. Was there anything else?'

'I don't think so,' said Baasteuwel. 'Assuming you really do have all the documentation you say you have . . . I've scraped together a few thousand wasted working hours, of course, and I can fax you documentation about those if you like.'

'That's not necessary,' said Reinhart. 'We've got more of such stuff than we can cope with already. But if we come across a light shining in the darkness, maybe we could meet and talk things over?'

'There's nothing I'd like better,' said Baasteuwel. 'And don't forget to give that inspector a kiss from me.'

'If I dare,' said Reinhart, and hung up.

Ten seconds later Baasteuwel phoned again.

'There's one thing I forgot to ask,' he said. 'Have you any recent similar cases? I mean, he might have been busy between the Kristine Kurtsmaa case and the one we're busy with now.'

'It doesn't seem like it,' said Reinhart. 'There's nothing that's been documented at least.'

'That's a pretty long gap,' said Baasteuwel. 'Over a year. But then, you never know how bastards like him operate – not until you meet them, at least.'

'I've set my mind on meeting this particular bastard,' said Reinhart. 'I'll be in touch as soon as I get a sniff of him.'

'Good hunting,' said Inspector Baasteuwel.

During the course of Thursday Ewa Moreno talked to seven persons in all that Rooth had dug out of Martina Kammerle's somewhat worse-for-wear address book, and it was a pretty depressing operation.

All seven admitted that they knew what had happened, thanks to reports in the newspapers and on the television. All seven admitted reluctantly that they knew who Martina Kammerle was. All seven insisted that they were not close to the murdered woman in any way, and that they hadn't seen her since her husband died four-and-a-half years ago.

Two of the seven were colleagues from one of the short periods when Martina had had some sort of job. Two were women she had met in hospital, one of them in Gemejnte, and the other out at Majorna. One was a man she had had a brief affair with eighteen years ago, one was a retired therapist she had visited three times, and the seventh was an old schoolmate who had been confined to a wheelchair for the last twenty years, and hadn't seen Martina since they were in class seven together, he claimed.

Depressing, Moreno thought as she clambered into her car after visiting Martina's former classmate out at Dikken. What the hell was the point of Martina Kammerle keeping an address book? Why all these names which must have been of no relevance whatsoever to her current life? It was as if she had listed them because it would seem bad if she hadn't.

What an incredibly cheap life she must have led, Moreno thought.

Cheap? Where did that word come from? Surely a life couldn't be cheap?

And she recalled once again those old maxims on the bed-room wall:

It's better to regret what you have done, than what you never did. Give significance to your life.

What had Martina Kammerle's and her daughter's lives really been like? Did they have any significance at all, despite their seemingly having been immured in their own loneliness? Was there any sort of light that she hadn't yet discovered?

Presumptuous questions, perhaps: but justified, beyond doubt. The seven people Moreno had interviewed had come up with absolutely nothing about the murdered woman's life, and when she thought about the two teenagers covered in black make-up who had irritated her so much at Café Lamprecht the other day, she realized that . . . Well, what did she realize, in fact?

Like mother, like daughter, perhaps?

Moreno sighed in despair and stopped for a red light at the Zwille–Armastenstraat crossroads. It was half past five, and traffic was racing pell-mell for the suburbs and housing

255

estates. It had stopped raining, but a strong wind was now blowing in from the coast.

Light? Moreno thought. Meaning? In this grey city at this time of year? A presumptuous assumption. She shook her head and turned her attention back to the investigation.

Wanted notices in the newspapers and on the television had drawn a blank. No reaction whatsoever. A few pupils from the Bunge Grammar School had rung and said they knew who Monica Kammerle was, but they hadn't seen her for ages. A girl from Oostwerdingen had said she was a friend of Monica's when they were about ten; and a notorious, neurotic informer by the name of Ralf Napoleon Doggers had reported that he had seen both mother and daughter in mysterious circumstances in a churchyard at Loewingen only three days ago.

Martina and Monica Kammerle hadn't exactly led their lives in the spotlight: that was obvious after just over a week's investigations. But Moreno reminded herself that many lives looked worse from the outside than they did from the inside. That was something eleven years in the police force had taught her. Nevertheless, what was it that enabled these mal-treated, abused, worn-out women to survive? There must be something, surely? Something to cling on to. Some sort of consolation, some kind of deceptive hope, because . . . Well, what else could there be?

Otherwise there was not much else apart from Hamlet's monologue, full stop.

Better the devil you know . . .

In other words, the usual biological toughness, Keep Buggering On. She shook her head in disgust, and pulled up at another red light, this time in Palitzerlaan.

And there were always contradictions to be taken into account, of course. There were lives that seemed tolerable and normal when you contemplated them from the outside, but hidden inside them could be bottomless pits of darkness. Totally incomprehensible abysses.

Perhaps that's the kind of murderer we're looking for, it occurred to her. An apparently normal person who acts perfectly normally ninety-nine days out of a hundred, but then, when something snaps – or surges up inside him – can commit the most hair-raising acts? Yes, when she thought about that it seemed very plausible.

Or possible, at least. It could well be such a person behind these horrific acts: but then again, it could be somebody entirely different. It was risky to speculate too much, she knew that; but what else was there for her to devote here energetic brain to, for Christ's sake? What?

And why was she so casually drawing these comparisons between Martina Kammerle and her own life? What was the point? She had a tendency – an increasingly clear tendency with every new case, in fact – constantly to see herself in relation to these poor people who were always involved. The victims and the warped lives they led.

Was she trying to make contrasts? To see herself as a shining light in contrast to their darkness? Was it as simple as that? Was it just that things could have been worse for her?

She decided that was how it had been to start with, perhaps. And it was natural enough, when she came to think about it. Vicarious suffering and all that. But that was no longer the case. Now it felt as if she were searching for some sort of common ground. A point at which she could identify with it all – with the suffering and the misery and the dark forces. At which she could understand the wretchedness of it all. Creep under its skin. Surely that was more like it?

But why? Moreno thought. Why am I doing this? Is it because I can't find any significance in my own life? In this grey city in these grey times?

When she got out of the car outside her home in Falckstraat, she knew she was on the verge of a rhetorical question.

Jung was sitting at the computer.

It was not a situation he particularly enjoyed in normal circumstances, but Maureen had acquired a new computer so that she could do some of her work at home – and as it was standing on their shared desk in the bedroom, he thought he might as well run it through its paces and see what it was capable of. It was large, yellow and streamlined. Apparently worth over five thousand, if he had understood it rightly, and with a memory far in excess of that of a whole police force.

So it could no doubt be used in the interests of law and order.

That was what he had thought when he sat down in front of the monster half an hour ago, and that is what he was still thinking. And somewhat reluctantly he had to admit that the technology was quite impressive. The confounded thing was certainly practical!

It was half past ten by now, and he was alone in the flat. Maureen was on a two-day course connected with her work, and Sophie was sleeping over at her boyfriend's place: his name was Franek, and it was beginning to look as if he was about to become her other half.

The flat was almost as new as the computer. Recently acquired, at least, and it was with a feeling of humble astonishment that Jung was beginning to accept that this was his home. His and Maureen's new home. And Sophie's, of course, who would soon be celebrating her twentieth birthday, was in her first year at university, and would no doubt fly the nest shortly. Any day now, if he had interpreted the signs correctly.

Four rooms and a kitchen in Holderweg. On the fourth floor with a view over the southern part of Megsje Bojs and Willemsgraacht. Newly refurbished with ceilings three-and-a-half metres high, and underfloor heating in the bathroom. And an open fire.

When he thought about it – and he did so almost all the time – he thought he was happy. That things had turned out so well in his life that he ought to find himself a god and thank Him on his bare knees. All that, and Maureen as well!

Plus a super-computer for use at home whenever the mood took him. Such as now. Such as this November evening, sitting at home in the darkness with the rain pattering against the window panes and Lou Reed whispering quietly on a CD in the background.

Benjamin Kerran. That was his opening move. The only name he had left to investigate. The only one remaining from the forty-six he had started with.

A name that had frustrated him and his colleagues, as there was no such person in Maardam according to their enquiries that afternoon. Not in the whole surrounding area either. And not even – assuming Rooth was right in what he claimed shortly before they shut down for the day at the police station – not even in the whole damned country!

It had taken Jung some time to venture out into the Internet, and more time before he realized what he needed to do in order to set up a search. He had no luck at all, using the first of the programs he tried. Just a number of faulty hits, in which the surname – usually wrongly spelled – was right, but not the first name. But then, when he worked out how to use a more powerful program, it suddenly turned up on his screen.

Benjamin Kerran.

Ha! Jung thought. Let nobody come and tell me I don't know how to handle computers.

He leaned forward and began reading. In increasing astonishment – rapidly increasing, as it was only a matter of a couple of lines.

Benjamin Kerran was not a living person. Nor a dead one, come to that. He was a literary character. Fiction. Evidently.

Created by an English author by the name of Henry Moll, according to what it said on the screen. Jung had never heard of him, but when he carried on clicking he discovered that this Moll had written a number of little-known travelogues at the beginning of the twentieth century. Plus a series of even less well known crime novels – yes, it actually said 'even less well known'.

And it was in one of those novels that this character Benjamin Kerran appeared.

In a book with the bizarre title *Strangler's Honeymoon*, to be precise. First published (and no doubt for the only time) in London in 1932, by a firm called Thurnton & Radice. As far as Jung could gather, Benjamin Kerran was a sort of leading character – a serial killer, one of the very early ones, who prowled around in the badly lit areas of the capital strangling prostitutes wholesale, in accordance with instructions given to him by voices addressing him from inside his head, in accordance with some sort of perverted divine ordinance.

Jung stared at the screen.

What on earth could this mean? He read the text one more time.

Could it be anything other than pure coincidence?

He went into the living room and switched off the CD. Could Martina Kammerle have read *Strangler's Honeymoon*?

That seemed implausible. There had not been many books in the flat in Moerckstraat, but the ones that were there were in Monica Kammerle's bookcase. The girl had evidently read quite a lot.

But an obscure crime novel from the thirties? Henry Moll?

Hardly credible, Jung thought and returned to the computer. And even if she had read it, why should she write down the name of this literary murderer in her notebook?

No, the link was too implausible, he decided. It must be pure coincidence. A coincidence and a hit in over-informative cyberspace where almost anything at all could happen. Where no end of strange knowledge was stored, and where the most hair-raising cross-fertilizations could take place.

A name without a telephone number in a missing girl's notebook, and a fictitious English murderer?

No, thought Jung. There are limits after all, even to what these computers are capable of.

He switched off the computer and went to bed.

But the name Benjamin Kerran persisted in the back of Jung's mind, and when he woke up in the middle of the night, a few hours later, he knew immediately why he had dreamt of those strangled women and those narrow, crowded streets in Covent Garden and Soho where he had spent a week on holiday with Maureen a couple of years earlier.

And as he stood there on the warm bathroom floor, having a pee, he decided he would tell Rooth what he had hacked his way through to that evening.

After all, you never know.

22

Afterwards – when he told his wife and their children, or told Gandrich and Kellernik at the pub in Lochenroede – Henry Ewerts blamed everything on the wind.

The change in wind direction, he explained with a brief, grim smile. If the wind hadn't veered from south-west to north-west during the night, I wouldn't have changed my usual route. In which case, we'd never have found her.

Not that day, at least. And not me and the dog.

And when his listeners (especially Kellernik, who never believed anything except *in vino veritas*) looked at him in sheepish incomprehension, he explained with an even shorter and grimmer smile that he always followed it. Always. The wind.

Headwind out, following wind home: that was how he had planned his jogging routes every damned morning for the last nine years, ever since they had bought that house in Behrensee after selling the company at exactly the right moment just before the depression in the nineties. He'd got wind of it just in time, you might say.

*

The wind was always blowing from the west, of course, but often from the south-west. That's how it had been for eleven or twelve days at a stretch, if he remembered rightly: but now there was a touch of colder air from the north, and he branched off onto one of the paths that headed in that direction over the dunes and down to the beach. Thatcher had only needed a little gesture for her to catch on to the change of plan. She was more receptive than most human beings: he'd told Kellernik and Gandrich that lots of times, and even if they didn't really agree or understand what he was getting at, that was merely proof that he was right on this matter as well. He had often thought he was pretty fed up with the pair of them, but didn't want to hurt them by cutting them off.

But on the other hand, he could always rely on Thatcher. That morning she had kept abreast with her boss until they passed over the crest of the hill and saw the sea down below, grey and tossing gently as always at this time of year. He tapped her on the head, and she set off at a fast pace in solitary majesty. As usual, free to do whatever she wanted. Henry pulled off the outermost of his jogging tops and hung it over one of the benches. Noted that his watch said 07.10, headed down towards the firmer sand at the edge of the water, and increased his pace.

He soon realized that Thatcher must have got scent of a rabbit, because there was no sign of her all the way – but it was only when he came to his turning point next to Egirs pier that he began to wonder if there was something wrong. No matter how engrossed the retriever was, obeying her basic instincts and chasing the rabbits who always escaped anyway, she was usually waiting for him when he got to the turning point, and would accompany him all the way back. The fact that Thatcher wasn't lying by the little boatshed just before Egirs, gasping away with her tongue lying out on the ground – or that she had not grown tired of the pointlessness of trying to catch a rabbit long before then – that was an indication, quite definitely.

An indication that something was wrong.

Henry slowed down and stopped. Climbed part of the way up towards the crest of the hill, flopped down onto the soft sand and started doing sit-ups.

He had only got as far as thirty to thirty-five when he heard the dog barking in the distance.

From somewhere in among the dunes – it was hard to say exactly where the sound was coming from, since the wind and the waves distorted everything. Perhaps also the pulsating in his temples caused by his physical efforts. He paused and stood up. The barking continued, and there was virtually no doubt that it was Thatcher. For a trained ear a dog's bark is just as individual as a human voice, he used to explain to friends and acquaintances. That was an old and reliable fact.

He turned his head and listened. Immediately he had a slightly better sense of its origin: somewhere diagonally in towards solid ground to the south-east. Muffled, persistent barking that didn't seem to be moving. The dog was standing still, and barking to draw attention to itself – nothing could be more obvious. To draw its boss's attention.

He walked up over the crest of the hill and made his way through the dunes towards the origin of the sound. Glanced at his watch and was somewhat irritated by the delay: he wouldn't get back home until after eight o'clock, and in order to get to work in time he needed to be in his car by a quarter to nine. A shower and breakfast would take at least half an hour: but if Thatcher was standing at bay, barking away at something, he didn't have any choice, of course. He would have to find her, and find out what the hell was going on.

Looking back – not while he was recounting what had happened that chilly morning to family and friends and the police, but when he was sitting alone at his desk in the evening, gazing out through the window and thinking things over – he couldn't make up his mind whether he had seen the dog or the dead body first.

It didn't matter either way, of course: but as he found himself sitting there, thinking about it, maybe it did mean something after all. God only knows what.

In any case, the dog was standing there in front of its find, completely still – in a sort of watchful, ready-to-attack posture he vaguely remembered from the training course he had attended at the kennel club several years ago: back bent, leaning forward over the widely spaced front paws. What could be seen of the female corpse – the back of her head, shoulders and her right arm – was partly concealed by sand and scraps of black plastic: but nevertheless it was clear enough for him to see in a flash how serious the situation was.

Crystal clear.

He took hold of the dog and began automatically calming

it down, pressing it against his right leg and patting its neck. For a brief, confused moment he wondered if somebody else might turn up and calm him down in the same way. Then he stood up and looked round to see if he could see any sign of a house.

A steep red-tiled roof was sticking up from behind the dunes a bit further inland, and when he came to the top of the next little grass-covered incline he realized that it was Willumsen's house.

Good, thought Henry. Thank God I know who lives there.

'Out jogging as usual?' asked Tom Willumsen, pulling a face. 'Isn't it too windy today? The wind's veered to the north as well, I think.'

'I know,' said Henry. 'But we can talk about the weather some other time? Thatcher has found a dead body out there.'

'A dead body?' said Willumsen.

'A woman,' said Henry. 'Or rather, a girl. Looks horrendous. Ring the police and give me something to drink, please.'

It was a few minutes past half past seven in the morning when Van Veeteren unlocked the door of the flat in Moerck-straat 16. Before doing so, he looked around carefully in all directions, but there was no sign of any curious heads. He stepped inside and closed the door behind him.

His first impression was the smell. Stuffy, dirty. He couldn't make up his mind if there was also a trace of the characteristic sweet smell of rotting flesh as well, or whether that was merely his imagination and a sort of perverted expectation.

He switched on the light in the cramped hall, and stepped into the kitchen on the left. Found the light switch and turned it on, but went over to the window and closed the Venetian blinds.

There was no need to advertise his presence, he thought. No reason at all. Even if tenants had no interest in their neighbours, according to what Reinhart and Moreno had reported, Van Veeteren was keen to remain incognito. Undisturbed and invisible. That was how he had described his mission to Moreno when he asked her to produce a key, and he really hoped he could rely on her promise of keeping everything under the counter. There was nothing to be gained from the whole of the police station becoming aware of his being involved. From their knowing that the bookseller in Kupinskis gränd simply couldn't keep out of police business any longer.

Any longer? Rubbish, he thought as he continued into the living room. There was no question of time, nor of his reverting to police duties: it was just that confounded priest whom he couldn't get out of his mind. The man of God he had turned away with catastrophic consequences, and whom he dreamt about at night. That was all. Nothing more. Was that so odd?

And in any case, why was he wandering around making excuses for himself? What was the point of that? He muttered away in irritation, and took out his cigarette machine.

As I'm here, I must look round about me rather than into myself. Stop feeling sorry for yourself, for Christ's sake!

He looked around the room. It looked dreary. The furniture seemed to have been collected by pure chance: the sofa and armchairs were covered in typical light-coloured nineties material, but several large wine stains (as far as he could judge – and let's face it, he was not exactly unacquainted with such phenomena) tended to undermine the impression of newness. There were large clumps of dust under the table, and the wallpaper pattern seemed to be more suitable for underpants than anything else. The bookcase along one wall contained more ornaments than books, and the black plastic audio-visual set-up opposite – television, video recorder plus a Korean hi-fi device he thought he recalled having seen on sale at a rock-bottom price in a petrol station – all of it could well have been a part of the flat's basic equipment, just like the blinds, the linoleum floor-covering, the cooker, refrigerator and kitchen sink.

What am I doing here? he thought, lighting his cigarette. What am I looking for, and with what justification am I trampling around through all this hopeless gloom?

Good questions. He moved on into the daughter's room. Monica? he thought. Monica Kammerle, who were you? Or who *are* you? The girl might still be alive, after all. Stranger things have happened.

The room was small and narrow. No more than four by two-and-a-half metres, or thereabouts. A bed with a worn, red bedspread. A basic desk and chair. A bookcase and a free-standing wardrobe in a corner. Two posters on the wall, one black-and-white featuring two hands reaching towards one another without quite meeting, the other a face he thought he recognized. A singer, he thought. Died a year or so ago after an overdose, he thought. A small noticeboard with a calendar, a school timetable and a few black-and-white drawings of horses.

The desk was full of the usual things – notepads, pen-and-pencil stand, lamp, diary, a red clock-radio that had stopped working, a framed photograph of a man and a girl aged about ten: he guessed that was Monica herself and her father, who had died in a road accident.

Father, mother, daughter, he thought. And now they were all dead – he had difficulty in believing that Monica was still alive, but of course, you could never tell. He went over to the bookcase and began examining the books. There were quite a lot. The girl had been quite a reader, it seemed. And it was not rubbish. He found Camus and Hemingway and Virginia Woolf. How old was she? Sixteen? Pretty advanced literary tastes, there was no denying that. He hadn't read Camus when he was sixteen.

And Blake!

He took the book out and began leafing through it. *Songs of Innocence and of Experience*. With illustrations and all – it was a handsome little edition, leather-bound, and must have been very expensive. He wondered if it had been a present, but there was nothing on the flyleaf, not even her name. He thumbed through to the end of the book, and read what he found there:

> *Cruelty has a Human Heart*
> *And Jealousy a Human Face*
> *Terror, the Human Form Divine*
> *And Secrecy, the Human Dress*

My dear little girl, he thought, replacing the book on its shelf. What did you get out of that?

And what had he got out of this visit?

Absolutely nothing, in all probability. He moved on into Martina Kammerle's bedroom, which was just as small as her daughter's. But even more messy and with an unmistakable touch of resignation. The walls were bare except for a couple of wall lamps. The curtain rails had come apart at the edges. Plastic carrier bags all over the floor, and a pile of dusty magazines on the window ledge. A dead pot plant. The bed was still unmade, and occupied about half the floor area. He bent down and looked underneath it – that was where she had been lying. For a whole month. The stench suddenly hit him: he stood up and took a deep breath.

For Christ's sake, he thought. I can't cope with thinking about this sort of thing.

He walked around the room one more time, then switched off the light. Checked that there were no curious faces around outside before slinking out of the door and locking it behind him. He hurried down the steps and to his car, parked in the street outside.

Checked his watch. A quarter of an hour, that was all the time he'd been inside the flat.

I changed my job in the nick of time, he thought.

*

Both Inspector le Houde's team and the medical officers were on the spot when Reinhart and Rooth arrived at Behrensee. The rain that had started falling an hour ago was now pouring down, and le Houde looked as if he had been lying down and rolling about in the soaking wet sand for quite some time. But he was dressed in waterproofs from head to toe, so Reinhart assumed that was nothing to talk about.

Besides, he could hardly have been forced to miss a football match this time round.

'Well?' he said. 'Is it her?'

'How the hell should I know?' said le Houde. 'It's a girl of about the right age, and she's been strangled. That's all I can say at the moment.'

'Who found her?' asked Rooth.

Le Houde gestured over his right shoulder.

'A bloke called Ewerts. He's standing over there . . . It was his dog, in fact. She was digging after a rabbit, and she found this instead.'

'How long has she been lying here?' asked Reinhart.

Le Houde shrugged.

'Don't ask me. But Meusse has just arrived. He can usually give you the family tree of a cow-pat.'

Reinhart nodded, and they walked over to the place where the body was found. A canopy of thin plastic had been erected, and three of the team were crawling around underneath it. The pathologist himself, Meusse, was standing close by under an umbrella, smoking. When he caught sight of Rooth and Reinhart, he greeted them curtly.

'Good morning,' said Reinhart. 'Have you had a look at her?'

'Of course,' said Meusse. 'Have you?'

'Not yet,' said Reinhart. 'But we shall do. What do you have to tell us?'

'Not a lot,' said Meusse.

'I see,' said Rooth. 'I suppose the awful weather doesn't help.' Meusse made no comment.

'What we are wondering is whether the body might possibly be that of Monica Kammerle,' said Reinhart. 'The daughter of that woman who—'

'I know,' interrupted Meusse, flipping his cigarette butt over his shoulder. 'I'm not senile. Yes, it could be her. The time's about right, she's been lying here for quite a while. And she was strangled.'

'Really?' said Rooth, for want of anything better to say.

Meusse glared at him, grinding his teeth for a while.

'Anything else before we go and take a look?' asked Reinhart.

Meusse produced a handkerchief and mopped his bald head.

'Maybe I should mention that her lower legs are missing,' he said.

'What?' said Reinhart.

'Her legs have been cut off at the knee. Both of them – but I don't suppose even you could avoid noticing that.'

'Cut off?' said Rooth. 'What the hell for?'

'Don't ask me,' said Meusse. 'Ask whoever did it. Anyway, if you'll excuse me, gentlemen . . .'

He went back to the canopy, crouched down and started giving out orders. Rooth looked at Reinhart.

'Shall we . . . ?' he said.

'I suppose we'll have to,' said Reinhart. 'That's a bonus that goes with the territory in our job. Legs cut off . . . Bloody hell!'

'Maybe he did it after he'd killed her,' said Rooth. 'Let's hope so.'

When Van Veeteren entered the antiquarian bookshop, he had been thoroughly soaked by the rain, and he had the feeling that his soul was dangling inside his body like the corpse of a sacrificed animal broken on the wheel. In an attempt to counteract all the misery he drew the curtains and locked himself in. Poured himself a beaker of port wine and flopped down in the wing chair in the inside room.

Stood up again after a minute and looked for Blake in the bookshelves: there were three volumes, and he sat over them for the rest of the morning. The rain came and went, pattering onto the pavement outside and against the windows, but not a single customer tried the door.

Perhaps it's just Blake and the rain and the port wine, he thought when the clock was showing half past eleven and his thoughts were starting to turn to lunch, but I'm beginning to get a sense of something particularly black and horrific at the heart of all this business.

The thought of something black and horrific reminded him of that fateful sandwich again. The olive.

And the broken filling.

The visit to the dentist's and the priest's beard and Stravinsky with the dead swallow in its jaws. There's no doubt that this case is a brew made up of remarkable ingredients.

And swimming around in the midst of the brew is a murderer. Feeling very sure of himself, it seemed. The police hadn't even begun fishing for him. Perhaps they hadn't yet found the right box of hooks to attach to the lines.

Van Veeteren heaved himself out of his chair and poured himself another glass. My range of vocabulary wouldn't even be adequate for a nightmare, he thought. Today is one of those days.

But the idea of the murderer wandering around in a state of total freedom was annoying. Extremely annoying.

23

He pushed the pile of newspapers to one side and leaned back on his chair. Gazed out of the window at the sick elm trees in the park, and the old observatory, whose blood-red-tiled façade formed a sort of backcloth behind all the branches and greenery.

Words, he thought. It's only when we put things into words that we begin to get a grasp of reality.

And images. The image of reality which is more important than reality itself, because all we see of it is the images. Even when it is a question of the reality of ourselves – it is always somebody else who paints a portrait of us. Somebody else putting us under the spotlight.

These were no new conclusions. On the contrary. He had wandered along these phenomenological paths many times before: but he had never felt it as distinctly as now. Action per se – *actions* per se – had hardly affected him at all after they had been carried out . . . Those women, and that unknown black-coated priest who had poked his nose in and got what he deserved: having killed a priest gave him far more satisfaction than he could ever have imagined, and he wondered why . . . And now, when he read about these people in the newspapers, or watched the television reporters leaning over backwards to be careful what they said, the whole business acquired an aura which struck him as strong and very much alive. Especially with regard to the girl and her mother, of course. It had taken over a month for things to become matters of immediate relevance. The priest had been headline news immediately after the incident in the Central Station: but it was decided that it was an accident, and not many lines had been devoted to him.

An accident, nothing more.

But all these weeks, all these days and nights that passed between that September night and the early Tuesday morning when he read about it at last in *Allgemejne* – all that time somehow endowed the actual events with sharper outlines . . . Portrayed them as reality, when they eventually presented themselves to him after all the lethargy and indifference. The clarity of it all seemed to be almost an obscene revelation, spotlighted after so much silence: it felt as if he had been stabbed in the chest, and for a brief moment he was afraid he had lost his footing, was staggering on the edge of a gaping abyss. Over a grave.

But there was also a strong and bitter taste of sweat and blood. Of life.

This is it, he thought. This is where my fires are burning. My life is just as derisively pointless as all other life. It came to an end on that damned Greek island, and since then death has been meaningless. It is no more than an irresistible force.

That same day he read about himself in six different newspapers, all the ones he could find; and each new headline and bold print introduction seemed to increase the pressure he felt on all sides. Enveloped him and raised him into some sort of extraordinarily significant context – an environment that gave (or seemed to give) him all the legitimacy that ought to be the incontestable right of every life. Every pointless individual life.

Justice and obligations. I am empowered, he thought. For the first time in my adult life I am empowered. People have seen me as I really am. Once again he tried to conjure up his mother's tired but irresistible look as she lay there in her sickbed, but she remained aloof. Was ousted by a mass of later images, more recent women, more recent naked bodies and faces and eyes that averted their gaze from him.

And this was the all-powerful force, these looks that avoided eye contact. They are dominating everything I do, he thought. My powers and my love. What do they think they are doing? I am completely justified in killing every one of them, all those who sooner or later reject me. Justified in blowing out the weak, flickering flames still burning in those disgusting lumps of flesh, growing colder by the minute. Nobody will ever understand me: there is a private and unique abyss inside every human being, and nobody else has one that can match up to mine. Nobody. A human being is a very hungry and very lonely animal: but we all have the same fundamental rights.

We must bear in mind that we are somewhat ironic creations of God.

And we must smile at that. It occurred to him that he was doing exactly that: sitting there, smiling.

There was a knock on the door, and fröken Keerenwert appeared in the doorway.

'Anything else before I go home?'

He looked through the papers lying on the desk in front of him.

'No,' he said, 'it's all in order. Have a nice evening. I'll see you tomorrow morning, then.'

'It's Saturday tomorrow.'

'Good Lord, so it is! Have a good weekend!'

'You too,' she said, and vanished.

He remained seated, staring at the closed door with its timetable of the term's various courses. Fröken Keerenwert's appearance had brought him to his senses. No doubt about that. A rapid shift of focus from the right half of the brain to the left.

From the dark feminine and mystical side to the clear and analytical side – he could almost feel it like a purely physical movement inside his head. Perhaps it was a change for the better. What he needed at the moment was not deep thoughts and reflections, not the stifled, seductive truths, but uncluttered clarity. Distance and perspective.

Luck, he thought. I've had a hell of a lot of good luck.

That was undeniable. He had manoeuvred his way out of that triangular relationship with a minimum of planning. Killed three people, one after another, without leaving a single trace behind. Assuming he had interpreted what the newspapers wrote correctly, that is. Not a single clue for the police to follow up. They had been writing about Martina for over a week now; and about Monica as well from today. It must be pure chance and coincidence that the bodies were discovered with such a short gap between them, he thought. First a month of waiting, then they had both turned up within ten or twelve days. He spent a short time wondering whether it was to his advantage or disadvantage, the fact that there were now two of them: but he reached no conclusion. Presumably it didn't make any difference. It might have been better if that confounded dog had never got a whiff of the girl, but of course that was not something one could realistically hope for – that the body would remain hidden for ever and a day. He had been short of time when he disposed of her: it had been a risky business, even by his standards; but looking back, there was nothing for him to reproach himself with.

He hadn't noticed any suggestion that there might be a link with that damned priest – not in any of the many newspapers he had read. But why would anybody dream of making such a link?

No links to Kristine Kortsmaa either, of course. As far as he could understand, the police were working on the theory that Martina Kammerle and her daughter had both been killed by a man who was a friend of the mother, but there was no trace of a suggestion about what lay behind it all. Not the slightest hint of a possible motive.

For the simple reason that they didn't know anything. That there wasn't a motive that anybody could possibly understand. He smiled briefly again and looked at the clock: half past four. Time to start thinking about going home soon, there was probably hardly anybody left in the department, especially as it was Friday, as fröken Keerenwert had pointed out. She was usually one of the last to head for home.

Nobody knew, and nobody understood . . . Yes, it was as simple as that. The dark forces that compelled him to carry out these deeds were of course way beyond the comprehension of the police – way beyond . . . These profoundly enjoyable and necessary actions taken to eliminate these women, these trivial devils in the form of sexual beings who first received him gladly but then rejected him as something no longer desirable, just as you get rid of a household pet or throw away a worn-out toy. Who produced inside him this stifling, ever-increasing pressure in his chest, this pulsating rush of blood that needed to be expelled before he burst . . . No, it was impossible to expect an ordinary man to tolerate such things. Most certainly not. Such fundamental biological traits under the conventional veneer of what was regarded as civilization . . . They might have been tolerated in remote tribes living in remote corners of the world, in nomads and hunters thousands of years ago – but not now, not in people living in these perverted times. With the possible exception of the Taliban or the Fuegians.

It had taken him some time to reach these conclusions, to understand why it was necessary for him to dispose of these women: but after the whore in London and the whore in Wallburg the penny had dropped. He understood it now. A sort of unwavering certainty: he needed to take control over them at the same time as they humiliated him. As they robbed him of his dignity and he began to feel those choking sensations. When he started his relationship with Martina Kammerle he had known from the start what would happen – realized that one day he would reach that tipping point. That was why he had taken all those precautions. False name. No telephone number. Sporadic meetings in private . . . The fact that the daughter suddenly appeared and offered herself to him on a plate had been a big bonus for as long as it lasted. It had very nearly made him lose his stride – and the fact that her stab with the pair of scissors hadn't hit some vulnerable organ or other was nothing short of miraculous.

A miracle indeed, and a hint from an ironic God that he had the powers on his side. Certain powers, at least.

But the powers only help those who help themselves, and he would never have got away with it if he hadn't been careful to take precautions. A grand total of three visits to public places – two with the mother, one with the daughter. Three different restaurants that he never normally went anywhere near, and carefully chosen tables away from the limelight.

No unnecessary walks through town. Contact lenses instead of spectacles, which he always wore in normal circumstances. Haircuts and the removal of his beard when it was all over. Discretion, one hell of a lot of discretion; but nevertheless he was well aware that he was taking risks – and that knowledge was in itself a stimulus. A challenge which made the whole enterprise that much more satisfactory, that much more exciting.

But he must be stricter with himself in future, that was also a requirement. The next time. He suddenly found himself in a situation in which he had killed six people. Half a dozen, and he knew that there would be more. Kefalonia had been the starting point, the rest had been a sort of consequence, and in a way an irrelevance. A modus vivendi which was taking up more time and demanding more and more attention.

Another time. And another one after that. If he hadn't realized that inevitability after Kortsmaa, he certainly knew it now. After the mother and the daughter and the priest. He would meet women again and make love to them. Have sex with them and keep them satisfied until they reached the point when they began to waver: and then it would be time to allow himself the greatest satisfaction of all. He would place his strong hands around their thin necks and squeeze hard. Squeeze the life out of them, then stroke his hand over their still warm pussies.

That's the way things looked, there was no other solution to the equation of life. But he must raise his guard. As yet there were no indications in the newspapers suggesting a link between that whore in Wallburg and these latest victims: but the next time, when they found another woman strangled in that deeply biologically – I'm repeating myself, he thought in annoyance – that same deeply biologically necessary way . . . My mum, my mother, she would have understood why these women had to die – nobody else but her. They are asking for it, they actually yearn for this escape route deep down inside themselves, and my role is simply to do them a favour . . . There is a part of every human being that, without ever recognizing the fact in deed or thought, is identical with decline and extermination . . .

He suddenly felt the opposite. An intoxicating wave of happiness and inspiration surged up like a rainbow from the balls of his feet to the crown of his head, and the erection that accompanied it was flushed with an almost electric heat. He was obliged to rush out into the corridor and into the bathroom, and to deal with it in the only way possible.

Afterwards, he sat on the lavatory seat with a feeling of somehow being protected, and bathed in the light of an all-powerful star.

Nothing has any meaning, he thought. That is precisely why every little insignificant detail means everything. I am the world, and the world is manifest inside me. No, the world is a woman. A woman's identity and the centre of her power is her body. The useless navel of the world is a woman's body, and nobody must deny the existence of another world. Especially not the woman herself. It's as simple as that, so damned simple, and dying is no more difficult than looking at one's image in a mirror.

Somebody started up the photocopier in the corridor outside, and the noise reverted his attention to the left-hand side of his brain. Obviously he was not yet the only person in the building. And yet again he felt the physical movement inside his brain. The other reality. Left–Right.

He flushed the lavatory. Stood up and once again, as usual, felt a stab of pain from where the scissors had entered his body. A stab of pain and a reminder.

I must lie low for a while, he thought. I really must.

But that intention was not without its complications. Something had happened to his murky urges after the episode involving the Kammerle women. They were closer to the surface now. He had crossed a borderline, or passed over the crown of a hill. The intervals would have to be shorter from now on; he couldn't cope with not having a woman's skin under his fingertips for an unlimited length of time.

And presumably, he thought as he sat down again at his desk, presumably it was precisely those unusual words and images, the unadorned description of reality that started him worrying again.

Worry and unrest.

Dusk was approaching out there in the park, he thought. The red background provided by the observatory was shrouded in darkness.

I liked the girl's armholes, he thought. I wish it had been possible to preserve one.

He sighed, and decided it was time to go home.

MAARDAM

DECEMBER 2000

24

When it came to men, Anna Kristeva liked to ring the changes.

After an early, childless and painful marriage – plus two or three so-called serious relationships – she had come round to the view that ringing the changes was the best solution.

The solution to a problem that unfortunately existed, no matter how much she might have wished that it didn't. Men were necessary, that's all there was to it. First one, then another. Occasionally, but not in too large doses, and not all the time.

And above all: it was not something that needed to be taken too seriously. She tried not to become too deeply involved, or to stir up too many far-reaching emotions – that was what had scarred her when she was in her twenties.

Now she was thirty-five: a free woman with control over her own life and an income sufficient to ensure that she would never have to depend on a man in order to keep her head above water. Or on anybody else, come to that. For just over two years she had been a partner in the firm of solicitors she had been working for ever since she passed her law exams, and which had also borne her name ever since the

1930s: *Booms, Booms & Kristev*. Actual ownership had passed out of the family's hands for a while – her grandfather, Anton Kristev, had been a founder of the firm together with the Booms brothers: but her father, the next generation, had unfortunately been a child of the times. He became too involved with the lost souls of the 1940s, and at the beginning of the seventies had sold his share in the firm in order to finance his drug habit. Needless to say his daughter felt a certain satisfaction a quarter of a century later when she had been able to put things right again. Even if by then Henrik Kristev had passed away in a thin, blue cloud of hash smoke and remained ignorant of the restoration.

Needless to say it was an undeniable advantage to have a real, flesh-and-blood Kristev in such a reputable firm as Booms, Booms & Kristev – especially as she happened to be a woman, still young, still attractive.

A Kristeva. Jacob Booms, the third generation of Booms in the post of chairman – and with the biggest office in the premises in Zuyderstraat with two genuine Van Dermen oil paintings and a Persian Javel carpet – had suggested that they should change the name of the firm by adding that little feminine ending of '-a', now that joint ownership of the enterprise had reverted to its original state: but Anna had declined the offer.

She knew that she was a woman no matter what. There was no need for a little extra letter on the moiré-patterned glass doorpanel leading into her office. Or in the classic Garamond letter-heading that had been used by the firm since the very beginning.

All that was needed to satisfy this hackneyed PC obeisance to sex roles was a man now and then. Just for a week or two. Nothing serious.

'The most important difference between men and bananas,' her friend Ester Peerenkaas had remarked on one occasion, 'as far as we are concerned at least, is that men don't grow on trees.'

That was, of course, a perfectly correct observation. Even if they were only interested in satisfying an occasional need, it was naturally an advantage if the fruit was tasty. The men available in restaurants and bars and other slightly dodgy plantations were easy to pick; but the outcome, the satisfaction provided by the arrangement, was seldom all that great. Both Anna and Ester had reached that conclusion after a few years of half-hearted indulgence. The aftertaste was generally much more sour than the sweetness of the fruit itself: it was hardly ever a matter of more than just a rather anxious one-night stand, and neither of them was very interested in continuing to plough that furrow.

'Sleazy,' Ester had commented. 'It's so bloody sleazy. He came after only twenty seconds, then lay there crying for two hours. We really must find some other way of going about it.'

Ester was even more hardened than Anna when it came to men. Or so she used to claim, at least, and it was difficult not to agree with her.

At the end of the eighties Ester Peerenkaas had met an Egyptian man, as handsome as a young god, at a conference on international economics in Geneva. She was twenty-five years of age, had just completed her studies, and had been appointed to work on a project in the Ministry of Finance: her life lay before her like a sun-kissed dawn. She fell in love, they married and had a daughter – all within the space of a year. They settled down in Paris, where he had a job at the Egyptian embassy. After three years she found her young god in bed with one of their French female friends. They were divorced within two months. Ester was granted custody of their daughter and moved back home to Maardam; but as her former husband had certain rights of access, she eventually allowed Nadal to spend a month with him one summer. The girl was five at the time, and since then Ester had never clapped eyes on her again. There was no longer a secretary by the name of Abdul Isrami at the embassy in Paris, and Egypt is a big country.

So Anna didn't use to protest when her friend occasionally seemed to be somewhat cynical with regard to their sex lives.

So what other way did they find of going about it? Of making sure that they could occasionally enjoy a little of the sweetness that a damaged fruit still had to offer? *How?* It was Ester who came up with the answer.

Advertise.

At first it was not much more than a joke; but even jokes can become serious with the passage of time. It didn't cost anything to try, and one warm, promising Friday in May 1997 they placed their first advert in the Contacts section of

Allgemejne. The love market was considerably bigger and broader in *Neuwe Blatt*, but that was all the more reason for plumping for *Allgemejne*: in so far as there might be a promise of a little sophistication and class in this as yet untried area, it was of course important to explore those possibilities. Worth having a go.

Written responses required. Age, brief biography and photograph. Preferences with regard to art, music and literature. There was no need to make do with conceited idiots or introverted stay-at-homes. On the contrary, this was all about intellectual, cultivated and stimulating experiences.

There was also a proviso written into the advert to the effect that what was being proposed was not a possibility of spending their lives together: they had been very careful about the wording, but once they had got that right they didn't bother to vary it from one advert to another. Nor was there any reference to the fact that two women were involved: but as both Anna Kristeva and Ester Peerenkaas were talented, well-educated and outgoing women aged about thirty-five, there was no question of any attempt to deceive. Not at all.

The first advert produced sixteen responses: they spent an extremely stimulating evening at Anna's with cheese and wine, allocation of marks, eliminations, and drawing of lots – a process which eventually resulted in five meetings (three for Anna, two for Ester), and on the whole a very enjoyable summer. With no especially unpleasant aftertastes in the mouths of any of those involved, males or females – with the possible exception of an excessively possessive doctor's wife who was apparently incapable of understanding details of the conditions.

So the method worked. Or at least, it was more satisfactory than many others: and when Anna Kristeva called in at the *Allgemejne*'s office in Rejmer Plejn that Friday afternoon at the beginning of December 2000, and collected a bundle of responses from hopeful candidates, it was the fifth time of asking.

In other words, a little jubilee. They had agreed to celebrate in style at Ester's place with a lobster and a bottle of Chablis.

Twenty-three responses.

After the first so-called elimination of the idiots (those who hadn't understood that it is not possible to submit a handwritten response using a computer – or the ones who were obviously only interested in showing off their muscles or beards before masturbating inside a woman), there were fourteen left. Plus one wild card: it was Anna who had invented and introduced that device – on pretty good and, it would transpire, foresighted grounds – after their third fishing expedition exactly a year ago.

After the next rather more careful run-through – after the lobster and the Chablis, but before the coffee and cognac, concentrating on such simple but important criteria as graphology and the ability to put thoughts into words – the number of possible candidates was down to four. Plus the wild card.

They took a break. Put on a Nick Drake CD and did the

washing up. Prepared a tray with coffee and cognac glasses, moved into the living room and settled down in armchairs. It was ten o'clock, and time for the final round.

'What about this one,' said Ester, 'what do you think of him? I must say he appeals to me much more than any of the others.'

'Read it out,' said Anna, leaning back in the armchair and sipping her cognac.

Ester started reading.

'"I have to say I'm not a regular reader of these Contacts pages, but your advert attracted my attention – and why not. I'm a pilot and spend most of my time roaming around the world, but I have a base here in Maardam. Two marriages have stolen my youth, two children have ruined my finances, but at forty I'm too young to die. My first wife taught me to read – Maeterlinck, Kafka and the great Russians; my second wife took me to the opera. I still burst into tears when I hear the duet from *The Pearl Fishers*, but why should I sit sobbing to myself? I have a house on a Greek island, but even Greece is lacking in charm at this time of year. I suggest a dinner and *La Traviata* instead: that's on until the New Year."'

'Hmm,' said Anna. 'He certainly has a point, no doubt about that. If half of what he says is true he has a lot going for him. Can I have a look at his photo again?'

Ester handed it over. A powerfully built man, smiling, half-length. White shirt, open-necked. Thinning hair and his eyes perhaps a bit too close together – but what the hell? There surely can't be any doubt that he must be one of the chosen two.

They had changed the rules of the game after the second advert, so that there were now just two finalists: one each. It would have felt wrong in the long run to have more than that, simply in order to have back-ups. Neither Ester nor Anna had been attracted to that model – it would have been cowardly, to put it bluntly. Too vague and not sufficiently uncompromising. You needed to play this sort of game with a certain elan, to take a few chances in order to achieve a romantic outcome – otherwise there was a risk of everything being watered down, something neither of them could have tolerated. A yawning Amor? No thank you. Certain rules didn't need to be spelled out, but they were there even so.

'Okay, the pilot is one of them,' said Anna, handing back the photo. 'Nothing to argue about there. Do you have a number two?'

Her friend said nothing for a while, just read the submissions and studied the pictures.

'Not really,' she said eventually. 'Possibly this journalist, but it's up to you.'

Anna took over the documents and glanced through them.

'I'm a bit doubtful about him,' she said. 'Maybe I'm just biased, but that editor I wasted two months on last spring was really no Richard Burton. Even if he did knock back a few glasses.'

'Richard Burton?' said Ester with a laugh. 'If he's the one you're after I suggest that bloke from Wahrsachsen, whatever his name is. At least he has the right sort of impressive-looking facial expression.'

Anna picked up the photo of Angus Billmaar, a forty-four-year-old with a steel business of his own. And she also burst out laughing.

'Good God no!' she snorted. 'I mean Richard Burton before he became an old-age pensioner. Are you really telling me that this bloke is forty-four? I have to say I very much doubt it – he must have chopped a decade off when nobody was looking. How the hell could he get through to the last round?'

Ester shrugged.

'Lack of competition,' she suggested. 'Unfortunately. Who do you suggest, then?'

Anna contemplated the remaining two photographs, holding one in each hand and weighing up first one, then the other, several times. Checked their write-ups as well, before putting everything down on the table in front of her.

'No,' she said. 'I don't find any of them uplifting.'

'Nor do I,' agreed Ester. 'Mind you, I do have my period at the moment – but I don't think I'd find any of them inspiring under any circumstances. Not in the best of worlds. So what the hell do we do?'

Anna thought for a moment.

'I have a suggestion,' she said.

'Really? Let's hear it.'

'It goes a bit against the rules, but we've put them aside before now. I'm quite attracted to my wild card.'

Ester took a sip of cognac and pulled a face.

'A plunge into the dark,' she said. 'I know you find it hard to resist that kind of temptation.'

'Do you have a better solution?'

Ester shook her head.

'Only that we work our way through them all once again – but I don't suppose for a moment that it would help. But I'd like to make it clear that I wouldn't want to draw lots and take that kind of risk. You'd have to take him on.'

Anna smiled.

'We don't need to draw lots. You take your pilot, and I'll take on this mystery man.'

Ester frowned, and thought for a moment.

'No photo, no name,' she said. 'No address and no telephone number. You can hardly say that he's complied with the requirements. Read it out again, let me hear it once more.'

Anna cleared her throat and read out the short text written on a yellow card.

'"Saw your advert by chance. If you really are the person you say you are, it could be interesting to meet you. I'll reserve a table at Keefer's on the eighth. If you turn up at about eight, I'll treat you to a bite to eat and a chat. How to recognize me? A red tie and Eliot's *The Waste Land* in the same colour." That was all. What do you think?'

Her friend looked thoughtful and fingered the bottle of cognac.

'Eliot?' she said. 'Have you read Eliot?'

Anna thought for a moment.

'Nothing apart from the odd poem we had to study at grammar school. But he has neat handwriting – not T. S. Eliot . . . I like it. And the colour of the card he wrote on is rather attractive.'

Ester topped up their glasses, then nodded thoughtfully a few times.

'You sound impressively rational,' she said. 'I'm almost inclined to agree with you. Handwriting and a feeling for colours can tell you more than lots of other rubbish. When's the eighth? Next Friday?'

Anna worked it out rapidly inside her head.

'Yes,' she said. 'So, shall we say that we've made up our minds?'

'Let's do that,' said Ester with a smile. 'Fifth time lucky . . . A pilot and a mystery man. Cheers and good hunting, my lovely.'

'Cheers,' said Anna Kristeva. 'I have to say that when it comes to foreplay, you and I are unbeatable.'

'I reckon we're unbeatable on all fronts,' said Ester Peerenkaas. 'May the gods be with us on this occasion as well.'

'Of course they will be,' said Anna Kristeva.

And she washed away the sudden pang of fear that flashed through her consciousness with a draught of excellent Renault.

25

'Three weeks!' said Reinhart. 'Three bloody weeks since the girl was found out there on the beach! And we've got absolutely nowhere – did you hear that? Nowhere! It's a scandal!'

He leaned forward over his desk and glared at all those present in turn: but nobody seemed to have anything to say in their defence. Moreno signalled to him by means of a glance in the direction of the woman sitting diagonally opposite her.

'Ah, yes,' said Reinhart, with a sweeping gesture. 'You probably haven't met the brains trust yet . . . I'd like to introduce you all to Inspector Sammelmerk. She's been transferred here from Saaren, to fill the gap left by deBries. About time, some might say – it's been over a year . . . Anyway, from left to right: Krause, Moreno, Jung, Rooth, Münster, and yours truly, Chief Inspector Reinhart . . . Any questions?'

Nobody had any questions. Jung blew his nose into a paper tissue.

'Welcome,' said Rooth. 'Although we met yesterday, didn't we?'

Jung, Moreno and Münster joined in the welcome by nodding. Krause stood up and shook her hand, and Inspector

Sammelmerk herself did her best to avoid looking embarrassed. She was quite a tall and well-built woman in her forties: she had asked to be transferred from Saaren for personal reasons, this Tuesday was her second day in the Maardam CID, and of course there was no reason to make a fuss about it.

'Thank you,' she said in any case. 'I'm not usually difficult to work with – and I hope you aren't either. Anyway, shall we get going?'

'Excellent,' said Reinhart. 'We all have our pluses and minuses, of course, but several of us are fairly normal human beings. If you feel you'd like to make a good impression on us, we have just the case for you to take on. Let's call it the Kammerle–Gassel case, for want of anything better. I thought of asking Inspector Krause to spell everything out – he's the youngest and least depraved brain we have access to, and as I said, we haven't exactly been making progress these last few weeks. Let's hear it then.'

Krause moved over to the short end of the table and switched on the overhead projector.

'Okay,' he said. 'Thank you for having faith in me. I've prepared a short presentation of this case: I thought I might run through it, and then we could discuss what to do next . . .'

'Off you go, then,' said Rooth. 'We're all agog.'

'Perhaps I ought to explain,' Reinhart felt it necessary to mention for the benefit of Inspector Sammelmerk, 'that when Inspector Rooth isn't stuffing his face, things sometimes come tumbling out of his mouth instead. He doesn't know any better. Carry on, Krause!'

'Hey ho,' said Rooth. 'I'm misunderstood and slandered – but never mind: let's hear what you've got to say.'

Krause inserted his first slide, which spelled out the case in chronological shorthand.

'The first thing that happened – before anything started to happen, as it were – was that a certain Pastor Gassel paid a visit to our former Chief Inspector at the antiquarian bookshop where he now works. It's the fifteenth of September. The pastor has something he needs to get off his chest, but Van Veeteren hasn't time to listen to him. Just over two weeks later, on Monday, the second of October, Gassel falls – or jumps or is pushed – under a train in Maardam Central Station, and dies on the spot. No witnesses. At about the same time – we don't have exact data – two women are murdered: Martina Kammerle and her sixteen-year-old daughter Monica. Both of them are strangled. The mother was probably strangled in her flat: her body was found there a month later, eleven days before Monica's corpse was dug up by a dog in the sand dunes out at Behrensee. As far as the daughter is concerned, we haven't the slightest idea about the location of the actual murder. Nor do we know why the murderer sawed her legs off.'

'Her legs?' asked Sammelmerk.

'From the knees down, yes,' said Krause. 'It's totally incomprehensible: but nevertheless there are a few other things that we do understand.'

'You reckon?' said Rooth, but Krause ignored him.

'Unfortunately there is no conclusive technical evidence in either of these cases – no fingerprints, for instance ... And nothing else: although after a few days we did find a link between this Pastor Gassel and the murdered women . . . Or the daughter, at least. She had written down his name in a notebook she kept in her room, and this link led us to conclude that in all probability she had met him on one or more occasions in order to discuss something specific. He paid a visit to the Bunge Grammar School at the beginning of term, on church business – and that might well have been when she made contact with him. There is reason to believe that the reason for Gassel's visit to Van Veeteren was to do with Monica Kammerle – that is not definite, of course, but we don't have a better theory. Needless to say, this presumes that the priest's visit and the deaths of the women are connected.'

'I can add to that,' said Reinhart. 'An analysis of the pastor's estate produced no further evidence whatsoever. Le Houde and Kellermann completed their investigation into that yesterday – it was by no means easy to gain access to the place where his belongings were stored, it seems. But in any case, there was evidently no reference to any Kammerle anywhere at all.'

'No doubt he had it tucked away inside his head,' said Rooth.

'I'd have thought so,' said Reinhart. 'But it would be useful if we knew what it was. And what exactly was going on in Moerckstraat.'

Krause cleared his throat.

'That is obviously the key to it all,' he said. 'Both the mother and the daughter led pretty solitary lives – we haven't been able to find a single witness who could supply us with a bit more information about them. Martina Kammerle was a manic depressive, of course, and wasn't fit and well by any stretch of the imagination. And the girl was a bit of a hermit as well. She didn't seem to have any school friends. Neither of them apparently had any friends, no social life at all. The fact that nobody reported Monica Kammerle as a missing person seems to be connected with the fact that she changed schools – it's pretty disgraceful that the authorities didn't have a proper check on what was happening, but I suppose that's life. In any case, it seems there was a man involved. Fru Paraskevi, a next-door neighbour in Moerckstraat, says she heard a man's voice in the Kammerle flat several times in August, and a witness saw Martina Kammerle together with a man in Maardam. But we haven't managed to obtain anything remotely close to a detailed description of him. Anyway, we've since established a possible link with a case in Wallburg some eighteen months ago – perhaps it would be best if Reinhart were to go into that?'

Reinhart produced a document out of a red folder.

'By all means,' he said. 'It could well be relevant. And quite possibly is. On the fifteenth of June last year a woman by the name of Kristine Kortsmaa was strangled in Wallburg. Strangled in more or less the same way as our two victims. She met a bloke at a pub with music and dancing, and invited him back home. It seems pretty clear that he was the one who killed her. I've been through the case with Inspector Baasteuwel, who was in charge of it, but all we've concluded is that it . . . shall we say probably? . . . that it was probably the same murderer. The same bloody lunatic that we don't know so much as a little fingernail about. No fingerprints, incidentally.'

'A discreet type,' said Rooth.

'Extremely discreet,' said Reinhart. 'All we've managed to scrape together about him is that he must have very strong hands, that he's probably somewhere between thirty and fifty – otherwise Kristine Kortsmaa would never have seduced him, according to her friends – and that he doesn't have any unusual physical characteristics that would draw attention to him. Let's face it, he spent an hour or more prancing around with his victim at that disco!'

'Good luck,' said Rooth. 'He must have been incredibly lucky, for Christ's sake.'

'I'm sure you're right,' muttered Reinhart. 'Let's ignore this stupid perpetrator profile – at least for now. The man we're dealing with is as weird as it gets when it comes to sex – that's what we must bear in mind. He hasn't had sex with his victims before or after killing them. But both Kortsmaa and the Kammerle girl had their knickers removed. Hmm. If any of you happen to know a bloke like this, I'd be most grateful for a tip-off.'

Nobody had any comment to make, and Krause fitted in a new slide. There were two names, and a question mark by each of them.

Benjamin Kerran?
Henry Moll?

'Up to you now, Jung,' said Reinhart. 'Your turn.'

Jung nodded, and adjusted his posture so that he had eye contact with Inspector Sammelmerk.

'Well, I don't really know,' he said. 'What I have to say

could be pure coincidence: and even if there's more to it than that, it's hard to see what the implications could be in the long run.'

'Well said,' said Rooth.

'Shut up, Rooth,' said Reinhart.

'Thank you, Chief Inspector,' said Jung. 'Anyway, we discovered this name, Benjamin Kerran, when we were combing through the flat where the murder took place, Rooth and I . . . It was the only one of the forty-six names in all that we couldn't pin on a real person, if you see what I mean. So I did a simple search on the Internet, and discovered that this Kerran is a character in an English crime novel. The author's name is Henry Moll, and Kerran is the murderer in the book. It's pretty obscure, written in the thirties, but I managed to get hold of a copy from the university library and I've read it. I didn't think much of it, I have to say, but it was fun reading a crime novel in working hours.'

Reinhart started filling his pipe.

'I don't doubt that for a moment,' he said. 'Anyway, what conclusions did you draw?'

'None at all, to be honest,' said Jung. 'This Kerran character is a particularly nasty type. He's a strangler, just like our own killer, but there's no sexual motivation behind what he does. He's driven more by religion. He wanders around the streets of London and strangles female drop-outs, mainly prostitutes – I suppose you could say he's a variant of Jack the Ripper. But as I said, it's a pretty awful book. And completely unknown. I've spoken to a few crime novel fans – Kevin A.

Bluum among others – but nobody has ever heard of it. Nor have they heard of Henry Moll.'

'Who the hell posted him on the net, then?' wondered Rooth.

'The publisher,' said Jung. 'They've listed every single name in every book they've published since 1912. Don't ask me why.'

'We'll pass the book round,' said Reinhart. 'Nobody will be deprived of the pleasure of reading a crappy crime novel in working hours. I take it you've still got it?'

Jung nodded.

'And there's nobody else called Benjamin Kerran?' asked Moreno.

'Not as far as we know,' said Jung. 'It's possible there might be somebody of that name, of course; but we haven't found anybody in the whole of Europe so far.'

'But nevertheless one of our victims wrote down his name in her notebook,' said Reinhart. 'A literary strangler – how about that?'

Münster, who hadn't said a word so far, spoke up at last.

'She can't have read the book,' he said. 'That would be too improbable. And do we take it that there's no other information apart from the name? Nothing about her relationship with him, so to say . . . ?'

'Nothing,' said Jung. 'If we'd had an address or telephone number, all we'd have needed to do was to bring him in.'

'Yes, indeed,' said Münster. 'Of course. But in any case, there could well be a connection – I have to say I find it highly likely. Our unknown strangler has given her that name somehow or other – as a sort of perverted joke, I expect: he's not normal, we have to take that for granted. It could even be that he called himself by that name. Don't you think?'

He looked around the table, but there was no response. Neither positive nor negative.

'I'll bet you anything that's what happened,' said Münster. 'He called himself Benjamin Kerran.'

'Very possible,' said Rooth.

'Where does that get us if it's true?' wondered Moreno.

Münster thought for a moment.

'Nowhere at all for the moment,' he said. 'We're still standing on square one, but at least we know which direction to go to find square two.'

'I'm most impressed by the brilliant imagery our colleagues are using today,' said Reinhart with a tired sigh. 'Switch off the respirator, Krause. You don't have anything else to show us, do you?'

'Not at the moment,' said Krause, switching off the overhead projector.

Reinhart stood up.

'I'm going out now for a smoke, and to arrange for a tray of coffee and goodies from fröken Katz,' he said. 'We'll assemble here again ten minutes from now, and I'll tell you what the future has in store.'

'Ooh, a real Sibyl,' said Rooth.

'Shut up, Rooth,' said Reinhart for the second time this Tuesday morning.

*

'The fact is that I've sold us to the mass media.'

There was silence all round the table. Inspector Rooth took the opportunity of swallowing half a bun.

'You what?' he said. 'What the hell do you mean?'

'*Crime and Punishment*,' said Reinhart.

'Dostoyevsky?' said Moreno.

'Good God no, not him. The crime series on Channel Five, *Crime and Punishment*.'

'Oh, that,' said Jung. 'I didn't think it was one of your favourite programmes.'

Reinhart growled.

'It's not. But in any case, they are going to feature the Kammerle–Gassel case. It'll be on the day after tomorrow, between nine and ten, in case you're interested. I shall be interviewed, and so will the chief of police. They'll be recording it tomorrow.'

'Hiller?' exclaimed Münster, and couldn't help but smile. 'What the devil is Hiller going to do on a programme like that?'

'Perhaps he has a new suit he wants to show off,' Jung suggested.

'Perhaps he wants to calm down the general public,' said Rooth.

Reinhart scratched himself between the eyebrows with the stem of his pipe.

'It was Hiller who persuaded me to take part,' he said. 'Maybe it won't be a complete waste of time. We haven't exactly excelled ourselves lately, and there's always a chance that appearing in the spotlight and getting a bit of publicity might lead to a breakthrough. We haven't had much help from the general public so far, but you never know.'

'How on earth did he persuade you?' Rooth wondered. 'Hiller, I mean. Did he threaten to give you the sack?'

Reinhart seemed to be wondering whether or not to spit out a sour apple.

'It was even worse than that,' he said eventually. 'He wanted to invite me to dinner. So that we could discuss the case face to face.'

'Ugh,' said Rooth.

'Exactly,' said Reinhart. 'Anybody who dares to laugh will receive a punch on the nose. Anyway, they are going to devote half the programme to our strangler. I've been given an outline of how they propose to proceed, and I've decided to be liberal and drop any misgivings I have. I just wanted you to know that: we'll probably get lots of tips as a result of the broadcast.'

'I hope they're not going to go on about the case in Wallburg,' said Moreno. 'That could cause a few problems if they do.'

'I've put a stop to that,' said Reinhart. 'No, it'll be mainly narrators in the background, pictures from the places where the bodies were found, the occasional pedagogical explanation and a hell of a lot of speculation. And an interesting little introductory sequence in blood-red: "When will the Maardam strangler strike again?" I tried to put a stop to that as well, of course, but Hiller rather liked it. He reckons the police will be granted more money if we have the odd lunatic murderer on the loose . . .'

'Brilliant,' said Rooth. 'Thus spake a true strategist.'

'Very true,' said Reinhart. 'But it seems he's going to promise that we'll have the murderer under lock and key within a month.'

'Excellent,' said Münster. 'Presumably he'll have to take his suit off and roll up his shirtsleeves. Incidentally, Chief Inspector, have you got anything impressive to wear? A uniform, perhaps?'

'I grew out of that twenty years ago,' said Reinhart with another sigh. 'I thought I'd wear a pair of overalls and my usual understated charm. Anyway, shall we pack up now and get on with what we each have to do? Or does anybody have anything sensible to say?'

Nobody had. Not even anything stupid to say.

Moreno opened the door to Irene Sammelmerk's office.

'Hi! Do you mind if I come in?'

'Of course not,' said Sammelmerk with a smile. 'I hoped you might pay me a call.'

Moreno stepped inside and closed the door behind her.

'Really?' she said. 'Why?'

'Well . . . Why do you think?' said Sammelmerk, somewhat hesitantly. 'How many women are there in this police station?'

'Not many,' said Moreno. 'But now there are two of us on this floor, at least. I'm pleased about that – and I hope you'll like it here.'

Sammelmerk gestured towards the piles of books and unopened packing cases that lined the walls.

'I'm sure I shall,' she said. 'Once I get all this stuff sorted out. But I have the rest of today to make this room liveable in. I get the impression the team is pretty good – am I right?'

Moreno sat down on the window ledge and thought that over.

'Yes,' she said. 'I think so. But then, I've hardly ever worked with anybody else, so perhaps I shouldn't pass judgement. Why did you apply to transfer here?'

Sammelmerk shrugged.

'Nothing dramatic, I'm afraid,' she said, 'if that's what you'd hoped. My husband got a job in Maardam, it was as simple as that. As a computer geek at Dixnerland. We've been living apart for six months, so it'll be nice to start living as a family again.'

Moreno nodded.

'Children?'

'Three,' said Sammelmerk. 'Six, nine and twelve. As regular as clockwork. What about you?'

'Not yet,' said Moreno, looking out through the window at the dull grey landscape. 'But I reckon it's about time I got started.'

'I can recommend it,' said Sammelmerk. 'Assuming you have a bloke.'

'That would help, of course,' said Moreno.

Sammelmerk laughed.

'Things acquire the right level of importance when there are children involved – you can't cheat any more . . . Incidentally, this case involving the mother and her daughter seems absolutely horrendous. Please feel free to fill me in a bit more on the details. Assuming I'm going to be involved in one way or another. Although I suppose there is other business as well . . . ?'

'There certainly is,' said Moreno. 'But I'm afraid I must dash off. I just wanted to say I'm thrilled to bits that it's a woman who has moved into this office . . . And I'd like to suggest that we should have dinner together once you've got sorted out. Then I can fill you in on this case, and lots of other things besides.'

Sammelmerk seemed to be quite touched.

'My God,' she said. 'To tell you the truth I'm over the moon to discover that there's another woman in the team. I've spent the last ten years working exclusively with male colleagues. You have to sort of tune in to another wavelength every damned morning before you start work . . . Well, you know what it's like. And of course we must go out and have a meal together – just give me a week or so to sort out the family.'

'That goes without saying,' said Moreno. 'Just let me know when you're ready.'

Sammelmerk nodded. Moreno felt an almost irresistible urge to give her a hug, but didn't dare. It's not yet time for CID officers to start hugging one another, she thought.

Instead she gave her a slightly awkward wave, and slunk out through the door. She had barely closed it before the image of Intendent deBries appeared in her mind's eye. And she was reminded of what she had discussed with Münster – how quickly we forget all about people who are no longer around.

And how certain people – like Martina and Monica Kammerle, for instance (and perhaps also Tomas Gassel?) – took up so little space in this life that nobody noticed their absence when they vanished from the face of the earth.

Apart from the fact that a large number of CID officers were doing their best to track down the monster who had murdered them of course.

A paradox, a paradox, a most ingenious paradox, Moreno thought. I wonder if we shall ever find him?

Benjamin Kerran? No, put me right at the bottom of the list of those waiting to read that book.

26

For some reason Thursdays were always the worst. Ester Peerenkaas had often thought that many times before, and this Thursday – 7 December in the Year of Grace 2000 – was no exception. It was as if all the tasks that had been put on one side during the week had reached maturity and cried out to be dealt with at the same time on Thursday afternoon, otherwise they would probably be left until the following week. Friday was always Friday after all, and you couldn't count on anything serious being done on a Friday: too much time was spent drinking coffee, and planning and discussing possible or impossible activities lined up for the weekend.

Ester was conscientious and understood how important it was to do her duty and thereby gain respect – the respect of her colleagues, despite the fact that she was a woman, and a beautiful one at that. Or perhaps especially for that reason. It was by means of hard and single-minded work that she hoped eventually to be promoted to chief financial officer of the whole hospital – when Svendsen retired in six or seven years' time – and that was why she stayed at her desk making calculations and forecasts until six o'clock that windy and freezing cold evening. Only two weeks left to the Christmas holidays and a trip to Fuerteventura, so reward was beckoning in the shorter term as well.

She did what little shopping she needed to do at Laager's in Grote Torg, and got back to her flat in Meijkstraat at a quarter to seven. She had a shower, made an omelette and listened to her telephone messages on the answering machine before flopping down on the sofa in front of the television, thinking that she had no intention of moving a limb until it was time to stagger to bed at about eleven o'clock, and enjoy a well-deserved night's sleep.

She zapped around the channels for a while before sticking with Channel Five, where a discussion was taking place on the roles of men and women in the new century, to be followed by a crime programme at nine o'clock. Entertainment with a gesture in the direction of a social conscience, she thought as she adjusted the cushions under the small of her back and sipped away at the weak gin and tonic she generally allowed herself after a hard day at the office.

When the telephone rang it was twenty past nine, and the crime programme was well into its stride.

At first she couldn't hear who the caller was, but after a few confusing seconds she realized that it was Anna. Anna Kristeva.

'You sound odd,' she said.

'I am odd,' said Anna. 'What are you doing? Am I interrupting anything?'

'No. I'm just watching the telly . . . It's about some loony who strangles women and pushes priests under trains. No, you're not interrupting anything. What do you want?'

'I'm ill,' said Anna. 'It's a damned nuisance, but I can scarcely stand.'

'I can hear it's bad,' said Ester. 'There's a lot of flu about.'

'Yes, that's what I'm told I've got,' said Anna, coughing feebly. 'Three or four days in bed, and I'll feel fine after a week, according to my doctor . . . But just now I find it hard to see the light at the end of the tunnel. Thirty-nine degrees when I took my temperature an hour ago . . . Huh.'

'Poor you,' said Ester. 'Is there anything I can do to help? Do you need any shopping doing?'

'No, no,' Anna assured her, 'all the practicalities are taken care of. My neighbour – you know, that engineer who has a soft spot for me, he looks after all that. But there is one thing . . .'

'Really?' said Ester. 'Fire away.'

'My wild card.'

'Eh?'

'My wild card. The bloke I'm supposed to meet.'

'What about him?'

Anna coughed a few times again.

'I can't very well turn up in this state.'

'Ah! I see,' said Ester. 'When were you supposed to meet him?'

'Tomorrow.'

'Tomorrow?'

'Yes. Don't you remember? Keefer's with T. S. Eliot, and that other business . . .'

'Oh yes, of course,' said Ester. 'Red tie and red Eliot. Forgive me, I'm a bit on the dozy side today as well . . . Not that I'm ill, mind. It's just that I had to work overtime, there was so much that couldn't simply be left unattended to. So you'll have to put him off, is that it?'

'How?' said Anna.

'What do you mean, how?'

'What am I supposed to do in order to put him off?'

'Well, I suppose . . .'

The penny dropped.

'Oh yes, I see what you mean. You don't have his phone number, do you?'

'Nor his address, nor even his name, nothing at all. And I think it would be a shame to miss him. Not after we've completed the elimination process and all that . . . Are you with me?'

'Yes, I'm with you,' said Ester. 'But I don't see what you can do about it. Three or four days in bed means three or four days in bed. You can't just stagger into the restaurant in your state and go looking for Eliot.'

'Exactly,' said Anna, taking a deep, wheezy breath. 'That's precisely what I'm coming round to. That's why I'm ringing.'

'Really?'

'I thought you might be able to help me.'

'Of course. What do you want me to do?'

'Go there.'

'Where?'

'To Keefer's, tomorrow evening. That's where he's supposed to be going.'

'Oh yes?' said Ester, then sat in silence for a few moments. 'And what the hell do you want me to do?'

'That's up to you. You could simply pass on greetings from me and tell him that unfortunately I'm indisposed. Ask him his name, and whether he can suggest an alternative date. It doesn't need to be Big Deal.'

'Fair enough,' said Ester. 'I could just call in and pass on a message – no problem. But . . . Oh no! I've just remembered, I promised Karen I'd go to the cinema with her tomorrow evening.'

'Who's Karen?'

'A colleague of mine. We're going to the Canaries after Christmas. Shit, shit, shit! What do we do now, then?'

Anna sighed.

'Do whatever you like,' she said. 'I just think it would be silly to miss the opportunity. But if you don't have time, you don't have time. Can't be helped. How are things with your pilot?'

Ester thought it over while gaping at the television screen: two police officers, one in a blue suit, the other in a crumpled tunic shirt and a yellow scarf, were sitting there, talking to the presenter.

'I don't know yet,' she said. 'He's out flying, but we have spoken on the telephone. I'm going to meet him next weekend.'

'Sounds good,' said Anna.

'Yes, he sounded rather charming. But it's going to be hard for me to fit Keefer's in, I'm afraid. Can't you think of some other way of solving the problem?'

Anna seemed to be thinking that over. She was drinking

something as well: Ester could hear her swallowing with considerable difficulty.

'I can't think of anything else. Maybe we should just leave him to stew.'

Ester thought for a moment.

'I'll go and see him if I can fit it in,' she said. 'We haven't yet fixed a time for our cinema jaunt, Karen and me. If I have time, I'll call in. Okay? But I'm not promising anything.'

'All right,' said Anna. 'Let's leave it at that. No, I really must go to bed now – I haven't the strength to carry on talking any longer. Give me a bell and let me know what happened – tomorrow, perhaps? By the way . . .'

'Well?'

'If you do go there and discover that he looks awful, just turn round and leave the premises.'

She coughed again. Ester laughed.

'You bet I will!' she said. 'There must be a reason why he refuses to send you a photo.'

'I expect so,' said Anna. 'But you never know.'

She hung up. Ester remained seated on the sofa for a while, thinking. She felt for the remote control – the bit about the strangler had come to an end, and they were now discussing the drugs situation in big cities versus small towns and rural areas instead. She switched off. She finished off her gin and tonic, and decided that it was time to go to bed, even though it was nowhere near eleven o'clock yet.

No, she thought. Red tie and red Eliot? I don't fancy that at all.

*

Karen deBuijk called in at her office on Friday morning, and in only a few minutes they drew up plans for that evening. It wasn't all that complicated.

First a drink at Ester's at about seven o'clock, and perusal of what was on in the various cinemas. Then a film – probably at Cinetec or Plus 8, which had eighteen auditoriums between them. Then a bite to eat and a drink somewhere – and then they would see what was on offer after that. No point in cramping their style in advance, as it were.

She had finished her weekly reports by soon after four o'clock. She left the administration block of the hospital and drove out to Merckx in order to do some well-organized shopping for a change. It took her an hour, and lowered her irritation threshold very considerably. But that's life, she decided when she was finally able to clamber into her Peugeot in the gigantic parking area outside the shopping centre. I'm not made for supermarkets, and will just have to accept the fact.

Were any human beings made for supermarkets?

She switched on the car radio as she drove towards the town centre. A brief weather forecast informed her that it was plus two degrees, raining, and would continue to rain for the foreseeable future; and that a westerly wind was blowing at about ten metres per second.

She thought about Anna, and it occurred to her that if you wanted to catch flu, Maardam at this time of year was the ideal place to be.

*

Just how true this was became clear to her when Karen rang at a quarter to seven, and sounded as if she had lost three litres of blood and ended up under a refrigerator.

'I'm ill,' she groaned. 'Can't make it.'

'You as well?' said Ester.

'As well?' said Karen,

'Huh, another friend of mine gave up the ghost yesterday. As it were. It's on the rampage, this flu epidemic.'

'It certainly is,' said Karen, breathing heavily. 'I could barely manage to walk up the stairs when I got home from work. It's amazing how quickly it hits you . . . I'm sorry.'

'No problem,' said Ester. 'Go to bed. We can go to the pictures some other time.'

'Too right,' gasped Karen, and replaced the receiver.

Or dropped it, according to what it sounded like.

Now what? Ester Peerenkaas thought. What do I do now? All alone on a Friday evening, in the prime of life.

She checked her watch, and it dawned on her that she would have plenty of time to wander down to Keefer's restaurant.

27

Münster contemplated the man who had just sat down on the visitor chair.

He was tall and thin. Round about thirty-five, by the look of him, with a narrow, horsey face on which he was trying to grow a sort of reddish-brown beard with limited success. His mouth was thin and indecisive, and his eyes were wandering incessantly behind a pair of metal-framed spectacles.

'Your name?' asked Münster.

'I would prefer to remain anonymous,' said the man.

'Your name,' said Münster again.

'I . . . Mattias Kramer, but I'd prefer it if this . . . if it were possible to . . .'

'To what?' wondered Münster.

'If this conversation could be treated with discretion. My situation is far from easy.'

'I see,' said Münster. 'If you say a little about it, and why you have come here, we can see what we can do about it.'

Kramer adjusted his spectacles, and swallowed.

'Would you like something to drink? A cup of coffee, perhaps?'

'No thank you. No, that's not necessary. Can you promise

me that what I say won't be made public? It would be . . . It would be catastrophic for me if my wife got to hear about it.'

Münster leaned back in his chair and allowed a few seconds to pass.

'I can't give you any guarantees,' he said. 'I'm sure you understand that. Our duty as a police force is to combat crime, and if you tell me anything that—'

'It's nothing criminal,' interrupted Kramer fervently. 'Certainly not. It's a private situation, but it would ruin me if . . . well, if it became public knowledge.'

'I see,' said Münster. 'Tell me why you have come to see me – I obviously have no desire to make life difficult for you.'

Kramer cleared his throat and hesitated for a moment.

'Tomas Gassel,' he said eventually.

It took a second or two for Münster to recognize the name. 'Well?' he said.

'Pastor Gassel, who had an accident in September.'

'Of course. I know about that.'

'I saw something about it on a television programme last night. I've been meaning to contact you several times during the autumn, but haven't been able to raise enough courage. But when I saw the picture of him last night, and heard what they said, I realized that I really must talk to you.'

'Go on, then,' said Münster.

'We had a relationship.'

'A relationship?'

'Yes. Tomas was homosexual, I don't know if you are aware of that.'

Münster nodded.

'Yes,' he said. 'We know about that. So you are also homo-sexual, are you?'

'Bi,' mumbled Kramer, looking down at the floor. 'I'm bisexual. That's much worse.'

Münster waited. Found a blank page in his notebook and wrote down Mattias Kramer's name. It was not exactly news that it was more difficult to be bisexual than homosexual, and the way his visitor looked just now confirmed the truth of the matter. He seemed to have no idea how to sit up straight on a chair, was shuffling around non-stop, and he was exam-ining every inch of the floor as if he had dropped something and was desperate to find it.

'I'm married and have a little daughter,' he said in the end. 'We live in Leerbach.'

Münster made a note of that.

'Go on,' he said.

Kramer pulled himself together and straightened his back.

'My wife knows nothing about any of this,' he said. 'I didn't know myself when we got married, it has just sort of crept up on me. I can't do anything about it, it's a sort of murky compulsive drive and there is no way I can protect myself from it.'

'I can understand that it is difficult,' said Münster. 'So you had a secret relationship with Pastor Gassel?'

Kramer sighed.

'Yes. We have known each other for about a year – or had known each other, I suppose I ought to say. We met occa-sionally, and . . . well, it was sufficient for me if I could give vent to my feelings in this respect every other month or so.

Or less than that – I don't expect you to understand me, I'm just giving you the facts.'

'Of course,' said Münster.

'Whenever I think about it, and about my family, I sometimes get the feeling that I want to put an end to it, once and for all, somehow or other. My only hope is that it will pass. I mean, it didn't start until I was an adult, so perhaps there's a chance . . .'

He fell silent. Münster observed him for a while, thinking things over.

'You don't need to apologize any more,' he said. 'I understand your problems. But perhaps you could explain how you are mixed up in the death of Tomas Gassel instead? That's presumably why you've come here.'

Kramer nodded several times and adjusted his spectacles again.

'Of course. Sorry. I just wanted you to be clear about the background. Anyway, that evening . . .'

'The second of October?' asked Münster.

'Yes, the evening he died. I was on my way to meet him. My wife thought I was attending a course, but that wasn't the case. I was on that train to Maardam in order to meet him.'

'The train that ran him over?'

'Yes. It was horrendous. He was supposed to meet me at the station, and instead . . .'

His voice started shaking. He took a handkerchief out of his pocket and blew his nose.

'Instead, he ended up on the tracks?' said Münster.

Kramer nodded and put the handkerchief away. Then he

buried his head in his hands for a few seconds before straightening his back and taking a deep breath.

'It was so horrendous,' he said again. 'I got off the train. I'd been in one of the rear coaches, and when I stepped down onto the platform and started walking towards the station building I realized immediately that something had happened. People were screaming and running around and bumping into one another . . . And a woman grabbed hold of my arm and wept and told me what had happened.'

'How did you find out that it was Tomas Gassel who was the victim?'

'It took a while. At first I was looking for him among all the crowds of people – he was supposed to be meeting me, after all. And in the end . . . in the end I saw him.'

'You saw him?'

'Yes, as they lifted him up off the track. What was left of him. For Christ's sake . . .'

Kramer blinked several times like an owl in the sunlight, then buried his head in his hands once more – and Münster could see from his shaking shoulders that he was crying.

Poor bastard, he thought. How has he managed to survive, for Christ's sake?

But perhaps that was what bisexual people had to come to terms with? Surviving. Mind you, they were not the only category of human beings who had to do that.

He waited until Kramer had pulled himself together. Asked again if he would like a cup of coffee, but received only a shake of the head in reply.

'Then what did you do?'

Kramer flung his hands out wide.

'What could I do? At first I thought I was going out of my mind, but then all the shutters went up and I didn't feel anything at all. I found a hotel and checked in for the night. Didn't sleep a wink. The next day I went back home to Leerbach.'

'And you never thought of getting in touch with us?'

'Of course I did, as I said. I haven't thought of anything else since it happened. All this horrendous autumn.'

Münster thought for a while.

'How did you get to know each other?' he asked. 'You and Pastor Gassel.'

Kramer reduced his mouth to a narrow slit as he thought about his response.

'At a club,' he said. 'Here in Maardam. There are clubs like that . . . for people like us.'

His voice had a trace of desperate pride, and Münster could see that in spite of everything, he felt relieved. Coming to the police station and telling them what he knew had somehow endowed him with a degree of human dignity. But it was only a few seconds before he remembered the quandary he was in.

'What's going to happen now?' he asked grimly.

'What do you mean?' Münster asked.

'What are you going to do with me?'

'We'll have to see,' said Münster. 'I have a few questions for you first. Despite the fact that you were in shock, did you have any thoughts about how your friend ended up on the track under the train?'

Kramer shook his head.

'No. I have no idea . . . But I saw what they were inferring on that television programme last night. That's awful – can that really be what was behind it all?'

'We're far from certain about any such link,' said Münster. 'It's just one of several possibilities.'

'What are the others?'

'Well, only two really,' said Münster. 'That he committed suicide. Or that he fell.'

Kramer livened up.

'He certainly didn't commit suicide – he would never do that. He knew that I was on that train, he was a strong and considerate person who would never . . . No, it's out of the question: he would never do anything like that.'

'You are quite sure about that?'

'One hundred per cent,' said Kramer. 'I've always taken it for granted that it was an accident . . . That he stumbled, or something of the sort.'

'But did you have any other thoughts, after that television programme last night?'

Kramer looked confused for a moment.

'Well, yes . . . I suppose you could say that I did. But it sounds so incredible. Why should . . . ? Who would . . . ?'

'He never said anything about feeling threatened, or anything like that?'

'No, certainly not . . . But then we spoke so rarely. Only when we were arranging to meet.'

'Did he ever mention the name Monica Kammerle?'

'No.'

'Or Martina Kammerle?'

'No, certainly not. But we didn't see much of each other, you must understand that we didn't have that kind of relationship.'

'Okay, I do understand that,' said Münster, 'but I'm asking these questions so that we can exclude certain possibilities, that's all.'

'I see,' said Kramer.

'What about Benjamin Kerran?' asked Münster.

'Eh?'

'Have you ever heard the name Benjamin Kerran?'

'Never,' said Kramer.

Münster paused and leaned back on his chair, his arms crossed.

'What's going to happen now?' asked Kramer again when the pause became too long.

'We'll have to see,' said Münster. 'You can go home, and we might get in touch again if we need any more information.'

'No, don't do that,' protested Kramer, looking as if he were about to burst into tears. 'You promised to be discreet. Can't I ring you instead?'

Münster nodded and produced a business card.

'Fair enough. Give me a ring towards the end of next week. But I must ask you to provide me with your address and telephone number, just in case. But you don't need to worry: I have no intention of making things difficult for you.'

Kramer sighed in relief. Borrowed paper and pencil and wrote down his contact details.

'Can I go now?' he asked when he had done that.

'Of course you may,' said Münster. 'But I would like to ask you a few questions that are really none of my business.'

'Really?' said Kramer, looking surprised. 'Such as?'

'Do you have any more lovers apart from that one? Male lovers, I mean.'

Kramer stood up and looked as if he was wondering whether to be offended or not.

'No,' he said. 'I don't.'

'And you haven't acquired any more after Tomas Gassel?'

'No.'

'So you haven't been unfaithful to your wife since he died?'

'No, I haven't,' said Kramer. 'Why are you asking about that?'

Münster thought for a moment.

'I don't really know, to be honest,' he said. 'Human interest, I suppose. And a certain degree of concern about your family. Anyway, thank you for coming to tell us about this, herr Kramer.'

He held out his hand. Kramer grasped it with both his and shook it energetically, before hurrying out through the door. Münster leaned back on his chair.

Huh, he thought. So now we know why the priest was at the station.

But how does that help us?

He spun round on his desk chair and looked out of the window. Still no sign of any rain.

28

There was a ring on the door, and Van Veeteren woke up with a start.

He realized he must have dozed off. Remarkable. On his knee was a newly arrived edition of Seneca, which he had been leafing through, and on the arm of his chair – in a special mahogany-lined inlay for this very purpose – was a half-empty cup of coffee. Two portions of coffee to one of Gingerboom's, if he remembered rightly. Perhaps that was why he had fallen asleep.

He stood up and looked at the clock: half past eleven, he could hardly have been asleep for more then ten minutes. At most. He went out into the shop: a woman with a pram was on her way in through the door, but it was only when she turned to look at him that it dawned on him who it was.

Marlene Frey.

'Hello,' she said. 'Thank God you're in. I need your help.'

'Really?' said Van Veeteren, opening the rain canopy slightly and peering down at the baby. 'Dobidobido, how's Andrea today, then?'

'She's asleep,' said Marlene. 'But I hope you can keep an eye on her for a while. I have a job interview, and I don't think it will give a very good impression if I go waltzing in with a baby. That little cow Christa announced a quarter of an hour ago that she was unavailable.'

'Christa?'

'The babysitter. You're my only hope.'

'Me?' said Van Veeteren. 'Here?'

'Now,' said Marlene. 'I've only got five minutes.'

'But . . .' said Van Veeteren.

'I'll be back in three-quarters of an hour. She's just eaten and fallen asleep, you don't need to worry. An hour at most. You can take the blanket off her if you like, there are dry nappies in the basket under the pram if you need to . . . I'm off, see you soon!'

'Bye,' said Van Veeteren as Marlene rushed out into Kupinskis gränd.

He looked at the pram, and looked at Seneca which he was still holding in his hand. Put Seneca down. Carefully removed the rain canopy from the pram, folded down the hood and rolled back the blanket. Andrea didn't move a muscle, slept like a log with her dummy in one side of her mouth and a bubble of saliva in the other.

Good God, he thought. Let's hope she doesn't wake up. She could be damaged for life.

He carefully manoeuvred the pram further in among the bookshelves, but realized that the space between them was too narrow to move it into the inner room, which would have made an excellent bedroom: the sheltered corner with maps and crime fiction would have to suffice. If any customers turned up and asked about crime novels, he could always tell them to go to hell. Or to come back on Monday.

He fetched his cup of coffee and the Seneca. Sat down on the stair half a metre from the pram and looked at the clock. Five minutes had passed since Marlene had left. What had she said?

Three-quarters of an hour? An hour? He noticed that he had palpitations.

Calm down now, he told himself stoically. What's the matter with me? It's only a little baby.

Ten minutes later he had read page thirty-seven of the Lucilian letters no less than four times, Andrea had sighed deeply twice, but nothing else had changed.

The doorbell rang. He swore quietly to himself, and decided not to announce his presence in the shop. Why hadn't he locked the door and pulled down the blind? And did people really have nothing better to do than to potter around in second-hand bookshops on a rainy afternoon like this one? If they really had to read, surely they could buy a new book or two rather than old ones?

'Hello?'

It took him half a second to identify the voice.

Inspector Moreno.

He thought briefly. Perhaps it wouldn't be a bad idea to have a woman around. In case anything critical happened. Ewa Moreno had no children of her own, that was true: but then, she was a biological creature, was she not?

Very much biological, it struck him.

'Yes.'

Her dark-haired head peered round the corner from biographies and miscellaneous.

'Is that the *Chief Inspector*?'

He didn't even bother to correct her.

'It certainly is. Good morning, Inspector, but I think we need to talk rather more quietly. There's somebody here trying to sleep.'

Moreno came up and looked down into the pram.

'Good Lord, I didn't know . . . Who is it?'

'Andrea,' said Van Veeteren.

'Who's that?'

'My granddaughter. Eighteen months old. An absolute treasure.'

Moreno smiled, then turned serious.

'Granddaughter? How . . . I mean . . .'

'Hmm,' said Van Veeteren. 'Let's move away a bit so that we don't wake her up. Maybe I haven't told you?'

They moved further into the room overlooking the street.

'No,' said Moreno. 'You haven't mentioned it.'

Van Veeteren took out his cigarette machine, but changed his mind. No doubt it was not good for Andrea to breathe in so much tobacco smoke at such a young age.

'Yes, she's Erich's daughter,' he said. 'He managed to leave a trace of his presence on this earth before he died, despite everything. He never saw his daughter, unfortunately, but she's the one lying over there. I'm babysitting, his mother will be coming to fetch her shortly . . .'

Moreno sat down at the low counter.

'Good Lord,' she said. 'I had no idea. Nor does anybody else, I suspect. It must feel . . . well, how does it feel, in fact?'

Van Veeteren paused for a while before answering.

'It's a consolation,' he said. 'Of course it's a consolation, curse it. Life is so damned strange, you don't realize what's important and what's less important until long afterwards. If you're unlucky, it's too late when the penny drops, although . . .'

He paused, but Moreno simply nodded and waited for him to continue.

'Naturally it's not only your own life that needs to make sense – it never does, of course, and you have to make do with a certain degree of meaningfulness . . . No, the important thing is the bigger perspective, and that little lady in the pram is a part of something much, much bigger than anything an ancient second-hand bookseller could ever dream of . . . Hmm, I'm going gaga.'

Moreno looked at him, and he suddenly wished he was twenty-five years younger. Then he remembered Ulrike, and realized that being over sixty wasn't such a bad thing either.

'I'm touched,' said Moreno. 'Sorry to mention it, but it's a fact.'

'Hmm,' said Van Veeteren. 'It suits you. But I have the impression you came here for some other purpose. Looking for some Saturday night reading, perhaps?'

Moreno laughed.

'Not really,' she said. 'But maybe I can sort that out while I'm here anyway. No, it's the same old story, in fact. The Kammerle–Gassel case, as we call it, although it makes it sound like a make of motorbike . . . Or some disease or other. Anyway, I thought you might still be interested.'

'I am,' said Van Veeteren. 'Very much so.'

'You weren't watching the telly last night by any chance, were you?'

'The telly?' said Van Veeteren, raising an eyebrow. 'No. Why should I do that?'

'Some people do,' said Moreno.

'I'm not much of a one for popular entertainment. And I think our set is broken anyway – Ulrike said something about that the other day . . . What programme did you have in mind?'

'A crime magazine programme. They discussed our case. Hiller was on, and Reinhart as well . . .'

'Reinhart?'

'Yes.'

'The times are out of joint,' said Van Veeteren.

Moreno pulled a face.

'For sure,' she said. 'They usually are. Anyway, we thought a bit of publicity might help our investigation. It's been pretty hard going, as you probably know . . .'

'I've suspected as much,' said Van Veeteren. 'You still have no idea about a possible murderer?'

'No,' said Moreno with a shrug. 'That would be putting it too strongly. But we did get a few reactions to yesterday's programme – you had a bit to do with that business of the priest, didn't you?'

Van Veeteren placed a thoughtful hand under his chin and frowned.

'Well, we've found out why he was at the Central Station at that time, for instance. He was going to meet a lover who was due on a train. You recall that Gassel was gay?'

'I was the one who established that,' said Van Veeteren modestly.

'Ah, yes, of course. In any case, this lover turned up at the police station and gave us a detailed confession – that he was on the train, and why, that is.'

'Really?' said Van Veeteren, and thought for a moment. 'And where does that get us?'

'Not very far, I'm afraid,' said Moreno. 'But it's another piece to add to the puzzle in any case. He had nothing new to tell us about Pastor Gassel. They hardly knew one another, he claimed. They used to meet and, you know, a few times a year, that's all. It seems that some people are like that.'

'Evidently,' said Van Veeteren. 'Did anything else float up to the surface after the police force's venture into the bottomless pit known as popular entertainment?'

'A bit,' said Moreno. 'But not a lot. One witness claimed to have seen a man running over the tracks at the Central Station that evening. Very helpful to have kept quiet about that for two-and-a-half months, of course . . .'

'Is he reliable?'

'She,' said Moreno. 'It's a she. A young woman. At least, that's what both Reinhart and Krause say, I haven't spoken to her myself. According to her, this man left the station area and ran off in a northerly direction, towards Zwille in other words; it's quite easy to get away in that direction. The witness had just left the station building and only saw his back. From twenty metres away, probably more.'

'In the dark?' asked Van Veeteren.

'Semi-dark, at least. There was a certain amount of light there. Not a lot to go on, of course; but I reckon that if anybody still doubted that Gassel was in fact murdered, they can forget that now.'

Van Veeteren contemplated his cigarette machine and scratched himself under his chin.

'I've never doubted that,' he said. 'Anyway, a bit of new evidence is better than nothing. I'd better have a word with Ulrike about having the television set repaired. Is Reinhart thinking of doing any repeat performances?'

'I don't think so,' said Moreno. 'To be honest. But we had another interesting tip.'

'Go on.'

'A waiter out at Czerpinski's Mill. He says he served a meal to Monica Kammerle and an elderly man some time around the beginning of September.'

'*Monica* Kammerle?'

'Yes. The daughter, not her mother. When he says "elderly man" he means that he was significantly older than the girl. About forty, perhaps. He assumed at the time that it was a father and his daughter.'

'Description?'

'Unfortunately not. He can't remember details. He's not a hundred per cent sure it was Monica Kammerle either – unfortunately he was on holiday when the papers wrote about it that first time.'

'Typical,' said Van Veeteren.

'Yes,' said Moreno. 'Absolutely typical. Anyway, this was the latest news. You can hardly call it a breakthrough, but needless to say we are following everything up as best we can. Something will turn up sooner or later.'

'Let's hope so,' said Van Veeteren. 'As long as it's not another victim.'

Moreno sat in silence for a moment, contemplating that possibility as her eyes wandered over the row upon row of books.

'Do you think that's what's going to happen?' she asked.

'Yes,' said Van Veeteren. 'To be honest, that's what I expect to happen next. Not least if it is in fact linked with that business at Wallburg. I was playing badminton with Münster last week, and he claimed that it wasn't out of the question that the same killer was involved.'

'Yes,' said Moreno. 'That seems likely. But if nothing else, that television programme ought to have put women on their guard.'

'Let's hope that's the case as well,' said Van Veeteren.

Moreno stood up.

'I don't think I'll bother about my literary education today,' she said with an apologetic smile. 'But perhaps I could take another peep at Andrea before I rush off?'

'Of course,' said Van Veeteren.

They crept along the gap between the shelves again. Moreno bent down over the pram, and Van Veeteren stood behind her, feeling a sort of diffuse pride bubbling up inside him.

'She's sweet,' said Moreno. 'Incredibly sweet.'

Van Veeteren cleared his throat.

'Of course she's bloody sweet. She's my grandchild after all.'

When Inspector Moreno had left, he sat down again on the stair and also took a look inside the pram.

Then he checked the time. It was fifty minutes since Marlene had hurried off for her interview.

Time's running out, he thought, giving the pram a shake. It would be a pity if poor Andrea had to spend a whole hour with her grandad without actually seeing him.

He gave the pram another shake, a bit harder this time.

29

On the night of 8 December, Anna Kristeva dreamed that she was going to die.

Or that she had already died. Among the chaotic, feverish images that had come cascading down over her were some depicting the actual burial – she recalled those clearly when she woke up at about eight in the morning, soaked in sweat and wrapped in foul-smelling sheets. She opened her eyes, stared up at the ceiling and noticed that the room was spinning round. For a brief moment she thought that she hadn't been dreaming after all, but that it was real. That she really was dead. Then she closed her eyes again and remembered that she was ill. Before falling asleep for the night at about eleven the previous evening she had managed to get her temperature down as far as 38.1: it hadn't been possible to get it any lower than that, so no wonder she had been afflicted by unpleasant dreams.

She lay there in bed for a while before daring to test whether her legs would support her. It turned out that they did, albeit only just: she had to cling on to the walls in order to stagger as far as the bathroom, and when she had finished peeing she remained sitting on the toilet for five minutes, without a single rational thought entering her head. It was a non-stop procession of images of her death from her dreams. Lying there naked on the bedroom floor, unable to breathe. Tossing and turning convulsively back and forth, trying to grab hold of something – an illusory and elusive object that evidently didn't exist. Hovering there in mid air, something only she could see and evaluate, nobody else. Whatever it could possibly have been.

Then she was lying in a white coffin in Keymerkyrkan as her friends and relatives filed past, gazing at her with sorrowful, sometimes tearful eyes. Her mother. Didrik, her brother. Jacob Brooms. Leonard, her ex-husband and his new wife, whose name she could never remember. And Ester Peerenkaas, who unlike the others didn't seem to take it all too seriously. She smiled encouragingly at her instead, winking conspiratorially at her: for some inexplicable reason she was wearing a red tie round her neck.

At that point the dream sequence came to a sudden end. Anna remembered the conversation with her friend on Thursday evening, flushed the toilet and managed to stand up. Clung on to the washbasin and stared sceptically at her reflection in the mirror before splashing a few handfuls of cold water forcefully into her face. Almost immediately she had a headache, and started shivering like a dog.

Out into the kitchen. Aspirin, juice, vitamin C and a drop or two of Kan Jang – she had trouble in swallowing it, her throat seemed to have dried up during the night, but she managed it in the end. She staggered back into the bedroom and tumbled back into bed. Wrapped herself up in all the blankets and covers and pillows she could lay hands on, and went back to sleep.

She just had time to think: I really must ring Ester if I ever wake up again.

It was just turned half past ten when she did, and she couldn't remember if she had been dreaming again. But she did remember that she should ring her friend, and as she wasn't quite as feverish and sweaty as when she first woke up that morning, she picked up the telephone and dialled Ester's number without further ado.

But Ester wasn't at home. She wondered if she ought to leave a message on the answering machine, but decided not to – she couldn't think of anything to say, and she could always ring again a bit later on.

Happy with her efforts and decision, she emptied the glass of water – which she must have put on her bedside table the previous evening, it tasted somewhat stale – turned her pillow over and went back to sleep.

The next time she failed to get through to Ester it was a quarter past three. She had taken a shower and got dressed: admittedly only a T-shirt and a pair of baggy jogging trousers, but still . . . She left no message this time either, but instead telephoned that neighbour of hers who was always willing to run errands for her, and told him she had the flu. She asked if he could possibly nip down to the corner shop and buy her a couple of litres of juice; and if he had any spare aspirins, could he please let her have one or two as her own stock was dwindling.

Herr Dorff, the engineer, produced the goods within half an hour. He seemed quite worried and looked just as love-lorn as usual when he handed them over, and asked if there really wasn't anything else he could do to help.

Anna assured him that there wasn't, she had everything she needed now and it was just a matter of lying down in bed and getting some rest.

Dorff told her he would be at home all evening, and all she needed to do was to give him a call if she wanted anything. She thanked him, and ushered him swiftly out through the door, explaining that she didn't want to pass on the germs: in those circumstances there was nothing he could do but with-draw gracefully.

By way of variation she parked herself on the sofa and tried to read, but the plot and the series of harrowing events in Diza Murkland's latest crime novel, which had shot up to the top of the bestseller list over the last couple of weeks, soon sapped the life out of her and she fell asleep again.

It was not until getting on for nine o'clock that evening that she left a message on Ester's answering machine, and it was only then that she started to feel a bit worried.

What the hell was she up to? Why did she never come home and answer her telephone?

Needless to say there was no end of perfectly natural

answers to those questions. She might be out shopping, for instance. Visiting a friend. At the cinema (although she had evidently been there yesterday, surely?), or out enjoying herself in some way or other. It was Saturday, after all. There was no reason why she should sit at home, wasting time she could be spending on celebrating her youth. Always assuming she wasn't ill and feeling miserable as well, of course.

And miserable was exactly how Anna felt at the moment. She had had her evening shower and drunk as much fluid as would have satisfied a camel before a desert safari, but she still had a temperature and felt completely washed out.

Shit, shit, shit, she thought. I must ask Dorff to get me some more juice tomorrow.

He'll be only too pleased to do that for me.

Sunday began a little better, but not all that much. Instead of asking Dorff to run the errand, she managed to get to the corner shop under her own steam: but by the time she was back in her flat she almost fainted. She went back to bed, rested for an hour then read the Sunday paper for another two. She drank some more juice and water, eventually succeeded in getting down her a sandwich and a banana, and checked her temperature.

Exactly thirty-eight, what else? . . .

That afternoon she telephoned her mother and felt sorry for herself, and also rang Ester Peerenkaas: still no reply.

She didn't leave a message, but the unwarranted and somewhat surprising feeling of unease started nagging at her again.

Only for a moment, but it was there and she had to ask herself why.

Despite everything she began to feel a bit better by the evening. She read some more Murkland, watched the television and lay down on the sofa, listening to music. Bach's cello suites, which she had been given by her family as a thirty-fifth birthday present and were just right for an evening like this one. She telephoned Ester once again, and instructed the answering machine that her friend had better get her finger out and ring her back the moment she came in through the front door. What the hell was she up to? A woman friend was lying here ill in a state of misery and despair: couldn't she display even a tiny bit of sympathy? A tiny crumb of interest in the fate of a fellow human being?

She smiled wearily to herself. Hung up and noted that it was a few minutes to nine. She decided to watch that Canadian film on the telly after all – if it was a load of crap she could always switch off.

The film turned out to be not a load of crap: not exactly unmissable, but she watched it to the end even so. Switched off the television, took the last aspirin of the day and went to the bathroom. The telephone rang as she was halfway through brushing her teeth.

Ester, she thought, rinsing her mouth out rapidly. About time.

But it wasn't Ester. It was a man.

'Hello?'

'I'm sorry to disturb you at this time of night. Is that Ester I'm speaking to?'

For a confused couple of seconds she didn't know what to say.

'Hello? Are you still there?'

'Yes . . . No, I'm not Ester.'

'Could I speak to her, please?'

His voice sounded rough. She had a vague image of an unshaven docker in a string vest with a can of beer in his hand.

But of course, that was just prejudice.

'There is no Ester at this number. Who am I speaking to?'

'That's irrelevant. Ester Suurna, is she not there?'

'No,' said Anna. 'And no other Ester either. You must have the wrong number.'

'Oh, shit,' said the man and hung up.

Very odd, she thought when she had got into bed. Here's me waiting for a call from that damned Ester for two days, and all that happens is that some bloody layabout rings and goes on about a different Ester.

And the feeling of unease started nagging at her once again.

In fact it was Monday morning before Ester got in touch. She sounded as perky as a parrot on pot.

'Good morning, my lovely – I hope I didn't wake you up?'

'Yes, you did.'

'I didn't get home until late last night. I didn't want to ring then and disturb you. How are things?'

'I haven't had time to find out yet,' said Anna. 'What time is it?'

'Half past seven. I'm on my way to work, but I thought I'd give you a bell first. I heard your message on the answering machine. So you're still ill, are you?'

Anna raised herself into a half-sitting position, and felt that she certainly wasn't yet back on top form. She brushed aside some hair that had stuck fast to her forehead and cheeks, and took a firmer grip of the receiver.

'Yes, I think I'm still ill. It'll take at least a week, just as the doc said. Where on earth have you been? I rang several times.'

'I know,' said Ester. 'I've been with my parents in Willby – didn't I say I was going there?'

'No, you didn't,' said Anna.

'Huh. Ah well, never mind. I expect you want to hear about what happened on Friday evening.'

'Among other things, yes.'

'Well, I ended up by going to Keefer's after all.'

'Really?'

'He was sitting there.'

'And?'

'Wearing a red tie and with Eliot on the table.'

Anna waited. Then her friend suddenly burst out laughing.

'The fact is, it went pretty well. I've taken him over.'

'Eh?'

'Taken him over. I didn't bother to pass on any greetings from you, I simply spent a couple of hours having dinner with him. You can have my pilot.'

'Your pilot?' said Anna, then sneezed straight into the receiver.

'Bless you! Yes, the bloke with the house in Greece – he'd be absolutely right for you. We'll do a swap, just like that.'

'But that's not on. You can't . . .'

'Of course it's on,' insisted Ester, sounding thrilled to bits. 'Why not? It's already fixed, there's no going back.'

Anna felt something that was either a fever or an attack of anger – or a combination of both – welling up inside her.

'What the hell do you mean?' she snarled. 'You can't simply take over my bloke just like that. I asked you to go there and explain that I was unable to attend. What you've done is a bloody disgraceful way of—'

'Of course it is,' said Ester, interrupting her, 'but that's the way it turned out. My colleague also caught the flu on Friday, so I had nobody to go to the cinema with. I thought it would be much easier to test the bloke out, seeing as I was there in any case. Why are you kicking up such a fuss? Surely it doesn't matter, it's too late to change anything now, and you can have my pilot . . .'

'I don't want your bloody pilot!'

'Why not? There's nothing wrong with pilots. Get a grip, for God's sake!'

Anna sat there in silence for a few seconds, trying to hold back another sneeze. But in vain.

'Bless you!' said Ester again. 'We can't do anything to change this now, surely you can see that. He has no idea that there were two of us involved in the game. I don't think

he'd be impressed if another woman turned up next time
. . . Don't take it personally, but we're not twins after all.'

'And when is next time?' asked Anna.

'Not for quite some time. So if you're in a hurry you
haven't lost anything. He's busy until Christmas, and then I'm
going away for a couple of weeks. I shan't meet him again
until January.'

'January?'

'Yes. I don't understand what you're getting upset about. If
I hadn't gone to Keefer's you wouldn't have got anywhere
anyway. But as it is, I'm serving you up a cultured pilot on a
gold tray – surely you could thank me for that. Don't you
think?'

Anna had the feeling that she didn't have much of a
defence against this attack. Ester had a point, no doubt about
it. She thought for a moment again.

'And this golden boy up in the clouds,' she said. 'Isn't he
going to notice anything fishy?'

'Of course not,' said Ester, demonstrating her early-
morning good humour by laughing yet again. 'He's away
flying, like I said. I've only spoken to him on the phone.
Our first date is a week from now, so there's no problem:
I can fill you in on what we said on the phone, that'll only
take five minutes.'

'Really?' said Anna.

'As easy as winking,' said Ester. 'Stop moaning, concentrate
on getting fit again, and I'll talk to you in a couple of days.
I really must get to work now.'

'All right,' said Anna with a sigh. 'I suppose I ought to thank you.'

'Of course you should,' said Ester. 'Love and kisses.'

'Watch out, I'm infectious,' said Anna as she replaced the receiver.

What an ego-tripping bitch, Anna thought when she eventually got out of bed. I stake everything on a wild card with a high risk factor, and that damned Ester thinks she can just step in and steal him from under my very nose.

With friends like that, who needs enemies?

But she failed to work out any way of putting things to rights, despite spending all day thinking about it.

She didn't even know what the bloke was called, for God's sake. And in the end she began to realize that it would be best to give up and be satisfied with that pilot.

I hope you end up with a real shit, Ester Peerenkaas, she thought as she switched off the light for the night. That would serve you right.

During the next few years of her life she would frequently come back to that thought, and regret it deeply.

MAARDAM

JANUARY 2001

30

Inspector Baasteuwel looked for a suitable place to put his wet raincoat. As he didn't find anywhere, he simply dropped it on the floor just inside the door.

Reinhart looked up and nodded.

'Welcome to headquarters. Take a seat.'

'Thank you,' said Baasteuwel, lighting a cigarette. 'I happened to be passing, as I said, so I thought I'd pop in and see how things are going. I see you've been starring on the telly . . . A happy New Year, by the way.'

'Thank you, and the same to you,' said Reinhart. 'As for the telly, well, it was worth a try.'

'I actually watched the programme,' Baasteuwel admitted. 'And very informative it was, I must say. But I gather you haven't had much of a response?'

'Not a lot.'

'But a bit, even so?'

Reinhart scratched his head while wondering what to say.

'Chickenfeed,' he said, examining his fingernails. 'We had confirmation of what we already knew. That the priest was in fact pushed under the train, for instance. And that the Kammerle girl had met him – at least once. A young lad from her school had seen them together in a cafe.'

'A cafe?'

'Yes. You might think that was a somewhat unorthodox location for a confession, but maybe it wasn't really a confession.'

Baasteuwel nodded.

'So we can be pretty confident that it was the same killer in all three cases,' said Reinhart. 'A pretty meticulous type, it seems: he's wiped away more or less every single fingerprint in the flat where the woman was murdered, not just his own.'

'What does that indicate?' wondered Baasteuwel.

'Nothing in particular; but it could be that he'd been there quite often, and wanted to be on the safe side . . .'

'It must have taken him a hell of a time,' said Baasteuwel. 'Even if it's only a small flat it must have been a devil of a job.'

'He had plenty of time,' said Reinhart, starting to fill his pipe with elaborate care. 'Don't forget that it was over a month before we came into the picture. He'd have had time to repaper the walls and install a new kitchen if that had been necessary.'

'Hmm,' muttered Baasteuwel. 'I reckon it's the same bastard as in my case, no matter what. He didn't leave any fingerprints in Wallburg either – but he didn't need to be so careful there. He'd presumably only had time to wrap his fingers round the odd door handle and glass . . .'

'Plus her neck,' said Reinhart.

'Yes, indeed,' said Baasteuwel. 'We mustn't forget that. So you agree that we're both looking for the same bastard, do you?'

'Why not?' said Reinhart. 'It's always an advantage to be looking for just one loony rather than two.'

Baasteuwel nodded again.

'What was that name you mentioned? Kerran or something like that?'

'Benjamin Kerran,' said Reinhart, with a deep sigh of disgust. 'Yes, it's possible that's what he called himself – but it's no more than a guess.'

'The name means nothing to me,' said Baasteuwel. 'You'll have to fill me in a bit, I'm afraid.'

'With pleasure,' said Reinhart, lighting his pipe. 'Benjamin Kerran is a fictional murderer in an obscure English crime novel from the thirties. The Kammerle girl had written down his name in a notebook. That's all, really – we haven't managed to track down a real, living person of that name.'

'Remarkable,' said Baasteuwel.

'Very,' said Reinhart. 'Anyway, as I said it's only a shot in the dark – but the swine we're looking for seems to be a pretty unusual type, and it's as well we bear that in mind. Why did he saw the girl's legs off, for instance? Can you tell me that?'

'I don't know,' said Baasteuwel.

'Why did he hide the mother under the bed, but bury the girl on the sea shore? Any ideas about that?'

'Remarkable,' said Baasteuwel again. 'So they were murdered at the same time, were they?'

'More or less, as far as we can establish. It's not possible to be absolutely precise. But surely it's a bit odd if he murdered both of them in their home and then hid just the daughter away somewhere else.'

'Was he having an affair with the mother?'

'I expect so.'

'What about the daughter?"

'What do you mean?' said Reinhart.

'Nothing,' said Baasteuwel. 'I don't mean any bloody thing.'

'I know what you're getting at, of course,' said Reinhart.

He inhaled deeply, and breathed out a cloud of smoke over his desk.

'Thank God you allow me to smoke in your office,' said Baasteuwel. He stubbed out his cigarette and produced another one. Reinhart raised an eyebrow in surprise.

'Are you saying that you're not allowed to smoke in the station up at Wallburg?'

'I certainly am,' said Baasteuwel. 'The whole place has been a smoke-free zone for the last couple of years.'

'What a bloody scandal,' said Reinhart sympathetically. 'How do you manage?'

'It's not as bad as it sounds,' said Baasteuwel. 'I smoke despite everything.'

'Good for you,' said Reinhart.

Irene Sammelmerk contemplated the woman who had just sat down on the other side of her desk.

Between sixty and sixty-five, she thought. Not badly off. Platinum-blonde hair cut pageboy style (or was it a wig?), fur-trimmed coat and brown medium-high boots that must be calf-leather if not even more expensive. Handbag in similar style on her knee. Clear-cut features and restrained make-up.

If she hadn't been shrouded in a cloud of uncertainty, she could well have passed for a president's wife at a formal photo-shoot, Sammelmerk thought. Or a former film star.

'Welcome,' she said. 'Would you like anything to drink?'

The woman shook her head.

'Let's start from the beginning. My name's Irene Sammelmerk, I'm a detective chief inspector. Your name is Clara Peerenkaas: would you be so good as to tell me why you've come here?'

Peerenkaas licked her lips and adjusted her handbag.

'It's about my daughter, she's the one I'm worried about . . . I told another policeman all about it on the phone earlier on – I can't remember his name, but maybe you know . . .'

'I'd be grateful if you could tell me all about it again,' said Sammelmerk, 'so that we can have a proper record of all the details. I'll be recording this conversation, so it's important that we don't miss anything. It's about your daughter, you said? . . .'

Fru Peerenkaas nodded.

'Ester, yes. Our daughter. She lives here in Maardam. In Meijkstraat. My husband and I still live in Willby. Ester has disappeared, that's why I'm here. We haven't been able to make contact with her for a whole week – for God's sake, you've got to help us to find her . . .'

She broke off and clasped her hands over her handbag. Her

narrow nose was trembling non-stop. It seemed obvious to Sammelmerk that panic was lurking just below the surface.

'When did you last speak to her?' she asked.

'On Monday. Monday last week. We spoke on the telephone, and she was going to give us a ring on Wednesday – it was about a Christmas present that Ester had promised to try and change in a shop here in Maardam . . . It was a soup tureen: my husband and I are trying to collect a whole set, but the one we got for Christmas wasn't right, and we were – or rather, Ester was – going to go to Messerling's and try to swap it for the right design. And she was going to phone me about it on Wednesday.'

'I see,' said Sammelmerk, making notes. 'What's your daughter's job?'

'She's an administrator at Gemejnte Hospital – finance and all that sort of thing. She's good. She's been there for nearly five years now . . . I've rung and spoken to them, of course. But she hasn't been seen since last Tuesday.'

'And they don't know where she is?'

'No. She hasn't turned up for five working days without getting in touch with them. Nothing like that has ever happened before. Not for five years.'

'Who else have you been in contact with?'

'Nobody else,' said fru Peerenkaas in a low voice. 'Ester lives on her own, we don't know much about her circle of friends. She was married, but that was a pretty awful business – maybe we don't need to go into that?'

Sammelmerk thought for a moment.

'That's up to you,' she said. 'If you are sure that it doesn't have anything to do with the present state of affairs, then of course we don't need to poke our noses into that.'

Fru Peerenkaas seemed to hesitate, but decided not to go any further into it.

'Have you been to examine her flat?' Sammelmerk asked.

Peerenkaas took a deep, somewhat worried breath.

'No,' she said. 'We called in and rang the doorbell, my husband and I, but she wasn't at home. We don't have a key to her flat. There were no lights on, we could see that from the street.'

'When was this?' asked Sammelmerk. 'What time were you there?'

'About two hours ago.'

'Where's your husband now?'

'At his doctor's. For various tests. We'd planned to come to Maardam today in any case. We'll be having lunch at Kraus unless . . .'

The rest of the sentence remained hanging in the air. Inspector Sammelmerk said nothing for a while, studying the rough notes she had made. Ah well, she thought, this is why the tape recorder is running.

'You've no idea what might have happened?'

Fru Peerenkaas shook her head.

'None at all?'

'No. We saw Ester at Christmas, and everything seemed to be the same as usual – she was happy and positive, just as she always is. Then she went off to the Canary Isles, and came back home last Sunday.'

'And nothing like this has ever happened before? She's never cut herself off like this, for some reason or other?'

'Never. Not even when she was getting divorced. It's not like Ester at all.'

'Is there a man in her life?'

Fru Peerenkaas blinked a few times before answering.

'Probably. But she doesn't have a steady relationship – I'd have known if she did. Her marriage left her scarred, so she's been a bit more careful than most when it comes to committing herself. Nowadays, I mean.'

'I understand,' said Sammelmerk. 'Do you have any photographs of your daughter you could let us have for a few days? It's probably a bit soon to send out a Wanted notice, but if we need to do that eventually we shall need a photograph, of course.'

Fru Peerenkaas produced an envelope from her handbag, and handed it over.

'It's a few years old,' she said. 'But it's the only one we could find, and it's a very good likeness.'

Sammelmerk took out the photograph and examined it for a moment. That was quite long enough to establish that Ester Peerenkaas was her mother's daughter. The same clean-cut, delicate features, the same finely drawn mouth. Dark, straight hair, a generous smile.

About thirty, Sammelmerk guessed – and so a few years older than that now. Pretty. She wouldn't have had any trouble in finding herself a man, if she had wanted one. She wondered about the trauma evidently connected with the woman's marriage: it seemed to be more than just the divorce in any case.

She put the photograph back in the envelope.

'Thank you,' she said. 'We'll do all we can to throw light on this matter. If you just give me her address and tell me how we can get in touch with you, I'll get back to you – will tomorrow be all right?'

Fru Peerenkaas produced a card from her handbag.

'You're welcome to call this evening, even if you don't know anything by then. We'll be driving back home this after-noon. Our mobile number is on the card as well. Ester's address and so on is on the back of it.'

Sammelmerk promised to ring by seven o'clock at the latest. Fru Peerenkaas stood up, shook hands and left the room.

Inspector Sammelmerk switched off the tape recorder and leaned back.

A pretty woman has gone missing, she thought.

Not for the first time in the history of the world, and these things rarely end up happily. Rarely or never.

She started to think about what measures they ought to take.

Her first act was to pick up the telephone and call Inspector Moreno.

When Chief Inspector Reinhart got home, he noticed that his soul was itching.

His copper's soul, that is, not his private one. Although it wasn't always easy to keep them apart.

His wife and daughter were not at home, but there was a

363

note on the kitchen table: they were three floors below, with Julek and Napoleon.

Julek was Reinhart's daughter's fiancé – both of them were aged three. Napoleon was a tortoise, and considerably older.

Julek also had a mother, but unfortunately she had to attend a meeting: which was why Winnifred and Joanna had gone downstairs to step into the breech.

They would be back at nine or thereabouts, it said on the note. Reinhart was welcome to go down and join them if he felt like it; otherwise there was a pie in the fridge. It just needed heating up.

He looked at the clock: only a few minutes to seven.

He hesitated for a moment, then took out the pie and put it into the oven. Sat down at the table and started scratching his soul.

It was that confounded case, of course. Yet again. It would soon be four months: that was a hell of a long time.

And hardly a feather in the police force's cap. He'd gone in to work over the New Year as well: it was always worrying to be lumbered with unsolved cases at this time of year, he'd noticed that before. It was as if the Christmas and New Year holidays exerted some mysterious kind of malevolent infection on all criminal cases, and in January all the loose ends seemed to feel sticky and smelly, as if officers were dealing with some kind of archaeological work rather than criminological tasks.

But of course the main reason for his copper's soul being irritated was the visit by Inspector Baasteuwel and the conversation they had had. It had persisted all afternoon, not surprisingly.

They had eaten lunch together, and if Reinhart had not noticed it earlier, he certainly became aware then that Baasteuwel was not just any old detective inspector.

He was intelligent. That in itself was unusual. He was utterly lacking in respect for his superiors, indifferent to prestige. And evidently afflicted by the same vulnerability to an itch in the soul as Reinhart himself.

There was a murderer on the loose, that was the crux of the matter.

The whole point of a detective officer's work was to ensure that there were no murderers on the loose. There were other aspects of the job as well, of course, but to be lumbered with three – or even four if one included Baasteuwel's – unsolved murders, well, that was certainly nothing to boast about.

If one were to compare the situation with that of other professions, it was more or less on a par with a taxi driver who could never find his way to the correct address (or at least went to the wrong place four times in a row).

Or a locksmith who was never able to open a door, or a farmer who forgot to sow his seeds.

Shit, shit, shit, Reinhart thought and took the pie out of the oven even though it was only lukewarm: we really must make sure we get somewhere with this bloody strangler.

It's by no means impossible that he might strike again.

Not impossible at all.

31

When Inspector Moreno stepped in through the dark, heavy door of Booms, Booms & Kristev's solicitors' offices in Zuyderstraat, she felt the stab of an inferiority complex.

She felt no better after being ushered by a discreet secretary in tweeds into Anna Kristeva's room (with three windows overlooking the street, and furnished with solid, old Wanderlinck items, each of which no doubt cost about as much as Moreno earned in a year) and sat down in a leather armchair about the size of a small car.

And matters were not helped by the fact that when Anna Kristeva arrived ten minutes late, she turned out to be a woman more or less the same age as Moreno. She made no attempt to estimate the cost of the lawyer's clothes, that wasn't necessary. The situation was crystal clear already.

She heaved herself out of the armchair and shook hands.

'Ewa Moreno, detective inspector.'

'Anna. I know. Sorry to have kept you waiting. I hope it's okay to use first names?'

The temperature rose slightly.

'Would you like a sherry? I think I could do with one.'

Sherry? thought Moreno, and the temperature fell again.

'Yes please,' she said. 'Why didn't you want to talk to a male officer?'

Kristeva didn't reply immediately, but instead opened a corner cupboard made of rosewood with intarsia marquetry. Took out a large carafe of sherry and filled two bluish glasses. Sat down in the other armchair and sighed deeply.

'Cheers,' she said. 'What a bloody mess! I'm worried by what has happened . . . Dead worried, to be honest.'

Moreno took a sip of wine, Kristeva emptied her glass in one gulp.

'Anyway, that business of my not wanting to speak to a male officer,' she said. 'You'll understand. It wouldn't be much fun for me sitting here and trying to explain matters to a man with what you might call traditional views on sex roles.'

'Really?' said Moreno. 'As you know, I've come to talk about your friend Ester Peerenkaas . . . And what might have happened to her. I think it would help if you explained in more detail what you mean.'

Kristeva explained in more detail.

It took quite a while. Half an hour and another glass of sherry, to be precise, and Moreno had to admit that it was one of the most interesting conversations she had had for quite a long time.

To start with, at least. It had never occurred to her that there could be ways like this of looking at and solving sexual problems. Anna Kristeva described in detail how she and Ester Peerenkaas had developed their advertising adventure since embarking on it four years ago. About their selection procedures. About the excitement in advance of the meetings. About the outcomes (or the results, to put it another way), and about all these men they acquired a sort of control over in this way. Perhaps it was only an illusory control – but so what? Kristeva maintained: perhaps the whole of life was merely an illusion.

And about the negative sides, of course. How nothing seemed ever to be really serious. And about how one could create genuine hurt.

And about the fact that going in for this kind of activity implied that one had made up one's mind to lead a solitary life. Once and for all.

'Although you can never be really sure about nothing ever being serious,' said Kristeva, lighting a cigarillo.

'Are you thinking about your pilot?' Moreno asked, but received only a non-committal smile in response.

Anyway, now that all the cards were on the table, Moreno could understand perfectly why the young lawyer had preferred not to talk to one of her male colleagues.

Rooth wouldn't have had any sympathy at all with this approach, she thought. Probably not Münster or Reinhart either.

It wasn't even clear that she did: but she had to admit that it was interesting. The first twenty minutes, at least.

After that, it became increasingly unpleasant. When they started discussing the latest development in the hunt for these men. The innovation since the middle of December or thereabouts.

'A wild card?' said Moreno. 'You mean you actually selected a wild card? A man you knew absolutely nothing about? Not even his name?'

'That's right,' said Kristeva sombrely. 'But when I was due to meet him, I fell ill – so Ester took him instead.'

'Against your will?'

'Yes. She stole him from me, that's all there was to it.'

'And how did you react?'

'I was absolutely furious. But there wasn't much I could do about it. Ester and I haven't really met since it happened either, we've only spoken on the phone once or twice. That's why all I know is that she met him last Tuesday – the tenth, it must have been.'

'Where? Do you know where they were going to meet?'

'I've no idea.'

'What do you know about this man?'

Kristeva inhaled deeply.

'Nothing at all, really. I don't think they could have met very often yet – that was probably the second time. She said something about him being otherwise engaged over the Christmas period, and she was in the Canary Islands for a couple of weeks.'

'By herself?'

'No, she was with a colleague from work. You should probably be interviewing her – she's bound to know more about it than I do.'

Moreno turned back a few pages in her notebook.

'Is it Karen deBuijck you're referring to?'

Kristeva thought for a moment.

'I think so,' she said. 'I don't know her, but I think she's called Karen.'

'A colleague of mine is due to speak to her later this afternoon,' said Moreno.

Kristeva put her hand over her mouth.

'My God!' she exclaimed. 'You really are taking this seriously. Does that mean you believe something has happened to her?'

'We don't know anything for certain yet,' said Moreno. 'But it's obviously not good that she's been missing for a whole week.'

'No,' said Kristeva. 'Of course not.'

Moreno cleared her throat and put down the sherry glass she had been swirling around for the last few minutes.

'In any case, we obviously need to try to identify this man,' she said. 'All you can tell us about him is that Ester met him for the first time at Keefer's restaurant . . . That's in Molnarstraat, isn't it?'

Kristeva nodded.

'And that was the eighth of December, a Friday?'

'Yes.'

'How did she describe him?'

'Hardly at all. He seems to have been nice. I think he made a really good impression on her, but that's about all I know . . . I know no details, she said virtually nothing at all after that first meeting. Nothing later, either – but it could well be that the date last Tuesday was only their second meeting – or the first real one, as it were.'

'You think so?'

'Yes. Assuming it's true what she said about him being busy before and over Christmas. But I suppose she could have been lying to me.'

'Why should she do that?'

'So as not to make me jealous. I was very annoyed about the way she carried on – she was breaking the rules.'

'What rules?'

'Nothing written, of course. But there's always a network of invisible rules. That's something you learn in my trade, if nothing else.'

She stretched out her arms, and smiled apologetically.

'I understand,' said Moreno. 'But you don't have a name?'

'No.'

'Are you sure about that?'

'Absolutely certain. I would have remembered it if she'd mentioned one. The only details I know is that business about the tie and the book, but I knew about that before she met him anyway . . . A red tie and a red T. S. Eliot book, that was how I was going to be able to recognize him.'

Moreno nodded. They'd already spoken about that.

'Nothing about his job?'

'No.'

'Or his clothes?'

'No.'

'His age or his appearance?'

'Nothing. But you can take it for granted that he's pretty good-looking. Ester is very choosy.'

'And that meeting last week, you don't know anything about that? Apart from the fact that it was due to happen.'

Kristeva thought for a moment as she contemplated her well-manicured nails.

'No. All she said was that she was going to meet him, and she was looking forward to it.'

'Why did she mention it at all, if she thought you were going to be jealous?'

Kristeva shrugged.

'I told her I was quite pleased with Gordon – the pilot, that is – and I suppose she felt she ought to say something. I wasn't annoyed with her any longer – and that was why I rang her, in fact. I thought that . . .'

'Thought what?' wondered Moreno when nothing else was said.

'I suppose I thought I'd over-reacted a bit. I wanted to smooth things over and improve our relationship, that's all.'

'And did you manage that?'

Kristeva smiled wryly.

'I think so. We talked about meeting at the weekend – last weekend, that is. We didn't fix anything definite, we were going to get in touch. I thought it was her turn to ring, and I . . . Well, I was busy with Gordon, I suppose . . .'

'When did you last speak to her? What day?'

'Sunday last week. In the evening. She'd just got back home from Fuerteventura that afternoon.'

Moreno made a note, and wondered if there was anything else to ask about.

She couldn't think of anything, thanked Anna Kristeva for taking the time to meet her, and left the offices.

She did so with somewhat different feelings than when she

had arrived. She wasn't at all sure what she thought about Anna Kristeva – as a woman and a human being – but at least the feeling of inferiority she had felt when she first arrived had been blown away completely.

Is the bottom line that I feel sorry for her? she wondered as she emerged into the street. Or for both of them? Both Anna Kristeva and Ester Peerenkaas and their artificial love lives?

Yes, possibly.

Perhaps there was all the more reason to feel sorry for fröken Peerenkaas.

If her analysis of all the disturbing implications was correct, that is.

On Thursday, 19 January, nine days after Ester Peerenkaas had last been seen alive, the Maardam police entered her flat in Meijkstraat. In charge of the operation – appointed very hastily – was Inspector Rooth, as Inspector Moreno – very hastily – had been given other duties by no less than Chief of Police Hiller himself.

Rooth was accompanied by Inspector Sammelmerk and the two friends of fröken Peerenkaas the police had been in touch with the previous day: Anna Kristeva and Karen deBuijk.

Before he instructed the caretaker to open the green-painted door with his master key, Rooth bent down and shouted in through the letterbox. As he did so he noticed there was quite a large pile of mail on the floor in the hall, and concluded that in all probability the tenant had not been home for several days.

He stood up and gave the caretaker – a tall, fair-haired man with sleepy eyes and a burnt-out cigarette end in his mouth – the signal to unlock the door.

'Take it easy now!' he said when the door was open and the blond caretaker had left. 'Let's take our shoes off and leave them outside here on the landing, and creep inside like naked Indians.'

Naked? Sammelmerk wondered. Why *naked* Indians?

But she said nothing. Chief Inspector Reinhart had warned her that Rooth was a little odd.

'We don't know what to expect inside there,' said Rooth, 'but we must be prepared for the worst. The important thing is that we must not touch anything.'

'Huh,' said deBuijk. 'I don't want to be involved in this.'

'You *are* involved in this,' said Kristeva. 'You'd better accept that.'

Rooth entered the hall and beckoned the other three to follow him. At least there's no smell of a dead body, Sammelmerk noted optimistically.

'Stay here while I have a preliminary look round,' said Rooth. 'Then I'd like you two' – he nodded at the two friends – 'to go round the whole flat and see if you can discover anything unusual.'

'Unusual?' wondered deBuijk. 'What do you mean by "unusual"?'

'Anything that doesn't look like it usually does, that's all. Anything you haven't seen here before, or things that aren't where they usually are . . . You've both been here several times before. But don't touch anything, okay?'

'Of course we shan't touch anything,' said deBuijk. 'We're not complete idiots.'

Kristeva nodded, Inspector Sammelmerk sighed, and Rooth started to inspect the flat.

The first thought about a possible connection cropped up in Moreno's mind shortly after she had left the chief of police's office. She had sat in his greenhouse for an hour and a half, going through the documentation of the Surhonen affair with Hiller: comments had been made, both on the television and in the press, about the way in which the police had handled this delicate business which also involved a delegation of foreign police officers, and as usual Hiller had given several undertakings.

It struck her just after she had completed that distressing task. It was hardly a thought, in fact: more of a faint suspicion that flitted through her consciousness for a split second; but it left an impression even so.

And that impression suddenly became visible again not long afterwards when she sat down at a table in the canteen to eat her salad lunch. God only knows why, she thought, but all of a sudden, there it was. The suspicion.

That there might be a connection. Between the Strangler and that missing woman.

That he might have been the person Ester Peerenkaas had come up against.

Needless to say there was nothing specific to support this gratuitous hypothesis. Not a thing. And in all probability the chances were no more than one in a thousand. She started eating, and wondered why the thought had occurred to her. Presumably it was simply because the two tasks had collided by accident, merely because they both happened to be inside her head at the same time.

In more or less the same way that she used to connect true love with funeral parlours, because her first serious lover (she was about ten-and-a-half years old at the time, if she remembered rightly) happened to have a father who owned one.

Her suspicion was probably no stronger than that link, and when Reinhart came to join her she decided it would be silly to mention it.

Especially as Reinhart seemed to be more gloomy than usual. She couldn't help but wonder how he was. At first she managed to refrain from asking him straight out, but when he spilled coffee over his shirt and swore so loudly that his voice echoed all round the room, she put the question.

'I'm okay,' said Reinhart. 'It's just this damned case that is gnawing away at my soul all the time.'

'I didn't know you had a soul,' said Moreno: but the thought fell on stony ground. He simply ignored it.

'And then there's that other case as well,' he muttered instead. 'That missing woman. Have you spoken to Inspector Sammelmerk since yesterday?'

'No,' said Moreno. 'Why?'

Reinhart took a bite of his sandwich and thought for a while before answering.

'She spoke to one of the woman's friends, just like you did.

I bumped into her briefly this morning, and she'd been given this name.'

'What name?'

'I can't get it out of my head. Fröken Peerenkaas had mentioned the name of the man she was about to start a relationship with, and it's a name I can't get out of my head . . . I've been thinking about it for over two hours now. Damn and blast!'

'What was his name?' asked Moreno, and felt her heart beating faster.

'Brugger,' said Reinhart.

'Brugger?'

'Yes, Amos Brugger. I've looked it up in the telephone directory, but there's nobody of that name in Maardam and district . . . It rings a bell, but I can't think why. Amos Brugger . . . Is there the sound of a bell ringing in your pretty head when you hear that name?'

Moreno ignored the compliment, and listened out for bells. Five seconds passed, Reinhart was staring hard at her all the time, as if he were doing all he could to assist her.

'No,' she said in the end. 'I can't hear a single tinkle.'

'Damn and blast!' said Reinhart again. 'This smells of duck shit, as my mother used to say.'

He slid the sandwich to one side and lit his pipe instead.

32

After searching through Ester Peerenkaas's flat in Meijkstraat, Rooth and Sammelmerk walked as far as Café Renckmann just round the corner of the street leading down to Willemsgraacht. Peerenkaas's friends Kristeva and deBuijk had been thanked for their efforts and allowed to leave, and Rooth thought it was high time they had a bite to eat and an opportunity to summarize their impressions.

Sammelmerk had some difficulty in understanding what impressions he might be referring to, but she kept a straight face and played along.

'Well,' said Rooth as they sat down. 'That wasn't very productive.'

'No,' agreed Sammelmerk. 'Still, what we do know is that nothing happened in her flat. It looked very neat and tidy, I thought.'

'More or less like my own place,' said Rooth. 'But the fact that the two ladies couldn't even find so much as a strand of hair out of place must indicate that she hadn't had any strangers visiting her lately. Or what does your feminine intuition tell you?'

'I think that's right,' said Sammelmerk. 'But she hasn't

been at home either, for that matter ... Not since last Tuesday. The left side of my brain tells me that something odd is going on.'

Inspector Rooth was by now deeply involved with a Danish pastry, and didn't respond.

'We ought to pay a visit to that restaurant,' said Sammelmerk. 'Keefer's. Somebody might remember them, even though it was over a month ago. Or are there other things we ought to be doing?'

Rooth shook his head and carried on chewing.

'It's the only place we know for sure that she was together with this Brugger character ... But I don't really know. You are more familiar with the details of the case, it's up to you.'

Rooth swallowed and looked at the clock.

'That's not a bad idea,' he said. 'If we sit here for a bit longer, it will be time for lunch, and we can have it at Keefer's. I'm told they do a beef stroganoff that's up there with the best of them – and Reinhart likes us to take the initiative.'

So that was that.

'Brugger?' said Münster. 'No, it doesn't ring any bells. I'm afraid.'

'Not for me either,' said Inspector Krause, looking for a moment as if he'd just been informed that he'd failed an exam. 'Amos Brugger, did you say?'

'Yes,' said Reinhart with a sigh. 'That's apparently what he was called. And there's nobody by that name in the whole of this area, as far as we can tell. I suppose it's possible he came from further afield, but talk about Blind Date! Anyway, if you could chase the name up in other parts of the country, we can see if there's anything worth following up.'

'I'll do my best,' said Krause, and left the room.

Münster waited until he'd closed the door.

'Why are you putting so much effort into this missing person case?' he asked. 'I thought we had other priorities.'

Reinhart snorted and shuffled all the piles of documents on his desk around.

'Priorities? Do you mean Surhonen? Or are you suggesting that we turn over every bloody stone in the Kammerle–Gassel case one more time? Or what are you getting at?'

'I don't really know,' said Münster, rising to his feet. 'In any case, I think it's probably best to leave you in peace. You seem to be a bit premenstrual, if you'll pardon the expression.'

'Go to hell,' said Reinhart, looking round for something to hit him with – but Münster was already in the corridor.

The distance from Café Renckmann to Keefer's restaurant in Molnarstraat was no more than three hundred metres, but as it had started raining they took the car. Even so they had to walk quite a long way through the downpour – it was lunchtime, after all, and the shortage of parking spaces was as severe as usual.

Rooth thought it best to sort out the food first before turning their attention to the staff. Sammelmerk voiced no objections, and as it was quite early they managed to get a window table with a view over the canal.

'It's a bit much to hope that they will remember details about customers they had a month ago,' said Sammelmerk. 'Unless they've been here again since then, of course.'

'I would avoid that,' said Rooth. 'If I found a woman I wanted to kill, I hardly think I'd take her out to a restaurant several times before bumping her off. Certainly not the same one.'

'We don't know that he did kill her,' Sammelmerk pointed out. 'We don't even know that she's dead.'

'There's quite a lot we don't know,' said Rooth. 'On the other hand, we do know rather a lot about this particular aspect of this particular case. So I suppose that's why we keep making guesses. What was it like working up in Aarlach?'

Sammelmerk shrugged.

'I quite enjoyed it. But even there we had to guess our way forward at times, I must admit.'

'It goes with the territory,' said Rooth, looking around the half-empty premises. 'Anyway, this is what we'll do. When we get our food, I'll give the photograph to the waitress, and she can hawk it around her colleagues while we're eating. If we do that, it will take care of itself as it were, and we shan't have to do anything.'

'A good idea,' she said.

'I wasn't born yesterday,' said Rooth, with a routine smile.

Even if the method had a touch of genius, it didn't produce any results.

When Rooth and Sammelmerk left Keefer's nearly two

hours later, the whole of the staff on lunch duty – ten in all – had examined the picture of Ester Peerenkaas.

None of them could recall seeing her as a customer in the restaurant, neither on 8 December nor on any other occasion. Nor anywhere else, come to that. Of the nine staff, only four had been on duty on the evening in question, but none of those recalled having seen a gentleman wearing a red tie sitting at a table together with T. S. Eliot. Red ties did turn up occasionally, they said, especially around Christmas time, but books were very rarely observed. Irrespective of colour.

Then again, of course, nobody could swear to *not* having seen a couple answering to that description. On a routine evening there were some sixty or seventy customers to look after, and on a Friday there could easily be over a hundred.

'We understand,' said Rooth. 'In any case, many thanks. The beef wasn't too bad. Even if it was on the expensive side. How many more staff would there have been working on that particular evening? And how can we get in touch with them?'

A woman in her fifties with dyed blonde hair and wearing spectacles that must have weighed half a kilo, looking as if she were some kind of manager, explained that there would normally be a dozen or so members of staff working the evening shift, plus one or two extra on Fridays and Saturdays. Naturally she had no idea who had been taking orders and serving food on 8 December, but she gave Rooth a scrap of paper with a telephone number he could ring. If he called he would get through to the chief financial officer, one Zaida Mergens: she had access to all the staff and wages details.

'Excellent,' said Rooth, folding the paper and putting it away in an inside pocket. 'We'll no doubt be in touch again.'

'Perhaps you might like to come for dinner,' suggested the woman. 'If you do, I recommend that you book a table in advance. What's happened? Or maybe you're not allowed to tell us that?'

'We'd love to tell you,' said Rooth. 'The problem is, we have no idea.'

Detective Inspector Ewa Moreno had been clear for a long time what a perfect morning would look like.

After making passionate and deeply satisfying love to the man of her life, she would wake up well rested. Stretch like a cat for a while, and eat a substantial breakfast in bed while glancing through the morning paper. Sleep for another quarter of an hour, then take a long, satisfying shower.

Then she would be ready to go to work.

At the moment – in January 2001, shortly before her thirty-fourth birthday – there were two serious obstacles in the way of her experiencing one of those ideal mornings.

In the first place, she was not sure that she had yet found the man of her life – although it was becoming more and more likely that Mikael Bau would take on that role. If he still wanted to, that is. But there was nothing to suggest that was not the case, and something told her that the crucial moment was rapidly approaching.

In the second place, she would have to get up at about four o'clock in order to fulfil all the requirements.

As she raced down the stairs that morning after no more than half a cup of tea and two minutes in the shower, she wondered how it would be possible to make passionate and deeply satisfying love, and then wake up well rested at four o'clock?

Impossible. So those perfect mornings had nothing to do with the meaning of life, despite everything.

Besides, she had slept badly. She had been dreaming about the Kammerle girl and her classmates caked with black make-up – the two young ladies she had talked to in that cafe a few months ago. In the dream they had been on a beach – a large and deserted sandy beach, with Monica Kammerle crying her eyes out and crawling around, looking for her missing legs while her so-called friends mocked her and wound her up. Moreno herself was lying on a beach towel some way away, trying to read a book, but unable to do so thanks to the girls.

What gave her food for thought was her own role in the dream: she couldn't shake off the feeling of shame. She hadn't bothered at all about the crippled girl, in fact, and just hoped she would crawl off in another direction so that Moreno could read her book in peace and quiet.

As she stood waiting for the tram, she found herself thinking once again about the link that had occurred to her the previous evening. The thought that there could be a connection between the Kammerle case and the disappearance of Ester Peerenkaas.

Always believe in passing whims! she recalled the *Chief*

Inspector saying on one occasion. Give them a chance, at least, it doesn't cost you anything.

The tram arrived and she elbowed her way on board. She even managed to find a seat – between an overweight man reading the Bible and a woman looking like an unusually thin Barbie doll – and continued thinking about it.

She started recapitulating the grim fate of the isolated family in Moerckstraat – was 'family' the right word, in fact? It was just a matter of two people: a mother and her daughter. Could such constellations properly be called families?

'My family consists of one person,' she recalled reading somewhere. 'Me.'

Anyway, both of them were no longer with us. Martina and Monica Kammerle. Dead.

Killed.

There's a murderer on the loose, as the saying goes. Perhaps he had murdered several women? That woman up in Wallburg, for instance? And maybe he had – this is where the passing whim came into it – maybe he also had something to do with the disappearance of Ester Peerenkaas?

It seemed to be beyond question that the man behind it all was the wild card she had gone to meet at the restaurant. The man who called himself Amos Brugger.

Ester Peerenkaas had told her friend that he'd said that was his name.

Amos Brugger.

But there was nobody by that name in Maardam, Reinhart had announced, and he had also suggested that it must mean something.

Mean something? Moreno thought. Names don't usually mean anything at all, surely?

She looked out of the window. The tram was just pulling up at the Ruyders Plejn stop.

She checked her watch.

A quarter to nine. She had another sudden thought, and got off.

'The day's starting well,' said Van Veeteren. 'I hadn't expected to see such a pretty detective inspector among all these piles of paper.'

'Come off it,' said Moreno. 'A hundred years from now and we're all nothing but a pile of bones. I think it was the Chief . . . that it was you who taught me that.'

'You're probably right,' said Van Veeteren. 'On both counts. But if you have something to talk to me about, you're lucky. I'm not usually here at work at nine in the morning . . . Would you like some coffee?'

'If you can supply a rusk or something to go with it,' said Moreno. 'I didn't have time for breakfast this morning. Perhaps I ought to phone Reinhart and tell him I'm going to be a bit late. It's just an idea I've had . . . That I'd like to discuss with you.'

'Really?' said Van Veeteren, looking somewhat surprised. 'I have lots of ideas I'm only too happy to discuss. Blame yourself . . . Anyway, let's lock the door and retire to the kitchenette.'

*

'Well, what's it all about, as it says in the Koran?' he wondered when the cups were on the table and Moreno had just taken her first bite of the ciabatta bread he had heated up in the oven. 'I take it that you haven't called on me simply because you're hungry and are interested in books.'

'No – although I'm not really sure,' said Moreno. 'I just wanted to hear what you think. I had an idea, as I said . . .'

'Might one guess that it has to do with the Strangler again?' asked Van Veeteren, starting to roll a cigarette.

'Hmm,' said Moreno. 'Of course it has . . . But I suppose that wasn't too difficult to work out.'

'Nothing new has happened, has it? I haven't seen a word in the press for several weeks now.'

'It's at a stand-still,' said Moreno. 'But we've had reported a missing woman. I got the feeling that there might be a link. That's my idea.'

Van Veeteren finished rolling his cigarette and gave her a searching look.

'When?' he asked.

'About a week ago . . . Well, a week-and-a-half.'

'Here in Maardam?'

'Yes.'

'Age?'

'Thirty-five.'

'About the same as you, roughly speaking?'

'More or less,' admitted Moreno.

'Although you look more like twenty-five.'

'Come off it.'

Van Veeteren lit the cigarette.

'And what makes you think there might be a connection?'

Moreno hesitated for a few seconds before replying.

'Nothing,' she said. 'Just intuition.'

Van Veeteren snorted.

'For God's sake, woman! If you start calling intuition nothing, you've forfeited the right to assistance from the supernatural. Well?'

Moreno laughed.

'All right, I take it back. But the fact is that there aren't any tangible links . . .'

'Have you discussed this with Reinhart or Münster?'

'No. They might be thinking along the same lines, I don't know. I didn't think about it until yesterday.'

Van Veeteren inhaled and thought.

'Tell me,' he said. 'Tell me about this new woman.'

'Amos Brugger?' exclaimed Van Veeteren ten minutes later.

'Reinhart said the name rang a bell – that's what he said yesterday, at least. But he couldn't think of what the connection was.'

She looked up and met Van Veeteren's gaze. And stiffened.

Before he spoke she knew that he knew. There was no doubt about it.

His face seemed to have frozen in a strange way. Coagulated, perhaps. His mouth was half open, and a thin stream of smoke oozed slowly out of one corner and crawled up his cheek. His eyes seemed to be switched off. Or pointing inwards.

The expression only lasted for less than a second, but Moreno knew that this was how she would remember him. Always remember him. The *Chief Inspector*.

Like Rodin's famous Thinker, when the thought finally occurs to him and he raises his head from out of his hand.

'You're right,' he said. 'You can bet your life you're right. Shall I tell you who Amos Brugger is?'

'Please do . . .' said Moreno, swallowing. 'Are you saying . . .?'

Van Veeteren stood up and went into the bookshop. Returned half a minute later with three books that he placed on the table between them.

'Musil,' he explained. 'Robert Musil. *Der Mann ohne Eigenschaften* – The Man Without Qualities. One of the greatest works of the twentieth century. On a par with Kafka and Joyce, some people maintain. I'm inclined to agree with them.'

'Really?' said Moreno, picking up the first of the volumes.

'Unfinished, alas. He spent over twenty years writing it, if I remember rightly, but was never happy with the ending. Anyway, there is a murderer in the book. A murderer of women, to be more precise. A brilliant psychological portrait, in fact. Do you know what he's called?'

Moreno shook her head.

'He's called Moosbrugger,' said Van Veeteren, taking a swig of coffee.

'Moosbrugger? . . . Amos Brugger?'

'Exactly, said Van Veeteren. 'Or why not A. Moosbrugger . . . *I am A Moosbrugger* . . . I don't think it can get much clearer than that.'

'Oh my God . . .' said Moreno.

'Didn't he borrow a name out of a book the previous occasion as well?'

'Yes,' said Moreno. 'Benjamin Karren. We're not certain but we think he might have got it from an English crime novel from the thirties. You're right. So you think . . . ?'

'What do you think yourself?' asked Van Veeteren. 'Anyway, I suggest you hurry along to the police station and urge your colleagues to commit all available resources to this business.'

'I'm on my way already,' said Moreno, getting to her feet. 'Thank you . . . Thank you for your help. And for breakfast.'

'You're welcome,' said Van Veeteren. 'But make damned sure that I'm kept in the picture. Don't forget that I have a finger in the pie myself . . . If I hadn't sent that blasted priest packing, things would have been rather different now.'

'I promise,' said Moreno, hurrying out of the shop.

The perfect morning? she thought. For Christ's sake . . .

33

'So it's one hundred per cent clear,' growled Reinhart. 'Hands up all those who've read Musil.'

He stared at his colleagues and allowed five seconds of silence to flow past before slowly raising his right hand, then lowering it again.

'One,' he ascertained. 'What a bloody scandal! In this brains trust there is just one worn-out chief inspector who has ploughed his way through *The Man Without Qualities*, and he didn't have the nous to see the connection. What a shower, what a useless shower!'

'We'll let you off this once,' said Rooth. 'Is it any good?'

'A brilliant book,' Reinhart maintained. 'Absolutely brilliant. But it's a quarter of a century since I worked my way through it, so I'm also prepared to go easy on myself. Anyway, Van Veeteren's explanation means we know where we stand now. I'll offer odds of ten to one on fröken Peerenkaas having come up against the same lunatic as our victims last autumn. Does anybody disagree?'

'Maybe we should be careful of being too hasty,' said Münster cautiously. 'But I agree that it's a major breakthrough . . . Amos Brugger must be a reference to Moosbrugger. We seem to be dealing with a pretty unusual character.'

'Unusual?' said Jung. 'You can say that again. What's his point, using these strange names? If he really feels he must introduce himself to his victims, why couldn't he just use any name that came into his head? Rooth, for instance.'

'What?' said Rooth.

'You could think that,' said Reinhart. 'But this name fixation must tell us quite a bit about him, surely?'

He looked around again, with a question mark engraved on his forehead.

'I volunteer to take a week's leave and read Musil's book,' said Jung. 'It must be pretty thick?'

'My edition has about twelve hundred pages,' said Reinhart. 'No, I reckon it was enough that you were already allowed to read a crime novel in working hours. But what can we say about our contemporary Moosbrugger? What do we know about him?'

Nobody spoke for a few seconds.

'He has strong hands,' said Moreno. 'But we've said that before.'

'He likes playing games,' said Sammelmerk.

Reinhart nodded.

'Yes, it seems so. We can take it for granted that he's mad – but there's method in his madness, to quote another great writer.'

'*Hamlet*,' said Rooth. 'Even I know that. Shall I tell you who wrote it as well?'

'That won't be necessary,' said Reinhart with a smile. 'You can have a brownie point even so. Tell us something more about our strangler instead.'

'He's well educated,' said Krause.

'He reads books, at least,' said Moreno.

'He's bold,' said Münster. 'If he did in fact kill Ester Peerenkaas, it was pretty cold-blooded of him to take her to a restaurant first. A place where anybody at all could have seen them together.'

'He might have chosen a table hidden away in a corner,' said Sammelmerk. 'Rooth and I checked up on that when we were at Keefer's: there are several tables that are more or less out of sight. But of course, he couldn't have been totally invisible – not to the staff, at least.'

'Hang on a minute,' said Jung. 'Hadn't he ordered a table, using a name? In which case he might have called himself Amos Brugger when he did that as well. That might tell us a bit more about how he—'

'Unfortunately not,' said Reinhart. 'Isn't that so, Rooth?'

'Yes,' said Rooth. 'We checked at Keefer's this morning. They still had the lists of table orders, but there was nobody by that name that evening . . . Or the evening before, come to that. But they had quite a lot of bookings for two customers round about eight o'clock on the eighth of December: that's the time we should be aiming at, so it must presumably have been one of those couples.'

'I assume that we might eventually discover what name he used then,' said Münster. 'Assuming we can trace all the others. But I don't quite see what good that would do us.'

'Probably no good at all,' said Reinhart. 'He probably won't have used his real name in any case. But are there any conclusions we can draw about herr Kerran-Brugger? Even if we're only repeating what we've concluded already.'

'Handsome and well-built,' said Moreno. 'Ester Peerenkaas fell for him, and she wasn't in the habit of falling for anybody who happened to come along, according to what her friend said about her.'

'Between thirty-five and forty-five, presumably,' said Sammelmerk.

'He doesn't kill them straight away,' said Jung. 'He starts a relationship first – that's rather unusual in this line of business, as I understand it.'

'Line of business?' said Krause.

'Like a cat that plays with its prey before devouring it,' suggested Rooth.

'Ugh,' said Moreno.

Reinhart pointed at Krause with the stem of his pipe.

'Krause,' he said. 'Would you mind noting down all these points. I'm not exactly a fan of perpetrator profiling, but this particular bastard seems to lend himself to the practice unusually well.'

Krause looked up.

'I've done that already,' he said, tapping at his notebook with his pen.

'Well done,' said Reinhart. 'I should have realized that. Anyway, our main line of attack now is that Ester Peerenkaas has been murdered, and we shall devote all our resources into following that up. But officially, she's just a missing person – don't forget that. We'll soft-pedal the link with Musil as far as the press is concerned – those halfwitted berks won't have a clue who Musil is anyway. Go easy on the link with previous cases as well, even if we need all the help we can get from the media. It's the same unholy alliance as usual, no special tricks. Anything else?'

There was nothing else, it seemed.

Not as far as the murderer was concerned, that is. But there was plenty of speculation with regard to what might have happened to Ester Peerenkaas. Rather grim speculation: even if they tried to bear in mind Intendent Münster's warning about jumping over-hastily to conclusions, it was difficult to imagine any optimistic possibilities.

It was also possible to speculate about the timing, and they duly did.

If it could be assumed that Kerran-alias-Brugger was behind the murder of Kristine Kortsmaa in Wallburg as well, and that Ester Peerenkaas had suffered the same fate, the number of victims was now five. The number of known victims, that is. Spread over about eighteen months, more or less. One-and-a-half years.

The first one in Wallburg in June 1999.

Numbers two, three and four in Maardam in September 2000.

Number five in the same town in January 2001.

Inspector Krause noted down these facts as well, and read them out.

A period of silence followed.

Then Reinhart leaned forward over the table and pointed his index finger in the air as a sort of warning.

'Let's avoid using the term "serial murderer",' he said. 'In theory we could be looking for five different murderers – even if I myself wouldn't bet so much as a matchstick on that possibility. And in theory, we don't know if number five really is a victim. She might just have run off with that Brugger bastard, and they could be lounging back lapping up sun and champagne on some picturesque little island in the South Pacific at this very moment. It's not impossible to grow tired of the charms of Maardam in January, perhaps I don't need to remind you of that – and for as long as we don't find her, she remains officially a missing person.'

'Well said,' commented Rooth. 'Even if we do have our thoughts. I must say I don't like the way she has disappeared . . . I'm not exactly enthusiastic about murder either, come to that: but if you have been murdered, you surely don't need to disappear as well. It's difficult to make sense of anything until the dead body is found. What the hell are we going to do? What are we going to do right now, I mean?'

Reinhart checked his watch.

'I assume that's a roundabout way of proposing a coffee break before we start allocating specific duties?'

'Such a thought had never occurred to me,' said Rooth. 'But if you're desperate for a cup of coffee, don't let me stand in your way.'

★

The allocation of duties lasted over two hours, and eventually took the form – at least in Inspector Krause's spiral notebook – of a five-point programme.

In the first place there should be an immediate and wide-ranging search for the missing thirty-five-year-old Maardam woman Ester Peerenkaas. Or at least, as immediate as was possible in practice. The chief inspector promised to remain at his desk smoking and preparing statements after the others had gone home to feed the chickens. Or whatever they usually did when they left work.

Secondly, and following on from the Wanted notices, there should be a comprehensive appeal to everybody who had visited Keefer's restaurant in Molnarstraat on 8 December the previous year to get in touch with the police in Maardam. For obvious reasons, this also landed on Reinhart's desk.

Thirdly, everybody who was acquainted with, or in one capacity or another was regularly in some kind of contact with the missing fröken Peerenkaas – friends, relatives, colleagues – should be interviewed. For obvious reasons it was difficult to forecast how many people might be concerned in such a complicated operation, but for the time being Jung and Krause were put in charge of it.

In the fourth place, it was decided that renewed contact should be established with Inspector Baasteuwel in Wallburg, more specifically to look once again at the Kristine Kortsmaa case in an attempt to find possible links with the September and January cases in Maardam. Inspector Moreno volunteered for this task.

And finally, it was decided to continue to uphold productive contacts with the bookseller at Krantze's Antiquarian Bookshop in Kupinskis gränd, one herr Van Veeteren.

'So, that's that then,' said Chief Inspector Reinhart after Krause had read out the programme once more. He wondered if anybody had anything to add.

But it was already twenty minutes to seven in the evening, and nobody could think of anything to say.

Ewa Moreno had just finished vacuuming the living room, taking a shower and opening a bottle of wine, when there was a ring at the door.

Irene Sammelmerk had a bouquet of red and yellow gerbera daisies in one hand, and a carrier bag of Chinese food in the other.

'A hell of a good idea, this,' she said. 'We need to be almost lying down to eat it – I don't have the strength to sit upright.'

'Same here,' said Moreno, ushering her in.

They had finally got round to arranging a meeting on their own. It was about time, too. Plan A had been a visit to a restaurant, of course, but when they happened to meet in the canteen at lunchtime, they had only needed to look at each other for a second to know that neither of them felt like sitting around in a public place.

Not in mid-January, when they were feeling exhausted and washed out.

Not with masses of other people hanging around and disturbing them.

What was needed was a comfy sofa.

And no cooking, God forbid.

So a Chinese takeaway and a bottle of wine in Moreno's cosy two-room flat in Falckstraat was just what the doctor ordered. An ideal solution.

'Excellent,' said Sammelmerk an hour later. 'I don't understand why we insist on cooking food seven days a week in our family.'

'Seven?' wondered Moreno.

'Well, five to seven,' said Sammelmerk. 'Sometimes the computer genius takes the brood out to a hamburger bar, and sometimes we settle for a pizza. I had a friend up in Aarlach who wouldn't hear of her children having less than two healthy home-cooked meals per day. She had her first heart attack when she was forty-six. Her two children are nervous wrecks. So much for that . . .'

'Yes, everybody's short of time nowadays,' said Moreno.

'Or they divide it up badly,' said Sammelmerk. 'Some people work their arses off, and others have nothing better to do than sit around scratching them.'

Moreno laughed.

'Yes, there's no denying that the balance could often be better than it is. But you have got your family sorted out now, I take it?'

'Oh yes indeed,' said Sammelmerk, taking a sip of wine. 'I can't complain. What about you? When are you going to take the momentous step? It would be stupid to wait until the menopause.'

Moreno hesitated, but only for a second.

'He lives here in the same building,' she said. 'On the next floor down. I'm the one with my foot on the brakes.'

'Why's that? Have you been burnt?'

Moreno thought that over. It was a good question. Had she been burnt?

Not really, if truth were told. You had to reckon with the occasional scratch and the odd dent in your soul as you tramped along the path of thorns that was life. She had birthmarks, of course, but she hadn't suffered any more than anybody else.

She didn't have much to complain about. In fact.

'No,' she said. 'Not burnt. Just a bit scorched at the edges. I suppose I'm just a bit sluggish ... And hard to please, perhaps.'

'Like our missing woman?'

'Not really. I shall never turn up at a restaurant on a blind date in any case, I promise you that. Do you think you could find yourself a man like that?'

Sammelmerk shrugged.

'I've no idea, to tell you the truth,' she said. 'I met my Janos when we were twenty-one. We have three kids and we've both been unfaithful ... I simply don't know how to find my way through the labyrinth of love. I'm not sure I want to know either.'

Moreno smiled.

'What about your lover?'

'He was a copper,' said Sammelmerk. 'That's the way it goes, I suppose. Cheers.'

'I understand,' said Moreno. 'Cheers . . . It's great to see you outside the police station at last.'

'This Kerran . . . Or Brugger . . .' said Sammelmerk.

'What about him?'

'What do you think about him?'

'Think? What exactly do you mean?'

'Well, what sort of a person do you think he is?'

Moreno swirled the wine around in her glass.

'I've no idea. Or rather, I do have an idea of course, but I haven't constructed a detailed psychological portrait of him. But it's obvious he's yet another of those perverted, frustrated stallions . . . There are a lot of them around.'

'There certainly are,' said Sammelmerk. 'Most crimes of violence are committed by aggressive males between twenty and forty, of course, blokes who didn't get their end away although they badly wanted to – but of course, deep down they are kind and gentle.'

'Bang on,' said Moreno.

'That's the way it is, unfortunately,' said Sammelmerk. 'But the bloke we're after doesn't have sex with his victims, neither before nor after, it seems. For Christ's sake, he just kills them. Why does he do it? That's what I can't understand.'

'He's sick.'

'Of course he's sick. But perhaps it's possible to diagnose his illness?'

'It could be. Huh, I suppose the problem is that we are so

badly constructed in the biological sense, if we try looking into the crystal ball, as it were.'

'Eh?' said Sammelmerk. 'I think you need to explain yourself a bit better than that.'

Moreno clasped her hands behind her head and decided to spell things out.

'Well,' she said, 'what I mean is that men – if they just follow their instincts and basic needs – are programmed to achieve sexual satisfaction within about twenty seconds . . . So the Good Lord can hardly have expected that we women would get any pleasure out of that, surely? Don't you think?'

'I understand that God is a bachelor,' said Sammelmerk with a wry smile. 'But they usually learn what to do, the ones – or rather the one – that I know.'

'In time, yes,' said Moreno. 'That's right. But you must agree surely that it causes a lot of unnecessary suffering, this difference in tempo.'

Sammelmerk leaned back in her corner of the sofa and burst out laughing.

'This difference in tempo!' she snorted. 'My God, yes! You certainly have a point. But what about our friend Kerran-Brugger? Why do you think he does it? From his point of view. If we try to penetrate his perverted mind.'

Moreno took a deep drink of wine and thought about that. Blew out a candle whose flame was coming dangerously close to her cuff.

'Power,' she said eventually. 'If you want a one-word answer. If you can't get love from the person you desire, you can at least get submission . . . You can control the object of your desire. It's a motive that's as old as the hills, but it's probably a variation on that which drives our strangler. That's what I think, at least.'

'Very likely,' agreed Sammelmerk with a frown. 'I remember reading something once: "When a man says no to a woman, she wants to die. When a woman says no to a man, he wants to kill." – That seems to sum it up rather neatly, don't you think?'

'In a nutshell,' said Moreno. 'We're on pretty good form this evening, aren't we?'

'It must be the wine,' said Sammelmerk. 'And the company. Anyway, I'll be blowed if it isn't time for me to go and see to my flock.'

Moreno looked at the clock.

'Half past eleven. Ah well, another working day tomorrow, I suppose.'

'The first of many,' said Sammelmerk with a sigh. 'I think I'll have to ask you to ring for a taxi. I've no great desire to come up against unknown men in the dark.'

'"When a woman says no to a man . . ."' said Moreno, standing up. 'Yes there's a lot of truth in that. Ugh.'

'Ugh indeed,' said Sammelmerk. 'I hope we find him soon.'

'It's a matter of time,' said Moreno, picking up the telephone. 'Only a matter of time.'

34

Five minutes before Inspector Rooth was due to meet Karen deBuijk, he was seized by acute depression.

He had just entered the square Grote Torg from Zwillesteeg, and very nearly fallen into the arms of Jasmina Teuwers. He would have had nothing against that – in different circumstances. They had both attended Italian classes, and also met as a couple three times in November and December – at a cafe, a cinema and a restaurant, in that order, and although those meetings could best be described as very slow progress, there had nevertheless been some progress made.

Or at least, Rooth thought that was the case.

Until this grey, damp, windswept January morning when their eyes had met and he felt as if his heart had just burst.

Jasmina Teuwers had not been alone. Anything but. She was very obviously in close contact with a superficially handsome type in a light-brown ulster and with a ponytail. His arm was wrapped around her shoulders, they were gazing into each other's eyes, and laughing at some shared joke.

Until she became aware of Rooth for just a fraction of a second.

A podgy lady with a dachshund blundered her way in between him and the loving couple, and they didn't even need to pretend they hadn't seen one another. Rooth and Teuwers, that is. They continued on their way as if nothing had happened. *Tra la perduta gente.*

A ponytail! Rooth thought when the analytical side of his brain started working again some five seconds later. Bloody hell!

Frailty, thy name is woman!

He staggered on across the square as far as Olde Maarweg. Karen deBuijk lived in one of the old warehouses that had been converted into flats from the mid-1990s onwards – way beyond the means of a mere detective inspector, for instance. DeBuijk's flat comprised just one large room, but it was at least fifty square metres, and the exposed wooden beams in the ceiling were ideal if one had any intention of hanging oneself.

Thought Rooth as he sat down together with his depression in a basket chair under a roof window. The sky was grey, he noted. He cleared his throat and took a notebook and pencil out of his briefcase as if in a dream.

I've done this ten thousand times before, he thought. I wonder how many bloody notebooks I've filled and how many bloody pencils I've worn out?

How many pointless questions I've churned out, and how many daft answers I've written down?

Karen deBuijk had left him alone for a moment, but now came back in carrying a ridiculously small tray with two ugly coffee cups. And a dish of what looked like dog biscuits. She sat down in the other basket chair, crossed her legs and smiled faintly and somewhat insecurely at him. He registered that she was pretty. Suntanned and blonde-haired.

The devil's illusion, he thought. From today onwards I shall never ever look at a woman again.

'Well?' she said, and he realized that it was time to get started.

'I'm not feeling too good,' he said.

That wasn't what he had intended saying, but he could hear for himself that those were the words he produced.

'I can see that,' said deBuijk. 'Have a drink of coffee.'

'Really?' said Rooth. 'Can you really see that?'

'Yes ... But I thought you'd come to talk about Ester Peerenkaas rather than the state of your soul.'

'I don't have a soul,' said Rooth.

'If you can feel lousy, that must mean you have a soul. That's where the pain comes.'

Rooth thought that one over. It sounded plausible.

'Okay,' he said. 'Just a drop. But what the hell, Ester Peerenkaas it is. What do you think?'

'What do I think?'

'Yes.'

'About what?'

'About all kinds of things. About what's happened, for instance. About that man she had begun meeting. You spent a couple of weeks with her on one of the Canary Islands recently: my experience tells me that in those circumstances women tend to talk to each other. But correct me if I'm wrong – I don't understand women.'

She laughed, but put her hand over her mouth – as if laughing was wrong in the circumstances. A friend who had gone missing and a depressed police officer.

'Please forgive me. But you're funny. It's true, of course.'

'What's true? That I'm wrong?'

'No, that we talked quite a lot while we were on holiday.'

'What about?'

'About everything under the sun, of course.'

'What, for instance?'

She paused, and took a bite of a dog biscuit.

'That little spot of danger, for instance.'

'That little spot of danger?' said Rooth.

'Yes.'

'Go on.'

'That little spot of danger,' said deBuijk again, sucking in her lower lip like a little schoolgirl, and looking too enchanting for words . . . 'What it is that makes one interested in a man, but which is also . . . well, dangerous. Exciting.'

'You don't say,' said Rooth, starting to draw a matchstick man with horns in his notebook. 'What exactly do you mean?'

'That's the way it is with men,' said deBuijk, and it struck him that she had effortlessly struck a chord of intimacy that he didn't feel he had earned, and that some idiotic impulse told him to destroy.

'Really?' he said in a neutral tone.

'That man, Brugger. She talked a bit about him. Only a bit, mind you. She said she felt ambivalent about him.'

'Ambivalent?' said Rooth, drawing a vertical line right through the middle of his matchstick man's head.

HÅKAN NESSER

'Yes. She said she felt attracted to him, but at the same time there was something that made her feel unsure. I suppose she didn't quite know what to make of him.'

'Perhaps that little spot of danger wasn't all that little?' Rooth suggested.

'Yes, maybe . . . Ugh.'

'Did she say anything about what he looked like?'

'No, only that he was rather attractive. I think she said his hair was dark.'

'And she'd only met him once?'

'Yes.'

'When was that?'

'At Keefer's in December.'

'What was he wearing?'

'She didn't say.'

'Job?'

'I think he had a business.'

'What sort of business?'

'I don't know. But he was self-employed. I don't really know what he did. We didn't talk all that much about him. It was mainly on the plane home – she was going to meet him a few days later . . . Are you really sure that he has something to do with her disappearance?'

Rooth took a dog biscuit.

'Pretty sure,' he said. 'Various things point in that direction.'

'What sort of things?'

She hasn't read Musil either, Rooth thought. We have something in common, at least.

'I can't go into that, I'm afraid,' he said. 'What else did she have to say about Brugger?'

'Not a lot, in fact. She talked about their advert – hers and Anna Kristeva's. I didn't know they went in for that kind of thing . . . Anyway, we talked more about that than about Brugger.'

Rooth munched away at the biscuit, and thought hard.

'Why did she feel ambivalent about him?' he asked. 'Surely she must have said something more about that?'

DeBuijk also thought hard.

'No, I don't think so. Maybe "ambivalent" is a bit over the top . . . She claimed that she liked the man when she met him. They sat talking for quite some time at that restaurant, it seems, and then she spoke to him on the phone once or twice, and . . . well, she evidently wasn't sure how interested in him she really was. Whether or not there was a solid basis to build on.'

'I see,' said Rooth, examining his matchstick-man who now had both a tail and large breasts. 'You say they spoke on the phone: do you know if she rang him, or whether it was the other way round?'

'How on earth would I know that?'

'I'm only asking in an attempt to discover if she had his telephone number.'

'Ah,' said deBuijk. 'No, I haven't the slightest idea, as I said before. What . . . What do you think has happened? I mean—'

'It's too early to have any theories about that,' said Rooth.

How many times have I churned out that line, he wondered. Or words to that effect. It must be several hundred. He turned over to a new page in his notebook, and sat quietly for a while.

'She could defend herself,' said deBuijk out of the blue.

'Eh?' said Rooth.

'Defend herself. Ester could do that.'

'Against men?'

Jujitsu? he wondered. Karate? Tear gas?

'A woman can find herself in difficult situations,' explained deBuijk.

'You don't need to tell me that,' said Rooth. 'I've been a police officer for twenty years. How could she defend herself?'

'There are all sorts of ways,' said deBuijk.

'I know,' said Rooth.

'Ester used hydrofluoric acid.'

'Hydrofluoric acid?'

'Yes. She always carried a little bottle in her handbag which she could throw into the face of a man if he went too far . . . She showed me it.'

Good God, thought Rooth, wondering if it was usual practice. Did lots of women wander around with bottles of hydrofluoric acid in their pretty little handbags? Or some similar brew. Had Jasmina Teuwers been sitting there, fingering a similar little bottle, when they had dinner at Mefisto's a few days before Christmas?

'I see,' he said. 'It sounds horrendous . . . That kind of stuff can produce terrible injuries, can't it?'

DeBuijk shrugged.

'I don't really know. But I suppose that's the point.'

'Has she ever used it?'

'No . . . But she's a tough cookie, our Ester. When it comes to men, that is. Nowadays. I take it you know about how her ex ran off with their daughter?'

'Yes,' said Rooth. 'I know about that.'

There followed a few seconds of silence once again, and deBuijk squirmed uneasily in her chair.

'Ugh,' she said. 'I'm scared stiff something has happened to her . . . Something awful. She's simply not the type to hide herself away like this for such a long time. Do you really have no idea if . . . ?'

'No,' lied Rooth. 'I'm afraid not. But we're working all out to get to the bottom of this business.'

She hesitated for a moment, then she looked him in the eye and said:

'Do you think she's . . . dead?'

Yes, Rooth thought. I think so.

'No,' he said. 'She's gone missing. That's not the same thing.'

'Really?' said deBuijk.

Huh, what the hell can I say? he thought.

'There are lots of other possible explanations,' he said.

Can you give me a single one, Mr Detective Inspector? he asked himself when he emerged into the street again.

Just one single explanation that would imply Ester Peerenkaas was still alive?

What had Reinhart suggested? Sun and champagne in the South Pacific?

That would have to be the only possibility. He couldn't think of any others, and as he crossed over Grote Torg the image of Jasmina Teuwers and that bloody ponytail cropped up again.

Evening classes in Italian! thought Inspector Rooth as he kicked to one side a fat pigeon that hadn't enough sense to get out of his way.

Lasciate ogni speranza, voi ch'entrate!

He was damned if next week he wouldn't go there and stick that notice on the classroom door. Abandon hope, all ye who enter here!

Then he would never set foot inside the building again.

'Can you explain what happened?' asked Jung, leaning over the counter.

The woman on the other side sighed deeply, as if his question incorporated some sort of attack on the peace and quiet of her working environment.

'It's not exactly rocket science,' she said. 'You just put them in, and then you take them out – assuming you've had a written answer, that is.'

'Put them in and take them out?' said Jung. 'What do you mean by that?'

She shook her head almost imperceptibly, presumably in response to what she perceived to be his mental capacity, and raised her head from the computer.

'People place an advert and provide a contact address. Punters respond, and after a few days the advertisers come to collect the responses.'

'I see. So these responses stay here with you for that short period of time?'

'Yes, of course. I don't know what the practice is as far as other newspapers are concerned, but here at *Allgemejne* we've been using the same system for twenty-five years. Any responses that haven't been collected after a month are thrown away.'

'Do you get a lot of these adverts?'

'A lot? You can bet your life we do. A few thousand a week, at the very least.'

'Wow,' said Jung. 'So we're looking for a response that presumably came in towards the end of November last year. I assume it's impossible to find out any details about it now?'

'Too right,' said the woman. 'It will have been either collected or thrown away. What kind was it, incidentally?'

'Kind?'

'Boats or stamps or pets or dating or—'

'Dating, I'd have thought,' said Jung.

'What kind?' she asked again.

'The usual . . .' said Jung.

'Him looking for her, or vice versa?'

'Vice versa.'

'Huh,' said the woman. 'Those are the most popular ones in fact. About ten a day.'

'So many?' said Jung. 'How many responses do they usually get?'

He realized that the hope of finding any clues about Amos Brugger in this way had long since flown out of the window; but he was beginning to get curious.

'That depends,' said the woman. 'Young women get twenty to thirty per week. Older ones ten to fifteen. But now I really must get on with my work. I assume you've had answers to all your questions?'

'Yes, thank you very much,' said Jung. 'I had no idea there were so many people indulging in . . . in this kind of activity.'

'Huh,' muttered the woman. 'There's no end of lonely people around.'

That certainly seems to be the case, thought Jung as he settled down in his car again. Paradoxically enough, that seemed to be the lowest common denominator among people. Loneliness.

Why on earth did I come here at all? he asked himself. Anna Kristeva had said they had thrown away the response from Amos Brugger – as they had done with all the other letters hoping to exploit the favours on offer from her and Ester Peerenkaas. He would never have even dreamt that the newspaper would retain a copy.

Besides, he had been acting on his own initiative. Reinhart hadn't told him to follow it up – although he might well have given it his blessing.

That morning's meeting had convinced him that now was the time to act on one's own initiative. And to chase after straws.

After a while Jung realized he was sitting in his car with his hands on the steering wheel, staring out through the windscreen at the rain. Sitting there and thinking about that Kerran-Brugger character.

He probably doesn't have a wide circle of friends either, he thought, thinking back to his conversation in the newspaper office. Perhaps he's the most lonely bastard of them all. Yes, that's highly likely to be the case.

It was hardly an earth-shattering thought. Murderers were seldom good mixers.

He realized he was feeling cold. Dawn had passed over into dusk. He checked his watch, started the car, and drove off to collect Maureen from work.

35

Münster switched off the engine, but left the music on. Dexter Gordon, the tenor saxophonist, live from the Village Vanguard in the early 1950s.

He had been given the CD by Reinhart. You'll think better if you have a sax in your ear, he had said.

Perhaps Reinhart was right. The atmosphere inside the car wasn't that of the usual barren desert, and there was a melancholy sharpness in the tone that could well help to banish the sludge polluting his brain.

He was parked in Moerckstraat. It was half past four in the afternoon, rain was drizzling down and a dirty, dusky gloom enveloped the housing estate in a sort of compassionate shroud. You didn't need to see it.

But maybe it wasn't really that bad, Münster thought. No worse than a lot of other places, in any case. The whole town looked pretty awful at this time of year. The bluish-greyness and the frosty mists. The rain and the persistent winds blowing in from the sea . . . No, there was very little chance of Maardam ever being allocated the Winter Olympic Games, that was for sure.

He contemplated the buildings with their frequent patches

of damp. Most windows were still dark. Presumably people haven't come home from work yet, Münster thought. Or haven't noticed that it's getting dark.

Or haven't had the strength to shake off their lethargy and switch the lights on, perhaps. There must be a high proportion of unemployed and people on the sick list in a housing estate like this one. The three windows of the flat where Martina and Monica Kammerle had lived were all dark. Münster knew that the furniture and household goods were in store, but that no new tenants had moved in. He wondered why. Did people still believe that it was dangerous to live in a building where somebody had recently been murdered? Maybe. People were more superstitious than one might think.

But he suspected that it was difficult to let flats here irrespective of that. Stopeka, as the district was called, was one of the least attractive areas of Maardam as a whole, and the developers had probably over-reached themselves. Strict curbs had been placed on immigration in recent years, so it was not easy to find natural tenants for a 1970s ghetto, and not surprising that there were empty flats here and there.

He sighed. Do something! Reinhart had instructed him. Anything at all. Try to make some sense of this damned case – I'm making as much progress as an ice skater in a paddy field.

Yes, they really were stuck. Münster had no objections to Reinhart's analysis. New cases came and went at the police station, but with regard to the murders of the priest and the two women in Moerckstraat, over four months had now passed with barely a glimpse of a clue of any kind. Apart from that business of the names. Benjamin Kerran and Amos Brugger. Names the murderer himself had let slip, possibly in order to tease the authorities – it was easy to imagine him grinning sardonically somewhere in the background. A long way away, at the far end of a dark cul-de-sac.

The link with the disappearance of Ester Peerenkaas was far from one hundred per cent established, of course, but Münster believed it. As did all the others, as far as he could judge. It made sense. There was a pattern. Even if the similarities were shadowy rather than clear-cut as yet, it was easy to imagine the same culprit behind the Peerenkaas murder as behind the two other murders – and also in the Kortsmaa case in Wallburg last summer.

But it was only a suspicion, no more than that. Not the slightest trace of anything more concrete. After all this time, and all these efforts . . . No, it was not difficult to understand Reinhart's feelings of impotence. Not at all. They wanted to believe in something, and so they believed in a link. Perhaps there was no more substance to it than that? Münster sighed, and glared at the black windows.

Behind them, Kerran-Brugger had murdered Martina Kammerle. Possibly her daughter as well, although that murder was more likely to have taken place somewhere else. It seemed highly implausible that he would have removed the body of one of his victims but left the other one where it was. He hadn't been in a hurry. He'd had all the time in the world, it seemed, especially when you thought of how long he must have spent wiping away all the fingerprints.

He must have visited that flat several times even before the murders. How often?

Nobody knew. Probably not all that often, Münster thought. None of the neighbours had noticed him. Fru Paraskevi thought she had heard a voice, that was all.

So quite sporadically, in all probability, and for quite a short period of time. About a month at most? A few weeks?

The most likely background was an affair with Martina Kammerle. Possibly even the only explanation. But why had he felt compelled to kill her?

Compelled? Münster thought. Crap. Lunatics feel compelled to do anything that clicks inside their sick minds.

What about the daughter? How did she fit into the picture? Had she witnessed the murder of her mother, or was simply knowing who he was a sufficient reason? Was it just too dangerous for him to have a living witness still around? Had she played some additional role? If so, what? . . .

Stop it now! Münster told his own thoughts. That's quite enough! I'm making it sound as if he had legitimate reasons for killing Martina Kammerle, but not Monica. My engine's running in neutral, they are the same questions as we were asking in November, the same damned ice skating in a paddy field that is keeping Reinhart busy, the same bloody . . .

He turned up the volume of the music in order to increase the stimulus. Dexter Gordon's sax was screaming and wailing now. Harsh, alienating screams in a tone that wouldn't have been out of place in a jet engine.

What about the names, though? he thought. Kerran and Brugger. Why did the murderer think it was necessary to flaunt these sinister literary characters? What was the point?

He leaned the seat back as far as it would go. Closed his eyes and spent a few minutes trying to convince himself that there might be a new way of approaching the problem – something they hadn't thought about. A clue they had missed, a possibility they hadn't tested.

But he found nothing. Because there wasn't anything, he concluded. We have done all that we could. The fact that we haven't got anywhere is because it's all so irrational. The reasons and motives originate in the same perversions that tell him he must kill. That is the root of all his evil – his accursed strangler-brain: we shan't be able to understand why he does what he does until we find him. And perhaps not even then.

But he's a well-read person, that's beyond all doubt. An academic, perhaps. Those who have studied at university are always the worst, Reinhart had declared the other day. The more they use their brains, the more likely it is that they'll go off the rails.

Münster found it hard to go along with such a depressing claim . . . It implied consequences that were too absurd to contemplate, and the officer in charge of the investigation had been very tired these last few days.

He started thinking about loneliness instead.

The loneliness that everybody experienced, but that of Martina and Monica Kammerle in particular. They must have felt very isolated, incredibly so. They had lived there behind those dark windows, and their world didn't seem to have extended all that far beyond the cramped three-roomed flat. They had had each other, presumably – a sick mother and her isolated daughter. No social contacts – apart from a man who killed them both when he thought the time was ripe . . . What a depressing state of affairs: but that is evidently how things were. Exactly like that. Some people's lot is allocated in so miserly a fashion, Münster thought. They never have a chance to influence the course of their lives.

Not the slightest chance. Monica Kammerle lived to the age of sixteen. Sixteen! His own son Bart would reach that age two years from now.

That thought crawled around in his brain like a freezing cold worm, and he shuddered uncontrollably. What kind of a monster would wipe out a sixteen-year-old girl? Take away her life? Kill her, saw off her legs and bury her among the dunes at the edge of the sea?

Saw off her legs!

He felt fury welling up inside him – a fury that was like an old acquaintance he could never get rid of. A hopeless and desperate relation that constantly reared its ugly head and held him captive by means of its inescapable blood relationship. Anger and impotence.

Was there really any logic behind actions like this? Patterns that could be discovered?

Oh yes. He knew that was entirely possible. If only one could overcome one's disgust, suppress one's personal feelings of impotence and fling wide the gates – then, perhaps, it might be possible to detect indications.

But what? he thought. What am I looking for? The portrait of a murderer? Would it be possible to establish that at this stage? Of course not! We don't know a thing, for Christ's sake.

He switched off the music. It was a piano solo now. Did there always have to be a piano solo in a performance of jazz music? he wondered. That wasn't something it was appropriate to think about just now, it was somehow too lightweight. Like a thin, blue cloud of smoke. He made a mental note to ask Reinhart about that. If there were CDs with exclusively woodwind. Or woodwind, bass and percussion, perhaps?

Intendent Münster shook his head. Took one final look at the unlit and meaningless windows, and started the engine.

He drove slowly through the narrow streets of Stopeka. It was high time: his badminton match with the *Chief Inspector* was due to begin at half past five.

Detective Inspector Ewa Moreno had eaten a lot of excellent dinners in Mikael Bau's kitchen, but his bouillabaisse took the biscuit.

'It comes down to the stock,' he said when they had finished eating. 'All fish soups taste of salt, of course: but there is a qualitative aspect to the salt you put in the stock, and not merely a quantitative aspect as most people seem to think.'

'Really?' said Moreno.

'Poor quality stock kills lots of other tastes, whereas a good quality stock can highlight them instead . . . The same applies to that little drop of lemon juice . . . Or the dash of angostura . . . Or that half-drop of tabasco.'

'You don't say.' Moreno lay back in her chair, feeling well satisfied. 'And how exactly did you make the stock in this evening's meal? To tell you the truth, it's one of the best I've ever eaten.'

Mikael Bau didn't reply. He merely sat there, looking at her with his warm blue eyes. Then he cleared his throat and looked up at the ceiling instead.

'The basis is lobster shell, of course. But if you marry me, I'll give you the whole recipe.'

'All right,' said Moreno.

When she came back up to her own flat she didn't switch on the light. Instead she dragged the armchair forward so that it was facing the window. She flopped down into it and gazed out at the violet-blue sky.

Am I out of my mind? she wondered. He actually proposed, and I actually said yes.

The motive was a recipe for the right kind of stock in a fish soup. Lobster shell?

Mikael Bau had proposed to her several times before. Not always directly. But she had never said yes.

She had now, though. She was going to marry him. That was what was expected of you if you said yes in a situation like that.

Oh my God, she thought. I didn't even think about it.

She could feel the butterflies in her stomach, and she was close to tears. Or to bursting out laughing. Or something in between. But she could feel tears on her cheeks – on the right one, at least.

When we have children, she thought, they are bound to ask how it came about that we decided to get married. And I shall have to tell them that the trump card their dad played was a fish soup.

She smiled up at the dark sky, and suddenly recalled one of the quotations Van Veeteren used to come out with.

Life is not a walk over an open field.

How very true.

Before going to bed she listened to her answering machine. There was only one message, and it was from Inspector Baasteuwel in Wallburg.

Could she please ring him before midnight. Yes, it was important.

She looked at the clock. Five to twelve. She dialled his number.

He answered after a mere second.

'Ewa Moreno,' she said. 'You wanted to tell me something. I'm sorry it's so late, but you said it would be okay until midnight.'

'No problem' said Baasteuwel. 'Or rather, there is a problem, that's why I rang.'

'Go on,' said Moreno.

'The old man's had a heart attack, we'll have to postpone it.'

'I beg your pardon? Who's had a heart attack?'

'My dad. His third, they don't think he'll survive it, so I have to sit up with him.'

'Your dad?'

'Yes. He's eighty-nine, I don't think he's aiming to get to ninety. But I'll have to sit up tonight with him, and maybe for a few more days and nights. So I'm afraid we shall have to put off that discussion about the strangler.'

'Of course,' said Moreno. 'Obviously you must be with him. The case is only marking time anyway. Do you have any brothers and sisters?'

'No,' said Baasteuwel. 'I'm afraid not. And my mum died ten years ago, so . . . Well, you know how it is.'

'Yes,' said Moreno, thinking at the same time that in fact she didn't, of course. Sitting at a parent's deathbed must surely be one of those experiences you couldn't possibly understand properly unless you had actually done it yourself. She tried to think of something appropriate to say, but words seemed to be as distant as death itself.

'I'll phone you in due course,' said Baasteuwel. 'Take care.'

'And you,' said Moreno. 'Is there . . . Is there anything I can do for you?'

Baasteuwel laughed drily and briefly.

'No, dammit,' he said. 'It feels very strange, I must admit. I can't really get my mind round it, but I've never believed that business of eternal life. Not even for my old man. Sleep well, my lovely.'

'Thank you. The same to you.'

'No chance of that.'

'Oh no, of course not,' said Moreno.

As soon as she had replaced the receiver she started thinking about her own parents' state of health.

And about her brother.

And Maud.

Her spirits fell like a stone, and suddenly she recalled another one of those mottoes she'd had on her wall as a teenager:

> If you don't dare to trust in your love,
> you must trust your loneliness.

Or had it said *your freedom*, in fact? Or *your strength*? She couldn't remember.

Then it occurred to her that she wouldn't now need to get up at six the next morning in order to drive to Wallburg, and she picked up the receiver again.

'I'm scared,' she said. 'Please come up to me. If we're going to go along that path anyway, I mean . . .'

'Ten seconds,' said Mikael Bau. 'You can start counting now.'

36

He rubbed his aching throat as he read through the Wanted notice in the morning paper.

Studied the photograph on the front page, and decided that it did her more than justice. The photograph must have been taken quite a long time ago, maybe even ten years ago, he thought. The same eyes, the same self-assured smile but more vital. More naive, healthier. He wondered what had happened to her since the photograph was taken – and what it would have been like to meet her then, instead of that December evening when she was on the verge of middle age.

Ten years?

That was an aeon. Such an enormous expanse of time that his mind couldn't cope with it. Nor could he convince himself that he had been the same person in 1991 as he was now.

There was no continuity. No calm river representing his own existence that could be followed from the clear, sparkling spring of his childhood and over the flat landscape of his life towards the estuary where it flowed into the sea in the autumn of his days. As he had been thinking only the other evening as he sat reading Auden . . . W. H. Auden, one of his favourites – but then, he had several. It was only in poetry that he could rediscover himself and the spirit of his earlier life. Nowadays.

A shift had taken place, and pointlessness – his own and that of everybody else – had extended its sterile desert to include all the dried-out furrows and streams – his own and those of everybody else: he had tried to write poems about precisely that, but given up. Emptiness didn't need any words. Any fuss.

Death does us the greatest of all favours, he had decided instead. But being its agent was neither noble nor evil. Just pointless.

He was sleeping better at night now that the new year had dawned. He hadn't remembered any dreams at all for several weeks, only that fragment of a memory that kept returning at regular intervals. It didn't matter if he was awake or asleep . . . My first murder, he thought . . . It was so close to that source, but it wasn't me, she was the one who arranged it, who planned it and staged it. The house burning away that freezing cold February morning, her even colder hand squeezing his own as they stood there in the wet village street together with all their neighbours, the smell of wet soil and coldness despite the raging fire as they watched the flames devouring their home and his father . . . It was remarkable that both the air and her hand could be so cold when the fire must have been so hot . . .

'If anybody hurts you, eliminate him!' she had said, and kissed his mouth. Those were her remarkable words, and that evening he had slept in her bed in the boarding house where they stayed for some days after the event . . . Eliminate him.

Or her. He felt a longing to be back on that Greek island once more, for some kind of homecoming, but he suppressed it. Squeezed out another dab of yellow ointment onto his fingertips instead, and rubbed it in carefully where his throat was hurting. The slightest touch was very painful, but nevertheless it was more bearable than it had been at the beginning. The first few days, not to mention the first few hours: he had never been so close to the core of pain and madness before . . . Never any closer than that.

He turned to page twelve and read more about the speculations.

The police had zoomed in on that night at Keefer's in any case, but that was just about all they had achieved. They knew that Ester Peerenkaas had met a man she didn't know on 8 December, and that this man might have had something to do with her disappearance.

They were keen to get in touch with him, and urged everybody who had been to the restaurant that evening to contact the Maardam CID as soon as possible.

Or their nearest police station.

He checked today's date at the top of the newspaper, and counted backwards in his head. Fifty-four days had passed.

More or less eight weeks.

Eight weeks had passed since somebody might have noticed them at the hidden table behind one of the trellises at Keefer's. No more than two-and-a-half weeks since her 'disappearance', but there were no other persons present at the meeting which preceded that. No presumptive witnesses.

Just him and her.

He smiled hastily, his skin tightened over his cheeks and neck.

And no mention of the other happenings.

Not a word to suggest that the murders in September – nor the one last summer in Wallburg – could have any connection with that vulgar Ester Peerenkaas.

Dilettantes, he thought with a weary sigh, and a sort of cold feeling of satisfaction took possession of him. A pleasure that was worth no more than a pale, austere smile, but nevertheless a positive force in the barren landscape of his emotions.

The barren landscape of my emotions? he thought. No, that won't do.

And what about the name? What did they have to say about the carefully composed name he had used on that latest occasion?

Nothing. Not a word.

Pearls, he said, folding up the newspaper. Talk about casting pearls before swine. I could kill one of their own, and they still wouldn't catch me.

The thought struck a chord. One of their own?

He noticed that the thought interested him no end.

WALLBURG, MAARDAM

FEBRUARY 2001

37

The coastal town of Wallburg was enveloped by a thin sea mist when Moreno arrived at about half past eleven in the morning – and Inspector Baasteuwel was surrounded by a similarly thin cloud of tobacco smoke when she finally found his office in the police station at Polderplejn a quarter of an hour later.

He smiled broadly and wryly, stubbed out the day's eighth cigarette and opened the window.

'Time to let some fresh air in,' he said. 'Nice to see you again. No problems getting here, I hope?'

'No, the drive was straightforward,' said Moreno. 'God had forgotten to switch the lights on, but that's how it usually is at this time of year.'

She took off her coat and hung it over a filing-cabinet, and looked around for somewhere to sit. Baasteuwel removed a crate of empty bottles, a leather jacket, a broken snooker cue and a heap of old newspapers – revealing a tubular steel armchair. After a moment's hesitation, she sat down.

'I must do some clearing away this afternoon,' he said. 'Work has been piling up a bit while I've been away. It's bloody disgusting that they can't find a stand-in for somebody as indispensable as I am when I happen to be indisposed – don't you think?'

Moreno nodded. He had explained on the telephone that he had been off for over three weeks as a result of his father's illness, death and burial. He had started work again on Monday, and today was Wednesday. She agreed that his office looked somewhat cluttered, especially on his desk.

And it didn't exactly smell of violets either, to be frank.

'So the criminal classes have had a bit of an extra start,' said Baasteuwel. 'That can't be helped, but it's only a short period of grace – I'll soon nail them anyway. Mind you, I'm not referring first and foremost to our damned strangler. He seems to have quite a lot of a start, if I understand things rightly.'

He reached out for his packet of cigarettes, which was somewhere among the junk on his desk, but then changed his mind.

'Rather a big one, yes,' said Moreno. 'We haven't exactly gathered a bunch of feathers for our caps. The fact is that we've made zero progress these last few weeks – apart from using up a few more hundred working hours that is.'

'That's the way it goes in our line of work,' said Baasteuwel. 'And this new woman who's gone missing – I don't supposed she's turned up, has she? In one way or another . . .'

Moreno sighed and shook her head.

'No sign of her.'

'But you reckon he's the one behind it, do you? Our strangler friend?'

'Very possibly,' said Moreno. 'But not certain. If you twisted my arm, though, I'd say it was him.'

'Hmm,' said Baasteuwel. 'I've been thinking about what you said regarding that name. It seems very plausible, but it's a blasted nuisance that he can't leave anything more substantial behind. Something concrete.'

'That's why I'm here,' said Moreno. 'My chief inspector is starting to get a bit desperate, but he thinks we ought to work a bit more closely together on searching for links with that old case of yours. It's worth exploring every possibility when you're as stuck as we are.'

'We mustn't let the bastards get us down,' said Baasteuwel optimistically. 'Let's see what we can do. I take it you're fully informed about fröken Kortsmaa?'

'Yes, indeed,' said Moreno. 'But it won't do any harm if you run through it all once more. I don't suppose this palace you work in can produce a cup of coffee out of nowhere? I didn't bother to stop for one on the way here.'

Baasteuwel smiled again and dug his fingers into his tousled hair.

'Mon dieu,' he said. 'Forgive my disgraceful lack of courtesy. Sit back here and meditate – I'll be back in two shakes of a puppy dog's tail. Sugar and milk?'

'Milk,' said Moreno. 'But just a drop.'

Baasteuwel's oral recapitulation of the Kristine Kortsmaa case took about half an hour, but contained no significant information that Moreno didn't know already. As he held forth, a feeling of despondency began to undermine her concentration. Despite the strong coffee. To undermine it very significantly, in fact: she felt she had heard it all before, and it wasn't until he took a dark-brown cardboard box out of a desk cupboard that a flicker of interest raised her spirits slightly.

A cardboard box, she thought: something concrete at last. Something substantial.

'What's that?' she asked.

'Technical evidence,' said Baasteuwel, lighting his eleventh cigarette of the day.

'Technical evidence? You're rambling again.'

'I only ramble in my spare time,' said Baasteuwel. 'Hardly ever then even, in fact. But never mind. Proof would be too strong a word.'

He took off the lid and began taking plastic bags out of the box, placing them quite meticulously on the desk in front of him. Moreno watched him in silence. He summed up the result.

'Thirteen significant pieces of circumstantial evidence,' he said. 'Let's call them pieces of circumstantial evidence, fröken, since you are so finicky . . . I assume you are still a fröken?'

'Just about,' said Moreno. 'What exactly is it?'

'What is it?' said Baasteuwel. 'Bits and pieces from her flat, of course.'

'Kristine Kortsmaa's flat?'

'Who else's? Needless to say we have a hell of a lot of other plastic bags with fibres and fluff and God only knows what other crap, but these are a bit more tangible.'

He held up one of the bags so that Moreno could see the contents.

'A pen?' she said.

'Give her a prize,' said Baasteuwel. 'I'm glad to see that there are still officers in the force with powers of observation like that. Anyway, I asked three of fröken Kortsmaa's friends to look through the flat and point out any items they didn't think seemed to belong. Things that *might* – this is obviously one of the case's most dodgy *mights* – have been left behind by that bloke she took home with her from the music bar. Her murderer, in other words. And so I'm sitting here with thirteen mysterious objects. I'm sure you agree that life in the CID is one big thrill after another.'

He held up another plastic bag that seemed to contain a bus or a tram ticket.

'I've spent quite a lot of time contemplating them,' said Baasteuwel glumly. 'Turning them over and staring at them from all angles for nineteen or twenty months now, or however long it's been. You're welcome to take over the whole caboodle.'

Moreno stood up and tried to get an overview of the thirteen significant pieces of circumstantial evidence that he had laid out over the top of the piles of paper on his desk.

A beer-bottle cap. A matchbox. A little nail file.

She couldn't help but laugh.

'A nail file? Why in God's name should he have left a nail file behind at the scene of the crime? Are you pulling my leg?'

'Not at all,' said Baasteuwel in a serious tone. 'I never pull anybody's leg, not even in my spare time. The nail file was found under the table in the room where the dead body was found. None of Kortsmaa's friends was sure that it belonged to her.'

Moreno sat down again.

'Good,' she said. 'Brilliant detective work – he filed his nails before he strangled her. I don't suppose you found any bits of nail among the dust and fluff?'

'I'm afraid not,' said Baasteuwel. 'You can forget DNA. No, seriously, I'd be only too pleased if you took care of this crap . . . Although there is one item that's rather interesting.'

'You don't say,' said Moreno. 'What?'

He held up another of the bags so that she could see the contents. It seemed to be a little lapel badge of some sort. He took it out of the bag and handed it over to her.

Moreno examined the badge somewhat sceptically, twisting it around between her thumb and index finger. The badge itself was yellow, presumably brass or something similar, she guessed. Four or five centimetres in diameter, and at the top a little triangular plate, pointing downwards, no more than half a centimetre square. Dark green enamel, and a little red strand that might have been a letter S, or possibly a stylized serpent.

'Some club or other?' Moreno wondered. 'A membership badge?'

Baasteuwel nodded.

'Something like that,' he said.

'Or maybe one of those badges people wear to indicate that they are suffering from some disease or other – epilepsy or diabetes, for instance?'

'No,' said Baasteuwel. 'I've checked every disease that occurs north of the South Pole, and none of them has a symbol anything like that.'

Moreno thought for a moment.

'So a club, perhaps?'

'Possibly.'

'What kind of a club?'

'I haven't the slightest idea,' said Baasteuwel.

'Have you checked?'

'What do you think? . . .'

'Forgive me.'

Baasteuwel scratched his head again, and looked melo-dramatically devastated again.

'Her friends didn't recognize it in any case. The only association she ever belonged to was a handball club when she was in her teens, and they were short of cash and didn't have club badges. This is the kind of badge people like to wear on their lapels because they want to show off the fact that they are members of some association: Alcoholics Anonymous or Siegbrunn's Rowing Club or Left-Handed Vicars Against Abortion – anything you like as long as they can show that they belong. But we don't have a register of badges in this country, and I don't suppose they have them in other countries either. Believe you me, I spent a week chasing up that damned badge.'

'Where was it found?'

'That's what makes it interesting,' said Baasteuwel. 'Assuming you don't have too ambitious pretensions, that is. It was lying inside a shoe in the hall. Under the coat rack and hat shelf. One of the victim's shoes, of course – the badge could well have come loose and fallen off an overcoat or jacket. It could have belonged to the murderer. Or some other visitor . . . But I'm fed up of seeing it now. We put a picture of it in the local newspaper, but nobody got in touch. I expect she bought the damned thing in a flea market in Prague or Casablanca or somewhere like that.'

'Shouldn't it be possible to find out where it was made?'

'We tried, but we didn't find that out either,' said Baasteuwel with a sigh. 'I think you should take it, so that you have something to keep yourself occupied.'

'With pleasure,' said Moreno. 'If you pack all the circumstantial evidence into the cardboard box, we'll be delighted to solve all the problems for you.'

'Excellent,' said Baasteuwel, checking his watch. 'By all means. But I'll be damned if it isn't time for lunch. I hope you'll allow me to treat you to a bite to eat in return for your help.'

'I think I'm the one who should be doing the thanking so far,' said Moreno. 'And as I still owe you at least two restaurant meals from last summer, I reckon this lunch should be on me.'

'Miserliness and equality of the sexes have always been my guiding stars,' said Baasteuwel. 'Lead the way.'

During the two-hour drive back to Maardam, Inspector Moreno's attention was concentrated more or less equally between two things.

The first was the western sky, where the sun suddenly burst forth in spectacular fashion as it sank down behind the sea in a festoon of red and purple . . . Ragged clouds were lit up from beyond the horizon by rogue beams, creating a slowly fading extravaganza as darker and duller tints spread with almost apocalyptic implications. *Der Untergang des Abendlandes* cropped up in her mind as she stood next to her car in a lay-by, making the most of the view for several minutes. *The Decline of the West . . .*

The other was the carton with Baasteuwel's plastic bags on the front passenger seat of her car.

Thirteen presumed pieces of circumstantial evidence, less substantial than strands of hair. Twelve of them, at least. That badge was the only thing worth devoting time and energy to, it seemed.

A red S against a green background.

Or a snake in the grass? Why not? It must mean something, after all.

Somebody must have been wearing it. The little pin securing the badge must have come loose, fallen out and ended up inside a shoe. Unfortunately not one of the black court shoes Kristine Kortsmaa had been wearing the evening she was murdered, Baasteuwel had explained, so it could have landed up there on some previous occasion. At more or less any time.

But nevertheless it must be an indication of something or other? A tiny piece of information that could turn out to be a key, in fact?

An unintended greeting from a murderer?

Wishful thinking? she thought.

Most probably, yes.

The third thing that occupied her thoughts – especially during the last half-hour of the drive into Maardam, when the sun had set and the plastic bags on the passenger seat beside her were almost invisible in the near-darkness – was a mathematical calculation.

It was quite straightfoward, but had nevertheless been the cause of the distraction she had felt while discussing matters with Inspector Baasteuwel – both in his office at the police station and at the Restaurant Bodenthal, where they had eaten an excellent lamb fricassee and an equally excellent lemon sorbet, and talked quite a lot about life and death and the point of being a copper.

Her period had been due last Saturday.

It was four days overdue.

38

'Why are we sitting here?' said Rooth.

'It was something to do with one of those lapel badges on a pin,' said Jung. 'Reinhart sounded almost enthusiastic – maybe we're on the verge of a breakthrough?'

'You're talking about the Strangler, are you?' said Rooth with a yawn.

'I think so,' said Jung.

'That would be good,' said Rooth. 'If we got somewhere at last, I mean. It'll soon be half a year since the murders, and my investigation instincts tell me that's a bit on the long side.'

'Ester Peerenkaas was only a month ago,' said Jung.

'If she really was one of his victims,' said Rooth. 'I must say I'm beginning to have my doubts . . . But I did have a thought this morning.'

'Really?' said Jung. 'Are you telling me you actually start thinking in the morning?'

Rooth frowned and gazed out of the window. It was raining. Wollerimsparken looked as if it would love to sink down into the earth. Or had even begun to do so.

'Well?' said Jung. 'Have you had a stroke?'

'Hang on,' said Rooth, raising an index finger as a warning. 'Any minute now.'

Jung sighed.

'It's always interesting to be present when a great mind is at work,' he said, also looking out of the window. 'It looks horrible out there! I can't understand where all that rain comes from. It's as if—'

'Yes, now I've got it!' interrupted Rooth. 'Her parents, that's what I was thinking about.'

'Whose parents?'

'Ester Peerenkaas of course. Or her mother, to be more precise. She doesn't pester us any more.'

'Eh?' said Jung. 'What do you mean?'

'She's stopped contacting us.'

'I heard what you said,' said Jung in exasperation. 'So what?'

'I don't· know,' said Rooth flinging his arms out wide. 'Krause mentioned that she'd been phoning us twice a day the first few weeks, but then she suddenly stopped.'

Jung thought for a moment.

'I don't understand what you are getting at. Fru Peerenkaas has stopped pestering the police every day with questions about her missing daughter. Are you suggesting that has some special significance?'

'I don't know everything,' said Rooth. 'Just almost everything. Where the hell has Reinhart got to? I thought he said—'

'He's here,' said Reinhart as he entered the room. 'You're not sitting on eggs by any chance are you, Inspector?'

'Not just at the moment,' said Rooth. 'Easter's a bit too far away for that.'

'Unusually clear instructions,' said Jung when Reinhart had left the room again. 'We can't complain on that score.'

Rooth nodded sombrely and stared at the badge he was holding in his hand.

'We have to find out where this thing comes from and report back by tomorrow afternoon's run-through at the latest, otherwise we shall be skinned alive. Yes, you're right: that's pretty clear.'

'It's good to know exactly what's expected of us,' said Jung. 'How do you reckon we should go about it?'

Rooth shrugged.

'What do you think? The telephone directory is always a good place to start.'

'Okay,' said Jung, standing up. 'Get going on that – I have half an hour's paperwork waiting on my desk. We can start hunting as soon as you've got wind of something.'

Rooth rummaged around in his jacket pocket and produced two or three sweets that he tossed into his mouth.

'Your word is my command,' he said. 'What do you reckon the chances are?'

'Of what?'

'Of this little badge really belonging to Kristine Kortsmaa's murderer.'

'Not very high,' said Jung. 'About zero.'

'And the possibility that she had anything at all to do with our Strangler?'

'More or less zero,' said Jung.

'Bloody pessimist,' said Rooth. 'Leave me in peace so that I can get something done.'

The shop itself was no bigger than about ten or twelve square metres, but perhaps there was more space behind, overlooking the courtyard, where manufacturing and repairs could be carried out. In any case, the firm was called Kluivert & Goscinski, and was squeezed in between a warehouse and an abattoir at the far end of Algernonstraat – a dark, slightly curved apology of a street running from Megsje Boisstraat down to Langgraacht, and was hardly an ideal location for anybody wishing to run a business. The abattoir seemed to have been boarded up for ages.

But perhaps Kluivert & Goscinski was such a niche enterprise – as Jung gathered the term was – that the actual location of the premises didn't matter much. Medals, plaques, cups, trophies, badges – Manufacture and sales! – Matchless prices! – Rapid delivery! – Brand leaders since the forties!

All this was printed in gold lettering on the chest-high teak counter with a glass top on which Rooth had carefully placed the plastic bag with the Wallburg badge. The shop assistant – a slim black-suited gentleman in his sixties with a nose like a ship's keel and a moustache like a hairy sausage (and which presumably did little to facilitate the partaking of food, always assuming he ever ate anything, Jung thought) – slid his spectacles up above the bridge of his nose and examined the object in front of him with a degree of seriousness that would not have been out of place had it been the Queen of Sheba's navel diamond. Jung noticed that he was holding his breath. Rooth as well.

'Well?' said Rooth after ten seconds.

The shop assistant put the badge back into the bag and allowed his spectacles to slide down the ship's keel. There was a red strip where they landed, and Jung assumed this must be an elegant manoeuvre he performed several times every day.

'I'm afraid I don't recognize it,' he said. 'It's not one of ours. Not from the last twenty years, that is – it could be older, of course.'

'Really,' said Rooth. 'Do you recognize the symbol itself?'

'I'm afraid not.'

'Could you guess?'

He hesitated.

'I think it's quite old. Thirty or forty years old.'

'What makes you say that?'

The man turned the palms of his hands upwards and moved his fingers slowly up and down, whatever that might mean.

'Made in this country?'

'Impossible to say for sure, but I think so.'

'Why?'

'The mounting of the enamel disc. What exactly are you looking for?'

'A murderer,' said Rooth. 'The fact is that we are rather

keen to identify this little bastard. You don't happen to know who we would turn to for assistance, by any chance?'

The man fingered his moustache and his eyes glazed over behind his thick spectacle lenses.

'Goscinski,' he said in the end.

'Goscinski?' said Jung. 'The man who—'

'Eugen Goscinski, yes. The founder of this firm. He's eighty-nine years old now, but what he doesn't know about heraldry and symbols isn't worth knowing . . . Even in the most prosaic connections.'

'Prosaic?'

'He knows the badges of every single football team in Europe, for instance, then the two or three hundred biggest clubs in South America. If you give him enough time, he can also—'

'Excellent,' said Rooth, interrupting him. 'How can we get in touch with him?'

'Wickerstraat, next door to your police station, in fact. But you should be aware that old Goscinski's a bit special. He never sets foot outside the front door during the winter months, for instance. I think it would be best if you phoned him first, he has a reputation for not allowing people into his flat, and he's not always easy to—'

'We're from the CID,' Rooth pointed out. 'And this is in connection with a murder investigation, as I said.'

'Hmm,' said the man. 'If you'll forgive me for saying so, I'm not convinced that Goscinski would pay much attention to such details. He's become a bit . . . well, a bit special.'

'We shall have to see what we can do about that,' said

Rooth. 'If you can give us his address and telephone number, we can sort that out. Inspector Jung here has a degree in psychology and is an outstanding judge of human beings, so it shouldn't be too big a problem.'

'Really?' exclaimed the man in surprise. He pushed up his spectacles once more and looked hard at Jung with renewed interest. 'I didn't think—'

'Address and telephone number, please!' said Rooth.

'Something ought to be done about that tongue of yours,' said Jung when they were back in the car. 'Cutting it off might be the best option.'

'Rubbish,' said Rooth. 'The funny thing is that you don't even have the decency to say thank you for a compliment when you receive one. Get driving now and shut up while I ring Goscinski.'

Jung started the engine and began driving at snail's pace back along the narrow street, listening to how Rooth dealt with the ancient eccentric in Wickerstraat. Despite what the toucan man in the shop had predicted, Rooth had no difficulty in arranging to visit Goscinski and ten minutes later they parked the car in the basement garage at the police station. His apartment was only a stone's throw away from the station, and when they rang the bell at the entrance to the block of flats down the street, Jung realized that he could probably see the building from his office window.

Let's hope to God that we're on the right track, he thought. This improbable proximity to Goscinski was a typical example of the ironic games the gods love to play with us, and it would be surprising if it weren't significant.

Needless to say there was no rational justification for thinking along those lines – but where had five months of rational thinking got them? wondered Inspector Jung, as he began to feel the familiar butterflies in his stomach that always suggested something was about to happen. A breakthrough, or something similar.

There was a crackling sound in the speaking-tube. Rooth explained who they were, and there was a faint click as the lock on the entrance door was released.

It was quite stifling in Eugen Goscinski's flat, and perhaps that wasn't so surprising. It was small, dark and stuffy, and the two cats that came to rub up against them in the hall probably had the same constricted winter habits as their owner. But at least the latter was the only one who smoked, and Jung was grateful for that: it was bad enough already with the ingrained stench of old cigarillos and old man. Their host lit a new Pfitzerboom as soon as he had ushered them into his kitchen and served up three small cups of pitch-black coffee without asking them what they would like in the way of refreshments.

'Well?' he said. 'Fire away!'

Rooth took the plastic bag out of his inside pocket. Goscinski took out the badge, held it by the pin and contemplated it. Jung noticed that once again he was holding his breath.

'Hmm,' muttered Goscinski, taking a deep drag of his

cigarillo. 'What have we got here, then? No, er, good Lord – yes, I do believe I recognize it . . .'

'Excellent,' said Rooth.

'. . . Recognize it, but it only rings a very faint bell at the moment, I regret to say . . .'

Jung took a sip of the coffee. It tasted of burnt meat and tar.

'Yes!' exclaimed Goscinski. 'I've got it!'

He hammered away at his forehead with his fist a few times, as if to emphasize that the machinery was still well oiled and in good working order.

'Excellent,' said Rooth again. 'This is what we'd hoped for. But what exactly does it signify?'

'The Succulents,' said Goscinski.

'The Succu-whats?' said Rooth.

'Yes indeed,' said Goscinski, sounding very pleased with himself, emptying his cup in one gulp and twirling the pin of the badge. 'Of course it's them, by Christ! I actually dealt with the order, but they were made up at the Glinders factory in Frigge. Fifty-six or fifty-seven, if my memory serves me rightly. Two thousand badges. Payment in cash on delivery.'

'What are the Succulents?' asked Jung calmly.

Goscinski snorted.

'God only knows. Some association or other. At the university. Something to do with the Freemasons, I assume, but I don't really know what they got up to.'

'Some kind of university society?' said Rooth.

'Yes. They were ordered by a dean or somebody like that in the Theology Department. A man of the cloth. I don't remember his name, but that's how it was in any case. Why are you so interested in this thing?'

Jung exchanged looks with Rooth. One of the cats jumped up onto the table and started to lick Goscinki's cup clean.

'It's a long story,' said Rooth vaguely. 'We can get in touch with you again if you'd like to know how it goes . . . Or if we need some more information. I assume we can get the information we need from the university. From the registry, perhaps?'

'No doubt,' said Goscinski. 'From the bloody pen-pushers. But put your heart and soul into it. What's the weather like out there?"

'Grey and wet,' said Rooth. 'And windy. As usual.'

'I'll be going out again in April,' said Goscinski, glancing sceptically out of the window. 'Around the fifteenth, or thereabouts. Was there anything else you wanted to know, while you're lounging around here?'

'No,' said Rooth. 'Thank you for your help. The Succulents are exactly what we wanted to know about.'

'Okay,' said Goscinski. 'Be off with you, then. It's time for my afternoon nap.'

They paused for a while in Wickerstraat before going their different ways.

'What do you think about that?' wondered Jung. 'The Succulents? What on earth are they when they're at home?'

'I don't think anything at all yet,' said Rooth. 'But that was the worst bloody coffee I've ever drunk in all my life, no doubt about that. Still, we did what we had to do in just one afternoon. I reckon we've earned a lie-in tomorrow morning. What do you say to that?'

'I agree entirely,' said Jung. 'Shall we say we'll turn up at about ten?'

'Make it half past,' said Rooth.

39

It was Saturday morning before Chief Inspector Reinhart was able to arrange an audience with one of the pro-vice-chancellors of Maardam University. In the meantime he managed to work up an impressive amount of anger.

'What's the matter with you?' asked Winnifred as they were eating breakfast in bed. 'You've been grinding your teeth all night.'

'They're a lot of half-witted bloody idiots,' said Reinhart. 'There are people in the university administration who would be locked up in a loony bin if they weren't allowed to prance and strut around and collect a fat salary in Academe.'

Winnifred looked at him with an expression of mild surprise for a few seconds.

'I'm well aware of that,' she said. 'I also work in the talent factory, remember? It's not something to grind your teeth about.'

'They're my teeth,' said Reinhart. 'I'll grind them as much as I like.'

He turned his head to look at the clock.

'Anyway, it's time I was off. Professor Kuurtens, is that somebody you know?'

Winnifred thought hard.

'I don't think so. What's his field?'

'Political science, if I heard rightly. Bone idle.'

Winnifred shook her head and went back to her news-paper.

'Say goodbye to Joanna before you go.'

Reinhart paused on his way to the bathroom.

'Have I ever forgotten to say goodbye to my daughter?'

He could hear her chatting away to herself through the open door of the nursery, and noticed that he relaxed his cheek muscles when he started thinking about her. Presumably what his wife had said was true: he really had been grinding his teeth all night.

Pro-Vice-Chancellor Kuurtens, he thought, you'd better tread extremely carefully.

Kuurtens received him in an office on the third floor of the registry. Reinhart estimated the ceiling height at four metres, and the floor space at about seventy square metres. Apart from a few free-standing columns in black granite with head-less busts on top, a display cupboard from the seventeenth or eighteenth century and a few drab oil paintings depicting long-dead pro-vice-chancellors, there was really only one item of furniture in the room: a gigantic desk made of a black wood Reinhart reckoned was probably ebony, with a high-backed red armchair on each long side.

In one of them sat Professor Kuurtens, gazing out over the world and the empty desk as he slowly and deliberately wrote a few gems of words with a priceless fountain pen on a sheet of hammered white paper.

Reinhart sat down in the other one without waiting to be invited.

A hint of a sneer formed on the professor's face, which was highly aristocratic in appearance. A classic Greek nose. A high forehead that disappeared under an Olympian mass of greying curls. Deep-set eyes and a firm, trust-inspiring jaw.

An immaculate grey suit, an ivory-white shirt and a dark-red tie.

He's been given the job on the basis of his looks, Reinhart thought. He's as thick as three sawn planks.

'Welcome, Chief Inspector.'

'Thank you.'

'Or should I address you as Detective Chief Inspector?'

'My name's Reinhart,' said Reinhart. 'I haven't come here to be addressed, nor to play cricket.'

'Hmm,' said the professor, glancing at his wristwatch. 'I can give you fifteen minutes. Cricket?'

'A metaphor,' Reinhart explained. 'But never mind that. The Succulents, what are they when they're at home?'

Pro-Vice-Chancellor Kuurtens screwed off the cap of his fountain pen, then screwed it back on again.

'I think I must ask you to enlighten me somewhat more on the circumstances before we proceed any further,' he said.

'Murder,' said Reinhart. 'Now you are enlightened. Well?'

'I would not say that was an adequate enlightenment,' said Kuurtens, clasping his hands over the sheet of paper. 'If you bear in mind that Maardam University has been in existence for over five hundred years, I trust you will understand that I must protect values that cannot be swept aside as casually as that.'

'What the hell are you babbling on about?' asked Reinhart, regretting that he hadn't brought his pipe with him: it would have been an ideal moment just now to envelope this overweening prat in a thick cloud of tobacco smoke.

'Might I beg you to adopt a more seemly tone of conversational discourse.'

'All right,' said Reinhart. 'But if you are so simple-minded as to claim that this university has had nothing at all to hide for several hundred years, you are doing your Alma Mater a disservice, as you must surely realize. Anyway, the Succulents. Let's hear about them. I don't have unlimited time at my disposal either.'

The professor leaned back in his chair and adopted an expression of deep thought. Reinhart waited.

'An association,' he said in the end.

'Thank you,' said Reinhart. 'More details, please.'

'Statutes from 1757. An association of scholars active in various faculties of the university, with the aim of promoting research and progress.'

'Why the name "Succulents"?'

Kuurtens shrugged.

'The original founders of the association were biologists. The title was a reference to an ability to reproduce and persist over a long period of time – applied to knowledge, for instance. But perhaps you don't—'

'I understand,' said Reinhart. 'So we're talking about free-masons, are we?'

'There are no freemasons any longer.'

'That's an assertion open to discussion. But I'm talking about those days.'

Kuurtens paused and contemplated his fountain pen.

'Sort of.'

'And the Succulents have continued to exist ever since then, have they?'

'Continuously.'

'With a red S against a green background as their symbol?'

The professor moved his head in a way vaguely reminiscent of the shape of a banana. A combination of affirmation and protest.

'Yes, although it's a comparatively recent invention. Quite late in the twentieth century.'

'I see,' said Reinhart. 'And how many members are there today?'

'About a hundred.'

'Men and women?'

'Men only.'

'And you are a member yourself?'

'It is forbidden to inform outsiders with regard to membership.'

'How can you know that if you're not a member?'

Professor Kuurtens did not reply. As I said, Reinhart thought: he's not exactly Nobel prizewinner material.

'I happen to know that you are a senior member of the Succulents, and I take it for granted that you will allow me to take a look at the membership list. Right now, I can't see any objections to that.'

'But that's . . . That is out of the question!' exclaimed Professor Kuurtens. 'Do you think you can come barging in here and demand to look at . . . at whatever you like?'

Reinhart crossed his arms.

'Yes,' he said. 'That's exactly what I think. If you happen to have a lawyer among your band of fellow-travellers, he will doubtless be able to explain to you that I have every right to – as you so neatly put it – come barging in.'

The professor stared at him for a moment, then put the fountain pen in his breast pocket and sat up straight.

'I have no intention of handing over to you a list of members,' he said belligerently. 'The Succulents are a totally independent organization and have no official links with the university. This is not my pigeon.'

Reinhart eyed him severely and slowly shook his head.

'Don't be silly now,' he said. 'Don't behave like an academic jackass. We're talking about murderers, not pigeons. I'll give you five minutes in which to sort yourself out and be reasonable. If you continue to be uncooperative, I'll have you collected by a police car and arrested for obstructing a murder investigation. Is that clear?'

The pro-vice-chancellor turned pale.

'You . . . You are exceeding your authority,' he muttered.

'That's not impossible,' Reinhart admitted, 'but I don't think so. In any case, it would be worth the trouble of shoving you into the back seat of one of our police cars – and I think I'd take the opportunity of having a chat with one of our local newspapers first. Can you imagine the headlines on the front page? Have you ever tried handcuffs, by the way?'

Now I've gone too far, he thought. But Professor Kuurtens looked appropriately pale as a result of the seriousness of the situation, and the hair-raising images that had been suggested to him. He sat motionless and straight-backed for half a minute while wringing his hands over the white sheet of paper on his desk. Reinhart began to feel deeply satisfied.

He looks like a plaster cast, he thought. It would be possible to put his skull on top of one of those headless busts, in fact. It would be most appropriate. I don't think I'm going to need to grind my teeth tonight.

'Let's see now,' said Pro-Vice-Chancellor Kuurtens in the end. 'If you give me a few more details, perhaps we can reach a solution . . .'

'There's not much more I can say,' said Reinhart patiently. 'In the course of murder investigation we have come across a membership badge of the Succulents. One of your colleagues told me on the phone that these badges were made in 1957, and were given to new members as they enrolled.'

'Which colleague was it who told you that?'

'That's not something you should worry about,' said Reinhart. 'But the bottom line is that this membership badge plays a significant role in our investigation, and that's why I need a copy of your current membership list. I can't tell you any more than that, I'm afraid.'

Kuurtens swallowed a few times, and kept glancing up at the stucco decorations.

'Well, those badges . . .' he said. 'They haven't been all that significant. As you said, they were made in 1957 – for our bicentenary year. And, as you also said, every member receives one when he's elected as a member.'

'How do you elect them?'

'On the basis of recommendations. There must be at least three recommendations from at least three existing members.'

How many per year?'

'Not many. Half a dozen at most. And applicants have to have a doctorate as well, of course.'

'Of course,' said Reinhart. 'Well, have you made your mind up yet? If you want to avoid being up to the ears in a scandal, I suggest that you should produce that membership list. You can probably imagine what the media would make of it if you – a semi-secret gang of freemasons in the academic world – were exposed as being involved in a murder investigation . . . I can tell you that it's not just a matter of one victim, but several. And if you make things worse by refusing to cooperate . . . well . . .'

Professor Kuurtens took two deep breaths then stood up. Held onto the desk just in case . . .

'I don't like your methods,' he said in a feeble attempt to sound uncooperative. 'I really don't approve of them at all. But you leave me with no choice, I'm afraid. If you come with me to my office, I'll give you a copy of our membership list. I assume you will treat it with maximum discretion.'

'Discretion is one of my strongest sides,' said Reinhart.

'Let's go. So you have an office as well? What exactly is this room, then?'

'This is what's called an Audi – a reception room,' said Kuurtens. 'It's been used as such ever since 1842 when this building came into use. Yes, indeed.'

'Yes, indeed,' agreed Reinhart, following the pro-vice-chancellor down the stairs.

The total number of current members of *Sodalicium Sapientiae Cultorum Succulentorum*, which was the official name of the association in accordance with the statutes of 1757, proved to be 152 persons.

Reinhart glanced quickly through the columns of names, year of entry and academic specialities. Then he folded the four sheets of paper in two and put them in his inside pocket. Glared for a moment or two at Professor Kuurtens, then shook his hand and wished him a fruitful Saturday before turning on his heel and leaving the university building.

So, that's that done, he thought as he took the short cut through the park towards Keymerkyrkan. We've narrowed it down nicely.

Narrowed what down? he thought in his next breath. What the hell am I trying to fool myself into imagining? Do I really believe I've got the murderer tucked into my inside pocket?

One of the hundred and fifty-two?

He put on his gloves, raised his shoulders as a defence against the strong wind, and thought about that.

It must be pure wishful thinking, he told himself – as inevitable as an attack of mildew or the growth of a cancerous tumour after all those unproductive weeks and months. Figuratively speaking.

Or was there in fact a realistic possibility?

Hard to say, thought Chief Inspector Reinhart. Right now, when the excitement engendered by the revelations about the Succulents is so fresh, it's difficult to distinguish between genuine thoughts and mere emotions or hopes. Having the name of the murderer hidden away with a hundred-and-fifty-one others is not exactly an ideal situation to be in – but it's significantly better than the barren desert to which we've been banished hitherto, with not so much as a lump of fly shit for a clue.

So, it's now a question of making progress. In principle, at least. We suddenly have a field to start ploughing. The murderer may well be one of a large group: but the group is clearly defined.

What he needed to do now was to sit down and work his way through the personal details of these dodgy academics, and that should shrink the size of the group of suspects significantly – their age is an obvious starting point. It seemed highly unlikely that the average age of a group like this would be all that low: Reinhart assumed that they remained members for life, and as the statutes required that members should have doctorates and also be recommended by a number of their peers, it was unlikely that any of them could have joined the association before the age of thirty-five at least.

And the Strangler could hardly be older than forty-five: several friends of the victims had stressed that aspect.

So let's face it: this list of members should infuse new life into the investigation. That must surely be the case?

It occurred to him that he was now walking at *tempo furioso* and had started whistling. He obviously needed to calm down and get a grip.

Hold your horses, you berk! he told himself. If you assign all your resources to this line of investigation and it turns out to be a dead end, you'll never solve this case. Bugger that for a lark!

That blasted badge could have landed up in Kristine Kortsmaa's shoe in God only knows how many different ways. Or? She might have found it somewhere. One of the Succulents might have paid her a visit in a perfectly innocent context – erotic circumstances, for instance – and happened to drop it. Somebody else might have found the badge somehow or other – come to think of it, Reinhart thought, the murderer could have come across the badge lying in the street, picked it up, and purposely left it in the victim's flat in order to mislead the police . . . Well, maybe that was a pretty far-fetched possibility, more appropriate to a fifth-rate English 1930s crime novel than the real world . . .

Anyway, there were plenty of possible variations, that was clear. And there were plenty of the badges in existence – two thousand were manufactured in 1957. Pro-Vice-Chancellor Kuurtens had said that there were over three hundred still available in the store, so there would be no need to make any new ones for quite a while yet.

Oh, shit, thought Reinhart. Do I believe in this, or don't I?

As confused as a donkey faced with a hundred-and-fifty-two wisps of hay, he emerged into the relative hustle and bustle of Keymerstraat – and that's when it happened. One second, that was all it took: no more.

Without really registering how it happened, he bumped into one of the other pedestrians and stepped to one side, into the road. The bus pulling into the stop at Keymer Plejn hit him with its right wing and sent him flying across the pavement and into the display window of the cheese and delicatessen shop Heerenwijk's – he was a regular customer most Saturdays, for fancy dessert cheeses.

But not this Saturday. Even before he hit the ground, Chief Inspector Reinhart had lost consciousness and was mercifully unaware of all the bones in his body that were broken, and of the young lady in a light-blue quilted jacket who screamed in such a way that the hearts of all those who heard her missed several beats.

Her name was Vera Simanova: she was a student at the opera college and the possessor of a soprano voice that for a brief moment that Saturday afternoon resounded throughout the whole of central Maardam.

But not in the ears of Chief Inspector Reinhart. Or at least, he had no recollection of it afterwards.

40

Van Veeteren lifted up his granddaughter, and smelled her.

Well, more than smelled her.

He inhaled every aspect of her being. He sniffed at the back of her neck, then breathed in deeply, ecstatically, over and over again.

My God, he thought. Absolutely divine.

How can there possibly be anything so ambrosially delectable in a world like the one we live in? It's incomprehensible.

Andrea giggled. He realized that she was ticklish. Erich and Jess had been ticklish as well.

Especially there, at the back of the neck.

And they had smelt exactly the same. Just as exquisitely.

He lifted her up into the air, arms stretched. She squealed in delight, and a strand of saliva came trickling out of her mouth.

'There are times,' said Ulrike, who was sitting at the other end of the sofa, with tears in her eyes, 'there are times when I wish I'd met you rather earlier in life. Twenty-five years or so ago.'

'It's a sufficient blessing to have met you at all,' said Van

Veeteren. 'But by Christ, she's so lovely! Can you understand how it's possible for anybody to be so damned lovely?'

'No,' said Ulrike. 'It's incomprehensible. But you'll teach her how to swear when she reaches the right age, I've no doubt about that. Yes, Andrea is an absolute pearl. I think it's excellent that her day nursery is closed on Sundays . . . It's exactly what you need – the chance to be a grandad for a few hours every weekend.'

'It certainly is excellent,' said Van Veeteren, placing Andrea on her back in his lap.

'Goo,' said Andrea.

'You can say that again,' said Van Veeteren.

Ulrike stood up.

'I'd better put the gratin in the oven. Marlene will be here in half an hour. But be honest, do you think we would have found each other if we'd had the opportunity when we were younger?'

'Of course,' said Van Veeteren. 'I'd have dug you up from the bottom of the sea if it had been necessary. I read somewhere – Heerenmacht, I think – that the paths to one's goal are legion, if only—'

He had no opportunity to enlarge on that thought as the telephone rang. Ulrike answered.

'Yes?' she said.

Then she said, in order: 'yes', 'yes', 'what?', 'no' and 'yes, he's sitting here'. She put her hand over the receiver and whispered:

'The chief of police.'

'Eh?' said Van Veeteren.

'Hiller. The chief of police. He wants to speak to you.'

'I'm not at home.'

'He sounds very persistent.'

'Tell him it's four years too late.'

'But he—'

'And it's Sunday afternoon. Can't he understand that I'm busy?'

'It's something to do with Reinhart.'

'Reinhart?'

'Yes.'

'What about Reinhart?'

'That's what he wants to talk to you about.'

Van Veeteren thought for two seconds. Then he sighed and exchanged his lovely granddaughter for a telephone receiver full of an ugly chief of police.

The call lasted for almost half an hour, and just as he replaced the receiver, in walked Marlene Frey, having finished her weekend stint at Merckx, the supermarket she'd been working at for two months now. So there was no opportunity to discuss the chief of police's unexpected and cunning disregard of all conventions regarding the Sabbath until after dinner – when mother and daughter had left for home, and host and hostess had once more flopped down on the sofa.

'It's remarkable,' said Van Veeteren, 'but it's as if I'm being hounded down.'

'Really?' said Ulrike circumspectly. 'Hounded down by what?'

Van Veeteren pondered.

'Something.'

'Something?'

'Yes. I can't pin it down, but I'm being persecuted whichever way you look at it. That olive stone, and the priest, and Stravinsky's poor swallow . . . Do you remember that morning last autumn when we'd just got back from Rome?'

Ulrike nodded.

'Those strangled women . . . and Robert Musil! And now perhaps there's another one.'

'Another Musil?'

'No, unfortunately not. A new victim.'

'Another strangled woman?'

'Yes – or at least, that's what the indications suggest. They haven't found her yet. She's just missing, so there might be some hope.'

'Oh, shit!'

'You could say that. And it's not exactly an uplifting story this time round either – although that's the rotten core of police work, when all's said and done . . .'

'What is?'

'That you never feel good when you've solved your case. When everything is laid bare. There's no satisfaction while you're working away at it, and none afterwards either. Apart from . . . well, what you probably feel after a successful amputation.'

'I understand,' said Ulrike. 'And what has been amputated?'

'A part of your soul,' said Van Veeteren. 'The bright side of your soul. But I've packed it in, thank God – why are we sitting here making ourselves feel miserable?'

Ulrike nodded thoughtfully and took hold of his hand.

'What's happened to Reinhart?' she asked.

'He's in Gemejnte Hospital,' said Van Veeteren. 'Run over by a bus.'

'What? Run over by a bus?'

'Yes. How the hell could that possibly have happened? Yesterday, in Keymerstraat. Leg broken in three places. Other fractures all over the place. He was in the operating theatre for over eight hours – but they've sorted everything. It all went well, according to Hiller.'

'So it was an accident?'

'Yes. But it happened at a most inopportune moment – it seems they've just got a new lead on that strangler, and now the leader of the investigation is a cripple. That's why Hiller rang.'

'What?'

'What more can I say?'

Neither of them spoke. Van Veeteren looked up at the ceiling. Ulrike eyed him over the top of her reading glasses. Five seconds passed.

'Well?'

'. . .'

'Come on. You don't need to say it in blank verse.'

Van Veeteren sighed.

'All right. Hiller wants me to step in as a freelance chief inspector, and take over the helm until the ship has docked. They're snowed under with other work as well . . . He was pretty convincing – he'd probably been practising in advance.'

'I see.' She leaned over towards him. 'Might one ask what you told him?'

'I didn't commit myself,' said Van Veeteren, eyeing her thoughtfully. 'To be honest, I've no desire to get involved again: but I must have a word with Münster and Moreno before I make a final decision. And Reinhart, when he's capable of rational thought again. There's a murderer on the loose out there after all.'

He turned his head and gazed out of the window.

'I suppose that's the quintessence,' he said, caressing her arm. 'I'm sitting here all snug and secure on this sofa with a devoted woman – but things are a bit different out there in the wide world.'

'They certainly are,' said Ulrike. 'Although perhaps you don't need to spend all your time looking out of the window. When are you going to speak to them?'

'Tomorrow,' said Van Veeteren. 'I'll meet all three of them tomorrow. Then we'll see.'

'No doubt we shall,' said Ulrike. 'I think we ought to go to bed now, so that you are thoroughly rested.'

Van Veeteren looked at the clock.

'Half past eight?' he said in surprise. 'What do you mean?'

'Can you possibly misunderstand me?' Ulrike wondered as she ushered him into the bedroom. 'What's happened to your famous intuition?'

He noticed that she was smiling.

41

'I drank an American beer once,' admitted Van Veeteren. 'Only once – please note that. But apart from that error, this must be the weakest brew I've ever come across.'

He eyed his two former colleagues with an expression of restrained displeasure.

'The *Chief Inspector*'s imagery has not deteriorated since he became a bookseller,' said Münster drily. 'It certainly is a bit on the thin side, but the implications are quite clear even so, I think.'

'I agree,' said Moreno. 'It might be a little wishy-washy, but there's no denying the taste.'

'Ah, well,' muttered Van Veeteren, taking a swig of Adenaar's significantly more full-bodied ale. 'I understand what you're getting at. We're looking for an academic, I gather. Somebody employed in some capacity or other by Maardam University. A professor or a reader, presumably, and a member of the Succulents. I actually know of them, but only by name. Anyway, forgive my teasing: there clearly is a pattern. But let's face it, anybody at all could have dropped that little lapel badge in Wallburg.'

'Of course,' said Moreno.

'But the suggestions of a literary murderer fit in well with what we've concluded already,' said Münster. 'Benjamin Kerran and Amos Brugger. We've thought all the time that the killer must be quite well educated.'

'You don't need to be well educated to read a tenth-rate English crime novel,' said Van Veeteren.

'It links all the murders together,' insisted Moreno. 'The priest, Monica and Martina Kammerle have been connected from the start, but now it's pretty sure that he has Kristine Kortsmaa and Ester Peerenkaas on his conscience as well. If you have the choice, it's always better to be looking for just one murderer rather than several – as I seem to recall a certain chief inspector saying on several occasions.'

'If you have the choice, yes,' said Van Veeteren, still looking sceptical. 'So you reckon there are five victims?'

'Yes,' said Münster with a sigh. 'It seems so. A handful. But the big question, of course, is how we're going to get anywhere with these damned freemasons. We have to investigate them, even if it turns out to be a false track. It won't be easy to persuade them to cooperate. The whole set-up is one of those fraternities in which everybody supports everybody else to the hilt, irrespective of the facts. That seems to be the bottom line – you brush my teeth, and I'll cut your toenails . . .'

'The Camorra,' said Van Veeteren. 'A sort of state within a state: no doubt what you say is absolutely right. But for Christ's sake, they surely don't have much influence in this day and age . . . Apart from in purely academic circles. Appointments and so on. I don't suppose you've started poking your noses into their affairs yet?'

Münster shook his head.

'We have to try to narrow things down a bit before we get going. Eliminate the most unlikely candidates. There are eleven Succulents who are over eighty – presumably we can exclude them without further ado.'

'Presumably,' said Van Veeteren.

'If we set an age limit at fifty, for instance, that leaves us with forty-three Succulents to investigate . . . Although that isn't the real problem.'

'What is the real problem?' wondered Moreno.

'As I understand it,' said Münster, 'and as Reinhart understands it as well, if I interpreted his slurred mumblings correctly, it could well be a mistake to simply jump in and start interrogating them all, one by one. No matter how many we pick out as possible candidates. Reinhart obviously had trouble in extracting the list of members from the top dog, Pro-Vice-Chancellor Kuurtens. If we just go barging in, they might very well keep mum once they realize that we're after one of their number.'

'Good Lord,' said Moreno. 'What century do they live in?'

'Not this one in any case,' said Münster with a sigh. 'Maybe not the last one either.'

Van Veeteren leaned back and lit a newly rolled cigarette. Münster exchanged glances with Moreno and decided it could well be best to say nothing at the moment. They had been sitting at one of the usual window tables for over an hour now. The *Chief Inspector* had been provided with all the information he could reasonably need as a basis on which to make a decision, and was immune to any persuasive arguments or ploys by this stage. As far as Münster could judge, at least.

If he felt like joining them in their efforts, he would no doubt do so. If he didn't, they would simply have to make do with the resources they already had. That was the long and the short of it. Münster looked out of the window and noted that the sun wasn't shining today either.

'Anyway,' said Moreno after a while. 'That's the way it is.'

'So I've gathered,' said Van Veeteren.

'Is the situation clear to you?' asked Münster tentatively.

Van Veeteren took another drag at his cigarette.

'As clear as a Budweiser,' he said. 'That's what it was called, that wishy-washy Yankee piss.'

'Oh, a Bud, was it?' said Münster. 'I have to agree that that's nothing to write home about. Still, one has to feel sorry for Reinhart. Especially as it's happened just now.'

Van Veeteren shrugged.

'There isn't a good time to get run over by a bus,' he said. 'Ah, well, I'll think about what I'm going to do. Don't take it for granted that I'll join you.'

Moreno and Münster nodded in unison, and waited.

'I'll drive out to the hospital this evening and have a word with Reinhart. You can tell Hiller that I'll let him know tomorrow morning what I've decided. Is that okay?'

'Yes, of course,' said Münster. 'But we could certainly do with your help. There are several other cases on the go, in parallel to this one of ours, so we're under quite a bit of pressure. Rooth claims he's lost a couple of kilos.'

'That's a bad omen,' said Van Veeteren. 'But as I said, don't take it for granted that I'll be joining you.'

He drained his beer glass and checked his watch.

'Oops,' he said. 'It's high time I opened the shop if we're going to sell any books today. Thank you for my free lunch.'

'The pleasure was entirely ours,' said Inspector Moreno, and received a tap on the head in return.

'I . . . collided . . . with . . . a . . . bush,' spluttered Reinhart.

'So I see,' said Van Veeteren, pulling a chair up to the side of the bed.

'Number . . . fourteen . . . I . . . remember . . . it . . . wash . . . number . . . fourteen.'

'Bravo,' said Van Veeteren. 'There speaks a real police officer.'

This is going to take some time, he thought.

'I . . . haven't . . . become . . . an . . . idiot,' Reinhart insisted. 'But . . . it'sh . . . shmashed . . . my . . . jaw . . . bone.'

Van Veeteren gave him an encouraging tap on his plastered jaw and looked hard at his bruised and swollen face.

'You look an even bigger mess than you usually do,' he said in a friendly tone. 'So you took the main force of the blow on your face, did you?'

Reinhart coughed and wheezed for a while.

'There . . . ish . . . a . . . crack . . . in . . . every . . . shing,' he panted, gesturing towards his head with his unbandaged arm.

'Do you remember what happened?' asked Van Veeteren.

Reinhart tried to shake his head, but the effort was too much and he pulled a face.

'Only ... the ... bush ... number ... and ... I ... thought ... about ... thoshe ... bloody ... Shuccu ... lentsh ... Woke ... up ... in ... the ... ambulansh ... God ... I'm ... sho ... tired ...'

'Hiller rang,' said Van Veeteren.

'I know,' said Reinhart in one go.

'He wants me to go back and join the team.'

The expression on Reinhart's face was impossible to interpret.

'I haven't made my mind up yet.'

'It ... washn't ... my ... shuggeshion,' Reinhart insisted.

'I believe you. But it looks as if you're going to be off work for a few days.'

'It'll ... be ... shome ... daysh ... yesh,' said Reinhart. 'But ... I ... have ... a ... favour ... to ... ashk.'

'Really?'

'Nail ... that ... bashtard ... shtrangler!'

Reinhart slurped noisily down some juice from a cardboard pack and groaned.

'I have a question,' said Van Veeteren when the patient had lain back down on the pillows. 'I'd like to know how you interpret the situation. Does that badge business really hold water? Do you believe it?'

Reinhart closed his eyes and kept them closed for five seconds before answering.

'Fifty-one ... pershent ...' he stuttered. 'I'm ... fifty-one ... persh ... ent ... con ... vinshed!'

'Excellent,' said Van Veeteren.

He stayed there for a while, listening to the faint swishing sound from the air-conditioning system, and recalled his own operation some six years previously. When he saw that Chief Inspector Reinhart had fallen asleep, he stood up carefully and left the ward.

He walked home from Gemejnte Hospital through persistent light rain. He recalled having taken an umbrella with him that morning, but it was presumably still in the antiquarian bookshop. Or at Adenaar's. He certainly hadn't left it by Reinhart's bedside, he was sure of that.

Indecision gnawed away inside him like a well-deserved bout of sickness, and he realized that he would have to devise a way of solving the problem. Something irrational – such as whether the first person he met after turning the corner into Wegelenstraat was a man or a woman . . . Or whether there was an odd or an even number of bicycles parked outside the Paradiso cinema.

Draw lots, in other words, and dodge having to make a decision in that way.

Because it certainly wasn't easy.

Becoming a chief inspector again – albeit for only a short time – was an exceedingly unpleasant thought.

But not doing one's bit to help solve the case was at least as unpleasant a thought. Especially as he had that confounded priest on his conscience.

Pastor Gassel, who had concluded his journey through this life on a railway line of all places.

And Hiller was expecting to hear his decision the following morning. Oh, shit!

But then again, it struck him just as he had passed by Zuydersteeg and resisted the temptation to nip down to the Society for an hour, perhaps there was a third way? A compromise?

That thought accompanied him all the way home. Was there perhaps a way of turning down Hiller's offer but nevertheless fulfilling his duty in this peculiar case? Was it possible to find such a solution? A moral short cut.

It would be worth its weight in gold if there was. And most certainly worth thinking about in any case.

Ulrike was not at home – he recalled her having said something about a friend who was having some difficulties. He switched on the standard lamp in the living room and flopped down into the armchair in front of the window. Got up again and set up a CD of Preisner's *Requiem dla mojego przyjaciela* before flopping down again once more.

He started recapitulating in detail everything that had happened since the day last autumn when he had bitten into that disastrous olive.

Pastor Gassel.

The lonely – and murdered – women in Moerckstraat.

The baby-faced vicar in Leimaar with his liberal views on sexuality.

Benjamin Kerran.

Moosbrugger.

The Wallburg woman and the missing fröken Peerenkaas, who appeared to have advertised for her murderer. And that unlikely little lapel badge with a pin pointing directly into the superior university world.

And to crown all, Reinhart run over by a bus!

What a story, he thought. What an absolutely improbable story! Thinking about it felt like an extremely dodgy walk over quicksand. A swamp which was mostly bottomless and unknown, and with long distances between the tussocks that would carry your weight.

And the thread linking everything together was thin, just as thin as Moreno and Münster had claimed it was at Adenaar's.

Nevertheless, it was there. Thin, but strong. It was exactly as they had said, his former colleagues: he had nothing against their analysis.

Five murders, one killer. When he thought about that, all other variations seemed significantly less plausible. It's better to be looking for one murderer rather than several, Moreno had said – something he'd come out with himself on some occasion or other, she had claimed. That seemed highly likely.

But there was something else he remembered . . . No, not remembered, that was too strong a word.

An association. Some sort of link to something that was as yet hidden away in the depths of his subconscious, but with a bit of luck it would come bubbling up to the surface without his needing to strain himself. Or to sacrifice a night's sleep in order to think about it.

An association that was in fact a confirmation?

Yes, that was presumably the case. He understood the

THE STRANGLER'S HONEYMOON

function before he could establish the content, which was quite remarkable. It was a detail that fitted in with all these somewhat bizarre circumstances: Kerran, Moosebrugger, the university world . . .

But what? he thought.

What the hell can that detail be?

He went to fetch a dark beer in order to stimulate the mysterious mechanisms of his memory, and just as he was swallowing the final mouthful he received his reward.

By Christ yes, he thought. You can bet your life on it.

He remained sitting there for another quarter of an hour, thinking, and the requiem proceeded via *Agnus Dei* and *Lux aeterna* to the *Lacrimosa*, the most beautiful of all the movements. When the music had finished, he fetched another bottle and sat down at his desk in order to write a note to Chief of Police Hiller.

42

'You look different somehow,' said Inspector Sammelmerk, eying Ewa Moreno up and down as she came in through the door. 'Has something happened?'

'I'm relieved,' said Moreno with a smile. 'Hence my pink cheeks. But it's pretty banal in fact.'

Sammelmerk thought for a couple of seconds.

'Your period?'

'Yes. It started this morning. Ten days late. Can you tell me why we women have to have these kind of problems?'

Sammelmerk shrugged.

'It's in our contract. In the next life you might be a man or a potted plant, then you won't have any periods.'

'Can one choose?'

'Choose?'

'Between being a man or a potted plant.'

'I think so. Incidentally, I thought you said you'd made up your mind to join forces with the laddie on the floor below.'

'That's true,' said Moreno, sitting down in the window-bay. 'We've done a deal – but only to move in with each other. Well, I suppose we've also agreed to get married – but don't you think it's a good idea to see if you can put up with each other when living cheek by jowl before you start bringing children into the world? I seem to remember reading that somewhere.'

Sammelmerk puckered up her brow.

'That's one way of looking at it,' she said. 'But I have to admit that I've never tried it myself. I never seemed to have time. But that's enough philosophy for today. What's on your agenda?'

Moreno sighed.

'Desk work,' she said. 'But I suppose there's a time for everything. And if you're bleeding, perhaps it's just as well . . . No, for God's sake, I didn't mean that! What about you?'

'Same here,' said Sammelmerk. 'Regarding the desk, that is . . . But only this morning, with a bit of luck. If all goes well I shall be gallivanting off to Willby after lunch.'

'Willby? Why?'

'A good question,' said Sammelmerk. 'To see Clara Peerenkaas: she's the one I have my sights on. Rooth thought she had been suspiciously quiet lately. As you may recall, she phoned us every day at first, after her daughter disappeared. But then, all of a sudden, she stopped . . . Well, it might not mean anything – but it could be worth looking into, at least.'

Moreno thought that over.

'Could be,' she said. 'But in any case, if you can miss half a day of shuffling paper around, that has to be a good thing. But I gather you haven't been given the green light yet, is that right?'

Sammelmerk flung out her arms.

'How could that have happened? We don't even know at

the moment who'll be responsible for switching on the green light. Do you think the notorious VV will step into the breech? It would be interesting to meet him.'

Moreno shrugged.

'I don't know,' she said. 'I have no idea, in fact. But aren't you also due to see Hiller at ten o'clock to find out what's going on?'

Sammelmerk looked at her wristwatch.

'I certainly am,' she said. 'I'm one of the chosen few. It's two minutes to – shall we go?'

Chief of Police Hiller was not at his best that murky February morning – but then, he rarely was.

Moreno thought for a moment that he reminded her of a fanatical German stamp collector and child murderer she'd seen in a tenth-rate film a few months ago – and she wondered how on earth it could be that he had five children and a wife who had stood by him all these years. It must be getting on for forty by now, she was horrified to realize.

'Now, let's see,' he began. 'Is everybody here?'

He checked all those present. So did Moreno. Münster, Rooth, Jung. Herself and Sammelmerk. And the promising Inspector Krause.

They were all the ones who had been summoned, it seemed. The criminal circle.

But then, there was nobody else available. She sat down next to Jung on the shiny leather sofa and closed her eyes while she waited for Hiller to write down the names of all present in his notebook. She tried to recall how things had been when she first joined the CID eight years ago. Who was still there – and above all, who wasn't.

Heinemann had gone, of course. Old, timid Intendent Heinemann who always stuck to his own leisurely tempo, but often edged his way forward to answers and solutions that the others had blustered their way past . . . And deBries, who had committed suicide six months ago. To avoid facing up to the shame of what he had done. Even now the only ones who knew what that shame entailed were she herself, Münster and Van Veeteren. The real reason for his suicide. An excessive interest in young girls. Very young girls. She couldn't avoid shuddering at the thought of it.

Was there anybody else no longer there?

Van Veeteren, of course. The *Chief Inspector*. Was he really going to turn up once again? She found that hard to believe. Very hard. He'd sounded less than enthusiastic at Adenaar's.

She opened her eyes, and concluded from the grim, stamp-collector-like expression on the chief of police's face that her presumption was correct.

What about the new faces? Compared with those from eight years ago?

Krause had forced his way into the regular team. Thanks to hard work, meticulousness and ambition. Perhaps he would become a good police officer one of these days. But she also wondered if he would ever become a man.

And she wondered why such a condescending thought had occurred to her. There was nothing wrong with Widmar

Krause, of course. But was he a man or a potted plant? What prejudiced thoughts occurred to her at times . . .

Sammelmerk had joined them. Moreno felt a sudden rush of gratitude, and hoped from the bottom of her heart that Irene had come to stay.

There were no more new recruits. There were fewer of them now, in fact, than there had been eight years ago, despite the fact that there had been no decline in the rate of criminality. Even fewer today, of course, in view of Reinhart's accident. That was why they were assembled here. Because of Reinhart. Moreno put her hand over her mouth to conceal a yawn.

'Anyway, good morning,' intoned the chief of police as he turned to a new page in his notebook.

'Good morning, sir,' said Rooth.

Nobody else spoke.

'The situation is grim. Unusually grim.'

He ran his hand over his head, to check that what remained of his hair was in place, and clicked a few times on his latest ballpoint pen.

'We are very sorry to note the mishap that has befallen Chief Inspector Reinhart. We had hoped that it would be possible to persuade Van Veeteren to step into the breech for a limited period of time, but alas, that has not been possible – despite the fact that I had a long discussion with him on Sunday . . .'

He fished out a sheet of paper from his inside pocket and waved it in the air.

'I have received his reply this morning, and he declines . . .

Regrettably but definitely, he says. On the other hand, he says – and I quote – he intends to "undertake certain investigative work on his own initiative". What the hell does that mean? Any comments?'

Rooth made a point of sneezing, but nobody else had anything to say.

'So that's the way it is,' said the chief of police. 'And that's the way Van Veeteren is. Anyway, we need to reorganize our resources in view of Reinhart's absence . . . Münster, you can take over as investigator in chief of this old Kammerle–Gassel case – or whatever you call it. I take it for granted that we shall soon solve it – there appears to have been a new development recently, and we can't have this strangler on the loose much longer: people's respect for the upholding of the law is being undermined. Use the resources at your disposal as you think necessary – but remember that we have a lot of other cases on our hands, so only use them if it is necessary – remember that!'

'Thank you for the trust you are placing in me,' said Münster courteously.

'And for Christ's sake keep in touch with Van Veeteren. God only knows what he's up to. Private detective work? – it's enough to give you goose pimples!'

He demonstrated his impotence by crumpling up the *Chief Inspector's* fax and throwing it into the waste paper basket.

'I have no intention of interfering in the practical operations in connection with this case – unless it is absolutely essential, and I repeat the word *essential*.'

Nobody seemed to think that such a circumstance was

likely to occur in the near future, and since nobody had anything else of relevance to say, Hiller declared the meeting closed.

'Make sure you sort out this mess!' was his final order. 'That's what you are paid to do. The general public has a right to expect a certain percentage of success when it comes to solving criminal activities.'

An inspiring run-through, Münster thought as he closed the door behind him. Five-and-a-half minutes. Perhaps one ought to have oneself encased in plaster for a few weeks?

Van Veeteren was slumped back in the armchair in the back room of the bookshop. In the shop itself two customers were wandering around discreetly among the bookshelves: he could hear the sound of them leafing through books, almost like a whispering echo from another world; but he had informed them that they could shout for him if they needed any assistance. Or if they even wanted to buy something.

In his lap was a copy of the Succulents' membership list – the one received from Münster at Adenaar's on Sunday. Four pages. A hundred-and-fifty-two names.

One hundred and fifty-one needed to be eliminated. Only one would remain. Benjamin Kerran alias Amos Brugger alias the Strangler. That was his task. The ideal solution.

He took a drink of coffee from the mug in the holder on the arm of his chair, and had a sudden and totally idiotic thought comparing what he was doing to the culinary reduction of sauce (when you began with two litres of cream and ended up with half a litre of ambrosial nectar). Then he started work.

After ten minutes he had eleven names left.

After fifteen minutes, six.

After another five minutes, four.

That was as far as he could get.

It was not possible to reduce his sauce any further. There was a limit to how thin a sauce could become. He wrote the names down on a loose sheet of paper, and memorized them.

> *Erich Lambe-Silbermann*
> *Maarten deFraan*
> *David Linghouse*
> *Mariusz Dubowski*

The first two – Lambe-Silbermann and deFraan – were professors. Linghouse was a reader. Dubowski a lecturer with a doctorate. Their ages were respectively, 48 – 42 – 38 – 41.

One of them, he thought. One of these men has murdered five people. I must have faith in the method used – any doubts must remain locked up in the wardrobe for the time being.

That was easier said than done, but he gritted his teeth and ignored any objections. It was just as well that he wasn't in charge of the investigation: the method he was using was light years apart from normal, acceptable police work. He shook his head at himself, and dialled the number of Gemejnte Hospital.

After being connected to various operators, he finally had Reinhart at the other end of the line.

'How are you feeling today?' he asked.

'A lot better, thank you,' said Reinhart. It was obvious from the tone of his voice that he was telling the truth. 'You were here visiting me yesterday, weren't you?'

Van Veeteren confirmed that he had indeed paid Reinhart a visit.

'I'll be buggered if I can distinguish between dream and reality,' said Reinhart. 'Until now, that is. I'm afraid they've shovelled a few kilos of morphine into me, but that's the routine in this abattoir. Still, from today onwards I'm in charge of my own healing process.'

'Thus speaks a real man,' said Van Veeteren. 'You'll be running in the Maardam Marathon in May.'

'No chance,' protested Reinhart. 'What the hell do you want? Don't tell me you're in harness again? I really don't want you to—'

'No chance,' said Van Veeteren. 'But I'm playing at being a private detective. I've dreamt of doing that since I was eight years old, and it does give you a free rein . . .'

'A private detective?'

'Something like that. You can call it whatever you like. I've had an idea regarding that murderer you're looking for, but it's a bit unorthodox and so I'm staying in the background.'

'Old bookseller, he talk in tongues,' said Reinhart. 'Ouch! . . . Sorry about that, I forgot I'm handicapped . . . Anyway, I'm also a shadow of my former self. Come on, tell me what the hell you are on about!'

'I'd thought of making use of your wife,' said Van Veeteren.

'My wife?'

'Yes.'

'Winnifred?'

'Do you have more than one?'

'No. But . . .'

'Good. You have no objections, then?'

Reinhart coughed, and groaned.

'What are you proposing to do with my wife?'

'She works in the English Department, isn't that right?'

'Yes . . . Of course.'

'Hmm. I've worked out that the Strangler also works there.'

There was silence at the other end of the line.

'Forgive me,' said Reinhart eventually. 'I needed to check and make sure I was awake. Why the hell do you think that he works in the English Department?'

'I'll come and explain it to you in the next day or two,' Van Veeteren promised generously. 'I just want to test the validity of my theory first. But I take it you don't have any objections to me consulting Winnifred?'

'Why should I?'

'Good. She's a woman of sound judgement, isn't she?'

'She has chosen me as her husband,' said Reinhart. 'What more proof do you need?'

'Hmm,' said Van Veeteren. 'Presumably none. I'm glad to hear that you are in such good spirits. Do you know if she's at home this evening?'

'She will be unless she comes to visit me, like a loyal and loving wife. Joanna thinks hospitals are great, so I expect them to turn up for a while.'

'I see. Then perhaps you could mention to her that I'm intending to get in touch.'

'You can rely on me,' said Reinhart. 'Do the others know what you're getting up to?'

Van Veeteren paused.

'Not yet. Münster is in charge of the investigation in your absence: I'll keep him informed if things turn out well. But only if they do.'

'If I weren't in plaster,' said Reinhart, 'I'd squeeze out of you whatever it is you're up to. I'd like you to be quite clear about that.'

'But you *are* in plaster,' said Van Veeteren. 'I'm quite clear about *that*.'

He hung up, and drank the rest of his coffee.

43

It was a few minutes past ten in the evening when he rang the bell of Zuyderstraat 14. It was Winnifred Lynch herself who had proposed such a late time for their meeting, but Van Veeteren thought she looked very tired indeed when she answered the door.

'I'm worn out,' she admitted without beating about the bush. 'Work, nursery, hospital, cooking, bathing, putting to bed, reading a story . . .' A day in the life of, no doubt about that. 'I need a whisky – would you like one as well?'

'Yes, please,' said Van Veeteren, hanging up his overcoat. 'I promise not to be long-winded, but you need to be pretty well on the ball. Reinhart said you usually are.'

'I'm the bright one in the family,' said Winnifred. 'Don't worry. Sit yourself down in there, and I'll fix us a couple of glasses. Water? Ice?'

'One centimetre of tap water, please,' said Van Veeteren, and headed for the living room.

He liked the look of it, as he always did. The unfussy, well-filled bookshelves. the piano. The almost bare walls and the large, comfy sofas. No television. A streamlined, black music centre and a potted palm touching the ceiling. Discreet lighting.

He realized that he hadn't been here for four or five years
. . . Not since Reinhart had married his pretty wife, in fact.

Why not? he asked himself. What do we do with our lives
and our friends? After all, Reinhart was one of the nicest
people he had ever met.

Winnifred arrived with a glass in each hand.

'Cheers,' she said, flopping down on the sofa opposite him.
'I have to say you've aroused my curiosity. Not to mention
what you've done to my dear husband.'

'I'm sorry,' said Van Veeteren. 'It's not my intention to be
mysterious, it's just that it would be damned stupid to enlighten all and sundry with regard to what I have in mind. But
I need your help.'

'So I've gathered,' said Winnifred.

'The fact is that I'm trying to cut corners, to take a short
cut to what I'm after. If it turns out that I'm barking up the
wrong tree, it's better that as few people as possible know
about my stupidity.'

'I'm with you,' said Winnifred. 'I'm worn out, but my
brain's wide awake, don't worry.'

'You must agree to say nothing to anybody about this.'

'I wasn't born yesterday.'

'Good. I shall worry you no end.'

'I'm worried stiff already.'

'And I shall cast aspersions on the reputation of your colleagues.'

She smiled.

'I've already had a certain amount of information from the

hospital, don't forget that. You don't need to run through the preliminaries.'

'Okay,' said Van Veeteren. 'I just want to make sure that we're both singing from the same hymn sheet, and in the same key.'

She didn't respond. He took out the sheet of paper with the names. He said nothing for a while, but Winnifred looked just as calm and relaxed as a goddess after a bath.

Or after making love.

And this despite the fact that she had seemed to be so tired only a few minutes ago: it was remarkable how quickly she had acquired a new aura. There's something special about certain women, he thought, and realized he was losing the plot. He cleared his throat and leaned forward, pushed the folded-over sheet of paper across the table, but kept two fingers on it.

'Here are the names of four of your colleagues in the English Department,' he said slowly. 'I want you to study those names, and concentrate on the persons behind them. Visualize them as best you can, you mustn't rush it – we can sit here in silence for half an hour if that's what it takes. What I want to know is which of them is capable of killing five people.'

She didn't respond. Just nodded rather vaguely. He realized that she must have been expecting something of this sort. Despite everything.

She had spoken to Reinhart, and they had reached their conclusions together. It would have been odd if they hadn't.

'If you can't intuitively decide on one of them, then let it drop. This has nothing to do with normal police work, but you can rely on my judgement. If it isn't one of these four, or if you pick out the wrong one, that will remain a matter between you and me. It will have no significance in any circumstances. But . . .'

'But if I pick the right one?'

'That will make the whole process easier, and enable us to nail a murderer.'

'Really?'

'I hope so, at least. The responsibility is entirely mine. Are you prepared to accept these conditions?'

She looked at him for a few seconds with something about her mouth that suggested amusement, before answering.

'Yes. I'll go along with all that.'

Van Veeteren removed his fingers from the folded sheet of paper and leaned back.

'Okay. Off you go, then.'

Inspector Sammelmerk had lots of good sides, but only one mania.

She loved taking a shower.

It had nothing to do with an exaggerated desire to be clean. Not at all. It had more to do with her soul than with her body in general, even if the physical pleasure was of course the direct link with her soul.

When the hot jets – so hot that they were barely tolerable – came into contact with the area around her seventh cervical vertebra and her first thoracic vertebra, a sort of electric well being spread out over the whole of her body; and she some-times asked herself whether the Good Lord was guilty of a careless error when he placed her G-spot in a different part of her anatomy.

Mind you, it didn't work that way when she was touched, only when she was subjected to a jet of hot water: so perhaps she wasn't all that abnormal after all.

Whatever, she liked nothing better than to take a long shower – the longer the better. Sometimes she could almost lapse into a trance in the bathroom, to the rest of the family's increasingly perplexed surprise. A twenty- or thirty-minute soak was nothing unusual, but eventually both the IT genius and their offspring came to terms with it. Every human being has a right to have their fundamental needs satisfied, she used to maintain, and if she were to try to overcome this harmless perversion, no doubt something much worse would turn up to replace it. The sum of one's vices is constant.

Besides, it wasn't always a case of sinking into a trance. Not every time. While in the shower she could also experi-ence an enhanced feeling of insight and clarity of thought, and very often she was able to make important decisions and solve complicated problems while in this meditative mode. Confused thinking was ironed out and irritations rinsed away. If she ever tried to work out why such remarkable things hap-pened while she was in the shower, she usually found that the most congenial solution was that she was born under the sign of Pisces.

The rest of her family were born under earth and air signs,

and could hardly be expected to fully appreciate the significance of water.

That evening she was in the shower a mere twenty minutes after arriving back home, and there was only one problem that occupied her thoughts as she wallowed in the hot jets of water. Only one.

The conversation with Clara Peerenkaas.

Without a second thought Intendent Münster had accepted her suggestion that they should renew contact with the worried parents out at Willby – which happened to be his home town, he informed her. She had rung and given notice of her arrival time, and at four o'clock she had been received in a neat, yellow-painted house on the bank of a canal in the idyllic little town on the River Gimser.

The husband had been otherwise engaged. Inspector Sammelmerk had drunk tea and eaten biscuits while sitting on a somewhat slippery plush sofa, trying to work out what it was about fru Peerenkaas's behaviour that disturbed her.

Or 'disturbed' was too strong a word: surprised her.

There was certainly something odd about it.

Elusive and hard to pin down, but odd even so.

Her worry about what might have happened to her daughter seemed to be genuine enough, there were no two ways about that. When Sammelmerk asked bluntly why the Peerenkaases had stopped telephoning the police, the reply was that they had lost heart when no progress was made. They had discussed the possibility of employing a private detective, but still hadn't made up their minds. Instead they had been concentrating on their efforts to contain their worries and fears.

This seemed quite a plausible explanation, Sammelmerk thought. They were religious and had received stalwart support from their parish, fru Peerenkaas maintained. Prayers were said for Ester several times a week, for instance: when one was unable to do anything concrete to solve a problem, it was a person's duty to put his or her trust in God. Calmly and without hesitation.

It had all sounded very convincing, and it was not until she was in the car on the way back to Maardam that Sammelmerk began to doubt the evidence of her senses. When she could contemplate what had happened from a distance, as it were.

And now, as she stood there in the shower, it soon dawned on her what the problem was.

She was lying.

Somehow or other fru Peerenkaas was not telling the truth.

God only knows about what, exactly, she thought. That could be literally true, in view of what had been said about prayers and the other world.

But there was something wrong in any case. Fru Peerenkaas was holding something back, and had not quite been able to conceal the fact that she was doing so.

That was the top and bottom of it.

But what?

What exactly had she been keeping to herself? Sammelmerk

wondered, and raised the temperature of the water by half a degree.

It didn't help.

Nor did it help that she stayed in the shower for thirty-five minutes. Nor that she raised the temperature another half-degree, so that it really was at the very limit of what was bearable. Nor did it help that her youngest son came and belted on the door, wondering whether she intended to spend the whole night in there or was turning into a seal.

Nothing helped.

But something was wrong, she was sure of that. Fru Peerenkaas was lying about something.

But she didn't know what. It was maddening.

Winnifred Lynch folded up the sheet of paper and drank the remains of her whisky.

'I'm ready,' she said.

Van Veeteren gave a start and realized that he had almost fallen asleep. He looked at the clock. Only a few minutes had passed, but the silence had been manifest. Very manifest indeed. Like a vacuum.

She slid the paper back across the table just as he had done. Like the final hidden card to complete a straight flush, he thought. He picked it up and unfolded it.

'Who?' he asked.

'Maarten deFraan,' she said. 'Number two.'

He looked at the name. Allowed a few seconds to pass

while stroking his cheek. He realized that he hadn't shaved today.

'DeFraan?' he said. 'Are you sure?'

It was only a name as far as he was concerned, nothing more.

'If it is one of that quartet, yes. The others are impossible.'

'How can you know?'

'I just know.'

He thought for a moment.

'Is he a plausible candidate? Or just the least unlikely?'

She hesitated before answering. Pressed the fingertips of each hand against one another and contemplated them.

'I can . . . I can imagine him in that role. He has always made me feel uncomfortable.'

'Do you know him well?'

'Not at all. Remember that there are over thirty members of staff in our department. I come across him occasionally, but our offices are a long way apart. It's mostly at meetings and suchlike.'

'What do you know about him?'

'Not a lot. Hardly anything. He came to the department the year before I started, I think. Was awarded the chair in English literature – there's another chair but that's for somebody more linguistically inclined: that's my own field. DeFraan used to be in Aarlach, unless I'm much mistaken. He's regarded as a big talent – it's rare to get a chair before you're forty.'

'Married?'

'I don't think so.'

'Do you know where he lives?'

'No. Quite close to the university, I think. But I can find out all his details from the computer, if you'd like me to.'

'Excellent,' said Van Veeteren. 'Can you get them for me by tomorrow?'

'Of course. Is one allowed to ask the oracle a question?'

'The oracle will only respond to the question if he knows the answer,' said Van Veeteren.

'Fair deal,' said Winnifred with a fleeting smile. 'What made you narrow everything down to . . . well, to this quartet in the English Department?'

Van Veeteren thought for a moment.

'All right,' he said. 'A few somewhat vague indicators, in fact. Do you know the details of the case?'

'To some extent,' said Winnifred. 'We've discussed it in the bath a few times . . . And this afternoon at the hospital, of course.'

'In the bath?' said Van Veeteren. 'Reinhart and you?'

'Yes, that's where we have our best conversations. Hmm . . .'

'I see,' said Van Veeteren. 'Well, there was nothing special – there never is when I'm under way. It was obvious at quite an early stage that the person the police were looking for had a fair amount of literary education, and when we had a tip suggesting he was in the university world, it was just a matter of finding the right faculty. And subject area. Robert Musil is what you might call public property – you don't need to be a German language expert to know about him and his books;

but that Benjamin Kerran from an obscure English criminal novel . . . coupled with T. S. Eliot at Keefer's restaurant – well, I would suggest that settled it.'

'Could well be,' said Winnifred tentatively. 'But it's not a cut and dried case, surely?'

'I've never claimed that it is,' said Van Veeteren. 'However, there are eleven of your colleagues who are members of the Succulent society. Seven could be excluded on the grounds of their age. But as you say, they are by no means indisputable observations. And bear in mind that we are talking about a method, nothing more than that: the possible margins of error border on the grandiose. The moment I discover deFraan has nothing to hide, we can forget the whole business and no harm will have been done . . . . Incidentally, do you happen to know his area of special expertise?'

Winnifred thought for a moment, and he could see that a penny had suddenly dropped for her.

'Good God!' she said. 'You could well be right. I'm pretty sure that his doctoral thesis was on English popular literature. Underground and crime novels and such stuff. Around the beginning of the twentieth century, I think.'

'Aha,' said Van Veeteren. 'That really could put him in the spotlight. Anyway, I mustn't disturb you any longer. I hope I don't need to tell you how significant your contribution could turn out to be?'

'Nor that I should hold my tongue,' said Winnifred. 'Many thanks, this has been very . . . interesting. Would you like me to fax his personal details to the bookshop tomorrow?'

Van Veeteren shook his head.

'I'd prefer to come to the university and fetch them in person. It would be useful for me to have a look around.'

'Your word is my command,' said Winnifred. 'You'll find me in my office at any time between twelve and four – but ring first just to be on the safe side.'

Van Veeteren promised to do that. He put the list of names in his pocket and stood up. When he had finished putting on his street clothes in the hall, Winnifred had one last query.

'How many has he killed?'

'If he really is the one, he could well have killed five people.'

'Good Lord,' whispered Winnifred, and he realized it was only now that all the implications of the situation had really registered with her. That this wasn't some kind of theoretical riddle.

'Go to bed now and think about something else,' he recommended.

'I shall just have another whisky first,' said Winnifred. 'How about you?'

He declined the offer, and left.

Ulrike was already asleep by the time he got home in Klagenburg.

Perhaps that was just as well. He wouldn't have been able to resist discussing with her the outcome of his conversation with Winnifred, and the sensible thing was of course to avoid involving anybody else in this ploy. Not even Ulrike. Not even as a sounding board – the method and what he planned to do next would probably not be able to cope with no end of viewpoints and female intuition.

What he planned to do next wasn't all that clear at the moment: but he had a name now.

A name without a face. He hadn't yet seen Maarten deFraan, neither in a photograph nor in real life. It felt odd. An odd way to find a murderer. He wondered if he had ever gone about tracking down a criminal in as clinical a way as this. Probably not.

He went to the larder and looked somewhat half-heartedly to see if there was a bottle of dark beer left, but decided not to bother. If there had been any whisky left in the house he would probably have allowed himself a wee dram: but he knew they had drunk the last drop during the Christmas holidays, and hadn't got round to replenishing stocks.

In any case, he was not into hard liquor. Red wine or beer. The darker the better. In both cases. And Ulrike's taste was the same in this respect, as in so many others.

But what mattered now was not drinking habits. All that mattered was the Strangler. He dug out a CD of Pärt's *Für Alina*, and switched it on at low volume. Stretched out on the sofa in the darkness, with a blanket over him.

Professor deFraan? he thought. Who the hell are you?

Private detective Van Veeteren? he then thought. Who the hell do you think you are?

Clever stuff. A way of proceeding that he might be able to make use of in his book of memoirs – if he ever got round to finishing it off. He hadn't added anything to it for over three months now. He was stuck in that accursed G File, and not for the first time. The only case he had failed to solve after thirty years in the police force – that wasn't too bad a record, of course, but G could still keep him awake at night.

Be off with you! he snarled at G. We're going to concentrate on the Strangler now!

He took a deep breath and closed his eyes.

The plan. What should he do? How should he approach him?

How should he go about tricking Professor deFraan into giving himself away, to put it bluntly? What was the best way of confronting him? In what situation could he be expected to be fooled into giving the game away sufficiently for a cynical antiquarian bookseller to be able to catch on?

To produce that absolutely unique expression that appears in every murderer's eyes. In certain situations.

Perhaps not every murderer, he decided after a couple of seconds. But in most of them.

At the moment when the murderer looks for the first time into the eyes of his nemesis – the person who knows.

That is the moment, Van Veeteren thought, that fraction of a second when a veil descends over the murderer's eyes, and nothing can be more explicit for anybody who knows how these things happen. Nothing.

But there is another sort as well, he reminded himself.

Another sort of murderer who is immune to a sense of shame. G, for instance. Van Veeteren was forced to make a mental effort to abolish his image.

And if Maarten deFraan was in fact guilty, but made of the

same hard stuff as G, Van Veeteren's method would never succeed.

But that remained to be seen. A lot remained to be seen, that was for sure.

He yawned. Wondered if he ought to remain lying there on the sofa and listen to the rest of Pärt. Or whether he ought to join Ulrike in bed.

It was not a difficult decision to make.

44

The lecture room looked as if it could accommodate about a hundred students, and was about three-quarters full. He chose a fairly discreet seat in the last row but one. Sat down, adjusted the shelf that turned his seat into a little desk, and tried to look like a twenty-three-year-old student.

This didn't come naturally to him. He looked around and reckoned that he was the oldest person present by a margin of at least fifteen years – only a few women sitting two rows diagonally in front of him looked as if they had passed the thirty mark, and provided him with a modicum of consolation. Swayed no doubt by jealousy and prejudice, he decided that they were a group of secondary school teachers making the most of the half-term holiday to brush up their English language and literature, and celebrate not having to teach.

The rest of those present were young and talented. More or less as they had been when he himself spent a few years at university round about 1960 – reading various subjects with varying degrees of success. To his surprise, he realized that he missed that experience. He would love to relive those halcyon days – and was decidedly jealous of all these young people whose lives were as yet an unwritten page.

But needless to say, it wasn't as straightforward as that. Obviously. It hadn't been the case then, and was not the case now. He had boobed left, right and centre in the course of his life: for these talented young people, most of their mistakes were yet to come. It was a toss-up when it came to deciding which of them was most to be envied.

He recalled the smell as well. He didn't know if it emanated from the spacious lecture theatre with its high, barred windows, worn seats and warm, dusty radiators – or if people aged about twenty-three always generated a smell like this. But it didn't matter. Neither then nor now. It also felt unexpectedly odd – as if he had ended up in a time warp which forty years of experience were incapable of sorting out . . . A kind of pocket of resistance, perhaps? Despite all so-called progress. The older we become, he thought, the more our conception of time becomes circular. There seems to be less difference between today and tomorrow. But that's not especially strange, of course.

He took out his notebook and the papers he had been given by Winnifred Lynch, and wondered if there might be some kind of attendance register. Not that it mattered all that much – Winnifred had assured him that it would be highly unlikely, and that in no circumstances would he be thrown out. Professor deFraan's lecture on Conrad, Borrow and Trollope was open to students enrolled for various courses, and it was not unusual for members of the general public to sneak in and listen simply because they found it interesting. So he didn't need to regard himself as an outsider. Even if that's what he was.

The personal details about Maarten deFraan took up two densely written pages. He had been given them by Winnifred in her office a mere five minutes ago, and hadn't had time to do more than glance at them. If the lecture turned out to be sleep-inducing, he could no doubt take a closer look at them – discreetly, of course.

This also felt remarkably familiar – having a sort of alternative occupation to keep him going during lectures. That was presumably how he had regarded the situation in the sixties, he now realized. No wonder he hadn't progressed very far in the academic circus, Van Veeteren thought, and yawned.

But there was presumably no reason to cry over spilled milk in this connection either.

DeFraan appeared at exactly fifteen minutes past eleven, and the hushed murmur became a more or less respectful silence. Van Veeteren had to acknowledge that he did not have an immediate impression that this was the man he was looking for. Unfortunately – but no doubt that would have been too much to ask for. DeFraan looked healthy and in quite good shape. On the tall side, quite sturdy and with a face that reminded Van Veeteren vaguely of an American actor whose name he had long since forgotten. Bushy hair, dark and with a trace of grey here and there; his thin oval-shaped spectacles and neatly trimmed beard gave him an air of strength and intellectual integrity. Dark polo-necked sweater and a modest dark grey jacket. It seemed highly likely that women would find him attractive.

He welcomed his audience. Took off his wrist watch, placed it on the lectern in front of him, and set off without further ado.

A short but elegant summary of the English nineteenth-century novel in barely five minutes, before he came to the first of the three authors named in the title of his lecture: Joseph Conrad.

He occasionally wrote on the whiteboard, and Van Veeteren was somewhat surprised to see that his audience were taking notes for all they worth. Some of the students even had small portable tape recorders on their desk lids – that had never happened forty years ago, and he began to realize that Professor deFraan was regarded as an authority.

But he soon found it difficult to concentrate. There was evidently a shortage of oxygen in the lecture theatre, and he couldn't ignore the influence of gravity on his eyelids. He had read both Conrad and Trollope; had his own views on Conrad at least, and wasn't really interested in having his judgements reassessed or modified.

Not by a potential murderer, in any case.

He only knew Borrow by name – and hardly that. He found himself yawning again, and it was remarkable how soothing it was, sitting there in that room.

DeFraan's voice was strong but restrained. As he delved into the white man's burden in *The Heart of Darkness*, Van Veeteren found it increasingly difficult to assign to this man the role that was the main reason for his being there.

DeFraan didn't act like a strangler, in fact. Didn't sound like a murderer.

Didn't act like a strangler?

Van Veeteren shook his head at that amateurish judgement. 'We need to be clear that even a criminal usually acts normally' – that was a rule that old Borkmann had inculcated into him many years ago. 'In certain circumstances it can even be impossible to distinguish between a bus-load of psychopaths and a totally harmless collection of unimpeachable citizens,' he had maintained, and grinned characteristically. 'For instance, a gang of undertakers on a Sunday outing.'

Van Veeteren smiled to himself when he realized that he had remembered it word for word.

He didn't sound like a murderer!

Borkmann would have laughed at that wording. You can never tell. Van Veeteren decided to leave the professor in the heart of darkness, and instead to look a little more closely at the information about him that Winnifred had found on her computer.

Needless to say it concentrated on academic qualifications. Examinations passed. Posts held. Published books and articles. Symposiums and conferences deFraan had attended, research projects he had been involved in. Van Veeteren skimmed quickly through all that. Noted that his doctoral thesis had been entitled *Narrative Structures in Popular Fiction*, and that he had been Professor of English at Maardam University since 1996. Before that he had spent four years as a lecturer at the considerably less venerable seat of learning in Aarlach, which is where he had studied as a student.

The more personal data took up about half the second page, and stated among other things that he was born in Lingen on 7 June 1958. That he had been married, but had been a widower since 1995, that he had no children, and lived at Kloisterstraat 24.

That was about all. Van Veeteren read through the whole document from start to finish once again, to see if there might possibly be something – the tiniest detail or circumstance – that might suggest he really was the man they were looking for. The Strangler. The notorious and elusive lunatic who had murdered three people with his bare hands.

The murderer with a capital M.

He looked up and contemplated the well-dressed man standing in front of the whiteboard. He was writing something now: several book titles with publication dates. Could these hands . . . this hand (which had a plaster on the back of it, Van Veeteren noted automatically) – could these fingers that were now holding the blue marker pen and writing these letters, in a different situation and in certain circumstances wrap themselves round a woman's neck and . . . ?

It seemed absurd. He had met wolves in sheep's clothing many times during his career, but this seemed too ridiculous for words.

The private detective sighed and checked his watch: there were twenty minutes of the lecture still to go. He was longing for something to drink.

In order to give himself something to occupy his mind he took *Strangler's Honeymoon* out of his briefcase and started thumbing through it. He had started looking for it in the beginning of December, and eventually received a copy from Dillman's in London in the middle of January. He'd read it, but not thought much of it.

It was just that damned name that haunted him.

Kerran. Benjamin Kerran.

He found it difficult to associate it with that neatly dressed academic berk holding forth from his pulpit. Very difficult.

No matter what Borkmann might have had to say.

Two of the female students – a short, plump, dark-haired one and a tall, blonde girl with a ponytail – had aspects of Trollope to discuss with deFraan, and Van Veeteren had to wait for a while before he could have a private word with the professor. But the girls finished eventually – although it was clear that they would have liked to carry on rather longer, but lacked the ability. Both the intellectual capability and the feminine guile, it seemed. They thanked him excessively and at great length, put their pens and notebooks away in their rucksacks, curtseyed and sauntered out of the room. DeFraan adjusted his glasses and looked attentively and enquiringly at Van Veeteren.

'Excuse me, but do you have a moment?'

DeFraan smiled and put his lecture notes away in a yellow plastic folder.

'Of course.'

'Thank you. My name is Van Veeteren. I'm joint owner of Krantze's antiquarian bookshop in Kupinskis gränd.'

'What's your problem?'

'I accepted a book the other day that baffles me a bit, and I wonder if you can help me. With the author, mainly. Henry Moll. I've never heard of him.'

He handed over the somewhat worse for wear paperback. DeFraan examined it for a couple of seconds with one eyebrow raised, adjusted his glasses again, looked at the title page and checked the copyright details and year of publication.

'I'm sorry,' he said. 'I've never heard of it. But lots of books of this sort were published in the twenties and thirties. Why are you interested in it?'

'I read it and rather liked it.'

'Really?'

DeFraan looked first at the book, then at Van Veeteren, with an expression that might have indicated scepticism or derision.

'It's not exactly high-quality literature,' said Van Veeteren, trying to look embarrassed (without succeeding, as far as he could judge), 'but there's something intriguing about the plot, and the main character . . . the murderer.'

DeFraan didn't react. He started leafing somewhat nonchalantly through the book.

'Benjamin Kerran. Do you recognize the name?'

'Kerran?'

'Yes.'

DeFraan closed the book and looked at his watch.

'No. I'm sorry, but I don't think I can be of any help to you in this matter, herr . . . ?'

'Van Veeteren.'

'Van Veeteren. I have a meeting in ten minutes, so if you'll excuse me . . .'

Van Veeteren took the book and put it into his briefcase.

'Ah well,' he said. 'Thank you for your time anyway. And thank you for an interesting lecture.'

'You're welcome,' said deFraan, leaving the room unhurriedly.

Van Veeteren followed him even more slowly. At the bottom of the imposing marble staircase, the steps worn and made shiny by the feet of masses of students for the last century and a half, flanked by unadorned columns, he found a cafeteria. He recalled having been there before – not a century and a half ago, but perhaps forty years. He sat down at an empty table with a cup of coffee and a cigarette, and tried to analyse the situation.

God only knows, he thought. Maybe, but maybe not.

That was as far as he got. It wasn't possible to get any further.

But the contest had begun, that was clear.

It took Winnifred less than ten minutes to find the dissertation. She didn't have a copy in her office, but after a visit to the departmental library she returned with a light-blue book in her hand. Its full title was: *Narrative Structures in Early Twentieth Century English Popular Fiction*. Van Veeteren thanked her, put it next to Henry Moll in his briefcase and left Maardam University to its fate, whatever that might be.

He bought a lunch sandwich (without olives) at Heu-welinck's and was back in the bookshop before half past one. He sat in the kitchenette, and while slowly eating the sand-wich and drinking a bottle of Bettelheim dark beer, he started reading.

When both the sandwich and the beer were finished, he gave up, and looked at the index instead, at the end of the dis-sertation.

There it was.

Moll, Henry p. 136

He looked up the page referred to.

Thirteen lines, neither more nor less, were devoted to Henry Moll. *Strangler's Honeymoon* was mentioned, as were two other titles. In positive if quite neutral terms.

He closed the book and slid it to one side. Drained the beer bottle one more time, in the hope that there might be a few drops left.

God only knows, he thought again. But surely the evidence is building up?

That evening he went to the cinema with Ulrike, and watched the old Russian film *The Commissar*, a forgotten masterpiece from the 1960s. Afterwards they sat at Kraus cafe for an hour, discussing how it was possible to produce such a perfect work of art in the conditions that held sway in the Soviet Union a mere ten years after the death of Stalin.

Talking about the sublime scene in which the Jewish cob-bler washes his wife's feet.

About the role played by salt and bitter things in life. And about both Karel Innings, Ulrike's husband, who was murdered by a vengeful woman exactly five years ago, and about Van Veeteren's son Erich who had been dead for more than two years by this time.

They didn't often discuss such matters, but they did now.

Was it the case that their respective sorrow had brought them closer together? Intensified their relationship, and in some respects made it stronger than it would have been in more normal circumstances?

Difficult questions, perhaps not ideally defined, and of course they did not reach any conclusions. Not this evening. But as they strolled home through the drizzle, he had the feeling that he loved her like a shipwrecked sailor must love a raft that comes floating towards him just when all his strength has been used up.

Yes indeed, that was the very image that haunted his mind's eye.

It was almost half past eleven by the time they got home to Klagenburg, and he decided to postpone the conversation until the following morning. People's guard was always lower shortly after they had woken up, and if he could ask his somewhat indiscreet question in those circumstances, it had to be a good thing.

He set the alarm clock for seven o'clock, and crept closer to Ulrike with a sardonic smile on his lips.

'What's the matter with you?' she wondered. 'You seem somehow brimming over with energy, Mister Yang.'

He had to admit that she was right.

'It's the old hunter inside me that has woken up,' he said. 'I think I've picked up a scent.'

'Me?' asked Ulrike, and couldn't help giggling.

He closed his eyes and tried to work out how much a fifty-eight-year-old woman who could still giggle like a child was worth.

Quite a lot, he decided.

'Of course it's you,' he said. 'But there's something else as well.'

'A prey?'

'Something like that.'

'Switch the light off and hug me more tightly.'

He did as he was bidden.

'DeFraan.'

'Van Veeteren here. Good morning.'

'Who?'

'Van Veeteren, the antiquarian bookseller. We met briefly after your lecture yesterday.'

'What can I do for you?'

'It's about that book by Henry Moll.'

'Oh yes, I remember you now. But why are you ringing so early? It's not even half past seven yet.'

'I'm sorry. I wanted to catch you before you went to work.'

'You've done that all right.'

'There's something I've been wondering about.'

'Really? I'm all ears – but I'd be grateful if you were quick about it.'

'Of course. I didn't mean to wake you up. But I have a question. Do you still claim that you've never heard of Henry Moll and that book I showed you?'

'Claim and claim. I don't understand . . .'

Two seconds of silence.

'What was it called?'

'*Strangler's Honeymoon*. Published by Thornton & Radice in 1932.'

'Ah, yes . . . No, I don't remember anything about that book. And I don't understand why you are harassing me like this. I think we ought to close this call now, I don't think . . .'

'I've been reading your thesis.'

'Eh?'

'Your dissertation. *Narrative Structures in Popular Fiction* . . . – that's what it's called, isn't it?'

No answer.

'There's something I've been thinking about.'

'What, exactly?'

Was there for the first time a trace of fear in his voice? Or was it just his own imagination and expectations that were playing games?'

'The fact that you wrote about Moll and that book in your thesis, but nevertheless you maintain that you've never heard of them.'

'Moll?' said deFraan thoughtfully. 'Hmm, I suppose it's possible that I've come across him . . . But you must realize that it's more than fifteen years since I completed my dissertation. If I remember rightly I referred to over two hundred authors and three times as many books – you can't expect—'

'And Benjamin Kerran?'

'Kerran? I don't know what you're talking about. What the hell are you getting at? I certainly have no intention—'

'So you don't remember the name Benjamin Kerran either? I think I mentioned the name to you yesterday. He's the murderer in the book I mentioned. A strangler.'

Silence again for five seconds, then deFraan hung up.

Van Veeteren did the same. And leaned back against the pillows in his bed.

End of round one, he thought. Honours even.

But if – *if* I'm on the scent of the right prey, he knows now that I know. No doubt about that. He's not an idiot. That's a fact that has altered the odds for all the coming rounds. Changed them fundamentally.

But nevertheless, he thought as he stood in the shower a quarter of an hour later. There's something missing.

The murderer's shame, for instance – that look, or that noticeably husky voice: he hadn't exhibited an ounce of that. Van Veeteren had played quite a high trump card and earned as a result . . . well, what?

Nothing, was the obvious answer to that. Damn and blast! He could feel the doubt and desperation beginning to nag away inside him, as familiar as the chronic pains he had been feeling as age crept up on him: but instead of scrutinizing everything in more detail he left the shower. Dried himself meticulously, switched on the coffee machine and devoted his attention to the chess problem in *Allgemejne*.

Mate in three moves with several unidentified snags. It seemed familiar.

45

Reinhart was dreaming.

Two different dreams simultaneously, it seemed, each one worse than the other. In the first one his daughter Joanna and her red-haired friend Ruth were busy baking his left leg inside some kind of dough – that was why it felt so heavy . . . They intended to bake the whole of him in order to present him as an unusually impressive exhibit at a birthday party at their nursery school, they had informed him. The resultant pastry would be decorated with all kinds of pretty little embellishments such as starfish, flags and various sparkling stones – and would win the first prize in a competition: a trip to Disneyland in Paris. The very thought sent spasms of disgust through Reinhart's whole being, but he was unable to protest because they had first given him a hefty dose of morphine. His tongue lay half-dead in his mouth like a beached jellyfish. The whole thing was disgustingly awful.

In the second one he was wandering though a noisy town on the way towards an accident. His own accident. Something was going to happen – it wasn't yet clear what, but he continued heading towards his fate just as inevitably as if it had been a repeat performance of an old film that he was watching for the seventh time. He lay there helplessly, with his baked-in and incredibly heavy leg, and watched as he was nudged and elbowed on the menacing pavements of the menacing town. His own Maardam and his own Zuyderstraat, if he was not much mistaken: but there were also odd and unfamiliar aspects that he didn't recognize at all: shattered bridges and ruined houses, as if from a country devastated by war. He tried desperately to attract the attention of Joanna and Red Ruth and his wife, and to beg them to stop the film before it was too late. But it was in vain. The jellyfish in his mouth was now no more than an insignificant single-cell organism that had died and was drying out completely, and adhering to the palate in the most hopeless way. It was clear to him that all his efforts were in vain and pointless.

All this became clear to him shortly before the accident happened. And just before what had to happen actually did happen, he felt the push on his left shoulder – and registered a fleeting glimpse of somebody disappearing into the mass of people in the street, before he woke up.

He lost his balance, his body suddenly felt weightless, and he woke up in a cold sweat. For a brief moment he didn't know who he was.

His leg hurt. His hip hurt. His arm hurt and his tongue was feeling sticky.

But the dream persisted. Not Joanna and Red Ruth and the nursery party with the leg encased in pastry adorned with flags. But that push.

That nudge on his shoulder.

He stared up at the clinically white ceiling. And at the plaster of Paris in which he was encased.

My God! he thought, making a heroic effort to loosen his tongue from his palate. There was somebody there.

Somebody pushed me.

Van Veeteren telephoned Winnifred Lynch again on Thursday, and was informed that Professor deFraan had a lecture quite late that same afternoon. Between five and seven, roughly speaking. He asked if she was still prepared to assist him in his somewhat dodgy efforts – and she said that she was, without much hesitation, he thought.

'There are a couple of things I'm wondering about,' he said. 'His contacts, for instance. Is there anybody in the department who is a close friend of his? Or who knows a bit about his habits? It would be very useful if we could get some information of that sort.'

'I'll look into it,' Winnifred promised. 'I know he goes for a drink with Dubowski occasionally. But what the hell are you after? I can't just go—'

'No, no, of course not' said Van Veeteren. 'You must be very cautious. He might well suspect that I'm onto something, but in no circumstances must he become aware that there's a spy in the department. The other detail is more important in a way, and if you could establish the facts it would be even more valuable to me.'

'Fire away,' said Winnifred.

'It's just a shot in the dark,' Van Veeteren admitted. 'But it would be stupid not to follow it up. June 1999 . . . Could deFraan possibly have been in Wallburg on some sort of university business then? If there's some kind of record and you can check it without giving yourself away – well, I'd be prepared to bet a beer on his being our man after all.'

'Hmm,' said Winnifred.

'What do you mean by "hmm"?' wondered Van Veeteren.

'That I'd have to go via Beatrice Boordon, I'm afraid. She's the departmental secretary and not one of my favourite people, but I expect I'll think of something.'

'Caution,' said Van Veeteren. 'Always keep that in mind. Don't take any unnecessary risks. DeFraan might have five lives on his conscience, and you must not take any chances.'

'I'm aware of the terms,' said Winnifred, and hung up.

Terms? Van Veeteren thought when he had done the same. Was he aware of them?

If deFraan really is the Strangler, he must surely start reacting in some way or other once he's understood that the confounded bookseller is rooting around.

But how?

How will he react? What action will he take?

Good questions. After all, this was the whole point of activating deFraan in this way; but if Van Veeteren had succeeded in his mission, it was hardly grounds for feeling satisfied.

Worry was more appropriate. It was a bit like collecting a sample of a chemical brew in a pipette and releasing some drops into a retort without really knowing if it would explode or not. Shit! Van Veeteren thought. Do I really have this business under control?

He really must think carefully about how he was going to manage whatever happened next.

He stationed himself in Kramer's Cafe opposite the steps up to the university entrance shortly after six o'clock. Sat there smoking and drinking a dark beer while keeping an eye on what was happening through the window. If deFraan took the same route out of the building as normal people did after his lecture, it would be difficult not to see him.

If he preferred to sneak out through some back door or other, so be it. There was no great urgency: if it was not possible to add a drop or two more to the chemical brew this evening, he could just as well do so on one of the next few days. Might it perhaps be preferable to take a little pause? To delay matters slightly?

It was hard to judge. Like everything else associated with this mission.

There was a fresh breeze blowing along the street between Kramer's and the university. Despite the noise inside the cafe he could hear the flag halyards slapping against the flagpoles. The gap between the rows of buildings acted like a sort of wind tunnel, and people hastening past were huddled up as best they could. A Muslim woman had pressed herself up against one of the pillars on either side of the imposing double-doored entrance, seeking shelter. She seemed to be waiting for somebody. It was obvious that she was feeling the cold, despite the fact that her hair and face were covered by a veil. This was certainly no weather to be out in: it had been raining in short bursts all afternoon. He had had no more than a handful of customers in the bookshop, and had locked up half an hour before the usual closing time.

In order not to neglect his duties as a private detective.

Occasional students emerged through the heavy doors from time to time – usually in pairs or small groups, but shortly after half past six a whole host came out and walked down the steps into the street within the space of a single minute. He guessed that Professor deFraan's lecture on Wilde and Shaw had come to an end – but of course, it could just as well be some other lecture that had finished. To be on the safe side, he emptied his glass of beer and made himself ready to get up and leave at a moment's notice.

Sure enough. DeFraan appeared only a couple of minutes later. Walked down the steps and paused for a moment at the bottom, as if wondering which direction to take. Knotted his scarf more tightly round his neck and buttoned up his overcoat. Van Veeteren left his table.

Now, he thought. It's make or break time.

When he came to Alexanderlaan deFraan turned left. So he's not thinking of going home yet, Van Veeteren concluded, and followed him some twenty or thirty metres behind. The Muslim woman had evidently not met whoever it was she was waiting for: he noticed her walking some ten metres behind the professor. When he came to Grote Torg, deFraan cut across between the parked cars and headed for Zimmer's, the restaurant on the corner of Vommersgraacht – not one of Van Veeteren's favourite eating places. He couldn't recall having set foot inside it for at least ten to twelve years.

He stopped at the little newspaper kiosk and watched the professor go in through the brightly lit entrance. He also noticed, to his mild surprise, that the Muslim woman followed suit.

He took out his cigarette machine, but when he discovered that he had run out of ready rolled ones, he closed the lid and put it back into his overcoat pocket. He thought for a moment before buying a copy of *Telegraaf* at the kiosk, then also went into Zimmer's.

If a pause really was needed, it would have to be another day. Now was make or break time.

It wasn't yet seven o'clock, and there were not many customers. He saw deFraan straight away at a table diagonally to the left of the entrance, where he was just being given the menu by a waitress. Van Veeteren waited until the dark-skinned girl was out of the way, then passed by deFraan's table without giving any indication that he recognized him and without establishing eye contact. But it was obvious that deFraan had noticed him. He saw from the corner of his eye that the young professor glanced at him for a fraction of a second, before continuing his scrutiny of the menu.

Okay, Van Veeteren thought and sat down at a table a few metres further into the oblong-shaped room. Another drop in the chemical brew. He knows that I'm here, and that I have him under observation.

And he must be wondering why I didn't say hello to him.

It was obvious that deFraan had come to Zimmer's for his evening meal. Van Veeteren restricted himself to some garlic bread and salad, and a small carafe of red wine. He started leafing through the *Telegraaf* while keeping half an eye on deFraan, and tried to relax.

That was not easy. He soon registered that the optimistic chemistry metaphor had begun to be replaced by nagging doubts – by the perfectly justified questions he had been keeping at bay so successfully all day. But after just a few seconds they had dug their claws into him in earnest. He had to confront them now, that was clear.

What on earth was he doing?

Why the hell was he sitting here?

Good questions. Extremely well-founded queries, in fact.

He took a mouthful of wine and sighed. Was there anything at all in the way Maarten deFraan behaved or reacted to suggest that he might be the Strangler? he asked himself. Anything at all?

That he didn't remember a book and an author – among hundreds of others – that he had written about fifteen years ago?

That he had been irritated when he was woken up at twenty minutes past seven by an importunate bookseller?

That he was sitting in a restaurant having his dinner after a lecture?

Oh, incredibly suspicious, Van Veeteren thought and drank another half-glass of wine.

Just as irrefutable as the chain of indications that picked him out in the first place, one could argue. A few sinister literary characters. A lapel badge in a shoe in Wallburg. An advanced process of elimination that reduced 152 freemasons to just one!

Oh, shit! he thought as he contemplated his pitiful salad with galactic indifference. I'm a complete ass!

After today's incontrovertibly correct conclusion – and his no-holds-barred self-criticism – he immediately felt a little better. After all, there was nobody who knew what he was up to, he tried to convince himself. Apart from Winnifred, of course (and presumably Reinhart as well, but he would have to try to cope with that). He picked out the thin mozzarella slices from the salad, and ate them. Then he slid the plate to one side, rolled a cigarette and smoked it.

DeFraan was still sitting there, eating. Completely at ease, it seemed. Van Veeteren drank up the rest of his wine and beckoned to the waitress, so that he could pay and go home. As the person he was shadowing (his prey? his quarry? the Strangler?) did exactly the same at almost exactly the same moment, the bloodhound decided he might as well continue trailing him for a bit longer – now that he had decided to play the role of an ass. A bloodhound ass? The odds on deFraan simply heading back home to his flat in Kloisterstraat were pretty good, so keeping a check on that shouldn't waste more than a few minutes of this already wasted day.

Make or break? Bollocks to that! Van Veeteren thought. I only hope he doesn't report me to the police.

But his straightforward plan was thwarted by the fact that deFraan received his bill first – and that he paid and got up to leave as soon as the procedure was finished. The ass of a bookseller tried in vain to attract the attention of his waitress, who had found other matters to attend to. He considered for a second simply leaving a more than adequate banknote on the table, but changed his mind when he saw the veiled woman emerge from one of the booths on the other side of the bar and cash desk, and follow deFraan as he left the restaurant.

Changed his mind and remained sitting there with a quite new thought in his mind. What the hell? he thought. What the . . . ?

He quickly conjured up his memories of her – how she had been standing up against one of the pillars outside the university building, evidently waiting for somebody. How she had moved on shortly after deFraan had walked down the steps. How she had followed him through the wind and rain, and slunk into the same restaurant.

And how she had left the premises only a few seconds after him.

Could that be coincidence?

Never, he thought.

Not on your life.

There were evidently several people interested in what Professor deFraan did and said on this miserable February evening.

But a veiled Muslim woman?

Shadowing a professor of English literature?

That seemed bizarre, to say the least. Van Veeteren re-mained sitting there for a while, smoking and drinking a glass of iced water. Then he paid his bill unhurriedly, and decided that he would phone Winnifred again the moment he got home.

Perhaps together with a representative of Maardam's blood-hound association.

For even if the chemical brew had not reacted quite as he had hoped, there seemed to be more ingredients in it than he had realized.

46

Detective Intendent Münster contemplated his wife's stomach.

He had never seen anything more beautiful – well, possibly twice before, when she was pregnant with Bart and Marieke. But that was years ago.

'I'm a bloody hippopotamus,' said Synn with a sigh. 'But not as agile.'

'Rubbish,' said Münster. 'You look so beautiful that I almost wish you were in this condition all the time.'

She slapped him with her pillow, rolled over onto her side and got out of bed.

'It's all right for you . . .' she said. 'But if it doesn't become a Nobel Prizewinner I shan't think it was worth the effort.'

'There are only two months to go,' said Münster, and got out of bed as well. 'Then I shall take care of everything.'

'The breastfeeding as well?' wondered Synn.

'Sure,' said Münster magnanimously, and began kissing her. 'How do you do it? I've almost forgotten.'

She laughed. Continued to embrace him, and played with his tongue.

'To tell you the truth, I like it,' she said. 'And it's so satisfying to make love when I'm in this condition – isn't that a bit odd? There can't be any biological justification for that.'

'There's always a point with love-making,' said Münster. 'It's the most natural thing there is – bollocks to whether it's biological or not . . . But I think I must go to work now.'

'Do you really have to?'

'I think so. Mind you, twice on an ordinary weekday morning wouldn't be a bad idea . . . Are you really serious?'

Synn looked at the clock.

'My God! Are the children awake? They'll never get to school on time.'

'So what?' said Münster. 'When I was a lad I was once late for school, I remember it clearly.'

In the car on the way to the police station he thought that he'd never been as happy as he was now.

It wasn't just this morning. It was the last few days, the last few weeks, all the time in fact. He had already written about it in his yellow notebook, in which he recorded the best and the worst periods of his life. It was naturally difficult to assess this period together with other times, to compare them – but that wasn't necessary. Spells of happiness didn't compete with one another, that was something he had learned. The most important thing – what made it feel stronger than any previous occasion – was that it persisted, and that he was beginning to believe in all seriousness that it would last for the rest of his life.

Him and Synn. And the children. Marieke and Bart, and another one whose name he didn't know as yet, nor even its sex.

What was new was the benevolent undercurrent: he would never need to look for another woman. Synn would never find herself another man instead of him. In thirty years' time or so they would sit next to each other on a beach in their deckchairs, and think about times gone by. Hold tightly each other's wrinkled hands and remember all the millions of details and events and thoughts that had bound their lives together . . . and gaze into the sun that was slowly setting behind the horizon.

I'm a romantic softie, Münster thought as he drove into the police station's garage. But so what?

The images of Synn and his family and the future faded away as he stood in the lift on his way up to his office on the third floor. It was always the same. The lift was the sluice between life and work. Over the years – especially since he was stabbed in the kidney in Frigge – he had begun to learn how to separate those two phenomena. Not to take his investigations home with him. Not to sit pondering about them when he was watching the television, or helping Bart with his homework. Or reading aloud for Marieke. Or when Synn required his full attention.

Not to think about work until he was in the lift between the garage and his office. That was easier said than done, of course, but perseverance pays off in the end – that was another thing he had begun to realize.

This morning, 25 February 2001, it was the conversation with Van Veeteren that first came into his mind. Of course.

The *Chief Inspector* had phoned him at about nine o'clock the previous evening. They had spoken for nearly half an hour: quite a remarkable conversation – he had thought that even while it was taking place – in which their old roles with Van Veeteren as the surly superior and himself as a sort of subordinate sounding board for thoughts and ideas, roles that had become ingrained after so many years, now seemed to have shifted somewhat. To start with, at least.

Münster himself was team leader of the investigation (in Reinhart's absence), and Van Veeteren was playing the part of a private dick (his own term). Without much success, to be honest, harrumph . . . A bit like a rheumatic hen at an exhibition of flying skills (that was also the *Chief Inspector*'s own modest assessment).

At the beginning of the conversation he had sounded almost humble, something he never normally did. He described how he was in two minds about Professor deFraan, described what he had been doing, and on the whole didn't sound especially hopeful. It was only when he came to the remarkable incident concerning the Muslim woman that he sounded rather more on the ball.

And it certainly was a mysterious situation, Münster had to agree. Why on earth should a veiled woman slink around after deFraan as if she were keeping him under observation? At first sight it seemed incomprehensible – although on the other hand they had no idea as yet about deFraan's habits and customs. There was no shadowy woman of this sort in the Strangler investigation, but even if she really was following him, this didn't by any means suggest that deFraan really was the person they were looking for. Not at all, both Van Veeteren and Münster were in agreement on that score. Surely everybody had a right to be followed around by veiled women? If they were of that turn of mind.

But the most important part of the conversation as far as Münster was concerned was not that mysterious woman, but the fact that the *Chief Inspector* had taken the liberty of booking in a visitor to come and see him. The following day. In other words, today, Münster thought, and checked his wristwatch.

She was due at ten o'clock – that is, in twenty minutes' time.

It was because of this tight schedule that Van Veeteren had felt obliged to disturb the family's peace and quiet with a telephone call so late at night. He had also taken pains to describe the situation in so much detail – something he would never normally dream of doing, he stressed several times. He hoped Münster would excuse him. But that's the way it was.

No, Münster thought, he had never sounded like this in the old days.

The visitor's name was Ludmilla Parnak.

She was an old acquaintance of Professor deFraan, and had agreed to talk to Intendent Münster as she happened to be in Maardam that day. She actually lived in Aarlach, so it was a sign, an indication from the finger of God, that Winnifred had happened to meet her in Maardam now, Van Veeteren had stressed.

Half ironic, half seriously, as far as Münster could judge. In so far as he had any views on the finger of God, he had kept them to himself.

The last five minutes of the telephone call had more or less restored the old ingrained relationship between the *Chief Inspector* and Münster. Van Veeteren had issued minutely detailed instructions, regarding the somewhat delicate situation fru Parnak was in, and how the intendent should conduct the interview.

Sensitive! he had said several times. Damned sensitive, very thin ice. In no circumstances must she suspect what we suspect deFraan of having done! You must handle this delicately!

Delicately? Münster thought as he entered his office. Huh. Van Veeteren's humility at the beginning of the call hadn't lasted all that long . . .

He looked at his watch again and saw that it was high time he started planning some smokescreens.

'It's important that you understand this conversation is totally unofficial. I don't know how much information you've been given . . .'

Ludmilla Parnak made a gesture with her hands that suggested she knew little about the situation. Münster eyed her discreetly as he moved around the office, producing cups and saucers and pouring out coffee. She was quite a slim woman in her forties, with an aura of energy about her. Dark hair in page-boy style, clean-cut features and lively blue eyes.

Unusually blue for such a dark face, he thought. As he understood it she was in Maardam on business, but he had no idea what kind of business.

'All I know is that it has to do with Maarten deFraan,' she said, 'so I'd be grateful if you could enlighten me somewhat.'

Münster gestured towards the two mazarins fröken Katz had managed to acquire at short notice, but fru Parnak shook her head.

'No, thank you, just coffee would be fine.'

'Me too,' said Münster, thinking that he could eat both the buns after she had left. 'Yes, you are right in thinking that I need to speak to you about Maarten deFraan, but I'm afraid I can't go into detail about the reasons why. Sometimes we need to work in that way in the CID.'

She looked at him sceptically.

'Why? Is he suspected of something?'

'Not directly. But he's one of a group of people – a very large group – of which we are sure that one, only one, has committed a crime. All the others are innocent, and we have to go through a sort of elimination process. It's absolutely essential that you say nothing about our conversation. Not to anybody. When we've finished I'll require you to sign a document saying that you agree to these conditions.'

'And if I refuse?'

'Then we won't take matters any further.'

She studied him for a few seconds with her intensely blue eyes.

'All right,' she said. 'But I don't understand why you picked on me.'

'What do you mean by that?'

'I don't know deFraan all that well. I don't know him at all, to be frank. I haven't set eyes on him for five or six years . . . Nor have I spoken to him.'

'But you socialized with him when he lived in Aarlach, didn't you?'

'A bit. Not very much. He and my husband were colleagues at the university. We occasionally met, all four of us – that was when Christa was still alive. After that summer when she disappeared, I don't think I've met him a single time.'

'What year was that?'

'The summer of 1995. My husband and Maarten used to meet during the autumn of that year, of course, both at work and in private, but he never came round to our place. And then he got a chair here in Maardam, and moved house. What . . . what exactly do you want to know?'

Münster shrugged and tried to look naive.

'Nothing specific. Just a few general comments about his background and his character, that's all. He doesn't seem to have much of a circle of friends in Maardam, so we need to spread our net a little wider.'

'How did you get hold of my name?'

'He gave you as a contact person in connection with his university appointment. Maardam University, that is. It's a standard procedure: the usual thing of course is to name a close relative, but deFraan doesn't seem to have any.'

She said nothing for a while.

'He must be a bit of a hermit, then?'

'Presumably,' said Münster. 'Our understanding is that he's a bit of a lone wolf.'

She took a sip of coffee, and he could see that she was weighing up what she wanted to say, and what she didn't. He looked down at his notebook, and waited.

'He was pretty distant in Aarlach as well.'

'Really?'

'Yes. To be honest, we didn't have much in common . . . I assume that you will be subject to the same degree of professional secrecy as I am?'

'Of course,' Münster assured her. 'You can regard me as a hole in the ground.'

She smiled. He could see that she appreciated this gesture of masculine unpretentiousness.

'But I liked Christa. The feeling was mutual. We socialized a bit, the pair of us – not a lot, but I was new to the town and I needed a bit of guidance . . . No doubt you can understand that.'

'Yes, of course,' said Münster. 'How did she die?'

'Don't you know that?'

'No,' said Münster. 'We haven't been interested at all in Professor deFraan until very recently.'

'She disappeared,' said fru Parnak. 'In Greece. She and her husband were on holiday there. It was assumed that she drowned. That she'd gone for a swim in the sea one evening and was carried off by an underwater current.'

'And her body was never found?'

'No.'

'Very sad,' said Münster.

'Yes.'

'It must have been traumatic for him. Why was it assumed that she died in the way you have described?'

Fru Parnak made the same gesture with her hands again.

'I don't really know. I think it had something to do with the fact that her bathing costume was missing . . . And I think they found a towel and some clothes on the beach, but I'm not sure. In any case, they never found her body. My husband talked to Maarten when he came back home after that trip, but as I said, I didn't.'

'Ninety-five, did you say?' asked Münster, writing the year down in his notebook.

'Yes. Perhaps he chose to leave Aarlach because he thought it would be easier to start all over again in a new location – that would be understandable. But then again, he was very keen on getting a professorship somewhere.'

'He has good academic qualifications, does he?'

'Oh, yes. Maarten deFraan has always been considered a bit of a genius. Even by my husband, and he's not one for throwing words like genius around.'

Münster made another note, and thought for a few moments.

'They didn't have any children, I gather,' he said. 'What was their relationship like?'

Fru Parnak hesitated.

'I don't know,' she said. 'Christa didn't want to talk about it – we didn't know each other all that well, after all. They'd been together for a long time, and I think she looked up to him in a way . . . A lot of people did. But perhaps it was wearing off a bit. Admiration is not a good basis for a relationship, don't you think? Not in the long run.'

'That's what my experience tells me,' said Münster. 'I don't suppose you know if he had other women as well as his wife?'

'No idea,' said fru Parnak. 'I don't think so – but then again, it wouldn't surprise me. In any case I think Christa was faithful to him for as long as I knew her. She was honest, never any shady dealings . . .'

'So she was a likeable woman, was she?'

'Very much so,' said fru Parnak. 'It was a damned shame that her life was cut short. She was only thirty-two or thirty-three. I don't think I've ever become reconciled to her death.'

Münster leaned back on his chair and looked out of the window. He noted that the sun actually seemed to be about to burst through the clouds.

'Thirty-three is a critical age,' he said thoughtfully. 'Jesus was thirty-three . . . And Mozart and Alexander the Great, if I'm not much mistaken.'

She looked at him in mild surprise. Then she looked at her watch.

'Do you think you've found out what you wanted to know now?'

Münster nodded.

'Thank you for taking the trouble of coming to see me,' he said. 'And what we have discussed will go no further. I don't think we need bother about signing that bit of paper . . . Would you like me to order you a taxi?'

Fru Parnak looked out of the same window as Münster, and smiled briefly.

'I think I'll walk instead. I don't have far to go, and it looks almost spring-like outside.'

She stood up, shook hands, and left the room.

When she had closed the door he hesitated for a moment, then rolled his desk chair closer to the window. Poured out more coffee from the thermos flask, put the plate with the mazarins on his knee and put his feet on the window ledge. Sat there and waited for the sun to appear, and began to discern the outline of a murderer.

Van Veeteren woke up with a start and looked around.

Books to the right of him, books to the left, and books straight ahead.

No doubt about it. He was sitting in the armchair in the antiquarian bookshop, and had fallen asleep. There was a cup half-full of coffee on the arm of his chair. He looked at the clock. A few minutes to five. So he had been asleep for about fifteen minutes at most. As usual.

Had the doorbell rung? He didn't think so, and he couldn't hear any sounds coming from the main area of the shop. But there was something. Must have been. He had been woken up in unnecessarily brutal fashion out of a dream: there must have been some detail, some little recollection, it was on the tip of his tongue. If only he could remember the dream itself; it would be remarkable if he couldn't . . .

Blake!

That was it. William Blake was on the tip of his tongue, and that name was so damned important that he hadn't been able to keep it hidden beneath the brittle surface of his dream. Neither the name nor himself. Remarkable.

Blake?

It took him five seconds to hit upon the connection.

Monica Kammerle – William Blake – Maarten deFraan.

He sat there for a while longer without moving a muscle, weighing up the links in the chain.

Kammerle – Blake – deFraan.

He recalled how he had stood and leafed through *Songs of Innocence and of Experience* that day some five or six months ago when he had visited the flat in Moerckstraat. Recalled how surprised he had been to find an author like that among the books of a sixteen-year-old girl.

It had been a high-class edition as well, he remembered that. Not a cheap paperback, it must have been expensive. Not something a young girl would run to a bookshop and buy with her pocket money.

A gift?

That was a very plausible assumption.

From somebody who was very fond of English literature?

That was feasible in any case.

'Professor deFraan,' he muttered as he stood up. What was that line? 'Rude thought runs wild in contemplation's field'?

Something along those lines at least. He went out into the shop to make sure there were no customers there, then returned to the kitchenette and filled the kettle to make some more coffee.

What next? he thought. How should I make use of this new piece of the jigsaw puzzle that has just turned up?

Potential piece, at least.

Another author. Another sort of literary clue. Surely that was convincing?

Or was it just him who was constructing this pattern, these links – against a background of some bizarre illness due to his profession? Why not? Books are the long route to wisdom and the short route to lunacy, as some bright spark once said.

It was hard to decide. Not to say impossible. It would make more sense to find a method of testing the validity of it all, he thought as he poured the boiling water over the coffee powder. Blake!

How?

How? What damned method could he hit upon?

Although he was only an old newly awakened antiquarian bookseller with highly doubtful mental abilities, it didn't take him long to find the answer. Half a cup of coffee and a cigarette, more or less.

He picked up the telephone and rang Münster at the police station.

The intendent has just gone home, he was informed.

He dialled Münster's home number.

'He hasn't come home yet,' said Münster's son Bart.

Blasted slowcoach, Van Veeteren thought, but he didn't say that. Instead he instructed Bart to ask his father to ring Krantze's antiquarian bookshop the moment he'd stuck his snitch inside the door.

'Snitch?' wondered Bart.

'The moment he gets home,' said Van Veeteren.

While he was waiting he checked the weather through the shop window. It was raining.

That's odd, he thought. Wasn't the sun shining when I fell asleep in the armchair?

It was half an hour before Münster rang, and his only excuse was that he had done some shopping on the way home. Van Veeteren snorted, but decided to err on the side of mercy.

'Where are their household goods?' he asked.

'Whose what?' said Münster.

'The personal property from Moerckstraat, of course. Get a grip! The belongings left behind by the mother and daughter Kammerle.'

'I don't know,' said Münster.

'Don't know? Call yourself an investigation leader?'

'Thank you . . . I expect they are in store somewhere. Why?'

'Because we need to get hold of them.'

Silence at the other end of the line.

'Are you still there?'

'Yes . . . Of course I'm still here,' said Münster. 'Why do we need to get hold of their personal belongings?'

'Because they might contain vital proof there to nail a murderer.'

'Really?' said Münster non-committally.

'A book,' said Van Veeteren. 'The girl had a book by William Blake on her shelves, and I have the feeling that the Strangler left his fingerprints all over it.'

Another brief silence.

'How can . . . ? How can you possibly know that?'

'It's not a question of knowledge, Münster! I said I had a feeling. But that's irrelevant, just make sure you find that book no matter where it is, and make sure the fingerprint boys do their job properly! You'll get another set of prints to compare with them in a day or so. If they correspond, it's game, set and match!'

Once again Münster was struck dumb for a few seconds. But Van Veeteren could hear him breathing: he sounded as if he had a cold. Or perhaps he was tense.

Or sceptical?

'DeFraan's?' he asked eventually. 'Are you talking about Professor deFraan's fingerprints?'

'Right first time,' said Van Veeteren and hung up.

He waited for a few minutes.

Then he rang Winnifred Lynch – who had got back home from both work and the hospital some considerable time ago – and gave her some new instructions and orders.

No, not orders. You don't give orders to women of Winnifred's calibre, he thought. You ask for help. And urge her to be careful.

After all that intricate bloodhound work he finished off his cold coffee, locked the shop, and walked home through the rain.

47

Time stood still on Saturday and Sunday.

At least, that's how it seemed to him. The rain came and went, daylight was sucked down into the wet earth, and he realized how deeply involved he had become in the hunt for this murderer. Whether his name was Maarten deFraan or something else.

Yet again. Yet again a criminal would shortly be captured. It was easy to imagine that such goings-on would never end.

On Saturday evening he played chess with Mahler at the Society, and lost both matches due entirely to a lack of concentration. Despite the fact that Mahler had just undergone an operation on his leg. Despite a spirited Nimzo-Indian defence.

On Sunday they looked after Andrea in the afternoon, as usual: but not even during that time could he prevent himself from thinking about Maarten deFraan. Ulrike wondered how he was, and in the end he gave up and tried to explain what the matter was.

The hunt. The scent of the criminal. The prey.

He said nothing about the moral imperative. Nothing about duty. Instead, she was the one who took up those aspects, and he was grateful to her for doing so. He had always found it difficult to attribute good motives to his own actions. Or to believe in them, at least, for whatever reason.

When they had finished dinner, and Marlene and Andrea had left, he picked up the telephone and dialled deFraan's home number.

No reply.

Perhaps that was just as well, he thought. He wasn't sure what he would have said if deFraan had answered.

After washing up and watching the television news, he wandered around the flat for a while like a lost soul. Then explained to Ulrike that he needed to go for a walk to clear his head, took his raincoat and went out. It's better for her to be rid of me for a while, he thought.

He started with a tour of the cemetery and lit a candle on Erich's grave; and since it was quite close by – and it was quite a mild evening – he walked to the professor's address in Kloisterstraat.

Without any real purpose and without any expectations. It was a few minutes past eight when he entered the enclosed courtyard of the big Art Nouveau complex. He couldn't remember ever having set foot in it before. Not a single time in all the years he had lived in Maardam – a fact that surprised him somewhat, although perhaps it shouldn't have done. There were plenty of addresses in the town that he had never had any reason to visit. Naturally, criminality was not rife, despite everything. Not really.

The courtyard was surrounded by dark buildings on all four sides. A bare chestnut tree on a small raised rotunda with two benches. A cycle shed with a corrugated iron roof. A low wooden shed for rubbish and refuse.

He counted five entrances with locked doors and entry-phones. Five storeys high on two sides, four on the other two. Steeply sloping black tin roofs and tall, old-fashioned windows, about a third of them lit up, and a third with blue flickering lights indicating that people were watching the television. Nobody out of doors. He sat down on one of the benches and lit a cigarette.

Is there a murderer lying low somewhere up there? he wondered. A brilliant and over-talented university professor with five lives on his conscience?

Do you know that I'm down here, waiting for you?

If so, what are you thinking of doing about it? Surely you're not simply going to sit there with your arms folded, waiting for me to come and fetch you?

It was that last thought that was the cause of his unease, he knew that. The deepest cause, in any case. Time certainly had sat still since Friday afternoon, but that only applied to his own time. The private hours. Just because he – the bookseller and former chief inspector and farcical bloodhound – was in a quandary and hadn't a single damned chess move to fall back on didn't mean that his intelligent prey was also sitting at home, biding his time. Like an injured bird or an ordinary blockhead.

Or had he not caught on, despite everything? Did he not suspect anything?

Or – a horrible thought – was he in fact completely innocent? Had he fenced in the wrong person?

That wouldn't be too much of a surprise, he thought
gloomily. No matter how you looked at it, the so-called chain
of circumstantial evidence linking deFraan to the murders
was so thin and drawn-out that any prosecutor worth his salt
would laugh to scorn the poor officer in charge of the investigation who presented it. No doubt about that. A few
abstruse literary characters, a lapel badge dropped in a shoe,
a gang of harmless academic freemasons . . . And all of it
drowning in an abundance of wild guesswork and speculation!

Firm proof? Don't make me laugh! Just the sort of dry,
cold laughter that five dead people might be able to produce.

Oh hell, Van Veeteren thought for the hundred-and-tenth
time since Friday evening. Let's hope to goodness those
damned fingerprints do exist in that book, otherwise I might
as well throw in the towel.

Take the king off the board and acknowledge defeat.

He stared up at the dark façades.

I don't even know where you live, he thought with a sigh
of resignation. I don't know if you're at home or not. You
didn't answer the telephone, but there's no law that forces
you to pick up the receiver, even if you hear the phone ringing.

He threw the cigarette butt onto the gravel and trampled
on it. Went back out of the entrance gates and into the street.
Just had time to see the person sitting in the car parked on the
other side of the road.

A woman behind the wheel. A streetlamp shone a certain amount of light onto the side window and he could see the hijab over her head quite clearly. He saw nothing of her hair, and only a glimpse of her face.

But he did meet her gaze for a brief moment before she started the car and drove off.

He never saw the registration number.

But he felt his heart pounding like the kick of a horse in his chest.

In the end, Monday finally came. When he met Winnifred Lynch in the morning, it felt as if a month had passed since he saw her last.

'Well?' he said, and thought that if he had a God he would have said a silent prayer at this very moment.

A prayer hoping that something at least had fallen into place. That not all the baited lines he had thrown into the waters would come up without even a nibble. Winnifred cleared her throat and took a sheet of paper out of her shoulder bag.

'I wrote it down,' she said with an apologetic smile. 'Although that wasn't necessary, of course.'

He clasped his hands. He had heard worse introductions than that.

'Fire away,' he urged her.

She studied what she had written for a few seconds.

'I think things are starting to shape up,' she said. 'But I suppose you are the one who should judge that.'

'I'll do my best.'

'Everything is witnessed and vouched for.'

'Come to the point now, never mind the preliminaries.'

'All right. In the first place, that Wallburg business seems to fit in. DeFraan took part in a symposium there lasting four days in June 1999, so he could very well have met that woman.'

'Excellent,' said Van Veeteren, fiddling with his cigarette machine. He could feel his pulse beating significantly more strongly.

'In the second place, I've arranged for some fingerprints. I took a few things from his desk – a few books, a tea mug, a few plastic files. I handed them over at the police station a few hours ago.'

She must get paid for this, Van Veeteren thought. If this bears fruit I shall personally squeeze a thousand out of Hiller. Two.

'And thirdly, my poor husband told me something that very nearly made my heart stop.'

'Reinhart?' said Van Veeteren. 'What do you mean?'

Winnifred took a deep breath before continuing.

'I went to visit him yesterday evening – incidentally, he's going to be discharged tomorrow or the day after . . . Anyway, he told me had a dream – or perhaps had begun to remember – about what happened when he was run over. He thinks somebody pushed him in front of that bus.'

Van Veeteren suddenly felt something short-circuiting inside him. A blinding white light flashed inside his skull, and he was forced to close his eyes for a second in order to control himself.

'What the hell . . . ?' he snorted, and noted that his temples were pounding like a steam hammer. 'Do you mean to say that somebody . . . ?'

She nodded solemnly.

'Yes. That's what he says.'

'He says that?'

'Yes. He lay there thinking about it for two days before mentioning it to me, so he must be pretty sure about it.'

He felt for words, but couldn't find any. Then he pounded on the table with his fist and stood up.

'For Christ's sake!' he groaned. 'What a damned . . . Good Lord, thank goodness he survived.'

'That's what I think as well.'

'A priest in front of a train, and a detective officer in front of a bus. Yes, by Jove, things really are starting to shape up, you're absolutely right!'

Winnifred bit her lower lip, and he suddenly became aware of how scared she was. He sat down on his chair again, and stroked her arm somewhat clumsily.

'Calm down now,' he urged her. 'We shall sort this out. The danger is over.'

She tried to smile, but it came over as a grimace.

'There's one more thing,' she said. 'He's cancelled all his lectures for this week.'

'What? Cancelled?'

'DeFraan. He sent a fax to the office on Saturday. Very brief. It just said he was going to be away, and the students should be informed.'

Four thousand thoughts exploded inside Van Veeteren's head, but the only one that came out of his mouth was an obscenity.

'Fucking hell!'

Spring arrived on Tuesday morning. Mild south-westerly winds swept the sky clear of clouds, and as he walked through Wollerimsparken on his way to the police station, he could feel the ground swelling under his feet. Small birds were hopping around busily in the bushes. The old ladies on the benches were hatless, and had unbuttoned their coats. He was passed by a jogger wearing shorts and a T-shirt.

So I've survived another winter, he thought with a sudden flush of surprise.

That was combined with a certain degree of willpower impelling him into the Maardam police station, especially on a day like this: but it was too late to do anything about it now. Intendent Münster had suggested this venue for a meeting to discuss developments, and he hadn't raised any objections. For whatever reasons. As he approached the shadowy entrance with the sun shining diagonally from behind him, he felt a bit like Dante approaching the gates of hell.

That's enough of literary allusions! he told himself. There have been more than enough of those in this case.

He marched in through the door and took the lift up to the third floor without looking round.

★

Münster received him with coffee and a wry smile.

'Wipe that grin off your face,' said Van Veeteren. 'This is just a lightning visit.'

'I know,' said Münster. 'But it's cool to see you here anyway.'

'Cool?' said Van Veeteren. 'Have you gone out of your tiny mind? Let's get going. Athens, did you say?'

Münster nodded and became serious.

'Yes. A plane from Sechshafen last Sunday morning. Due to land about noon. What do you think?'

'Think? That he's done a runner, of course. How's it going with the fingerprints?'

'It'll take a bit more time,' said Münster. 'They've only just started on that book.'

'Blake?'

'William Blake, yes. But Mulder says there are several fingerprints they can use. The ones from deFraan's office are ready, of course. But how the hell could you know that he'd had that book in his hands? He wiped the whole of the flat clean.'

Van Veeteren shrugged.

'I've also thumbed through Blake,' he said drily. 'Let's wait with the acclamations until we know whose fingers they find.'

'All right,' said Münster. 'They say they'll be ready by this afternoon in any case. But surely he's the one – we don't need to doubt that any more, do we?'

Van Veeteren sighed.

'No,' he said. 'I don't think we do. I'd bet quite a large beer

on him having murdered all of them – and tried to kill Reinhart as well. But proof! What proof have we got, for God's
sake? If we can't match those fingerprints, or if he doesn't
give up and confess – well, we're in a bit of a mess, aren't we?'

'I suppose so,' said Münster, looking out at the sunshine.
'Yes, I've been thinking about that as well. And it's not all cut
and dried even if they do find his fingerprints on the book.
We have to prove it beyond any reasonable doubt . . .'

'I know,' grunted Van Veeteren. 'Perhaps I haven't mentioned it, but I was also a police officer in the distant past.'

Münster produced a sheet of paper.

'We've started looking into his background. We haven't
got much yet, but there will be more – Krause and Moreno
are dealing with that.'

Van Veeteren took the sheet of paper and read it without
speaking. When he had finished he dropped it on the table
and muttered to himself for a while. Took out his cigarette
machine and started filling it with tobacco.

'What shall we do?' wondered Münster after half a minute.

Van Veeteren looked up. Closed the lid of his machine and
put it in his pocket.

'I want all the information about him that you can find,'
he said. 'Tomorrow morning. We'll wait until then, and I'll
make a plan. You can tell Heller that I shall be working full
time from now on, in the highest salary bracket.'

'That you—'

'You heard.'

Münster tried another wry smile.

'But I have no intention of sitting here while I'm doing it.'

'I thought not,' said Münster. 'It's pretty good weather out there.'

Van Veeteren stood up and looked out of the window.

'It's even better in Athens,' he said, and left the room.

ATHENS, KEFALONIA, MAARDAM

MARCH 2001

48

The hotel was called Ormos and was in an alley leading out into Syntagma Square.

Only a stone's throw from the Grande Bretagne, where he had stayed once in the distant past. So many years had passed since then, so much water and life and pain had flowed under the dark bridges. There wasn't much left now.

Not much at all.

He had started telephoning Vasilis before he left Maardam, without receiving an answer, and he continued doing so all the first afternoon and evening.

In the end, shortly after ten o'clock, the phone was answered by a woman called Dea – presumably his new wife. As far as he could understand, that is – she spoke only Greek, so he restricted himself to basic information. Vasilis was in Thessaloniki and wasn't expected back for another three or four days. No, it wasn't a conference: his mother was ill. But it wasn't all that bad – she wasn't on her deathbed.

Yes, he had said, Wednesday or Thursday.

He asked for his telephone number and was given two: one to his mobile, and the other to his mother's house, where he was staying. The mobile was apparently dodgy, she hadn't got through to it earlier in the day, despite several attempts. Dea.

Or Thea.

He thanked her and hung up. He suddenly remembered that Vasilis had said she had red hair. Could Greeks have red hair? Odd, he thought. Damned odd. He smiled at the thought, and began rubbing the wound on his throat. It wasn't irritating him any longer, but rubbing it had become a habit. He still had the sticking plaster on his hand – he could probably do without it now, but it could stay where it was. He didn't fancy the idea of having to stare at a wound every time he looked at his hands.

He smoked a few cigarettes after the phone call. Sat on the wicker chair on the tiny balcony and breathed in petrol fumes from the road below together with the tobacco smoke. He recalled the smell from the first time he was here, in July twenty years ago, a few years before the stay at the Grande Bretagne. It had been hard, almost impossible to breathe during the unbearably hot afternoons.

It was rather better now. The temperature was probably around twelve to fifteen degrees: his lungs would no doubt adjust to the atmosphere, and he wouldn't even notice the fumes. Everything becomes a habit sooner or later, he thought.

Everything.

Anyway, he was going to have to stay in Athens for a week. More or less. That was an unforeseen snag, but he had no desire to change his plans on that account. Everything would have to go ahead as he had planned, and as soon as he made contact with Vasilis he was bound receive the assistance he needed: they had that sort of relationship, and there was no reason to doubt that.

He went indoors and tried the mobile number. Despite what Dea had said, he had an answer after only three rings. Vasilis's husky voice, restaurant noises in the background, somebody playing a bouzouki.

'My friend! A voice from the past! Where are you?'

'In Athens, and in deep shit. I need help with something.'

'No problem, my friend! What do you want?'

'A gun.'

Silence at the other end. Only the background noise of the restaurant and the bouzouki for five seconds.

'A gun? What the fuck happened, my friend?'

'We can talk about that when you come back home. When?'

More silence.

'Wednesday. I promise you Wednesday, my friend! But what the hell . . . ?'

He gave Vasilis his own mobile number, but not that of the hotel.

'Take care!'

'I will.'

Now his throat really was itching.

To be on the safe side, he changed his hotel on the Monday. You never knew. That damned bookseller and that woman. He moved into a third-class boarding house out at Lykabettos, paid in advance and didn't need to show his passport. Lay on his bed for hours, thinking about Mersault in Camus's *The Outsider*. Felt neither hungry nor thirsty.

He had no desire to get up and sit by the window, looking at passing girls. Like Mersault. Even if there had been any in the narrow alley. Even if it had been overflowing with pussy.

He thought about his mother instead.

Thought about a Greek saying. A Greek man loves himself and his mother all his life. His wife for six months.

Anger had begun to boil up inside him; and disgust. He kept it hidden, but it bubbled away inexorably and made the room rotate slowly whenever he closed his eyes. The noise from the street and the rest of the building was also distorted when his eyes were closed, sounds became oppressive and insistent, seemed to join forces with the movement of the room and forced themselves inside him. Even so, he found it difficult not to keep his eyes closed. It was somehow alluring.

A sort of battle. A wrestling match with his mother, his anger and his disgust. Eyes closed. It was a blind struggle, with the noise and the rotation of the room its way of expressing itself. His mobile was switched off. At one point as darkness began to fall with incredible speed, he went out to the bathroom in the corridor and tried to be sick. But he failed. He lay on the bed again, ripped the sticking plaster off the back of his hand and contemplated the ravaged skin.

He waited until it was completely dark, then went out into the town.

Came back after midnight, slightly drunk on ouzo and cheap retsina. No food – there was no space inside him for food. Apart from a few olives and a lump of feta cheese one of the taverna owners had offered him without charge. He smoked another ten or twelve cigarettes while lying on the bed, and fell asleep, feeling sweaty and rather sick, at turned three.

There was a sort of emptiness that he soon felt unable to fill any longer.

He dreamed about the fire, and his mother. About how he sucked her nipples for the last time on the day of his twelfth birthday. *I have no milk any more, and you're a man now. Never forget that you are a man, and that no woman shall deny you anything you want – not even your mother. Believe me when I say this.*

Believe me.

Tuesday was an exact repetition of Monday.

Wednesday evening, Plakas. He wanted to sit outside, but Vasilis insisted they should go indoors. It was hardly spring yet, after all.

As if that mattered. They found a table that was more or less half-and-half, by a window looking out over Tripodon Street. The restaurant was called Oikanas. Vasilis had put on fifteen kilos since they had last met. Was that seven years ago, or was it eight?

He was already drunk, which was a damned nuisance; but his disgust had been nagging at him all afternoon, and he had forced himself to drink quite a lot. Vasilis kept on saying My Friend, My Friend, My Friend – and soon he no longer had the strength to listen to it. He urged Vasilis to Cut the Crap, commented Bullshit, and asked when he was going to deliver that damned gun? That was what all this was about, and nothing else.

When? My Friend.

It took time to convince Vasilis, but in doing so he didn't reveal an iota of his plan and intentions. Nor the story behind it all. He realized (and recalled) that basically, he was much brighter and more strong-minded than Vasilis, and had the Greek at his mercy even though he was drunk. As time passed, Vasilis had drunk more and more and become hesitant and sluggish, and eventually he gave up. Mediterranean apathy.

'Fuck you, My Friend. All right.'

'When? Where?'

Vasilis took another drink of the expensive Boutari wine, and ran his fingers through the Communist beard he had worn since the Junta era. More grey than black nowadays. More bourgeois pig than revolutionary.

'Friday evening. Here. Same place. All right, My Friend?'

'All right.'

Thursday was a repetition of Tuesday.

He bought a boat ticket at a little travel agent's. It was low season, and he would have to wait until Sunday. There was an Olympic Airways flight, but that was only in theory: the Saturday flight was fully booked. They asked him if he wanted to turn up on stand-by.

Ochi. No thank you. He sat in the National Park instead

and watched the women. Imagined them naked. Imagined them naked and dead.

The naked and the dead. Disgust bubbled up inside him once more. And he had an erection. The only thing that could fill the emptiness. Everything else was finished and done with. His fingers were seismographs again. He masturbated in some bushes. Shouted out loud when he came, but nobody took any notice. The park was almost deserted. It was an ordinary weekday, people were at work of course; it was cloudy, but quite warm.

Then he lay on his bed for five or six hours, smoking. Ate next to nothing, tried to masturbate again but couldn't even get an erection. His throat was itching.

He went to the bathroom and tried to be sick, but his stomach was empty. He went out and bought some sesame biscuits, a bottle of water and two packets of local cigarettes.

He drank quite a lot, and dreamed about his mother's pubic hair. It became quite sparse as the years passed by.

Friday was a repetition of Thursday.

Slightly drunk again. Short meeting with Vasilis in the same taverna in Plakas. He had cut off most of his Communist beard for some reason or other, and maintained that he was worried – but nevertheless handed over without more ado a pistol in a shoe box inside a plastic carrier bag. A Markarov, he said. Russian, nine mil. A bit awkward, but reliable. It should be loaded with eight bullets, and a whole carton was part of the deal. Thirty thousand drachma – that was cheap, he stressed several times. Damned cheap: what was he intending to use it for?

He didn't answer, paid up and left. He knew they would never meet again.

My Friend.

He didn't have many memories of Saturday. He lay on his bed. Smoked and drank several glasses of ouzo, but mixed with quite a lot of water. Masturbated occasionally, managed an erection but not an orgasm. Evidently empty there as well. On Sunday morning he was unable to dredge up any memories of the night's dreams. He took a taxi out to Piraeus and boarded the boat.

It was called *Ariadne* and wasn't very big. There was rather a strong wind blowing, and the departure was delayed as the sea was too rough: but he stayed on board rather than going back on land.

They set off in the end at two o'clock. He was quite grateful for the delay, having felt ill all morning. He went straight to the bar and ordered a beer, then started reading Isaac Norton's Byron biography – he had taken it with him as travel reading, but hadn't got round to looking at it until now.

Byron? he thought. I've waited too long before making this journey. People have suffered unnecessarily.

But he was in no hurry now.

49

When MS *Aegina* set off from the harbour in Piraeus at nine o'clock in the morning of Tuesday, 5 March, the sky was as blue as a faultless sapphire. The temperature was about twenty degrees in the shade, and there was no wind to speak of in B-deck's open after-saloon. Only a slowly rising morning sun. No blankets were needed over their legs, they didn't really need long trousers. Van Veeteren had even acquired a straw hat.

'Not too bad,' said Münster, turning to look at the sun.

'You ought to have been an astronaut,' muttered Van Veeteren.

'An astronaut?' said Münster.

'Yes, one of those Americans who flew to the moon. I heard how the first man on the moon tried to express his rapture to the dumbfounded masses back here on earth – do you know what he said?'

'No.'

'It's great up here.'

'It's great up here?'

'Yes. A bit on the inadequate side, you might think.'

'I see,' said Münster, looking out over the rail. 'And how

would an antiquarian bookseller express his feelings on seeing this panorama?'

Van Veeteren thought for five seconds, also gazing out over the sea, the sky and the coastline. Then he closed his eyes and took a sip of beer.

'O bliss to be young in the light of morning on the sea,' he said.

'Not too bad,' said Münster.

'Maybe we should exchange a few thoughts about our mission,' suggested Van Veeteren when Münster arrived back at the deckchairs with two bottles of lemon squash (a sort of primitive beer substitute: it was only half past nine in the morning, and their fluid balance needed some attention in view of the hot sun). 'So that we know where we stand.'

'By all means,' said Münster. 'Personally I'm not even sure we're on the way to the right island. But then, I'm only the one in charge of the investigation.'

Van Veeteren eased off his shoes and socks and splayed out his toes with an air of satisfaction.

'Of course we are,' he said. 'DeFraan is trying to complete a circle – I don't know exactly how, but we shall find out in due course.'

'Do you mean that he's returning to the place where his wife died?'

'Have you any other suggestion?'

Münster did not. They had not discussed the case properly for two days, even though they had spent nearly all the time in each other's company. On the flight Van Veeteren had slept from start to finish, and the previous evening he had resorted

THE STRANGLER'S HONEYMOON

to his old, familiar weakness for smokescreens and general mystification, Münster had unfortunately been forced to conclude.

But that's the way he was. The intendent had seen it all before. And now it seemed at last to be time to hint at an apology. Better late than never. Münster drank some water, and waited.

'We have no chance of proving any of this,' said Van Veeteren to begin with. 'Don't you think?'

'I agree,' said Münster. 'But surely it's deplorable that the prosecutor wouldn't allow us to search deFraan's flat, don't you think?'

'Deplorable is the right word,' said Van Veeteren. 'But it's pretty obvious what lies behind it.'

'The fact that Ferrari is a member of the Succulents?'

'Of course. He has a chance to obstruct us, and so of course he does just that. Don't forget that their motto is *"Singillitam mortales, cunctim perpetui!"'*

'What does that mean?

'On your own you are mortal, together you are immortal!'

'I didn't know you could speak Latin.'

'I looked it up,' said Van Veeteren. 'I work in a bookshop now and then, as you might know, so it wasn't too difficult. According to Reinhart, Ferrari is going to be replaced, so that detail will be sorted in a few days.'

'Presumably,' said Münster, turning to look at the sun again.

I'm doubtful about the whole of this, he thought. Does he really know what he's doing?

'If deFraan had had a bit more ice in his veins,' said Van Veeteren, 'all he'd have needed to do was to lie low instead of running off in this panicky way. He must have known the situation, he's no fool. What do you think it signifies?'

'That he ran away?'

'Yes.'

Münster thought for a moment.

'That he's tired of it all?'

'Exactly,' said Van Veeteren, adjusting his straw hat. 'That's the conclusion I drew. He knows that we know, and his lunacy isn't under control any longer. Not completely, in any case, and that's what will bring about his downfall. He just hasn't the strength to go on any longer. My guess is that he's utterly exhausted – no wonder, come to that.'

'The fingerprints in the Blake book were pretty convincing,' said Münster. 'Not conclusive, of course, but they prove that he had a link to the Kammerle family.'

Van Veeteren nodded. Sat in silence for a while, staring at the glass of lemon squash he had in his hand.

'Of course. But a good lawyer would produce ten innocent explanations from up his sleeve in as many seconds. The same applies to that confounded lapel badge. All the clues pointing to deFraan are so insubstantial that they would carry no weight at all in a courtroom, that's the problem. But I would really like to meet him eye to eye. I hope we can nail him.'

'Why?' wondered Münster. 'Why would you like to meet him?'

'Human interest,' said Van Veeteren, lighting a cigarette.

'Or inhuman interest, perhaps?' suggested Münster.

'Possibly, yes. I want to know what makes him tick, and what the hell lies behind it all. It's so damned unpleasant for a man of such high intelligence to be driven for so long by such high lunacy. He must be an emotional monster, I can't see it any other way. But even monsters are made up of flesh and blood and nerves – or so I've always believed, in any case.'

Münster put on his newly acquired sunglasses and unfastened a couple of shirt buttons.

'Nobody seemed to have known him particularly well.'

'Nobody at all, it seems. If that Dr Parnak was a pal of his for so many years and didn't have more to say about him than she did, well – who the hell could throw light on him?'

'His wife? Could have done . . .'

'We're on the way to her,' said Van Veeteren. 'It's a pity we weren't able to talk to her sister – that might have given us a few clues, at least.'

Münster nodded. They had managed to track down Professor deFraan's former sister-in-law, a certain Laura Fenner née Markovic, to Boston, USA, but just before they left Maardam Krause had informed them that fru Fenner was unfortunately on a skiing holiday at Lake Placid, and couldn't be contacted.

'What do you think about Christa deFraan's death?' Münster asked.

Van Veeteren said nothing for a while, merely sat twiddling his toes.

'I think what I think,' he said eventually.

*

It was four in the afternoon when they got out of their taxi in the square in Argostoli. Van Veeteren stood for a while beside his suitcase, looking around and nodding contentedly. Münster paid the driver, then followed suit. It was not difficult to understand the satisfied expression on the *Chief Inspector*'s face. The agora was large and square, surrounded on three sides by restaurants, tavernas and cafes. Low, pale-coloured buildings with flat roofs, and plane trees and oleander bushes to provide shade. The town climbed up the mountainside, and down towards the sea. Palm trees were making crackling noises in the warm breeze. Cyclists and small children were everywhere, pedestrians, elderly gentlemen playing tavli, and a few apathetic pigeons pecking away around an empty tribune with some kind of rudimentary loud-speaker set-up.

'Ah,' said Van Veeteren. 'We have come to the real world, Münster. Pascal never saw this.'

'Pascal?' said Münster. 'What do you mean?'

'He claimed that people are incapable of sitting still in the same place for any longish time, and that almost all wretchedness can be traced back to that fact – evil, for instance. But you could spend an eternity in this square, surely you can see that? If you have a beer and a newspaper, at least.'

Münster looked around.

'Yes indeed,' he said, picking up his suitcase. 'And that hotel doesn't look so bad either. That's where we'll be staying, isn't it?'

He pointed to the Ionean Plaza, the large building on the northern side of the square. The pale yellow façade was bathed in evening sunshine. Three storeys high, small balconies with wrought-iron bars, and a distinctly French look overall. Van Veeteren nodded and looked at his watch.

'That's right,' he said. 'But we mustn't forget that this island has a history as well. A recent history.'

'Really?' said Münster.

'It was one of the worst affected of all during the war, in various ways. The Germans massacred thousands of Italian soldiers, for instance. Burnt heaps of them on big fires. And there was a terrible earthquake here in 1953.'

'I thought Germany and Italy were on the same side during the war,' said Münster.'

'So did the Italians,' said Van Veeteren. 'But I suppose we'd better forget about the war and Pascal for a while, and check in instead. Perhaps we ought to get something done today. Or what do you think?'

'A good idea,' said Münster. 'For our peace of mind – especially if we are going to sit around here for an eternal evening.'

The Fauner travel agency had its office in the south-west corner of the agora, and Münster was served by two blonde women in blue uniforms. They looked to be in their thirties, could well have been twins, and for the moment had nothing better to do than sit in front of their switched-off computers with a cup of coffee each. Münster knew that the tourist season proper didn't start for another four or five weeks, and he was surprised to find the office open from as early as 1 March.

But perhaps there was the occasional island-hopper to look after. And an occasional detective intendent. He turned to the nearest blonde and introduced himself.

'Were you the one who rang?'

'Yes.'

She smiled a friendly charter-smile. Münster smiled back.

'I've looked into the matter for you.'

She took a sheet of paper from a file.

'Maarten and Christa deFraan were here for a fortnight's holiday in August, 1995, like you said. They bought the holiday from us, and stayed at one of the hotels out at Lassi. That's only a few kilometres from here – it's where the best beaches are, and most people want to stay there. The hotel's name was Olympos, but it's not there any more. It wasn't one of the better establishments, to tell you the truth, and we stopped using it about three years ago. They closed down altogether last year. I think they're converting it into a collection of boutiques, but I'm not sure.'

Münster wrote it all down in his notebook.

'I suppose you don't happen to know about an incident that took place while they were here?'

She shook her head.

'No. What are you referring to?'

'Were you not working here then? In 1995?'

'Oh no, I didn't come here until spring last year. Agnieszka as well.'

The presumptive twin looked up from her newspaper and smiled.

'I've just extracted the information from the computer.'

'I see,' said Münster. 'Am I right in thinking there are quite a lot of hotels out there?'

'Of course. We use about ten, but there must be twenty-five to thirty in all. Most of them haven't opened yet, of course. The usual season is Easter to the end of September.'

'I see,' said Münster again, and contemplated the slowly rotating fan on the ceiling for a few seconds. 'But you haven't had a booking from Maarten deFraan this week, have you?'

'No. There's very little to do at this time of year, to be honest. It's mainly planning for the season ahead – checking that the hotels are up to standard, booking buses for the excursions, that sort of stuff. But we are open for a few hours every afternoon, as you have noticed.'

Münster nodded.

'What's the situation regarding the police authorities?' he asked. 'Argostoli is the main town on the island, is that right?'

'Yes. The police station is down by the harbour. We don't have much to do with them – it's pretty quiet around here, thank goodness. But they have three departments: traffic police, tourist police and criminal police – well, I suppose the criminal police isn't really a department. His name is Yakos. Dimitrios Yakos.'

'He's gone home for the day,' said Van Veeteren an hour later when they sat down with a beer each under a green parasol outside the Ionean Plaza. 'Chief Inspector Yakos. I rang the station, but the secretary wasn't even sure if he'd been in at all today – she hadn't seen him, if I understood her rightly. You haven't considered moving yet, have you?'

'I'm sitting here,' said Münster.

'Hmm, so you are,' said Van Veeteren, taking out his cigarette machine. 'Anyway, she was going to tell him that I want to meet him tomorrow morning, no matter what. I wonder where the hell our friend has got to . . . He's got a few days' start on us, of course.'

Friend? Münster thought. He's taken the lives of five people, or however many it is by now. Whatever he is, he's certainly not a *friend*.

'Was it Chief Inspector Yakos who was in charge of the investigation in 1995?' he asked.

'In so far as you can call it an investigation,' said Van Veeteren, suddenly looking much grimmer. 'I hope he speaks better English than his secretary in any case. But perhaps it's intentional that the local population should look after criminal activities on the island, and not the tourists.'

Münster said nothing for a while, gazing out over the square, where a blue Mediterranean twilight had begun to descend and make outlines more blurred. It made everything look even more attractive, like a large living room under an open sky. The temperature was still around twenty degrees, he estimated, and there were rather more people out and about now. Elderly gentlemen sitting and reading newspapers, or chatting over tiny cups of coffee. Women with or without string bags, with or without widows' veils. Young people sitting on the little podium, smoking. A few motorcyclists standing around, preening themselves . . . Young girls laughing and shouting and chasing one another, and small boys playing football. Dogs and cats. Not many tourists, as far as he could judge: perhaps twenty or so in the cafes and tavernas he could see from their table.

How the hell are we going to find him? he thought. We don't even know for sure if he's on this island.

Has he really got a plan, this bookseller by the name of Van Veeteren?

He didn't bother to ask as he knew he wouldn't get a sensible answer. Was content to keep a discreet eye on his former boss from the side – just now he looked as inscrutable as a newly dug-up antique statue as he sat there sipping his beer with a newly rolled and newly lit cigarette between the index and long fingers of his right hand. But I suppose statues didn't normally smoke and drink beer, Münster thought. I suppose I'm an astronaut after all, at bottom.

He relies on his intuitive ideas no matter what, always has done. But sooner or later surely even he must step on a land mine? Or was that not the case? Wasn't the fact of the matter that Van Veeteren was always more sure about things than the impression he tried to give? Always knew more than he pretended to know? That could well be the case now, although on the other hand . . .

'Oh hell!' exclaimed Van Veeteren, interrupting his chain of thought. 'That wouldn't be an impossibility, of course!'

'What wouldn't?' said Münster.

'That Muslim woman.'

'What about her?'

'It doesn't have to be the case that . . .'

Münster waited.

'It could equally well be . . .'

Münster sighed.

'What are you on about?'

'Shut up,' said Van Veeteren. 'Don't ask so many damned questions, I'm trying to think. Have you got your mobile with you?'

The leader of the investigation sighed and handed over his mobile.

50

As they sat waiting in Inspector Sammelmerk's office, Ewa Moreno thought about the problem of time and space.

Or to be more precise, things that happen and when they happen. About the peculiar fact that events appear to have the ability to attract other events. Like a sort of magnetism, almost. She recalled having discussed this phenomenon with Münster at some point: how long periods of time can pass – in one's private life but more especially in police work – unbearable periods when nothing at all happens. Boring investigations when days and weeks and months pile up when nothing at all happens and zero progress is made: and then suddenly, without warning, two or three or even four crucial events occur more or less simultaneously.

Like now. Like this day in March with warm breezes and the promise of spring in the air. She had been sitting in her office with the windows wide open all afternoon. The phone call from the Greek archipelago had come at exactly ten minutes past five: a week's accumulated paperwork had just been completed, and she was the only person left in the much reduced CID. That was why she was the one to receive the call from the *Chief Inspector*.

She had spoken to him for barely five minutes: no longer was needed. Then she had hung up and sat staring out of the window for a while, thinking about what action needed to be taken.

And about what the hell he was up to out there.

And then the next phone call had come. Anna Kristeva. Passed on to her via the switchboard, like the previous one. When she had been listening for long enough – a few minutes at most – to be clear that a face-to-face meeting was necessary, she had agreed a time, hung up and looked at the clock. It was still short of half past five.

A quarter of an hour, then. No longer than that had passed between the calls from Van Veeteren and Anna Kristeva. Surely that was remarkable. What peculiar waves in the passage of time had caused this sudden concentration in the flow of events? And brought matters to a head more or less simultaneously.

Bookseller Van Veeteren and lawyer Anna Kristeva? Two people completely unknown to each other, several thousand miles apart.

Well, as far as the *Chief Inspector* was concerned, it hadn't been a question of making a decision, of course. It was more of an insight. Several thoughts that had suddenly rung a bell, and several observations that put matters into perspective. Intuition, as it is called.

But Anna Kristeva had made a decision, something she had been thinking about for days, even weeks. Something that had stretched her nerves to their limits, and reduced her night's sleep to several hours below the minimum necessary.

That was presumably why she had black rings under her eyes, Moreno thought, when fröken Kristeva turned up at the police station at a couple of minutes after seven.

'Two women police officers?' said Kristeva when the polite preliminaries had been completed. 'That's something I hadn't expected. Is this some kind of new interrogation psychology you are developing?'

'It's pure coincidence,' said Inspector Sammelmerk. 'Please take a seat. Coffee? Water?'

'Water, please.' She ran her hands over her somewhat creased blue jacket, and turned to Moreno. 'I gather it was you I spoke to on the telephone – I don't think we've met before.'

'That's right,' said Moreno. 'And I must say you really surprised me. So we'd be grateful if you could tell us the whole story from the beginning. We need to record it as well – it could be the crucial proof we are looking for. Then we'll write a summary which you must call in and sign within the next few days. It's standard procedure, so to say.'

'I understand,' said Kristeva, looking down at the floor. 'I know I ought to have come to see you much earlier, but I didn't get round to it. This business . . . well, it hasn't been easy.'

Sammelmerk switched on the tape recorder.

'Interrogation of Anna Kristeva at Maardam Police Station on the fifth of March 2001,' she said. 'The time is 19.15. Those present are Inspector Moreno and Inspector Sammelmerk.

Would you please tell us why you have come here, fröken Kristeva.'

Kristeva took a deep breath and looked a few times at each inspector in turn before starting.

'Ester Peerenkaas,' she said. 'It's about Ester Peerenkaas, my friend, who's been missing for . . . well, it must be a month and a half by now. Most people have probably assumed she's dead – that she was murdered by that man who has killed several women previously, it seems. But that is not the case. Ester is alive.'

She had been staring fixedly at the tape recorder during these preliminary remarks. Now she paused briefly, looked up and drank a sip of water.

'Go on,' said Moreno.

Kristeva put her glass back on the table and clasped her hands in her lap.

'I also thought she was dead, to be honest. But then one evening a couple of weeks ago, she phoned me. It was the nineteenth of February, a Monday evening. I was awfully surprised, of course . . . and awfully pleased. At first I thought it was somebody having me on, but nothing could have made me happier than that telephone call – although I hadn't yet heard her story. She asked if she could come and stay with me for a few days, and she begged me to promise not to tell anybody that she was still alive. I didn't understand why – not until I saw her and heard what had happened that night . . . And until I heard about her plan.'

'Her plan?'

'Yes.'

She paused again and shook her head slightly, as if she found it hard to believe her own words.

'She turned up with a suitcase that same night, and when I saw her face I had quite a shock. It looked awful. My first reaction was that it looked like severe burns – the kind of thing you see on the television and in the newspapers . . . But it was in fact hydrofluoric acid in Ester's case. I don't know if you are aware of what such acid does to your skin, what a mess it can make of a face.'

Moreno exchanged glances with her colleague, who frowned and looked vaguely doubtful.

'Hydrofluoric acid?' she said.

'Yes, it's much worse than hydrochloric acid and sulphuric acid and stuff like that. It sort of creeps though the skin and deep down into the flesh . . . Hmm, maybe I don't need to describe it in detail?'

'I think I've actually seen it once,' said Sammelmerk. 'What hydrofluoric acid does to you. I agree with you, it's horrendous. So you're saying that Ester Peerenkaas had got some of that in her face, is that right?'

'Yes.'

'How did it happen?' asked Sammelmerk. 'I recall another friend of hers telling us that she used to carry a little bottle of acid in her handbag. Was that what . . . ?'

Kristeva nodded.

'Exactly. She always had that bottle with her. The idea was to protect herself from rapists. And that's how it happened, but not quite in the way intended. I don't know exact details, Ester didn't want to discuss it . . . She has changed a lot, not just her face. She's . . . well, it's taken me quite a while to catch on, but she's gone mad. Crazy and dangerous. It was hard going, having her staying with me: she's like a . . . like a black hole. I've tried talking to her, tried to make her see some sort of light in the darkness, but she hasn't listened to me, not even for a second. When I've tried to come close to her she has simply pointed at her deformed face and told me to go to hell. She's obsessed by what has happened to her. Totally obsessed.'

'So what actually happened?' asked Moreno. 'You said she gave some indication of it at least.'

Kristeva nodded.

'Yes, I know what happened – but only in broad outline. He tried to kill her. Not to rape her, that wasn't his primary aim at least. He had his hands round her neck and was going to strangle her, but she managed to get the bottle out of her handbag to throw over him. He somehow managed to fend her off: I think he was standing behind her, and she got most of it in her own face. But a small amount landed on him, and that's what presumably saved her life. She somehow managed to run out of the flat, he rushed into the bathroom, bellowing away, and switched on the shower, according to Ester. She splashed cold water onto her face from the kitchen tap, gathered together her things and raced off with a wet towel over her head – and terrible pains, of course.'

'How much of her face was affected?' Moreno wondered. 'It must have been horrendously painful.'

'It was a miracle that she managed to make it home,' said Kristeva. 'The whole of her right cheek up to her eye is ruined, and part of her nose and forehead as well. She looks grotesque, like a leper. At least she can still see out of that eye, but her skin is . . . well, there's hardly any of it left. She sleeps with a wet towel over her face now.'

'Good Lord!' exclaimed Sammelmerk. 'Is it possible to . . . to repair it somehow?'

Kristeva sighed.

'I don't really know. She didn't want to talk about it, but I've been in touch with a doctor – without letting on what it was really all about, of course – and he says it's possible to restore a face to a certain extent. Even if it's very disfigured. It would take a series of small operations and transplants over a period of about five or six years. The problem is that Ester isn't interested in such a solution – not yet at least.'

'I can understand that,' said Moreno, stroking her cheek lightly with two fingers. She could feel that she had goose pimples.

'What did she do when she got home that evening?' asked Sammelmerk. 'I thought it was necessary to get medical care as soon as possible?'

'Yes indeed. But not in this case. She said she kept herself locked up in her flat for a whole night and a day, bathing her face in water and applying ointments and whatever else she had at hand. The next evening she took the night train to Paris with a shawl over her head and face, and dark glasses, of course. She stayed in Paris for a month.'

'A month in Paris?' said Moreno. 'Where? Why?'

'At a friend's. She knows quite a lot of people there. She lived in Paris during the years she was married. She went to a doctor specializing in skin conditions – apparently he is one of her circle of acquaintances there – and got some help. She hid herself away in her friend's flat. Lay low and prepared for her return.'

She paused again and eyed Moreno and Sammelmerk for several seconds. As if she were telling a story that wasn't true, Moreno thought, and needed to keep stopping to check that her listeners were still interested in what was coming next.

'She got in touch with her mother eventually. Explained that she was still alive, but said that her parents would never see her again if they gave the slightest indication to anybody that she had been in touch. And then she turned up at my door a couple of weeks ago. Disguised as a Muslim woman, so that she could keep her face hidden in a way that seemed natural, of course. The conditions were more or less the same for me as they had been for her mother and father. I wasn't to say anything at all about her to anybody, it was as simple as that. It was a shock for me to discover that she was still alive, and, well . . . I promised to do all I could to help her. As you might recall, I was actually the one who was supposed to meet that man at Keefer's in December. In fact. But I fell ill, and things turned out as they did . . .'

'Excuse me a moment,' said Moreno, interrupting her and glancing at the tape recorder. 'I take it you're talking about Maarten deFraan, professor of English at Maardam University, is that right?'

'DeFraan, yes,' said Kristeva. 'That's his name. She didn't want to tell me his name at first, but after a few days I managed to squeeze it out of her. But Ester Peerenkaas is no longer Ester Peerenkaas, that's the most horrific thing of all. She's not the same person. She has only one thought in her head, a single one, and that is taking her revenge on that man.'

She threw her arms out in a gesture of impotence.

'Why can't she simply go to the police?' wondered Sammelmerk.

'Do you think I haven't kept asking her that?' said Kristeva with a snort. 'Do you think I haven't spent many a day and night asking her just that?'

'But why?' insisted Moreno. 'Why not the police? This man has many more things on his conscience, not just Ester Peerenkaas's ruined face . . .'

Kristeva sighed deeply again, and sat up straight.

'Because that wouldn't be enough for her,' she said. 'A conventional punishment wouldn't be sufficient. Ester has been let down by the authorities in the past as well – I don't know how much you know about her background, but that man who took their daughter and disappeared, well, she spent two years fighting for her rights before she gave up. That sort of thing leaves its mark. Quite simply, she doesn't trust the police. She intends to kill Maarten deFraan with her own hands – and not just kill him, come to that.'

Moreno gave a start.

'What do you mean?' she said. 'Not just kill him?'

Kristeva took a drink of water and sat in silence for a while before answering.

'She intends to torture him,' she said eventually in a low voice. 'I think . . . I think she intends to capture him somehow or other, and then subject him to something horrendous.

Extremely painful, and lasting for as long as possible, before she finally kills him. Don't ask me how she's going to do it, but she's obsessed by it. It's the only thing that keeps her going, and it's as if . . . as if it's not really about her. I think she sees herself as a tool – a representative of all the women who have been tormented by men. She sees it as a mission to take revenge for all the oppression our sex has been subjected to since the beginning of time – and to take it out on him, of course. It's as if she had been chosen. As I've said, she's mad . . .'

She paused again.

'But I understand her, of course. It's not all that odd that she has become like she is: that's why I didn't want to betray her.'

She tried to make eye contact with both Moreno and Sammelmerk now, as if in the hope of receiving support. Or at least some kind of understanding. Moreno found herself trying to avoid Kristeva's eyes, and she nodded rather vaguely.

'Yes indeed,' she said thoughtfully. 'It's understandable. I think it would be understandable for a male detective officer as well – for most of the ones I know, at least.'

'No doubt about that,' said Sammelmerk. 'But I don't think we should get too deeply involved in the sex role aspects at this stage. In any case, I don't think you need to worry at all about having kept quiet about this. The whole business is bad enough as it is. But what's the current situation? I don't think you've quite brought us up to date, as it were . . .'

Kristeva cleared her throat and continued.

'Ester had that Muslim woman disguise – she'd bought it in

Paris somehow or other. Hijab and all. I don't know if you can just walk into a shop and buy everything, just like that – perhaps it is that simple. The problem when she came back here was that she didn't even know what the man was called. He hadn't used his real name, as you know. But she knew where he lived, and it wasn't long before she knew who he was. She shadowed him for a few days while she was making her plans. Presumably he noticed her, because one day she discovered that he'd upped and left Maardam. Last Sunday, I think it was. In addition somebody else had turned up, also shadowing deFraan, according to Ester. Some sort of sleuth or detective officer from your lot, if I understood her rightly.'

Moreno managed another movement of the head that committed herself to nothing.

'In any case, deFraan must have become aware of one of them, or perhaps both. He must have realized that no matter what, he was living dangerously, and one day he was simply no longer there. Ester was furious, she didn't sleep for two nights, didn't even go to bed. I really thought she was going to lose control – she must have been taking some kind of tablets too. And then, well, she simply disappeared as well.'

'Disappeared?' said Moreno.

Kristeva nodded.

'So you're saying that Ester Peerenkaas disappeared once again, are you?' said Sammelmerk, checking that the tape recorder was still functioning. 'After Maarten deFraan had left Maardam.'

'Yes,' said Kristeva somewhat wearily. 'That's what I'm saying. On Wednesday last week she was suddenly no longer there. She had left and taken her suitcase with her, without a word of explanation.'

Five seconds passed.

'Where is she?' asked Moreno.

Kristeva shrugged in resignation.

'I don't know,' she said. 'I don't have the slightest idea. But I know who she's after, and I wouldn't like to be in his shoes.'

Moreno looked at Sammelmerk. Sammelmerk looked out of the window and drummed lightly with a pencil on her underlip.

'Maarten deFraan,' she said slowly. 'The Strangler. Suspected of having taken the life of five people – or perhaps it's only four now. So you're saying that he's the one Ester Peerenkaas is after?'

Yes,' said Kristeva, with another sigh. 'I don't suppose you know where he is?'

'We have our suspicions,' said Moreno.

Inspector Sammelmerk switched off the tape recorder.

'For Christ's sake!' she said. 'Forgive me, but I really must swear a little off the record. What a dreadful story! Yes, as Inspector Moreno said, we think we've begun to nail him down – but the less said, the better.'

'Where?' asked Kristeva, but she received no reply.

'Thank you for coming to us,' said Moreno instead. 'It hasn't been easy for you.'

Anna Kristeva allowed herself a very slight and brief smile.

'No,' she said. 'It hasn't been easy.'

*

When they were alone, Inspector Sammelmerk went over to the door and switched off the light.

'Good God,' she said as she flopped down onto her desk chair again. 'What do you say to that?'

'What is there to say?' said Moreno.

Sammelmerk thought for a while, biting her underlip and gazing out through the window.

'If we continue to refrain from getting involved in the sex role aspects,' she said eventually, 'where do we land up?'

'In Greece, of course.'

'And what do you think?'

'What about?'

'About how things are down there. Do you think she's landed up there as well?'

'No idea,' said Moreno. 'But I reckon we ought to give them a ring in any case.'

Irene Sammelmerk waited for a few long seconds, then slid the telephone across her desk.

'You do it,' she said. 'You know our representatives down there better than I do. Shall I look the number up for you?'

'That's not necessary,' said Moreno. 'I have a good memory for numbers.'

51

The police station in Argostoli was a blue-and-white two-storey building in Ioannis Metaxa, opposite the harbour office. Van Veeteren was escorted by a young, fit-looking constable through a long corridor to a blue door with a hand-written plate saying Dimitrios Yakos. In both Greek and Latin letters.

The constable knocked gently, and after a few seconds the door was opened by a stocky, thin-haired man in his fifties. He had a cigarette in his mouth, a cup of coffee in one hand and a newspaper folded in two in the other. Van Veeteren couldn't help but wonder how he had managed to manipulate the door handle.

'Chief Inspector Van Veeteren?' he said solemnly, and put down what he was carrying. 'I am very pleased to meet you.'

Van Veeteren shook hands, and the young constable headed back towards the front desk. Chief Inspector Yakos invited his guest to sit down and apologized eloquently for not being contactable the previous day as he had been busy with a case that needed his presence and full attention: but now he was available one hundred and fifty per cent. Europe is one big town nowadays, isn't she?

Van Veeteren nodded and accepted a cigarette from a shiny

metal case. He looked quickly around the cramped room with barred windows overlooking the street and the harbour, and decided that (apart from the barred windows) it looked more like a sort of student room than an office. A low table with two armchairs. A bookcase with files, books and newspapers. At least twenty framed family portraits on the walls, and a small humming refrigerator from which Yakos produced two cans of beer and opened them dexterously without even bothering to ask.

He was speaking all the time, and Van Veeteren's worries about possible linguistic problems were put to shame in no uncertain manner. Yakos's English was almost as fluent as his own – apart from the imagery which was firmly rooted in the Greek cultural traditions – and when Van Veeteren had tasted the beer and sat down in one of the armchairs, he had the distinct impression that everything might click into place despite everything.

After five minutes the chief inspector had completed his introductory monologue concerning his family and professional circumstances. He lit a new cigarette from the butt of the previous one, clasped his hairy hands and contemplated his guest with eager interest.

'Perhaps you could now explain the nature of your business here. It will be a pleasure to work with you.'

Van Veeteren thought for two seconds.

'I'm looking for a murderer,' he said then.

'Ah,' said Yakos, smacking his lips slightly as if he had just enjoyed a fresh fig. 'Here? On the island of donkeys and heroes?'

'Yes, here,' said Van Veeteren. 'His name is Maarten deFraan, and I have reason to suspect that he is holed up here in Argostoli – or possibly in Lassi. We think he arrived quite recently, and has presumably checked into a hotel or boarding house. Possibly using a false name, but he's probably using his real one. I need your help to find him, and I need your help to arrest him. I assume you have received my authorization documents?'

Yakos nodded.

'Yes, of course. No problem.'

Van Veeteren handed over a photograph of deFraan. Yakos took it, held it carefully between his thumb and index finger as he studied it with his eyebrows assuming the shape of a circumflex accent.

'The murderer?'

'Yes.'

'How many lives does he have on his conscience? It's not clear from the picture.'

'We don't know for certain. Four or five.'

'Ah.'

He returned the photograph.

'Can we expect any complications? Is he armed?'

Van Veeteren thought for a moment before replying.

'Possibly,' he said. 'It's difficult to judge if he's dangerous or not. I suggest we wait with that aspect until we have located him. How long do you think you'll need?'

Yakos looked at the clock and smiled.

'Get in touch again this afternoon,' he said. 'Let's face it, we only need to carry out a check on the local hotels. That shouldn't take more than a few hours – I have several junior officers at my disposal. If we don't find him, then of course the situation will become more difficult: but why foresee difficulties that might not exist?'

'Why indeed,' agreed Van Veeteren. He drank the rest of the beer and stood up. 'I'll call in at about four, is that okay?'

'This afternoon, yes,' said Yakos with a smile suggesting a typically Greek indifference towards time. 'If anything happens before then, I'll be in touch.'

Before going out on watch the second day, she checked the contents of her cloth bag.

A short iron rod taped into a piece of sheeting. A nylon rope. Two bottles, one containing hydrofluoric acid, the other petrol. A packet of salt. Matches. Two different knives. A small pair of pliers.

She offered up a silent prayer, hoping to be able to use them all in more or less that order while trying to visualize the scenario in her mind's eye. She felt a sudden shooting pain down her spine and into her legs, and a moment of dizziness. Then she tied the thin headscarf around her hair and the lower part of her face. Good to be rid of those Muslim veils, she thought. Looked at herself in the mirror again before completing her disguise with the aid of a pair of large, round sunglasses.

She picked up the bag and left the room. Stepped out into the sunlight and warmth of the Greek morning. Looked around. The Lassi district, as it was called, was basically just one street. That was an advantage, an indisputable advantage. She adjusted her sunglasses and looked up at the sky. It was more or less cloud-free, and the temperature must have been eighteen to twenty degrees already. A warm day, but not too hot. There was a hint of promise in it, she told herself. Something that suggested the end was nigh.

It was a long street, two kilometres or more. The previous evening she had walked back and forth along it, past the tavernas and hotels, without attracting any attention. Bars, mini-markets and boutiques. And why should she attract any attention? Headscarves were a common item of clothing, sunglasses almost compulsory. It was perfect. Sooner or later she would get wind of him. Sooner or later. There were no other streets to walk along if you wanted to move around Lassi out of doors.

Sooner or later.

'What do we do now?' said Münster.

Van Veeteren looked up.

'We wait,' he said. 'There's not much else we can do. But we could take a stroll around the harbour district and have a look at the shops. Or would you like to go for a swim in the sea? I'd be happy to stand by with the towels.'

'It's only the seventh of March,' Münster pointed out. 'No thank you. But I'd like to know what you think about fröken Peerenkaas.'

They left the cafe and started walking towards Ioannis Metaxa. Van Veeteren took off his straw hat and wiped his forehead with a paper tissue. Münster's query remained hanging in the air for half a minute until the *Chief Inspector* felt called upon to answer it.

'I think she's highly dangerous,' he said. 'Unfortunately. Perhaps not only for deFraan. But I hope she hasn't found her way here. Perhaps you could keep your eyes skinned as we make our way through the crowds – your eyesight's better than mine. Do you have your service pistol handy?'

Münster tapped under his arm, and nodded to confirm that it was there. It had delayed their departure a whole day, but Van Veeteren had insisted that at least one of them should be carrying a gun.

That was most unusual, Münster thought. He never seemed to be especially interested in police officers carrying weapons. Certainly not as far as he himself was concerned.

'I suppose there is a risk, though,' said Münster. 'That she might be here, I mean. If she was already in Athens when we got there, as Krause maintains, well . . . I have to say that I don't honestly know what she might do.'

'Hmm,' muttered Van Veeteren, adjusting his straw hat. 'Maybe it isn't all that complicated. It's not deFraan she's been shadowing, it's us, my dear Watson. You and me. A couple of thick detective officers who book flights and hotels backed up by a fanfare of trumpets, and using their own names. DeFraan has no doubt done all he can to prevent her from catching up with him, but so what when we have been as obvious as brightly coloured hippos in a chicken run?'

Münster frowned, then relaxed again.

'All right,' he said. 'No doubt that's the way things are. But if we happen to catch sight of her in among all the crowds of people, what do we do then? Arrest her?'

'For what?' wondered Van Veeteren. 'As far as I'm aware she hasn't even acquired a parking ticket.'

Münster thought for a moment.

'That's true,' he said. 'But what do we do, then?'

'We wait,' said Van Veeteren. 'I tried to explain that to you. Have you already forgotten your Pascal?'

Hell's bells, thought Münster, gritting his teeth. Here we are, wandering around in peace and quiet – like brightly coloured hippos! – although in fact we're on the trail of a lunatic who has killed at least four people with his bare hands. And of a totally obsessed woman. And he goes on about Pascal! Life in the antiquarian book world has made its mark, it seems.

He adjusted his gun, which was chafing against his armpit, and ducked under a red awning to a stall where Van Veeteren had just slipped in to taste some unusually large and fat olives.

'Watch out for the stones,' thought Münster – but said it out loud.

'What?' said Van Veeteren. 'These are not bad at all. What did you say?'

'It was nothing,' said Münster.

She saw him out of the corner of her eye – she'd been a hair's breadth away from missing him completely.

Niko's Rent-a-car. On the extreme northern edge of the little town, where the road started to climb up the mountain towards Argostoli. She continued a few metres past the office, then stopped.

He was standing inside. Maarten deFraan. *Him.* Her heart rose up inside her chest, and suddenly she could feel a strong taste of metal on her tongue. It was strange. For a few seconds she just stood there, in the middle of the pavement, while the ground seemed to be revolving under her feet as the cicadas sawed away at her eardrums. It was as if something – or possibly everything – was about to burst.

It soon passed. She took two deep breaths and regained control of herself. Concentration surged into her like a fast-flowing river. No, she thought. We're nearly there. There's not far to go . . . But what's he doing?

He intended to hire a car. Or some kind of motorbike. That was as clear as day.

But why? What was he going to do? What was he doing on this confounded island in any case?

And what would she do?

She looked round. A white-and-green taxi was approaching slowly along the road, and she automatically raised her hand. The driver stopped and she jumped into the back seat.

At that very moment the car rental assistant – a flabby young man in a large-patterned shirt unbuttoned down to his navel – emerged from the office together with deFraan. The necessary papers had evidently been signed. All was in order. They walked over to a purple-coloured scooter that was standing by itself, slightly to the side of the other two-wheelers lined up on the pavement. She realized that deFraan must have picked out that one before entering the office. The assistant handed over a couple of keys and gave his customer some simple instructions. DeFraan nodded, and sat astride the scooter. Adjusted his rucksack and exchanged a few more words with the young man. Then he turned the ignition key and started the engine. He checked the road situation before gingerly negotiating the kerb edge and spluttering off in the direction of Argostoli.

'Where are we going, miss?' asked the taxi driver, looking at her enquiringly in the rear-view mirror.

She took a one thousand-drachma note out of her handbag and pointed at the scooter.

The driver hesitated for a moment, then took the note between his index and middle fingers, put it into the breast pocket of his white shirt, and set off.

'I understand,' said Van Veeteren. 'He's been located, but is still at large, is that right? Okay, we'll wait for your next report.'

He handed the mobile to Münster.

'You can switch it off. I don't know where the button is.'

Münster did as he was bidden, and put the phone in his breast pocket.

'Was it Yakos?' he said. 'Have they found him?'

'Not really.'

Van Veeteren paused and looked out over the whitewashed buildings that filled the whole of the western side of the bay.

They had crossed over the narrow stone bridge and were on their way back. It was half past eleven, and the sun had started to become really warm.

'No,' continued the *Chief Inspector*. 'Apparently they've found the hotel, in Lassi as we expected, but the bird had flown the nest. He went out at about ten o'clock, they thought. Perhaps he's lounging back in a deckchair somewhere, or maybe he has something else in his sights.'

'What, for instance?' wondered Münster.

Van Veeteren put his foot on the low stone balustrade and gazed out over the glittering water. Said nothing for a while.

'God only knows,' he said in the end, straightening his back. 'But he must have gathered that we are at his heels – and that a certain woman is hot on his trail as well. He knows the game is almost up, but perhaps he wants to have a hand in setting up the final showdown – or what do you think?'

Münster sat down on the balustrade, and thought that one over.

'It's hard to figure out the logic behind his behaviour,' he said. 'In many respects he's as mad as a hatter, but in other ways he seems to be acting more or less normally.'

That's not an especially unusual phenomenon,' said Van Veeteren, lighting a cigarette. 'We all have a few screws loose, including you and me; but it's a bit more complicated in the case of deFraan. He's presumably hyper-intelligent, and if there's anything we like to use our intelligence for it's trying to explain away those loose screws. To find motives for our peculiar behaviour and our murky instincts . . . If we didn't do that we would never be able to put up with ourselves.'

Münster nodded.

'Yes, I've never understood how certain people have the strength to carry on living. Rapists and wife-beaters and child murderers . . . How the hell can they look themselves in the eye the following morning?'

'Defence mechanisms,' said the *Chief Inspector* in a weary voice. 'That applies to you and me as well. We create safety nets over the abyss, and in deFraan's case he has presumably been forced to devote the whole of his abilities to making things work . . . We'll have to see if we ever get to the bottom of it all.'

'We'll also have to see if we ever catch him,' said Münster. 'I hope Chief Inspector Yakos can handle this.'

Van Veeteren shrugged and they started walking back to the harbour.

'I'm sure he can,' he said. 'Just as well as we could, in any case.'

Chief Inspector Yakos looked tired when he came to sit at their table shortly after nine o'clock that night. He beckoned to the waiter, ordered Greek coffee, beer, ouzo and peanuts. Stubbed out a cigarette and lit another.

'I'm sorry,' he said, 'but we haven't managed to catch him.'

'Things sometimes take time,' said Van Veeteren.

'He hasn't been at the hotel since this morning. I've had a constable posted outside Odysseus all afternoon, and he'd have been bound to see him.'

'What about that scooter?' wondered Münster.

Yakos shook his head grimly.

'He hasn't been back to the rental people with it. He was supposed to return it by nine o'clock, according to the contract – that's when they close. I'm afraid there's not much else we can do today. But my man at Odysseus will remain on watch – and if he turns up, we'll pounce on him immediately, of course.'

He placed his blood-red mobile on the table, as if to stress that the network was on red alert.

'Excellent,' said Van Veeteren. 'I assume you've instructed your constable not to try to tackle him on his own? We're dealing with a murderer, and he can be extremely dangerous.'

Yakos emptied his glass of ouzo.

'No chance,' he said. 'Constable Maraiades is the most cowardly donkey on the whole island.'

'Excellent,' said Van Veeteren again. 'And that scooter – are you following that up?'

Yakos observed his guests with a wry smile before answering.

'My dear friends,' he said slowly but firmly. 'I have been a chief inspector in Argostoli for twenty years. I was born here – two days after the earthquake and a week too early, it was the tremors that sparked off my dear mother's labour pains ... Anyway, I can guarantee that every police officer, every bar owner and every taxi driver on this island knows that I'm looking for a purple scooter, a Honda with the registration number BLK 129. Don't underestimate me.'

'I apologize,' said Van Veeteren. 'Let's drink a bottle of

good Boutari wine and eat a lump or two of cheese while we're waiting.'

Yakos flung out his arms.

'Why not?' he said.

52

'The problem,' her grandfather had said on his deathbed, 'is that there isn't a God.'

She often used to recall those words, and during the last few weeks they had kept on returning with a sort of somnambulistic persistency. *There isn't a God*. Her grandfather on her mother's side had died of cancer, had spent the last few months of his life in hospital, and two days before he died she had sat alone with him, by his bed. They had been taking it in turns: her, her mother and her aunt – they all knew that he didn't have long left.

She had sat there in a blue armchair in the special part of the hospital reserved for the dying. Terminal patients. A grandfather on his last legs, drugged up to the eyeballs with morphine, and a sixteen-year-old granddaughter. The cancer was in his pancreas. A part of it, at least. She had gathered that if you had to have cancer, you wouldn't choose to have it in your pancreas.

It was his last night but one, as it turned out, and as morning approached, shortly before half past five, he had woken up and reached for her hand. She must have fallen asleep in the chair, and woke up when he touched her. She tried to sit up.

He eyed her for a moment or two, with a serene expression on his face, and she almost had the impression that it was that notorious moment of clarity just before death – but it wasn't the case, in fact. He had over a day left.

Then he had spoken those words, in a loud and clear voice. *The problem is that there isn't a God.*

Then he let go of her hand, closed his eyes and went back to sleep.

He had been deeply religious all his life. At his funeral the church had been so full that she had to stand right at the back.

She was sixteen years old, and had never told anybody about what he had said.

No, she thought as she sat there in the taxi, her hands clasped tightly in her lap. There isn't a God: that's why we have to make sure justice is done ourselves.

The journey lasted barely a quarter of an hour. He had stopped at a hairpin bend at the top of a ravine. There was still some distance left to the pass over to the north side of the island, if she understood it rightly. When she looked back she could still see a bit of the old, narrow stone bridge over the sound leading into Argostoli's harbour. She asked the driver to continue past the next rocky outcrop, and then stop.

She thanked him and got out of the car. The taxi continued up the side of the steep hill – she assumed it was too difficult to turn round on the narrow strip of asphalt, and perhaps there were other roads leading down to the capital. When the car had left her field of vision, she went back round the bend and saw him again. He was standing next to the purple scooter with his back towards her, staring down into the ravine. The sides were steep, rocky and devoid of vegetation, but down at the bottom, some thirty metres deep, there was a mass of dry, straggly bushes and rubbish which unscrupulous motorists had thrown down. Paper and plastic carrier bags and empty cans. And something that looked like a refrigerator.

He was standing there motionless, with a small greyish-green rucksack at his feet and a revolver in his right hand.

She ran her fingers over the mangled, ravaged skin on her face, then put her hand into her shoulder bag. She took hold of the wrapped-up iron rod. As far as she could tell he hadn't noticed her presence. Good, she thought. The distance to him was no more than twenty metres: she gave no thought to why he was standing there, why he had a revolver in his hand or what he was intending to do. It was sufficient that she had her own plan clear and at the ready.

More than sufficient.

There isn't a God, she thought as she approached him cautiously.

He didn't notice her – or took no notice of her – until she was almost next to him. He seemed to be concentrating hard: but when he finally heard her footsteps and sensed her presence, he gave a start and turned to look at her.

'Excuse me,' she said in English, tightening her hold on the iron rod in her bag. 'Do you happen to know what time it is?'

'The time?'

It was a bizarre question to ask up here in this barren mountainous landscape, and he looked at her in surprise.

'Yes, please.'

He raised his hand, the one not holding the revolver, and checked his wristwatch.

'Twelve,' he said. 'It's one minute to twelve.'

She thanked him and adjusted the scarf over her face. He doesn't recognize me, she thought. He has no idea who I am.

'It's beautiful here,' she said, and took a step closer, as if she was about to pass him. He looked out over the ravine again. Didn't respond. The arm with the revolver was hanging down motionless by his side. She saw a bird of prey soaring up over the mountain ridge: it circled around then hovered high up in the air, almost directly above them. She took the rod out of her bag.

God . . . she thought as she raised it in the air.

He turned his head and stared at her for a fraction of a second with his mouth half open. Raised his gun so that it was pointing at his own head, his right temple.

. . . doesn't exist, she thought, and swung the rod.

53

Chief Inspector Yakos didn't look much more cheerful.

'He'd been asleep in bed with his mistress, that confounded taxi driver,' he said. 'That's why we haven't heard from him until this morning.'

He leaned forward, supporting himself with his hands on his knees, and breathed heavily. Münster looked around. The view was stunningly beautiful, and it was hard to shake off the feeling of unreality that hovered in the clear morning light . . . The feeling that he was in bed, dreaming, or perhaps taking part in some surrealistic film. To make things worse he had slept badly, unlike the taxi driver, all alone in his austere hotel room. It had been three o'clock before he finally dozed off.

Now it was half past ten. They were a few kilometres outside the town. The sun had risen a hand's breadth over the top of the mountain ridge, casting light onto the lower, barren slopes, and the olive groves down by the coast, and the scattered whitewashed dwellings on the other side of the sound. The bluish silhouettes of little islands faded away in the west towards the horizon, which was as sharp as a drypoint engraving, despite the fact that the sea and the sky were very nearly the same blue colour. Closer to them, a few hundred metres further along the road, were the equally sharply outlined ruins of a building – some sort of mill, Münster guessed – flanked by two olive trees.

And even closer, parked alongside the low, half-eroded stone wall that separated the road from the precipice was a purple scooter, a Honda. Registration number BLK 129.

Münster adjusted his police gun and turned to look over the edge. Straight ahead of them was a ravine – two steep sides forming a deep and rocky V deep down into the hillside with its point a long way below them, some thirty or forty metres at a guess, covered by a mass of prickly bushes and piles of rubbish. Completely inaccessible to everyone and everything.

Nevertheless the steep sides were crawling with people. Young men dressed in black with ropes and pickaxes and lots of other equipment. A helicopter was hovering over them, shattering the silence of the magnificent landscape. Münster turned his head a little more and observed Van Veeteren, standing two metres away from him with an unlit cigarette in his mouth. He also looked as if he had slept badly.

Or perhaps it was just the disappointment and frustration that was engraved in his grim facial expression. Disappointment at not having been able to capture Maarten deFraan alive.

Ever since they had heard from Yakos about the discovery shortly before eight o'clock, the *Chief Inspector* had been irritable and tetchy. Münster guessed – hoped, perhaps? – that it was the arrogant reference to Pascal that gave him a bad taste in his mouth. Among other things.

For Maarten deFraan was dead. Very dead. The idea of sitting face to face with him and poking around in his murky psychology would never become reality. Neither for Van Veeteren nor for anybody else.

Chief Inspector Yakos wiped the sweat off his glistening head with a towel. He had just clambered back up to the road from the finding-place, and the patches of sweat under his arms were as large as elephant's ears.

'Would you like to go down and take a look?' he asked, looking at Van Veeteren and Münster in turn.

'I don't think that's necessary,' said Van Veeteren. 'But I'd be grateful if you could give us a detailed description. I assume photographs will be taken?'

'Hundreds,' said Yakos. 'No, forget about all the climbing. It looks horrific down there. Absolutely horrific.'

He paused, as if he were tasting the word to make sure it was the right one.

'Two bodies. Or rather, to be precise, one body and a skeleton. Dr Koukonaris says the skeleton could be anything from three to thirty years old: but of course we'll get a more accurate assessment when all the analyses have been made. In any case, everything seems to indicate that it's a woman.'

'It's his wife,' said Van Veeteren. 'Her name is Christa deFraan and she's been lying there in that ravine since August 1995.'

Chief Inspector Yakos stared briefly at him with circumflex-shaped eyebrows, while blowing out a thin stream of air from between his lips.

'Really?' he said. 'Well, if you say so. Anyway, the other

body is of more recent vintage. A man who has been lying there for a day at most. There is no reason to doubt that it is Professor deFraan, who you have been hunting. But he has been badly mauled, so we can't be certain of that yet . . .'

'Mauled?' said Van Veeteren. 'How has he been mauled?'

Yakos inhaled deeply on his cigarette and gazed out over the sea.

'Do you want details?'

'Yes please.'

'Don't blame me . . . But of course you'll have to take a look at him when we've recovered him from the ravine. Horrific, as I said.'

'We've gathered that,' said Van Veeteren with a trace of irritation in his voice. 'Please tell us about it now.'

Yakos nodded.

'In the first place, he's been shot through the head. Entrance hole through one temple, exit hole through the other one. We haven't found a gun, but it is a pretty large-calibre weapon – nine millimetres, perhaps. We're still looking for it, of course.'

'Of course,' said Van Veeteren.

'But that's not the worst injury,' said Yakos.

'No?'

'Presumably he had injuries from the fall,' said Münster.

Yakos nodded grimly.

'Yes, he doesn't have many unbroken bones, according to the doctor, so it's obvious he's fallen from up here. Or been pushed . . . But those are not the injuries I'm referring to.'

He inhaled once again, and seemed to hesitate.

'Go on,' said Van Veeteren. 'The intendent and I have fifty years in the branch between us so you don't need to censor your description.'

'All right, if you insist. His body is almost naked and full of injuries in addition to those caused by the fall. There are stab wounds and slashes by a knife all over the place, and what seems to be corrosion, especially in his face – or what is left of his face. He is unrecognizable. His eyes have been dug out, and his . . . his penis and testicles have been cut off. His hands and feet are tied together with a nylon cord – his hands behind his back. Several of his nails have been pulled out. And in addition he has burns on large parts of his body, especially his chest and stomach – it looks as if somebody has poured petrol over him and set fire to it. Everything suggests that he has been tortured . . . down there . . .'

He pointed to a narrow ledge a few metres down the precipice. Münster noted a few black patches on stones, and sooty remains of some sort of cloth or clothing.

'If that happened before or after the bullet went through his brain, well, we don't know that yet. I have . . . I must say that I've never seen anything worse than this.'

He fell silent. Münster swallowed and looked up at the helicopter, which was flying away over the mountain ridge with something dangling on a rope underneath its grey-green bodywork. Van Veeteren stood there motionless, gazing down into the ravine with his hands behind his back. Somebody down below shouted something in Greek and was answered by Chief Inspector Yakos.

No, thought Münster. Why climb down there and look at

that unless you were forced to? We'll be faced with it soon enough anyway.

One of the police officers climbed up onto the road carrying a plastic bag containing some dark object Münster was unable to identify. Yakos accepted it and handed it over to Van Veeteren, who looked at it for two seconds before returning it to the young police officer. Yakos gave him a brief instruction in Greek and he clambered into one of the police cars lined up along the side of the road.

'For Christ's sake!' said Van Veeteren.

Yakos nodded.

'His penis. I told you it was horrific. What sort of a lunatic could have done that? Did you expect to find something like this? What on earth has been going on?'

It was doubtless no more than half a minute before Van Veeteren replied, but it seemed to Münster like an eternity. The shades of blue in the perfect morning that surrounded them on all sides became slightly lighter. A lone cicada started chirruping listlessly, a bird of prey flew in from the coast and more or less took over the space previously occupied by the helicopter. Chief Inspector Yakos threw his half-smoked cigarette down onto the edge of the road and stamped on it.

Münster began rehearsing the whole of this confounded case in his head, very rapidly. Almost against his will. Speedily and rhapsodically the images flashed past in his mind's eye: the cramped flat in Moerckstraat, the dead priest and his bisexual friend, Monica Kammerle's mutilated body in the dunes at Behrensee, the conversation with Anna Kristeva and all the others involved in this agonizingly drawn-out tragedy . . . The lapel badge in the shoe up in Wallburg, the Succulents and the veiled woman. Ester Peerenkaas. Nemesis. Had she got there in time, or what was one to think?

And the murderer himself. Professor Maarten deFraan. Who had evidently killed his wife almost six years ago at the very spot where they were standing now, and then continued along the same lines . . . Another four people had lost their lives, just in order to . . . in order to what? Münster thought. What was it that had lain hidden at the back of his insane mind? Was there an explanation at all? Was there any point in looking for one? For the *derangement*, as Van Veeteren used to call it.

Eventually, perhaps, Münster thought wearily. Just now I don't understand this case. But I do understand that it is closed.

He realized immediately that his latest assumption was also an over-hasty conclusion, but he didn't have time to revise it before Van Veeteren cleared his throat and addressed Yakos's query.

'What has been going on? . . .' he said slowly. 'Hmm, God only knows. But if we really want to know, we shall have to wait for the post-mortem results, of course. That body has been mutilated . . . The question is whether it happened before or after the bullet went through his brain . . . Either or, as it were. Personally, I have to admit that I couldn't care less which.'

Chief Inspector Yakos stared at him in genuine surprise.

'Couldn't care less? Forgive me, but I don't understand what you are saying. That man has been murdered, and—'

'Thank you,' said Van Veeteren. 'You don't need to enlighten me. But there is a possibility that he took his own life, don't forget that . . . And that those mutilations of his body were administered afterwards. When we get the post-mortem results, we'll know the answer to that.'

'Why?' wondered Yakos. 'Why on earth should anybody want to . . .'

Van Veeteren put a hand on his shoulder.

'My dear friend,' he said. 'If you come to our hotel this evening, I'll tell you a story.'

Chief Inspector Yakos hesitated for a moment. Then he nodded, shrugged, and gazed out to sea.

'It's a lovely morning,' he said.

54

The next day the same sun rose over the same mountain ridge. Poured its unblemished light over the same barren slopes and the same greyish-green olive groves.

And over the same pale-orange agora in Argostoli, with all its elderly gentlemen wandering around or drinking coffee, stray mongrels, clattering Vespas and children at play. Van Veeteren and Münster were enjoying a late breakfast outside the Ionean Plaza while waiting for Chief Inspector Yakos to arrive with the latest news from the pathologist and the technical boys.

'Those olive trees,' said Münster, pointing up at the hillsides. 'I've heard they can be several hundred years old.'

'So I gather,' said Van Veeteren. 'What do you make of this, then?'

He tapped his spoon on the five-page fax that had arrived from Maardam a few hours earlier. Münster had received it in reception and read it three times before handing it over to the *Chief Inspector.*

'Krause can be very efficient when he puts his mind to it,' he said diplomatically.

'He has always been reliable from a quantitative point of

621

view,' said Van Veeteren. 'But this really is a remarkable picture of deFraan that is emerging – or that can be deduced, in any case. I can't help but think about his childhood: that's where we start bleeding . . .'

'Bleeding?' said Münster, but received no response.

Instead Van Veeteren thumbed through the papers and cleared his throat.

'Listen to this: "When deFraan was six years old his father died in what where traumatic circumstances for the little boy. The family house in Oudenzee burnt down to the ground: unlike his son and the boy's mother, the father was unable to escape. In the investigation that followed in connection with the incident, the mother was suspected of arson at one point, but no charges were made." What do you say to that?'

Münster thought for a while.

'I don't know,' he said. 'I just have a sort of feeling.'

'A sort of feeling?' snorted Van Veeteren. 'Everything begins with a feeling – even you, Münster.'

'An interesting point of view,' said Münster. 'Perhaps you could enlarge upon it?'

Van Veeteren glared at him before consulting the fax again.

'Here!' he exclaimed. 'Listen to this! "At his mother's funeral in 1995, according to notes in the will her son was the only one present. After her death he was off work sick for four months." Four months, Münster! What do you make of that?'

'Yes,' said Münster, 'I noticed that as well. It certainly seems to have a whiff of Freudian implications. What should one make of it? But surely what they found in the freezer is what really turns your stomach over?'

Van Veeteren turned to the relevant section of Krause's fax and read it out.

'"Yesterday's search of deFraan's flat turned up a macabre discovery in the freezer in his kitchen: two human legs, cut off just below the knee. There is no reason to doubt that these are the missing body parts of Monica Kammerle. A plausible explanation is that deFraan cut the legs off the body of his victim so that it would fit into his golf bag: that was found in a wardrobe, and was overflowing with traces of spent blood."'

'Overflowing with traces of spent blood!' said Münster. 'For Christ's sake, what kind of language is that?! But still, it seems to fit in with the facts. He kills her, cuts off her legs, squashes her body into that golf bag and puts the tarpaulin over it . . . Takes her in his car and buries her out at Behrensee. For Christ's sake, I'm relieved not to have met him.'

Van Veeteren slid the papers to one side.

'Yes,' he said pensively. 'Perhaps it's as well that we didn't take him alive.'

'What do you mean by that?' said Münster.

Van Veeteren scratched at the stubble on his chin and seemed to be wondering what he meant.

'Just that I would never have been able to understand him,' he said. 'And as it is, I don't even need to try.'

Münster said nothing for a while, and looked out over the square. A dark-brown dog emerged from a side street and circled round them several times, then gave up, and lay down under a neighbouring table. A waiter came with a new pot of coffee.

'What do you think happened up there?' Münster asked in the end. 'And no mystifications, if you don't mind.'

'Mystifications?' exclaimed Van Veeteren in surprise. 'Surely I don't normally indulge in mystifications?'

'Tell me what you think, then.'

'All right,' said Van Veeteren. 'It's surely pretty obvious. Our friend deFraan had decided to close the circle and put an end to his days – in the same place as his wife, who he killed six years ago. It all started with her – or at least, the murders started with her . . . Anyway, fröken Nemesis caught up with him just in time, it seems. She followed him in that taxi – if it had been me I'd have used the scooter he'd hired for the trip back to Argostoli: but maybe she couldn't get it started, what do I know?'

'Just in time?' said Münster. 'Are you saying that she managed to torture him while he was still alive?'

Van Veeteren made a meal of wiping his mouth with his table napkin before responding.

'How could I know?' he said. 'Presumably it's not a problem for the pathologist to sort that out, so we shall soon know about it for certain.'

'No doubt,' said Münster. 'And we'll also find out how long Ester Peerenkaas can manage to hide herself away . . . But surely she must have got as far as Athens by now, don't you think?'

'I hope so,' said Van Veeteren, and started filling his cigarette machine with tobacco. 'I don't think you lot should put too much effort into trying to find her, if you don't mind my saying so.'

'You lot?' said Münster.

'Don't be so pedantic, Münster. That woman has lost her daughter thanks to a bastard of a husband, and she has been disfigured by an even bigger bastard . . . If she managed to achieve some kind of revenge up there at the ravine, my instinct is to congratulate her.'

Münster thought that over.

'Maybe you're right,' he said. 'It's a pity that taxi driver didn't see any more than he evidently did . . .'

Van Veeteren produced a cigarette from his machine, and lit it. Looked at Münster through the resultant smoke.

'I'm glad that I don't have to worry about that detail,' he said.

'So I gather,' said Münster.

'It's a pity we can't stay for a few more days,' said Münster when Chief Inspector Yakos had left them a few hours later. 'It must be getting on for twenty-five degrees today. What are those books?'

Van Veeteren placed his right hand on top of the pile of books on the table.

'A sort of canon,' he said. 'About this case. I couldn't resist taking them off the shelves. Perhaps there is some sort of thread.'

He handed them to Münster one by one: William Blake. Robert Musil. The lugubrious little crime novel by Henry Moll. Rilke's *Duino Elegies*. Münster took them and nodded, somewhat bewildered.

A sort of thread? he thought.

'But what about this one? Rappaport? *The Determinant*? The thing that we—'

'Exactly,' said Van Veeteren. 'But it's in Swedish, so I'm not going to try to read it.'

Münster sat there for a while without speaking, his gaze alternating between the books and the *Chief Inspector*.

'I understand,' he said eventually. 'Anyway, we've four hours before our flight leaves. Perhaps we ought to order a taxi, to be on the safe side.'

'Ah, well,' said Van Veeteren. 'Go on then, do that.'

Münster looked at him sceptically.

'What does "ah, well" mean?' he asked.

Van Veeteren shrugged and pushed his straw hat over the back of his head.

'It doesn't mean anything special,' he said. 'Just that I need a bit of peace and quiet in order to write my memoirs. *The G File*, among other things . . . Ulrike is due here tomorrow, by the way. We're going to stay for a week – didn't I mention that? She said it's been raining non-stop in Maardam. Ah, well . . .'

Münster took the last of the olives from the dish and put it in his mouth.

All right, he thought magnanimously. Part of me doesn't begrudge him that.

THE G FILE

1987. Maarten Verlangan, a former cop turned private detective, is hired by a woman to follow her husband. The request is hardly unusual; but then two events occur that turn everything on its head. First, Verlangan realizes that Barbara's husband Jaan 'G' Hennan is a man he helped put in prison many years before; and then, a few days later, Barbara is found dead at the bottom of an empty swimming pool.

Maardam police, led by Chief Inspector Van Veeteren, investigate the case. Like Verlangan, Van Veeteren has encountered Jaan 'G' Hennan before and knows only too well the man's dark capabilities. When it is then discovered that G is due to receive a huge insurance pay-out following his wife's 'accidental' death – and further information about his shadowy past comes to light – Van Veeteren becomes more desperate than ever to convict him. But Verlangan himself witnessed G sitting in a restaurant at the time of Barbara's fatal plummet – and no one else can be found in relation to the crime.

2002. Fifteen years have passed and the G file remains the one case former Chief Inspector Van Veeteren has never been able to solve. But when Verlangan's daughter reports the private detective missing, Van Veeteren returns to Maardam CID once more. For all Verlangan left behind was a cryptic note; and a telephone message in which he claimed to have finally discovered the proof of G's murderous past . . .

An extract follows here . . .

When Chief Inspector Van Veeteren came out into the street with Bismarck, it was just turned half past six in the morning and the sun had not yet managed to climb over the top of the line of dirty brown blocks of flats on the other side of Wimmergraacht.

Even so, it seemed like quite a decent morning. The temperature must have been round about twenty degrees, and bearing in mind that he lived in a city where near gale-force winds blew three mornings out of five and it rained every other day, he couldn't really complain.

Not about the weather, at least.

What he *could* complain about was the time. His wife Renate had woken him up with a prod of the elbow, and claimed that Bismarck was whimpering and wanted to go out. Without a second thought he had got up, dressed, attached a lead to the collar of the large Newfoundland bitch, and set off. He was presumably not properly awake until he came to the Wimmerstraat-Boolsweg crossroads, where a clattering tramcar screeched round the curve and scratched a wound in his eardrums.

He was now as wide awake as a newborn babe.

Bismarck forged ahead, her nose sniffing the asphalt. The goal was obvious: Randers Park. Five minutes there, ten minutes examining the plants and relieving herself in the bushes, then five minutes back home. Van Veeteren had been on this outing before, and wondered if the faithful old dog really was all that keen on this compulsory morning walk.

Perhaps she did it to keep the people she lived with happy. They needed to get out and have some exercise every morning, taking it in turns: it seemed a bit odd, but Bismarck did what was required of her in all weathers, rain or shine.

It was a worrying thought: but she was that type of dog, and how the hell could one know for sure?

At the beginning there had been no question of Van Veeteren being involved in the morning exercise. Bismarck was his daughter Jess's dog, and had been ever since she acquired her eight years ago. After eleven months of insistent pestering.

She had been thirteen at the time. Now she was twenty-one and was studying abroad for a year at the Sorbonne in Paris. She lived in a tiny little room in a student hostel where it was not allowed to keep Newfoundland dogs. Nor any other animals, come to that. Not even a French boyfriend was permitted.

So Bismarck had to stay behind in Maardam.

There was also a son in the house. His name was Erich, he was fifteen years old, and liked going out with dogs in the mornings. He was allowed to do that now and again after his big sister moved to Paris, but this morning he was not at home.

God only knows where he is, it suddenly struck Van Veeteren.

He had phoned at eleven o'clock the previous night, spoken to his mother and explained that he was out at Löhr and would be spending the night at a friend's house. He was in the same class – or possibly a parallel one – and his friend's father would drive them straight to school the following morning.

What was the name of the friend? Van Veeteren had wanted to know when his wife hung up and explained the situation.

She couldn't remember. Something beginning with M, but she couldn't recall having heard the name previously.

Van Veeteren also wondered if Erich had some clean underpants and a toothbrush with him, but hadn't bothered to pester his wife any further.

Bismarck turned into the entrance of the park, ignoring with disdain a neatly curled poodle who was on his way back home with his boss after a satisfactory outing.

I must have a chat with Erich one of these days, thought Van Veeteren, taking a packet of West out of his jacket pocket. It's high time I did so.

He lit a cigarette and realized that he had been thinking the same thought for over a year now. At regular intervals.

He had breakfast together with his wife. Neither of them uttered a word, despite the fact that they spent a good half-hour over the kitchen table and their newspapers.

Perhaps I should have a chat with Renate as well one of these days, he thought as he closed the front door behind him. That was also high time.

Or had they already used up all the available words?

It wasn't easy to know. They had been married for fifteen years, separated for two without having managed to go their separate ways, and then been married for another seven.

Twenty-four years, he thought. That's half my life, more or less.

He had been a police officer for twenty-four years as well. Perhaps there was a sort of connection, he thought? Two halves of my life combining to form a whole?

Rubbish. Even if you have half a duck and half an eagle, that doesn't mean that you possess a whole bird.

He realized that the image was idiotic, and during his walk to the police station he tried instead to recall how many times he had made love to his wife during the past year.

Three times, he decided.

If he interpreted the word 'love-making' optimistically. The last occasion – in April – didn't seem to come into the category of 'making love'.

And to be honest, in no other category either.

That's life, he thought – and avoided by a hair's breadth stepping into a pool of vomit somebody had left on the pavement. It could have been worse, to be sure; but for Christ's sake, it could have been considerably better as well.

*

On his way up to his office on the third floor he bumped into Inspector Münster.

'How's the Kaunis case going?' he asked.

'Full stop,' said Münster. 'Neither of those interrogations we talked about is going to be possible until next week.'

'Why not?'

'One of them is in Japan, and the other is going to be operated on this morning.'

'But he'll survive, I hope?'

'The doctors thought so. It's for varicose veins.'

'I see,' said the Chief Inspector. 'Anything else?'

'Yes, I'm afraid so,' said Münster. 'Hiller will no doubt be on to you. Something's happened in Linden, if I understood it rightly.'

'Linden?'

'Yes. If we don't have anything more important on – and we might not have now that—'

'We'll have to see,' said Van Veeteren. 'You'll be in your office if I need you, I take it?'

'Buried under a drift of papers,' said Münster with a sigh, and continued down the corridor.

Van Veeteren entered his office, and noted that it smelled rather like a working men's lodging house. Not that he had ever lived in such an establishment, but he had been inside quite a few in the course of his duties.

He opened the window wide and lit a cigarette. Inhaled deeply. Another morning and I'm still alive, he thought, and it struck him that what he would like to do more than anything else was to go and lie down for a while.

Was there anything in the rules and regulations that said you were not allowed to have a bed in your office?

'Yes, well, it's that business in Linden,' said Hiller, pouring some water into a pot of yellow gerbera. 'I suppose we'll have to drive out there and take a look.'

'What's it all about?' asked Van Veeteren, contemplating the chief of police's plants. There must have been about thirty: in front of the big picture window, on the desk, on a little table in the corner and on the bookshelves. It's beginning to look like an obsession, he thought, and wondered what that was a sign of. Growing roses was a substitute for passion – he had read that somewhere; but Hiller's display of plants in his office on the fourth floor of the police station was much more difficult to pin down. Van Veeteren's botanical knowledge was limited, but even so he thought he could identify aspidistra and hortensia and yucca palm.

And gerbera.

The chief of police put down his watering can.

'A dead woman,' he said. 'At the bottom of a swimming pool.'

'Drowned?'

'No. Certainly not drowned.'

'Really?'

'There was no water in the pool. It's rather difficult to drown in those circumstances. Not to say impossible.'

A slight twitch of the mouth suggested that Hiller was indulging his sense of humour. Van Veeteren sat down on the visitor chair.

'Murder? Manslaughter?'

'Probably not. She probably fell in by sheer mischance. Or dived in by mistake. But it seems to be not straightforward, and Sachs has asked for assistance. He's not quite himself after that little haemorrhage he had – no doubt you remember that? He seems to be aware of that himself. But he only has one more year to go before he retires.'

Van Veeteren sighed. He had met – and worked with – Chief Inspector Sachs on three or four occasions. He had no special views about him – neither positive nor negative – but he knew that Sachs had suffered a minor cerebral haemorrhage a few months ago, and that it might have affected his judgement to some extent. At least, that is what had been alleged: but if it really was the case, or if it had more to do with Sachs's lack of confidence after being a millimetre-thin blood vessel wall away from death – well, that was difficult to say.

'When did it happen?' asked Van Veeteren.

'Last night,' said the chief of police, running his fingers over the immaculate knot in his tie. 'You could delegate it to somebody, of course; but if you're not too snowed under I think you ought to drive out there yourself. Bearing in mind Sachs's situation. But there's nothing to suggest anything irregular, remember that. It shouldn't need more than a few hours and a bit of common sense.'

'I'll go myself,' said Van Veeteren, standing up. 'A car drive might do me good.'

'Harrumph!' said Hiller.

'Jaan G. Hennan!' exclaimed Van Veeteren as Münster started manoeuvring them out of the underground labyrinth that was the police station garage. 'I can hardly believe my eyes.'

'Why?' wondered Münster. 'Who is Hennan?'

But Van Veeteren didn't reply. He had received a three-page summary of the case written by somebody called Wagner and including a short statement by the pathologist Meusse. He was holding the documents in his hand and trying to absorb the contents. Münster glanced at his boss and realized that it was pertinent to wait, and meanwhile concentrate on driving.

'Hennan,' muttered the Chief Inspector, and started reading.

Wagner's report revealed that the dead woman was called Barbara Hennan, and that the police had been summoned to the scene (Kammerweg 4 in Linden) by a telephone call (received 01.42) from the dead woman's husband. A certain Jaan G. Hennan.

The police had arrived at 02.08, and established that the woman was lying on the bottom of an empty swimming pool, and was in fact dead. Hennan had been interrogated immediately and it had transpired that he had arrived at home about 01.15, and been unable to find his wife until he discovered her lying in the said empty swimming pool. Both local doctor Santander and pathologist Meusse from the Centre for Forensic Medicine in Maardam had examined the dead body, and their conclusions were identical in all respects: Barbara Henna had died as a result of extensive injuries in her head, spine, nape and trunk, and there was everything to suggest that all the injuries had been a consequence of falling into the empty swimming pool. Or possibly diving into it. Or possibly being pushed into it. The post-mortem was not yet complete, so further details could be expected.

The time of death seemed to be between 21.00 and 23.00. Hennan maintained that at this time he was in the restaurant Columbine in Linden; he had seen his wife alive for the last time at eight o'clock in the morning when she left home in order to drive to Aarlach. It was not known when she had arrived back home after that outing, nor how she had ended up in the empty swimming pool. All information received thus far had come from the said Jaan G. Hennan.

Meusse's brief statement merely confirmed that all fractures and injuries were consistent with the assumption that the dead woman had fallen (or dived, or been pushed) down into the pool; and that the alcohol level in her blood was 1.74 per mil.

'So she was drunk,' muttered the Chief Inspector when he had finished reading. 'A drunk woman falls down into an empty swimming pool. Kindly explain to me why the Maardam CID has to be called out to assist in a situation like this!'

'What about this Hennan character?' wondered Münster. 'Didn't you say you couldn't believe your eyes, or something of the sort?'

Van Veeteren folded up the sheets of paper and put them in his briefcase.

'G,' he said. 'That's what we called him.'

'G?'

'Yes. I was at school with him. In the same class for six years.'

'Really? Jaan G. Hennan. Why ... er ... why did he only have one letter, as it were?'

'Because there were two,' said Van Veeteren, adjusting a lever and leaning the back of his seat so far back that he was half-lying in the passenger seat. 'Two boys with the same name – Jaan Hennan. The teachers had to distinguish between them, of course, and it always said Jaan G. Hennan on class lists or in class registers. If I remember rightly we called him Jaan G. for a week or so, and then after that it was just G. He quite liked it himself. I mean, he had the whole school's simplest name.'

'G?' said Münster. 'Yes, I have to say that it has ... well, a sort of something to it.'

The Chief Inspector nodded vaguely. Fished out a toothpick from his breast pocket and examined it carefully before sticking it between the front teeth of his lower jaw.

'What was he like?'

'What was he like? What do you mean?'

'What sort of a person was he then? G?'

'Why do you ask?'

'Well, you seemed to suggest that there was something odd about him.'

Van Veeteren turned his head and looked out through the

passenger window for a while before answering. Tapped his fingertops against one another.

'Münster,' he said in the end. 'Let's keep this to ourselves for the time being, but I reckon Jaan G. Hennan is the most unpleasant bastard I have ever met in the whole of my life.'

'What?' said Münster.

'You heard me.'

'Of course. It was as if . . . I mean, what does that imply in this context? It can't be completely irrelevant, surely? If you—'

'How are things with you and the family?' said Van Veeteren, interrupting him. 'Still as idyllic as ever?'

The family? wondered Münster and increased his speed. Typical. If you've said A, under no circumstances must you say B.

'As a man sows, so shall he reap,' he said, and to his great surprise the Chief Inspector produced a noise faintly reminiscent of a laugh.

Brief and half-swallowed, but still . . .

'Bravo, Inspector,' he said. 'I'll tell you a bit more about G on some later occasion, I promise you that. But I don't want to rob you of the possibility of your forming an independent impression of him first. Is that okay with you?'

Münster shrugged.

'That's okay with me,' he said. 'And that business of him being the biggest arsehole the world has ever seen, well, I've forgotten all about that already.'

'Of course,' said the Chief Inspector. 'No preconceived

ideas – that is our credo in the police force. In any case, we'll
have a word with Chief of Police Sachs first. Whatever you
do, don't recall the fact that he recently had a cerebral haemorrhage when we meet him.'

'Of course not,' said Münster, 'An interesting call-out, this,
no doubt about that.'

'No doubt at all,' agreed Van Veeteren.

THE MIND'S EYE

An Inspector Van Veeteren Mystery

Janek Mitter stumbles into his bathroom one morning after a night of heavy drinking, to find his beautiful young wife, Eva, floating dead in the bath. She has been brutally murdered. Yet even during his trial Mitter cannot summon a single memory of attacking Eva, nor a clue as to who could have killed her if he had not. Only once he has been convicted and locked away in an asylum for the criminally insane does he have a snatch of insight – but is it too late?

Drawing a blank after exhaustive interviews, Chief Inspector Van Veeteren remains convinced that something, or someone, in the dead woman's life has caused these tragic events. But the reasons for her speedy remarriage have died with her. And as he delves even deeper, Van Veeteren realizes that the past never stops haunting the present . . .

Out in paperback now

BORKMANN'S POINT

An Inspector Van Veeteren Mystery

Borkmann's rule was hardly a rule; in fact, it was more of a comment, a landmark for tricky cases . . . In every investigation, he maintained, there comes a point beyond which we don't really need any more information. When we reach that point, we already know enough to solve the case by means of nothing more than some decent thinking.

Two men are brutally murdered with an axe in the quiet coastal town of Kaalbringen and Chief Inspector Van Veeteren, bored on holiday nearby, is summoned to assist the local authorities. The local police chief, just days away from retirement, is determined to wrap things up before he goes.

But there is no clear link between the victims. Then one of Van Veeteren's colleagues, a brilliant young female detective, goes missing – perhaps she has reached Borkmann's Point before anyone else . . .

Out in paperback now

THE RETURN

An Inspector Van Veeteren Mystery

An unmissable hospital appointment is looming for Inspector Van Veeteren when a corpse is found rolled in a rotting carpet by a young child playing in a local beauty spot. Missing head and limbs, the torso is too badly decomposed for forensic identification – bar one crucial detail . . .

Circumstantial evidence soon points to a local man, a double murderer who disappeared nine months before, shortly after being released on parole; a local hero turned monster after being convicted of killing two women over a span of three decades.

Recuperating after an operation, Van Veeteren is nevertheless directing investigations from his hospital bed, for he is convinced that only the innocence of this new victim can be the motive for his murder. But the two women have been dead for long enough for any evidence to have died with them . . . And is he simply on the wrong track completely?

Out in paperback now

WOMAN WITH A BIRTHMARK

An Inspector Van Veeteren Mystery

A young woman shivers in the December cold as her mother's body is laid to rest in a cemetery. The only thing that warms her is the thought of the revenge she will soon take . . .

Then a middle-aged man is killed at his home, shot twice in the chest and twice below the belt. He had recently received a series of bizarre phone calls where an old song is played down the line – evoking an eerie sense of both familiarity and unease. Before the police can find the culprit, a second man is killed in the same way.

Chief Inspector Van Veeteren and his team must dig far back into each man's past – but with few clues at each crime scene, can they find the killer before anyone else dies?

Out in paperback now

THE INSPECTOR AND SILENCE

An Inspector Van Veeteren Mystery

In the beautiful forested lake-town of Sorbinowo, the tranquillity is shattered when a girl goes missing from the summer camp of the mysterious the Pure Life, a religious sect buried deep in the woods.

Chief Inspector Van Veeteren's investigations at the Pure Life seem to go nowhere fast. But things soon take a sinister turn when a young girl's body is discovered in the woods, raped and strangled; and the sect's leader Yellinek himself disappears. As the body count rises, a media frenzy descends upon the town and the pressure to find the monster behind the murders weighs heavily on the investigative team. Finally Van Veeteren realizes that to solve this disturbing case, faced with silence and with few clues to follow, he has only his intuition to rely on . . .

Out in paperback now

THE UNLUCKY LOTTERY

An Inspector Van Veeteren Mystery

Four friends celebrate winning the lottery. Just hours later, one of them – Waldemar Leverkuhn – is found in his home, stabbed to death.

With Chief Inspector Van Veeteren on sabbatical, working in a second-hand bookshop, the case is assigned to Inspector Münster. But when another member of the lottery group disappears, as well as Leverkuhn's neighbour, Münster appeals to Van Veeteren for assistance.

Soon Münster will find himself interviewing the Leverkuhn family, including the eldest – Irene – a resident of a psychiatric clinic. And as he delves deeper into the family's history, he will discover dark secrets and startling twists, which not only threaten the clarity of the case – but also his life . . .

Out in paperback now

HOUR OF THE WOLF

An Inspector Van Veeteren Mystery

In the dead of night, in the pouring rain, a drunk driver smashes his car into a young man. He abandons the body at the side of the road, but the incident will set in motion a chain of events which will change his life forever.

Soon Chief Inspector Van Veeteren, now retired from the Maardam police force, will face his greatest trial yet as someone close to him is, inexplicably, murdered.

Van Veeteren's former colleagues, desperate for answers, struggle to decipher the clues to this appalling crime. But when another body is discovered, it gradually becomes clear that this killer is acting on their own terrifying logic . . .

Out in paperback now

THE WEEPING GIRL

An Inspector Van Veeteren Mystery

A community is left reeling after a teacher – Arnold Maager – is convicted of murdering his female pupil Winnie Maas.

Years later, on her eighteenth birthday, Maager's daughter Mikaela finally learns the terrible truth about her father. Desperate for answers, Mikaela travels to the institution at Lejnice where Maager has been held since his trial. But soon afterwards she inexplicably vanishes.

Detective Inspector Ewa Moreno from the Maardam police is on holiday in the area when she finds herself drawn into Mikaela's disappearance. But before she can make any headway in the case, Maager himself disappears – and then a body is found. It will soon become clear to Ewa that only unravelling the events of the past will unlock this dark mystery . . .

Out in paperback now